Breathing Room

Breathing Room

Patricia Elam

POCKET BOOKS

NEW YORK   LONDON   TORONTO   SYDNEY   SINGAPORE

POCKET BOOKS, a division of Simon & Schuster, Inc.
1230 Avenue of Americas, New York, NY 10020

Library of Congress Cataloging-in-Publication Data
    Elam, Patricia.
        Breathing room / Patricia Elam.
          p. cm.
        ISBN 0-671-02842-1
            1. Afro-American women—Fiction.   2. Female friendship—Fiction.
        3. Mothers and daughters—Fiction.   4. Washington (D.C.)—Fiction.
        5. Adultery—Fiction.   I. Title.

        PS3555.L185 B74 2001
        813'.6—dc21   00-057141

First Pocket Books hardcover printing January 2001

10 9 8 7 6 5 4 3 2 1

POCKET and colophon are registered trademarks of
Simon & Schuster, Inc.

Designed by Joseph Rutt

Printed in the U.S.A.

For my tributaries:
my ancestors, my parents, my siblings, and my children

Acknowledgments

I am indeed fortunate to have had support from family and friends at every stage of my life, and in particular while writing this book. Many times I have been overwhelmed by your love, prayers, daimoku, phone calls, notes, e-mail, attendance at readings, encouragement, confidence, guidance, gifts, loans, and other acts of kindness. I only wish I could name you all, because each of you is so very special to me, but the list would fill pages and I'd be panicked that I'd leave someone out. Please know that I love you, appreciate you, and want the very best for you with all my heart.

I must, though, acknowledge those who specifically contributed to this book's emergence at this time. My grandparents were all storytellers in their own way, and they passed it on. From earlier than we can remember, my parents, Barbara Clark Elam and Harry Justin Elam, read to us and thus began instilling the love of words in their four offspring. They never let up, and have been a steady source of sustenance for me throughout this process. My siblings, Jay, Keith, and Jocie, continue to inspire me with the manner in which they are achieving their dreams and goals. My children, Justin, Denzel, and Nile, give me joy and strength and were (most of the time) interested, proud, and patient. Debra Iverson, my "dog," as my teenage character Zadi would say, or best friend for almost thirty years, knew intuitively what was needed and then did it or gave it, over and over again. Without her, I simply could not have gotten the work done. Angela Baden offered boundless compassion and wisdom at crucial moments. Coles Ruff provided support along the way. Nisey and Lee Baylor unselfishly gave assistance when it was sorely needed.

I am awed by the majesty, prodigious skill, and clarity of vision my agent, Molly Friedrich, possesses. My talented, assured, and patient editor, Tracy Sherrod, has been an unwavering advocate for my book.

Their respective assistants, Paul Cirone and Calaya Reid, were always helpful and very tolerant of my many calls and inquiries.

My unofficial editor, Edward P. Jones, lent his Midas touch, sharp eyes, intellect, and vast compassion for, and understanding of, the human condition to my pages. Kenyatta Dorey Graves, with humor and wisdom beyond his years, picked up where Edward left off. Erica Hines-Sutton, a gifted young writer and former student, kept the "Zadi pages" real.

A host of talented writers has influenced, mentored, and inspired me over the years. Once again, I cannot name you all but please know that your work and your words have made mine possible. Eugenia Collier, Kay Brown, and Marcia Davis, of the early writers' groups, always encouraged and inspired. Marita Golden nourished me from early on with her books and workshops and push to "stop taking workshops and just write," as well as her inclusion of me in her many Hurston/Wright Foundation projects. Kenny Carroll urged me on with his storehouse of immense talent, energy, positive words, and information. Maxine Clair, with her generosity of spirit, shared jewels of advice as well as her agent with me. Patrice Gaines sat me down for lunch and lessons about writing and publishing. The masterful workshops of writing/teaching divas Julia Alvarez, Gloria Wade-Gayles, A. J. Verdelle, and the late Toni Cade Bambara are etched in my soul. University of Maryland professors/writers Michael Collier, Merle Collins, Joyce Kornblatt, Howard Norman, Stanley Plumly, Tova Reich, and Mary Helen Washington all gave of themselves, encouraging me to discipline and hone my reading and writing. Students at the University of Maryland, the Writer's Center, and UCLA Extension Online writing program furthered my development as a writer and teacher of writing. My intrepid writing sisters, Lisa Page, Robin Vazquez, and Sindiwe Magona, gifted writers all, are invaluable to my journey. And I sorely miss the prolific Arthur Johnson, who always spurred me on.

Debra Iverson, Kathy Aiken, Carl Clark, and Linda Day Clark provided insight into the passion and work of photographers. Julian Orenstein, M.D., Hunter Nicholas, M.D., and staff members at

Washington Hospital Center clarified and corrected medical terms and conditions. Lydia Curtis and Joseph Strong shed light on the lives of social workers, probation officers, and juvenile offenders. Causton Toney, Esq., and Gary Valby, Esq., discussed pertinent aspects of employment with large corporate law firms. Gail Gorlitz instructed me about the beauty and intricacy of gardening, flowers, and birds. Ballet grande dames Doris Jones and Elma Lewis and legendary dance instructors Jacqueline Curry and Tammy Odom inspired many of the ballet sections. Jacqueline Curry, Tiffany Glenn, Holly Hyman, and Brandye Lee shared their experiences as accomplished dancers. There were many teenage and young adult role models, including the students in my creative writing workshops at Dunbar High School and in the Black Student Fund summer classes. Other influential young people who contributed to Zadi's essence (and in many cases, read and commented on her sections) are Pyrrha Baxter, Kashira and Zakia Cummings, Jourdan Davis, Lindsey Holmes, Alia McPhail, Kennise Millner, Stacey Smith, Ismael Vazquez, Khadijah White, Khiana and Lanika Womack, and Audrey Yiadom. My son, Justin, who also helped immensely with teenage sentiments, crafted Octavius's rap song. When I was unsure, entrepreneurs Nisey Baylor, Brenda Belton, and Montsha Ofori persistently assured me I wouldn't regret leaving my day job, and they were right. My former boss, Erias A. Hyman, Esq., encouraged my writing even though it meant I would leave the law behind. Kathy Awkard embedded the seeds of this story in my mind, whether she knows it or not. Shirley Payne contributed her eagle copy-editing eye as well as her organizational talent and global thinking for marketing and publicity efforts.

Some of the establishments and institutions that provided structure, opportunities to read from my early work, financial support, and/or a place to write when I needed it are: The University of Maryland's Creative Writing Program, the Writer's Center, the District of Columbia Commission on the Arts and Humanities, the Virginia Center for Creative Arts, the Ragdale Foundation, the National Museum of Women in the Arts, the Bethune Museum and Archives, the African

American Writers' Guild and its workshops, Sisterspace and Books, and Vertigo Books. I am so grateful.

The practice of Nichiren Daishonin's Buddhism and the members of SGI-USA continue to focus and guide my forward movement.

Thank you, all.

The moment we break faith with one another,
The sea engulfs us and the light goes out.
                    —*James Baldwin*

a shadow of my past came
transformed
a specter
I know it is she
a flood of memories
released
echoes/distant voices
pleasant recesses
explored/re-explored
she is both a feeling
and a sight
a catalyst
a formalist
a beginning
                    —*Kenneth Clark*

Everything is determined by our
attitude, by our resolve.
Our heart is what matters most.
                    —*Daisaku Ikeda*

Breathing Room

One

He sleeps deeply, turned on his side with an arm draped across her shoulders. His slow exhaling crescendos to a jagged mixture of snorts and labored breaths. Norma wishes she could sleep as comfortably. She feels the weight of his elbow on her back and eases out from under his grasp.

She raises herself and sits close to the edge of the bed, which they never bothered to unmake, and examines her state of disarray. Her bra dangles from her shoulder, held by one intact strap. Her right breast, the one his mouth latched onto first, is exposed. She smiles at the memory and closes her eyes, trying to experience it all again. When she stands, a smoldering ache below her waist makes her wince.

In the bathroom, she adjusts her bra, lifting her heavy breasts up from where breastfeeding dropped them. She crosses her arms beneath, as she examines her body in the baroque mirror. She's gained weight this past year but doesn't harbor guilt about dropping the t'ai chi class or being a stranger at the fitness center she joined with lofty intentions. Her stomach is actually the only part of her form she is displeased with. The flesh immediately above and below her navel is creased and wrinkled like a huge prune, the reward of two C-sections—yet only one child.

A church bell chimes twice, sharp and clanging, startling her. She can't even imagine where there is a church nearby; the sound must travel quite a distance. She wants to wake up Woody. Half the day is gone and she still has to make major decisions about her first solo photography exhibit next month. She's unsure whether there should be an overall theme or just a smorgasbord of past and present work. Several assignments, in various stages of completion, also loom before her, and she doesn't want to wait until the last minute.

Coming to this hotel room was not originally in the day's plan, at least not for her. She and Moxie had talked about possibly getting together for lunch today. It's not that she's elevated trysting with Woody above lunching with her best friend. Moxie simply wasn't in when Norma tried to reach her. And then Woody called and suggested they meet at "our" hotel, as he referred to it because it would be their third visit. The Holiday Inn is near Union Station, not too far from Catholic University, where Woody teaches, or from Norma's Capitol Hill studio loft and the gallery where Norma had been earlier, checking on the available wall space.

It is the day before New Year's Eve, and there are several large signs announcing the hotel's scheduled festivities. The lobby is strung with gold wreaths and potted poinsettias grace every available flat surface. Woody and Norma had to wait several minutes to be seated in the restaurant. All the tables were filled by people in business attire or tourists with cameras dangling from their necks. Waiters in black vests and white shirts bustled about, balancing trays and half smiles. After only a few bites of the smothered chicken, Woody gently pressed his knee against hers under the table. When she looked up at him he said, "I want to kiss you badly. Let's get a room."

"Sure you have time?" she had asked, coyly.

"Yes. I'm still on winter break, remember? I've got papers and exams to grade, but I have time for you."

"Aren't you going to ask if I have time—or don't you think my time is valuable?" she responded, half-serious.

"Of course I value your time," he said, turning away from her to signal the waiter. "I have great respect for your phenomenal work and your time." He smiled, pressing more firmly against her leg. "It was a suggestion, not an assumption. Stop giving me a *hard* time. Note the emphasis on the word 'hard.'" She flashed him a look of mock chastisement, and both of their smiles ruptured into laughter.

His indelicate comment and their spontaneous giggling made her look around to see if anyone was in the hotel restaurant who might know her and guess what she was up to. She whispered, "And what makes you think I'm going to let you make love to me today?"

"Did I say that? I said 'kiss you.' That's all I said. My God, you've got a dirty mind." He laughed from way down deep as he always did, even when things weren't that funny. She wanted him to lean across and kiss her now, but was anxious about him doing so in public. Woody left her with money to pay the check while he went to the front desk to secure a room.

The first time he ever kissed her was right before Thanksgiving, a little over a month ago. He called and came by her studio under the guise of checking out her work. He walked around examining the many photographs Norma has taped, pushpinned, and framed on her studio walls. It helps her to hang the photos she's pleased with right after she prints them. If her positive feelings about a particular photo increase the more she studies it, she knows it's worth keeping. Observing her work in this unhurried way enables her to discover something that may be out of sync or that weakens the shot.

When Woody stopped in front of a framed series of deflated hot-air balloons, he called it "intriguing." The photo series had been featured, a few years before, in a local exhibit of D.C. photographers, and her photos were selected to accompany a subsequent newspaper review of the exhibit. She was pleased something had materialized from that disappointing day she and Miles traveled all the way to Pennsylvania to watch the balloons take off. She settled for photographing the airless balloons when the lack of wind made liftoff impossible.

Woody lingered before each photo, one at a time. As she explained how manipulating the toner resulted in the sepia hue, Woody inched closer. He seemed to breathe in the words she spoke, but she wasn't certain he was listening. By then he was so close that if she had moved an arm or a leg even slightly, she would have touched his. She forgot what she was talking about, aware only of the increased pace of her own breathing and the proximity of his lips. It made sense, at that point, for them to kiss. She almost lost her balance, so he held her by the waist, keeping her steady. "How do you get such richness from black-and-white photos?" he asked her when the kiss ended.

"It depends on the light. Light is everything."

"Everything?" He held her hand and wove his fingers in between hers, sliding them gently back and forth. "Does it matter if it's natural light or artificial?" He blew the question into her ear, grazing his mouth against the lobe.

A shiver made her shift her feet again. "I love natural when I can have it, but . . ." He took her words away with his lips.

"But what?" he asked, moving on to her neck.

She tried to answer, but too much was happening to her body. He looked around and at her, as if to ask where they could go to be more comfortable. She led him to a couch in the corner, but it was so lumpy and stiff they both started laughing. Although they wanted to finish what they had started, they waited until they could arrange to meet later at a hotel.

Now, in the same hotel's bathroom, she takes the floral-scented oval soap out of its package to wash her hands. She splashes water onto her face and returns to the bedroom to dress. Woody is still asleep on his stomach. How ordinary he looks lying there, as undistinguished as a sheet of paper. His hairline recedes, his lips are thin, and his stomach protrudes over the waist of his boxers. Yet moments ago he reminded her, once again, of the immense difference between making love to a man who is hungry for you and one who turns to you merely because you are there.

She sits on the bed beside him, leans over, and whispers, "Wake up and come back to me." He mumbles something and nuzzles the crook of her neck. She enjoys the easy familiarity she feels with him. She slips a hand onto his back, kneading his shoulders. Her fingers know just where they want to wander on him, unlike their hesitation about touching her husband.

"You must be really exhausted," she says. "It didn't take you ten seconds to fall asleep."

"I'm sorry," he says as he straightens to a sitting position. "I stayed up 'til the wee hours reading essays."

"What did they have to write about?"

"Where they think they'll be in five years. Sadly—many of them, seniors and juniors, don't think they'll be very far. They have this idea that we baby boomers messed things up irreparably," he says, melding his hand to the side of her face. "Are you sure we have to leave now?" He leans forward and kisses her hard. When they shared that first kiss back in her studio, her full lips had practically swallowed his thinner ones. After numerous practice sessions, she now knows to purse her lips gently and slowly press her mouth against his. Then she opens wide, letting his tongue glide on in.

Norma reluctantly peels his hands from her. "Woody, we have to stop. I've really got to go."

"Okay," he says. "Me, too." He reaches across the bed to gather his crumpled slacks from the floor. "Now, here's a real test for supposedly permanent-press pants." He chuckles at his corny joke and stares at her. "Hey, this was almost as good as spending New Year's Eve together, wasn't it?"

The pillars near the hotel entrance are wrapped with garlands of white pine and red velvet bows. Christmas lights outline the arched doorway, and piles of dingy snow cling to the edges of the walkway. Most of the previous week's downfall has been rinsed away by an early morning rain. The sky is lined, though, with row after row of transparent clouds. Tissue-soft snowflakes begin to sift about their heads. Even though both their destinations are only a few metro stops away, they agree to hail a taxi as the snowfall threatens to increase in pace and density. Norma took the metro today because the last time she drove to the hotel, she lost track of time left on the meter and ended up with a parking ticket.

Woody and Norma wait for a taxi to pull up into the semicircle. Norma rummages in her shoulder bag for her gloves and puts them on while Woody pats his pockets, searching for cigarettes. Usually, she dislikes people smoking around her, but Woody inhales like an actor in a subtitled movie. He holds the cigarette between his middle finger and thumb, the way you would a marijuana joint, blowing smoke away in a diagonal direction. Smoking cigarettes actually becomes him.

A yellow-and-black taxi drives up. The doorman lurches forward to open the taxi door for them. Woody folds a bill into his hand. Norma inadvertently glances into the taxi's rearview mirror and meets the driver's unflinching stare. His red eyes peer at her. Maybe African, she thinks, looking at his ink-toned skin. She and Woody ride without much talking. At stoplights, she stares at people in other cars and hurrying along the street. She wonders whether any of them have lives as complicated as hers.

It is a little too warm in the taxi. Norma unbuttons her coat, removes her gloves, and absently turns her grandmother's silver West Indian bracelets around on her wrist. Woody's fingers rest on her knee. She notices hair sprouting from small pores in his thick fingers; so different from her husband's long, dark hands.

They travel only about a mile or so to the Library of Congress, where he is meeting a colleague. Woody asks the driver how much the fare is to Norma's destination. Norma tells him she has enough money, but Woody pays anyway. Norma sighs because he has paid for everything today and it's not as if he's rich. As he scoots from the taxi, he presses his palm to her face, as is becoming his endearing habit. She is uncomfortably aware that the cabdriver is watching them. Woody waves as they pull away from the curb. He mouths, "Happy New Year."

The cabdriver coughs loudly, several times. "Generous guy. That your boss?" he asks. His voice is thick and gravelly, scraping its way out of his mouth. No trace of the African accent she expected.

She says nothing and begins rebuttoning her coat.

"Probably got you working real hard. Probably pays you real good, too?"

Ignore him, she tells herself.

"Maybe things the other way around. Maybe you *his* boss? Maybe he the one got paid!" A chuckle rattles low in his throat. Her studio is only a short distance away. The driver continues north on Independence Avenue. Norma shifts around on the slippery seat, her chest tight and hammering away at itself. She slides over nearer the door. "Excuse me, I changed my mind. I need to get out at the next corner." His pellet eyes rove over her.

"This ain't Eastern Market."

"That's okay. Just let me out right here," she says, trying to keep her voice from quivering. Norma accidentally looks into the mirror, as she adjusts the shoulder strap of her purse. His eyes are hard and sharp as glass. He runs a red light and she squelches the fear that he might not let her out at all. He pulls the cab over abruptly.

She is at Fourth and Pennsylvania, still a good walk from her studio on South Carolina and Eleventh. It has stopped snowing, but the chill nips at her ears nonetheless. She tightens the scarf around her neck. Norma begins walking more briskly. The people she passes seem to stare at her as if they know what she did on her lunch break. She wraps her arms across her body as she walks, trying to regain what she lost of herself in the taxi. Unsure of whether to hail another cab for the nine or so blocks remaining or to walk the distance, she is frustrated at her inability to make this simple decision. She can feel her hands trembling, although thrust deep into her coat pockets. She craves the comfort of her darkroom. She continues walking until she is there.

Climbing the stairs to the studio, her legs are almost numb. She turns the key in the lock quickly, as if someone were following her. Still wearing her coat, she tries to call Moxie but hangs up when the office voice-mail system comes on. Now that Norma's finally ready to tell Moxie what she has put off for the last month, Moxie's not available.

The coffeemaker beckons from its stand in the corner, and she adds water to the always ready, ground-and-measured coffee beans. When it's done, she takes a sip, scorching the tip of her tongue. An almost comforting pain after the taxi ride. She ties an apron around her waist and enters the darkroom. The odor of the developer is a fragrant herb. She turns on the enlarger and the faucet. The water from the hose splashes into the basin like a miniature waterfall. Usually she can lose herself here in the darkroom and forget the chaos in her life. She wants it to erase the grimy way the cabdriver made her feel. The phone rings outside the darkroom, but she doesn't interrupt what she's doing. When she prints, there is a magical feeling, a rush that comes watching the image emerge onto the paper. Photography is like writing a poem with light. She is never certain of what she caught or even what she saw or felt with the camera until the image is developed. Often there's a vast difference between what the mind sees and what the eye, the final arbiter, sees.

Norma holds the tongs, dipping the photo paper in the three chemical trays. She always dips a few extra times in the fix, for good measure, the way Arnold, her father, used to, in his garage darkroom. Her father, a retired army major, was an amateur photographer when she was growing up. He gave her an Instamatic camera for her fifth birthday, shortly before he left to serve a tour of duty in Vietnam. She remembers it was the gift she treasured most that day. She developed her own interest in photography, she now thinks, to become closer to him. That first camera still sits on one of the shelves in the darkroom, next to the chemical chart, along with her first photograph. A picture so shaky and blurred only she can tell it's her teddy bear from years ago.

Two and a half hours later she has printed the photograph she took of Moxie's father's hands, knuckles swollen and knotted by arthritis, as they lay in his lap. In the black-and-white photo you can't see him or the chair he sits in, just the tip of his knees and those hands.

Somewhere along the way, in printing the photo of Pa Dillard's hands, she has made a small mistake, but she's not sure what. Maybe when the image was exposed through the enlarger. There is a haze around the hands as if they're lying on a bed of clouds. She finds the end result stunning, but has no idea how to recreate it. When she was in art school, her photography instructor encouraged students to experiment with chemicals in order to stumble upon varied and often captivating results.

Satisfied with the printing and not as frazzled as when she began, she covers the chemical trays and pins the wet prints on a wire line that runs across the corner wall of the studio. Afterward she sits at her desk and dials Moxie's work number again. "Ms. Dillard is in with a client," the receptionist says. Norma wonders if it was Moxie who called earlier and leaves a message on Moxie's home answering machine: "Let's get together ASAP—I have something to tell you. Call me."

There, she has launched the confession.

Thursday, Dec. 31, 1998
Tommy jeans
cinnamon sweater
cinnamon Timberlands from Dad for
    Christmas

Dear Sistergirl:

   I know Anne Frank did it and also that girl from Bosnia, but writing Dear Diary sounds cheesy as far as I'm concerned. My mother's best friend, Norma, gave this diary to me for Christmas. Well, she said Kwanzaa, but only because of Ma. Norma's been calling me sistergirl probably since I was a baby. Ma wanted me to call her Aunt Norma, but Norma said that made her feel too old. She told me to treat my diary like a good girlfriend who I can trust and confide in. She says it'll be therapeutic. Whatever. I'm going to write all the important stuff about my life in here. Norma is my dog because she is off the hook. She's so pretty and she's almost forty!!! Three years older than Ma. In the last year Norma has let herself get a little on the heavy side, but she can still play the diva. When I first got my period, she took me to B. Smith's in Union Station for a special dinner. I was a little embarrassed that Ma told her, but Norma said it meant I was on the verge of leaving childhood and growing into a woman and that I should feel proud and beautiful. She should be the mother of a teenager because she tells you about when she was a teenager and how she did stupid stuff and she doesn't have to say don't do it because you get the idea. Like instead of bugging me about short skirts and tight pants like Ma does, she told me this: if a boy likes you just cause of your body and not your heart and mind, then all he'll want to do is screw you (her word), not talk to you or go places with you. I get her point but I think that advice is more for people who are old and ready to get married, not teenagers trying to have fun. But she's still probably the most off-the-hook grownup I know. She also went to a predominantly white boarding school more than twenty years ago, so she understands what I go through at Willow and helps me out with that, too. When she was in school, they were real ignorant (more so than now). Somebody asked her if she could wash her color off—be for real. When I talk to her about some of the things I go through, she always says, Damn, things haven't changed very much.

It's almost a new year. Not a great start, though. We lit the candles for Kuumba, the sixth principle, and poured our libation. Then we went to a Kwanzaa celebration. It was all right—drumming, dancing, African everything. Last week we had Christmas dinner at Norma's parents' house with Grandpa. Christmas Eve I stayed over at Dad's. This week I did the Kwanzaa principles and all that with Ma—tomorrow's the last night and she'll give me my gifts, finally. All I'm doing now is watching TV all night with Ma, who just fell asleep. Allegra was supposed to have this banging-ass New Year's Eve party, but she got an interim report before vacation for getting a D- on the Literature exam. Her parents shut that party idea down quick. Why don't grownups care that those kind of punishments affect more than one person? Parents shouldn't be allowed to ruin other teenagers lives, who they're not the parents of !!

Friday, Jan. 1, 1999!!!
white sweater
DKNY jeans from Fawna
black Banana Republic boots
with money from Grandpa

Dear Sistergirl:

Got my gifts from Ma this morning. They were good. I don't even have to take anything back. The necklace I showed her from that little store on Connecticut Avenue, Gap jeans, some books (of course), a Dance Theatre of Harlem calendar, and a basket with bubble bath, soap, and stuff. I didn't get her anything yet cause I don't have any money. Dad said he might take me shopping for her, though.

The last time I had a diary I was in third grade and it had a lock and everything, but my life was so unbelievably boring it doesn't count. Plus I couldn't spell for shit. I almost threw it out when I was cleaning my closet, but Allegra says if I become a famous dancer one day, my fans will want to read stuff like that. Norma says this is more like a journal because the pages don't have dates on them, so if I need to write three pages for one day I can. It has a lock and a key, but I still need to find a safe place for it.

I do plan to be a famous dancer with either Ailey or Dance Theatre of

Harlem. Saw Revelations *for the hundredth time (slight exaggeration)
tonight at the Kennedy Center. Dad kept clapping when everyone else
had stopped. Also his beeper went off—Fawna bugging out, I guess—
embarrassing for real. I love the part when the dancers use the scarves to
look like waves in the water. And there was a male dancer whose grand
jetés were amazing. Judith Jamison came out at the end and took bows,
and people threw her roses. Ma gave me her book a couple of years ago.
Skipped some of it, but the parts I read were jive interesting. Her dance
teacher looked like she was white and that's how she was able to get the
building where she taught all those black kids how to dance.*

*I am going to try out for Dance Theatre of Harlem's summer program.
Miss Snow says they'll conduct auditions at Duke Ellington in February.
She says I have a lot of work to do before then if I want them to even
glance in my direction. You know she's always tripping anyway.*

*Saturday, Jan. 2nd
Tommy jeans
red/black stretch top
black Nikes (Airforce Ones)*

*Dear Sistergirl:
    Our recital is only five months away. Next week the dance studio
opens back up. I miss it. At ballet I feel safe, like I do at Granddaddy's
house. I remember once when I was ten and Dad was taking me to
ballet. He told me in the car that he was going to marry Fawna and they
wanted me to be in the wedding. He thought I would be happy, he said.
He thought I liked her, he said. I did but not enough for him to marry
her. That really blew me because I was still hoping he would marry Ma
again. I stupidly hoped that I could hook them back up like in that
stupid movie* The Parent Trap. *And I hated Tiffany even more than I
do now because he was saying that she would be my sister—like I wanted
that. I ran out the car crying and feeling like I was going to throw up.
But when I got inside the dance studio everything calmed down.
Tchaivoksy's (how do you spell that?)* Nutcracker *music was playing—
"The Dance of the Sugar Plum Fairy." Everything—the music, the*

smells, the wooden bars, the rosin in the corner, even Miss Snow's big sub sandwich—rushed at me to make me feel better. My dancing was off the hook that day cause I put all my sad thoughts into it. Miss Snow gave me one of her fake compliments, and no one even knew I had been crying. I didn't feel sad again until I got back home.

At ballet no one stares at me and asks me whether I wash my braids when I take a shower. And nobody's playa-hatin cause I go to private school, like some of the kids in my neighborhood who go to public school. Most of the girls at ballet go to private school, too, or at least the better public schools. Allegra is my best friend at school. At ballet, I guess it's Zora. We think it's cute that we both have four-letter names that begin with Z.

At the end of the month Miss Snow will have the Swan Lake auditions. I'm trying out for the role of Odette/Odile (the good/bad swan). I want this part soooo bad. Ma says it's racist that the bad swan wears a black tutu but she won't say that to Miss Snow. All the parents are scared of Miss Snow cause they know she'll play them like a deck of cards. And anyway Ma thinks everything is racist.

Todd already knows he has the part of Prince Siegfried because he's so obviously the best of the boy dancers. I wish some of the white girls at school could see Todd, since they call black guys sexy who aren't even that cute. In the second pas de deux I do a pirouette away from him (if I get the part) and then pas de bourrée back into his arms. There's also a part where I have to lean back against his chest. When we practice we're close enough to kiss sometimes, and I just wish that once, he would. Maybe if Miss Snow was blind. Allegra and I are on the lookout for the ones we're going to get off the V train with. Todd, maybe?!

Two | On her first day back in the Office of Adolescent Services after the holidays, Moxie sits patiently beside her client, Antoine Sanders. She has moved her chair around to his side of the desk. She points to the high-lighted dates on the computer-printed chart in front of them, indicating the numerous times his urine tests were positive for drug use.

"Somebody lyin'," he says, rolling his chair back on its wheels.

"Nobody fills out this chart except me, Antoine, and no one else uses my computer. So am I lying? It's either drug treatment or probation revocation and back to Oak Hill." Moxie closes the case file, glancing up at the clock lodged between her Assata Shakur and Malcolm X posters.

"Damn, Miss D. That ain't no kind of choice." He groans loudly as he passes one hand over the top of his cornrowed head.

"Sorry, Antoine. Let's hope there's a drug program willing and able to take you. Most are full after the holidays, especially for juveniles. Call me back this afternoon before five." She hands him her card again, in case he's misplaced the previous ones.

"I need me a job," he says, frowning as he takes the card. "Not a drug program."

"What are you qualified to do, Antoine?"

He gazes off to one side of her. "Nothin'," he says angrily.

"Well, what's your prior job experience?"

"I scrubbed floors and cleaned the bathrooms before in a office on M Street. I was 'bout to go to job training on Monday, though." He remains in the chair, head bowed, while she stands in front of him.

Moxie touches the shoulder of his leather jacket, "Antoine, don't you think I'd love for you to be in job training? We've tried that before, but the reality is drugs keep rearing their ugly head. If you really want to go to a job training program, then let's put the effort in and get this monkey off your back," she pleads.

"You don't know nothin' about me." He moves away from her and rushes out of her office after opening the door like he's attacking it. Antoine, like many of her clients, is a high school dropout and has already been arrested for burglary, simple possession, and joyriding, all under the influence of marijuana and cocaine.

She shuts off her computer and walks down the hall, nodding to the security guard at the metal-detector station, and pokes her head into Voncella's office. Her supervisor's decor consists of framed pictures of her son in karate gear, holding trophies bigger than he is, and a bulletin board filled with photocopied quotes like: "I'm your boss, not your mother. Ask before you shit on me."

"Von, I'm about to leave," Moxie says.

A sturdy, chestnut-skinned woman in her late forties, Von wears a closely cropped natural. Hair is usually the first feature Moxie notices on other black women and the foundation upon which she bases her opinion of them. Moxie's respect for Von's hairstyle choice is diminished by its platinum shade, a kind of heresy. Von spins her chair around and glares at Moxie over her designer frames. "I'm not ready yet. I thought the funeral wasn't until noon."

"I'm picking Zadi up from school first, if that's okay. Hopefully she can learn something about making choices in life." Moxie stands just inside the door.

"Trying to scare that girl straight, huh?" Von smiles knowingly. "Go ahead then. I'll see if I can catch a ride with Leland or Mackie." She walks down the hallway with Moxie.

"When will your car be fixed?"

"Girl, my car has been ready, but it's thirty-five hundred dollars, Moxie. Would've been better off if it had been totaled. Contrary to popular belief, my paycheck's not that much bigger than yours."

"I hear you," Moxie says, not wanting to think about money or the lack thereof. At yesterday's staff meeting they received word there would be no cost-of-living increase, despite having been told the opposite before the holidays. She's glad she didn't already spend the anticipated extra money, as some of her coworkers confessed they had done.

Moxie stops at the elevator bank, and Von turns to her before continuing down the hall. "Oh, Moxie. I went over your reports. I don't see Bruno in there."

"Still working on it, Von. I gave you the others early. I'll do that one when I get back from the funeral." She adjusts the headwrap around her locks and puts on lipstick while she waits for the elevator.

Moxie's fifteen-year-old daughter, Zadi, grumbles for most of the trip down Wisconsin Avenue and across town to a sprawling white funeral home off Pennsylvania Avenue. "Ma, I can't believe you took me out of school for a funeral of some kid I don't even know. It's the first day back to school. I thought my education was so precious," Zadi mutters.

"Zadi, I don't care for your tone. How many times do I have to tell you that education doesn't just take place in books or at school?" Without looking, she knows those big eyes of Zadi's are narrowing with irritation. Moxie parks and walks quickly up the path to the funeral home. She waits at the entrance, holding on to the brass doorknob.

Zadi trails behind and kicks at some of the snow-covered gravel in the walkway. "Why does my education have to be about dying? Do I have to go in?" Zadi looks down at her short black boots. A small amount of snow outlines the tip of one. Leaning against the iron banister, she bends down and plucks the snow away with her fingertips.

"Yes, you have to go in." Moxie cautions herself to keep her impatience in check. While Zadi is bent over, Moxie takes one hand and runs it through Zadi's thick and plentiful braids. She loves the luxuriousness of her daughter's natural hair.

Zadi shakes her mother's hand off and stands up straight. "You said this guy Reebok was a drug dealer, Mom. So if he brought it on himself, then what's the point? What lesson can I learn from that?" Zadi's thick eyebrows collapse into a frown. She clutches her leather jacket close with one hand.

Moxie moves aside to let an older man and woman pass. "The point

is his life was lost needlessly. I don't want you to take life for granted."
She reaches out to touch Zadi's face. "Now come on, let's go in."

Zadi rolls her eyes and walks inside behind her mother. They follow
the line of mourners through the foyer into a large room with dim
lighting, folding chairs, and thin red carpeting—a makeshift church.
The mood of the group in front of them—mostly teens waiting to file
past the casket—seems inappropriately upbeat. They arrive in huddles,
whispering and profiling, clad in leather, suede, stone-washed denim,
and fake fur, hats and caps on backwards. They pop gum, mess with
each other's clothes and hair, giggle, and playfully push one another. A
young man gets jostled so hard he loses his balance and bumps into an
older woman, who glares at all of them wearily and blurts out *"Shhh."*
They all start sputtering and laughing. This is the way they grieve or
keep from feeling the pain, Moxie thinks. Some of them don't even
approach the casket. It's enough that they have put in an appearance.

"Ma," Zadi whispers, catching Moxie by the elbow. "Over there—
doesn't that girl look just like Missy Elliott?" Moxie nods distractedly.

The line of people inches forward slowly. Moxie puts her hand on
Zadi's back to move her along. A tall girl with a slicked-back ponytail
and a fur coat, giggling outrageously, accidentally steps on Moxie's toe
with her high-heeled boots. Moxie winces in pain. "Scu'me," the girl
says, without looking up at Moxie.

"That girl's boots are off the hook," Zadi whispers, in restrained
admiration.

Three of the clients from the juvenile unit were killed last year.
Moxie attended each funeral. One thing about her office, they may
have their squabbles but they always support one another at critical
moments. They'll come pay their respects to Reebok. She ponders the
irony of that word. *Respect.* Reebok was always pontificating about
respect. How much he got from who and what would happen if he
didn't get it when he thought he should. She had asked him once
whether he respected himself. He looked at her as if she were an extra-
terrestrial. "Respect myself? Yeah, I respect myself. I wouldn't get no
respect from nobody else if I didn't."

"If you really respected yourself," she told him, "you wouldn't be living like this."

Those frustrating conversations unraveled endlessly. She worked with Reebok from his first arrest for carrying a knife in school, through his many "possession with intent to distribute" cases, his eventual lock-ups and final release. He would have turned eighteen in a few months. She has to force herself to focus on her fifty or so other clients who are still alive, some of whom are actually trying to improve their circumstances.

In the far corner of the room, a wispy woman with curly gray hair and brown, folded flesh on her arms plays an organ. Her music sounds hollow, as if she barely has enough energy to lift her fingers. Moxie surveys the crowd for Octavius, a current client and one of Reebok's closest cronies. She's sure he feels the loss deeply, and she'd like to let him know she cares.

Reebok was fatally shot on the second day of the new year. He is propped up on a satin pillow wearing a burgundy leather bomber jacket and matching jeans, accessorized with a heavy gold chain, a gold bracelet and pinkie ring on one of his wooden-looking hands crossed at the wrists. The only hint of what happened is a round indentation, in the center of Reebok's forehead, that looks as if it could have been made by pressing down with a twist-off bottle cap, instead of a bullet.

Moxie stares at this Reebok, trying to see the other, vibrant one, again. She feels angry, instead of tearful. A funeral should be the culmination of a fully realized life. Moxie bends and whispers good-bye close to his ear. She can feel Zadi's disapproving stare. Poor Zadi, so easily embarrassed by her mother. They rejoin the line, which has slowed in front of Reebok's family. A young woman in a nylon warm-up suit and several strands of hair falling over one eye holds a squirming baby and pushes a pacifier into his mouth. Moxie is sure the baby is Reebok's son, whom he brought into the office not long ago, to show off like a trophy.

Reebok's mother stands with her eyes closed, tightly clasping a mourner's hand. Her black chiffon dress seems more suitable for summertime, and her head is framed by an overdone geri-curl. A second woman Moxie assumes to be Reebok's grandmother sits beside his mother, rocking sideways, Ray Charles style. She whimpers in monotoned intervals, "Maurice, oh, my baby, Maurice." She seems to be in a trancelike state, beyond comforting.

Moxie approaches Reebok's mother, whose hand remains extended, robotlike, after the previous mourner has held it. Moxie tries to meet her eyes, noticing they are misted over. "It's Moxie Dillard, Ms. Little, Maurice's probation officer." Ms. Little shows no sign of recognition. Just when Moxie thinks there will be no response, Ms. Little stretches past Moxie and grabs Zadi by the arm. "This your baby?"

Zadi's eyes open wide; she seems startled but not scared. Too cool for scared, Moxie knows. "Yes, this is my daughter, Zadi, Ms. Little."

"Baby, listen to your mama. *Please* listen to your mama before it get too late. Whatever she tellin' you she tellin' for your own good," she says, squeezing Zadi's arm longer than Moxie knows is comfortable for Zadi. Ms. Little reaches out to hug Moxie, hungrily and full of longing, before greeting the next mourner. "Come see me sometime, baby, all right?" Moxie wishes she had visited or at least talked to her more often.

Moxie and Zadi find seats near the rear of the funeral home. Moxie hadn't planned to stay for the entire funeral, but she is surprised at how brief it is. After everyone has viewed the body, a minister comes forward and rants about the violence "wiping out young black men like an angry volcano, spreading its evil lava from city to city." He points at the audience accusatorily. "What are you going to do about it today? We keep waiting for someone else to stop the violence, but who are we waiting for? Who is going to do it for us? This is *our* stain on *our* own community! We're the ones who have to be the stain removers. Don't let this young brother die in vain! Don't let this be just one in a steady stream of funerals you attend this year."

"Amen," everyone shouts. The casket remains open while someone sings "Lord, Take Me Home" and one of Reebok's cousins reads the eulogy. Moxie follows along with the program, halted by the phrase, "Reebok was known for his great smile and talent for making new friends." That's all they could come up with to praise, she thinks: his gold-tooth smile and some fast-living friends. What a legacy.

After the service, Zadi digs into her small purse until she finds a stick of gum, unwraps it slowly, and pops it into her mouth. "Did you understand Reebok's mother's point?" Moxie asks, her eyes skating over the crowd from where she sits, still looking for Octavius. She sees Reebok's grandmother, one hand raised in the air, swaying to the wailing sound from the organ. "Zadi?" Zadi doesn't answer. "Zadi?"

"Yessss." Zadi rolls her eyes again and leans back in the folding chair. "She thinks if her son had listened to the stuff she told him, he wouldn't be dead. So she's suggesting that I listen to you so I won't end up dead. Dang—I thought she was never going to stop digging her fingernails in my arm." She puts her hands in her jacket pockets. Moxie bends forward and turns to look at her, waiting for more.

"Why are you looking at me like that?" Zadi says.

"Well, did what she said mean anything to you? Or did you just dismiss it?"

"She doesn't understand that a lot of kids aren't pressed about being dead. After all"—she shrugs her shoulders—"everybody has to die sometime."

"I'm talking about you, though. Do you care about being dead before your time? Before you've achieved anything is this world?"

Zadi flutters her eyes, the way Moxie hates. "I'm not talking about me. I'm just saying that a lot of kids aren't afraid of being dead, so every time people say that stuff to them, it doesn't mean anything really. It doesn't change anything. And what does 'before your time' mean, anyway? I mean, nobody knows what their time is. Okay, I answered all your questions. Can we go now? Please?" She leans one arm on her mother's shoulder.

Moxie sighs. She stands, letting Zadi's arm drop down gently, and notices Octavius reclining against one of the pillars at the edge of the room. She leads Zadi by the elbow, and they make their way through the crowd to him. Octavius's face is wiped clean of an expression. "Octavius, I'm so glad to see you. I wanted to tell you how sorry I am about Reebok." She extends her hand.

He shakes it awkwardly, nods, and looks hastily from her to Zadi.

"This is my daughter, Zadi. Did you just get here?"

"Wasn't in no rush. Can't stand no funerals." He looks around the room as he talks, rather than at Moxie or Zadi.

Moxie tries to keep eye contact. "Well, I'm glad you came. Reebok would have wanted you here."

Octavius nods. "He look better than I thought he would. For real—look like he just chillin'." Octavius speaks in a monotone, as though the words are floating around in his mouth with nothing to latch onto. His eyes appear eager though, as if he hopes to convince himself of what he's saying.

"Octavius," Moxie says in a low voice, snapping her eyes up at him, "Reebok does not look good at all."

"Everybody gotta go out sometime, Ms. Dillar." She hates how he slurs the last letter in her name, rendering it nonexistent.

"Moxie. Moxie Dillard," someone calls. She turns and sees some of her coworkers, including her supervisor Von, Leland Jones, and two probation officers from the adult division. "Damn shame," Leland says when she approaches. The others concur.

Von reaches out and touches Moxie's arm. "I'm going outside to smoke," she says. Looking past her, Moxie sees Octavius and Zadi talking where she left them. When Moxie returns, they fall silent.

In the lobby on their way out, Moxie and Zadi pass the tall girl with the ponytail who stepped on Moxie's foot. She is in a heap on the floor, crying. Her ponytail has become lopsided. Two of her friends are before her on their knees, but looking unsure of how to comfort her. Moxie asks if she's all right, and the girl nods, sniffing and wiping her swollen eyelids. Outside Moxie and Zadi trudge past Von who waves, cigarette in hand. Their shoes make crunching sounds through the snowy gravel, all the way to the car.

As she lets the car warm up for a moment, Moxie reflects on Reebok. There was something loose about the way he lived, something Moxie could almost have envied if danger weren't so obvious an appendage. He saw no need to wait for the material things he thought would produce the respect he craved like a junkie. She tried to teach him that accumulating things didn't garner lasting, substantive respect. Maybe she should have hugged him more and chastised him less. The last time she saw him alive, he was sitting in her office eating a supersize order of McDonald's French fries drenched in ketchup. Clients were generally not allowed to bring food into their appointments, but he had a long explanation about how massive his hunger was and how long he had been forced to wait because he had returned one order, saying they weren't hot enough. ("Bama girl turned into Evilene and acted like she had to grow the damn potatoes and cut 'em up herself, but I let her do me like that 'cause she was phat as . . . you know what.")

He pled his case and Moxie made an exception for Reebok that day, mainly because his story had her laughing. She's glad now that she did. She had been eating a tofu and avocado sandwich herself before he came in. Reebok scrunched up his face in an exaggerated fashion and asked, "African food?" (He had asked if she was African the first time he saw her, she supposed because of her locks and mudcloth skirt.) Moxie had smiled and patiently explained the sandwich ingredients. She likes exposing her clients to worlds outside their limited file box of experiences. But the constant rhetorical question around her office is, How do you get someone to want something more than what they now want for themselves?

Zadi turns up the collar of her leather jacket. "Can you *please* turn the heat on?"

"I just started the car. It takes time to come on. I saw you talking to Octavius. What were you all talking about?" She looks at Zadi peripherally.

Zadi shrugs. "I don't know. Nothing. Why?"

"Just . . . curious. He's somebody I think has a chance to turn himself around and head in the right direction. Some of the kids who come through the court system—they're so lost nobody can reach them. We just go through the motions with them. But Octavius has got a good head; if he chooses to use it."

"What makes you think that?"

"The lights haven't gone out in his eyes yet. He's interested in a music career, and at least that's something. A lot of these kids aren't interested in anything. So . . . what was he talking to you about?"

"Huh? I told you. Nothing."

"Zadi, I *saw* you two talking," Moxie says in a playful tone, trying to make the question sound light. She reaches out and runs her fingers through Zadi's hair again.

Zadi shakes her hand off. "Ma, why are you always tripping? You need to just relax." She touches the radio dial. "Can I turn to WPGC? That funeral was jive depressing."

Monday, Jan. 4th
Express Classic Fit jeans
Gap black sweater
blk Banana Republic boots

Dear Sistergirl:
   First day back to school and Ma picked me up early to go to a funeral for one of her drug dealer clients. It was morbid as hell. The guy had this bullet hole smack in the middle of his head. Except for that, he looked like your average scrub you'd see out on the street who'd probably say, What up trick. But it wasn't all that bad cause I met a cute guy there! He's also Ma's client, but I don't know what kind of trouble he got involved in yet. Ma talks about her cases sometimes but she won't tell the private details cause she could get in trouble, I guess. We do know that his friend, the one who got shot, was a drug dealer—she only told me about him because he's dead and she thinks she's teaching me something. (Yeah, right.) Even though I can't see myself ever doing anything like selling drugs, I'm curious about that kind of life. You know? But for real I wouldn't do it. I mean do you like sit around weighing drugs all day and watching big screen TVs like they do in the movies?
   Anyhow, the cute guy's name is Octavius and he asked me for my pager number. I was like, I don't have a pager. Of course I didn't say my paranoid mother won't even let me have a pager when everyone else in the world has a damn cell phone.
   Anyway Octavius is tall with nice shoulders—I could tell by the way his jacket fit him. (Not as nice as Todd's at dance class but still nice.) I asked him if he works out, and he said yeah, I'm a baller. So anyhow, he goes to Woodson. I ignored him when he asked what school I go to, because most people who don't go to private school never even heard of Willow. He's dark brown like a Snickers bar, has small, sexy eyes that disappear when he smiles, a small hoop earring in his left ear (tight as a mug!), close haircut and wears CK One cologne. He was wearing a T-

shirt with the dead guy's picture on it, and underneath the picture it said Reebok, the date he was born and the date he died. On the back it said, For the brothers who ain't here. I thought that was so cute. More personal than flowers, for real. I gave him my phone number, which he wrote on the back of his hand! I told him to call late and hang up if Ma answers.

Ma saw us talking, but I didn't let her blow me. She's all right as long as she's not worrying about my business. I don't know what makes her think she's supposed to know everything about my life. I sure don't know everything about hers. It's obviously jive boring, since she spends so much time pressing me about mine. Ma got some real issues. If she wasn't my mother, Allegra would say—she needs to get some. Which she probably does.

Today was the first day back to the studio after the holidays. We were all really glad to see each other. Todd got his tongue pierced!!! Sexy as a mug!!! His tongue is still a little swollen and he's got this long silver thing in there. He said it didn't hurt that much, but I don't believe him. He can't eat spicy food for a month. Miss Snow told him our ancestors died so that we wouldn't have to be pierced or branded ever again and here we are doing it to ourselves. She is so overdone. The black swan dance is hard as shit. Sixteen fouetté turns as soon as you get on the stage. At first I could only do twelve, but now I can do all sixteen. Miss Snow showed us a video of Sylvester Campbell (a black dancer) performing the part of Prince Siegfried for the Royal Dutch Ballet in the 1960s! Miss Snow actually met him. We saw another video of a Russian dancer, Natalia Makarova, dancing Odile/Odette. She did thirty-two fouetté turns!! I'm jealous as shit. Miss Snow let me borrow the video and told me to give it to Sonya when I finish. Makarova was off the hook—amazing extensions, and her arms were fluttering like leaves on a tree in the dying swan part. I already watched it twice. I tried to do thirty-two fouettés in the living room and got so dizzy after twenty I almost bumped into the wall. Sonya is my competition for the role. Her dancing is like that, I have to admit, but she thinks she's like that, too. She has real straight hair—you know, what some people call good hair, although Ma says all hair is good. Miss Snow said everyone's hair has to be pressed and in a bun for the part. She was looking dead at me, knowing damn well my

mother won't let me get my hair permed. I said can't it just be in a bun,
without being permed? She was like, Zadi Lawson, I know that you are
neither deaf nor dumb. For real though, I'll die if I don't get this part.

Tuesday, Jan. 5th
gray miniskirt from Express/Gap jeans
gray leggings
white Bebe shirt
black Ban. Republic boots

Dear Sistergirl:
   During the holiday break, most of the girls in my class went on major
vacations. At least five went skiing in Europe, others went to Vale (sp?),
and several to the Caribbean. When they asked me and Allegra where we
went, Allegra was like, Southeast. I was like, Northeast. We just laughed
because most of them have only driven through the part of the city we live
in, on their way to Maryland or something. For a couple of years now
Ma has been saying that she's saving up for us to go to Senegal and see
Gorée Island, where the slaves were kept.
   I was thinking about how I wouldn't feel comfortable inviting
anybody to my house, except Allegra (who's already been over) and
possibly Windy Kaufman, especially after seeing Cherry Latham's house
last year and Mona Roberts's when we had the class dinner. Those people
are crazy rich, with mansions and whatnot. Some of the girls even have
black chauffeurs who bring them to school, and both Mona and Cherry
have black maids. I told Ma the maid at Cherry's house acted like she
was mad at me and didn't want to hang up my coat. Ma said she's
probably internally oppressed and only wants to take care of white folks.
Sometimes it gets to you, though. All the stuff the white girls have. All the
stuff I don't. Once in the bathroom I overheard Becky Sherwood call me
and Allegra scholarship girls. The only black people I know with big
mansionlike houses are Norma and her parents. They both have houses
that look like castles. When I used to baby-sit for Miles, I'd make believe
that I lived there, and I even took a bath in that Jacuzzi tub. Dad and

Fawna's house is pretty nice, but it's in Mitchellville, which does not count as far as I'm concerned, and it's not exactly a mansion.

Ma thinks my skirt is too short and swears I didn't have it on this morning when I left the house. She's right—I put it in my book bag and forgot to change back before I left school. It's not too short, though, and anyway, Fawna bought it for me, so what can Ma say? Style is one thing Fawna has more of than Ma.

I just checked my e-mail. One from Windy wanting to know how many pages we have to read in Othello. *What would she do if I didn't check my e-mail regularly? Also one from Allegra telling me to check out the Friends of Janet web site. I'm on my way. I counted—I have twelve pictures of Janet Jackson on my wall. You could say I'm obsessed.*

Wednesday, Jan. 6th
black Parasuco jeans
blk/white checked top
black Nikes

Dear Sistergirl:
These white girls are trying to drive me crazy up in this joint. There's a new black guy in the admissions office, and they think he's such a hunk. And me and Allegra are like, why don't you worry about guys your own color and leave the black guys for us? They think they have a right to everything. That shit gets on my nerves. And then they have the nerve to get mad because we black girls sit together at lunch. I mean, come on, Willow is only like fifteen percent black (they say twenty percent, but that includes the Asian, Indian, and Hispanic girls), so most of the time there is only one or two of us in a class together. We look forward to sitting together at lunch. It's how we relax and keep our sanity in this place. Jemmi Stockholm, a junior, and Ms. Marks, the lacrosse coach, started talking about how it is so separatist. Someone even brought it before the student council, and they were trying to make a rule that we would have assigned seating at lunch until I told Ma and she talked to the head of school. She said that if the shoe were on the other foot, the white girls would do the same thing, out of survival instincts. Ma can be good for

things like that. She's still kind of mad that I'm in a private school in the first place. She thinks she shouldn't have given in to Dad about it. I hate when they have fights about me. Anyway, we still have the black lunch table, thanks to Ma.

In the tenth grade, the students of color are me, Allegra, Maia Simms, and Lucy Parker, who keeps saying she's Puerto Rican even though her father is obviously negroid, as Beth Basheba says. Beth is cool as shit—I'll miss her when she graduates this year. Nobody tries to play her. And she knows how to keep it real and still have white friends, too. She tells them off in a second if she feels disrespected and always calls the girls who don't sit with us at lunch, The Negroids. Lucy sits at the black lunch table sometimes (a SemiNegroid), but Maia never does (a SuperNegroid). She even dresses like a white girl, wearing headbands and shit!!!! And huge bell-bottoms that are so long you can't see her shoes, which you wouldn't want to see because she wears Doc Martens! And sometimes she doesn't wear any socks—hello, it's wintertime. Allegra and I don't speak to her, not that she would care.

At our brother school there's only twelve black guys in the whole high school. I would say that at least seven of them are confused about their identity. Kwame Anderson is okay, but he acts like he's engaged to Tara Hicks, so forget him. Eugene Morris would be all right, but he still wears Reebok Classics!!!!!—now you know nobody in their right mind wears Reebok Classics. If boys only knew that shoes make the man! I don't go to the private school dances anymore unless it's a gogo. They play cheesy music, and if they do play a good song, most of the black guys dance with the white girls, and since the white boys don't ask you to dance either, you end up dancing with another girl or sitting down all night. The gogos I've gone to at Maret and Gonzaga have actually been damn near off the hook. I just don't see why people have to lose their blackness just cause they go to a white school. I absolutely refuse to do it. That's why I'm looking for a boyfriend who lives in the real world, not a criminal, or anything, but a thug-boy, like Allegra says (she got it from Master P). Yeah, that's what I want—a no-limit soldier!

	By Christmas vacation of her freshman year in
Three	1979, Moxie had observed a healthy sampling of
	the available men at Howard University. In her

mind, they seemed older and wiser and far surpassed what her high
school boyfriend, David, had to offer. She had no intention of spending her winter break with him but couldn't bring herself to tell him
directly. Instead she had her father say she was unavailable when he
called or came over, while she hung out with her new college friends.
Back in the dorm, in January, she stopped responding when summoned to the hallway phone, in case it was David.

Over the next few months, she was relieved that, having heard nothing, he had finally gotten the message. One Friday night in mid-
March, however, the front desk worker called upstairs in the dorm and
announced that David was there to see her. He said he wanted to give
her something. A thought flashed that perhaps she shouldn't take him
upstairs because her roommate was away for the weekend, but she
quickly decided that was silly and this was the last time she would have
to tolerate him. Once David was inside, she felt cramped in her own
space and knew she had made a terrible mistake. He told her he had
started using drugs because of her. He showed her his syringes and the
long rubber band he used to tie his arm up with. He showed her the
track marks. He said he wanted them to die together, that he couldn't
live without her. David held her by the shoulders, leaning against and
blocking the door. He pushed her down onto the bed, keeping his knee
pressed into her chest, took off his shirt, made a fist, and tied his arm
above the elbow. She wouldn't watch him inject himself, even though

he begged her to witness it. Moxie tried to scream, but no intelligible sound came from her throat. She reached past him for the doorknob while he was occupied with his works, but he jerked into action, kicking and punching her. She began to cry while he railed about how his life was destroyed and hers would be, too, before the night was over. When he let go, Moxie huddled near her roommate's dresser until he slid down the door into a crumpled nod on the floor. She tiptoed to the door and yanked it, making his eyelids quiver and his head jerk back, but she was free. She knocked on random doors, but it was a Friday night and no one seemed to be in their rooms.

She ran upstairs to the next floor and remembered the three dorm resident assistants who alternated weekend duty. She didn't know which one was on duty, but she knew there was one on each floor. She banged on the second-floor door labeled "R.A." A senior named Norma, whom Moxie recognized from her sociology class, opened the door. Moxie didn't realize how badly David had hurt her until she saw Norma's reaction. Norma stifled her gasp, though, and asked, "Are you okay?"

The words raced from Moxie's mouth, "My boyfriend tried to beat me up."

Norma ushered her inside, wet a washcloth, filled it with ice cubes from her small refrigerator, and gave it to Moxie for her wounds. Then Norma called the campus police. When they came to question Moxie, they informed her that David was no longer in her room. She declined their offer to transport her to the infirmary even though the left side of her face was puffed and swollen, slanting her eye. She winced every time she applied Norma's makeshift cold pack.

Between crying spells, Moxie told Norma that she and David became sexually involved in her last year at McKinley Tech High School. He didn't have enough credits to graduate but was insistent they remain a couple, despite her going on to Howard. "He didn't seem crazy then," she said. "I just thought he really loved me." Norma didn't know what to say because she couldn't imagine any boyfriend of hers even dreaming about doing anything of the kind. She listened though, played Frankie Beverly songs for comfort, and poured Moxie several paper cups of wine. While listening to "Joy and Pain" for the sixth

time, Norma helped Moxie onto the extra bed. Lying there, Moxie
noticed the many photographs Norma had taken and apparently
developed herself. A group of students doubled over in laughter on the
quad, a muscular guy skateboarding near Cramton, and several shots
from a Caribbean parade down Georgia Avenue. The photos were displayed carefully about the room, along with Norma's collection of
pink-and-green AKA paraphernalia. Some of the campus sisters had
tried to get Moxie to pledge, but she thought sororities were bourgeois
and trivial, a sentiment she didn't mention to Norma.

As a result of that night, they'd occasionally have lunch together
after their sociology class or drop by each other's room to chat. Once
when Norma was absent from class, Moxie brought her the next week's
assignment. She found Norma in bed with cramps, went to the lunch
hall and got her a bowl of soup, and then stayed with her until Norma
felt better. Though they came to appreciate and care for each other,
their lives remained mostly separate. Moxie became active with a Pan-
African organization that Norma thought too radical. And Norma, a
language major, was busy with graduation preparations and readying
herself to spend a year traveling throughout Europe. Moxie couldn't
help thinking that, given the opportunity, she'd rather journey to
Africa.

Norma sent postcards from her trip, and they met for coffee once
when Norma returned. Norma effervesced about Paris, London,
Rome, and Barcelona, and Moxie updated her about what was happening on campus. When they left each other that day, they vowed to
stay in touch, but over the next two years, the friendship was pushed
behind the demands of their lives. Norma embarked on further travels,
interspersed with apartment and job hunting. Moxie stayed busy with
studies, other girlfriends, and a young man she met in the Pan-African
group. Before graduation she became pregnant and married James a
week after they received their diplomas.

By October 1987, Norma was working as an art gallery bookkeeper
during the week and a photography lab assistant on weekends. She and
Moxie ran into each other one evening at an art exhibit. Moxie's afro
was shorter, closer to her head. She smothered her shock that Norma

had relaxed hers into a short, wavy style. They brought each other up to date and exchanged phone numbers. Moxie was a divorced mother of a four-year-old; Norma was still single. When Moxie called to ask if Norma would accompany her on a double date with two Georgetown law students, Norma agreed. Why not? She had already been through an endless chain of men, none of whom was long-term material.

Moxie and her date tolerated each other for the duration of the evening. But Lawrence, Norma's date, was an anomaly, someone whom she was attracted to *and* someone she knew her parents would approve of. The first time they made love, though, it was awkward. He was so much taller that when he was above her, she found herself pressed into his chest experiencing difficulty breathing. They moved around, bumping a knee here, an elbow there, but they eventually found a workable position. He came quickly that first time. "I'm sorry," he said, self-consciously. She didn't mind, though, because he held her for a long while, kissed her again and again, and stroked her face and arms. Her bed was positioned so that at night she could see the stars and the moon through the skylight. Lawrence, who told her later he was "inspired by the intimate yet vulnerable moment," made up a poem about the stars, the color of night, and her. She fell off to sleep before he did, and he woke her by making love to her again. This time he stayed afloat inside her and she held on to him tightly, thinking—I can work with this.

Norma impulsively asked Moxie to be her maid of honor. She had never really had a "best friend," per se. Just people she occasionally hung out with and talked on the phone to. Moxie had, after all, been instrumental in her meeting Lawrence and seemed to be genuinely interested in her happiness. When Norma expressed nervousness about the magnitude of what she was embarking upon, Moxie assured her she was doing the right thing. "But *your* marriage ended," Norma said. "How do I know for sure if we belong together?" Moxie told her there was nothing to guarantee a "forever-after" marriage, but she could see that Lawrence "loves your dirty drawers." Moxie was also the buffer between Norma and her mother, who had a more elaborate wedding in mind for her second daughter. (Norma's sister had eloped years earlier.)

A week before their July 1989 wedding, Lawrence moved into Norma's one-bedroom apartment on Fourteenth Place in the northeast section of Washington. The apartment was in a quaint two-story brownstone, with ribbons of plant-thriving sunlight gushing in from windows the size of some folks' doors. Lawrence had just taken the D.C. bar exam. A few months earlier, he had become an associate attorney with Davis, Lodge, and Badger, a large law firm on K Street. Norma was working at a gallery but planned to return to graduate school in Baltimore and major in photography. They fed off each other's energy and marveled at the progress of their lives, the richness they had uncovered in each other.

"We need a place that's ours," Lawrence said, "before we get started on our family." Norma agreed because she felt anxious at the thought of a baby growing in her. They began putting money aside to buy a house, which she felt would postpone things. "Of course your life will change with a baby, but it will all be worth it," her mother offered as comfort. And Moxie assured her she would be astonished at her ability to make the requisite changes.

Both the house and the baby took longer than initially anticipated. But by the spring of 1993, Norma had completed her graduate program and begun teaching photography to children at a Virginia arts center. Lawrence was certain he was on the track toward becoming the firm's second black partner, so Norma's father put them in touch with a realtor buddy. They purchased a modest three-bedroom on Aspen Street, NW, close to Walter Reed Army Hospital. Norma's parents offered to fund the down payment, but Lawrence was hesitant at first. Norma convinced him that they really wanted to do it and, after all, had done the same for her sister, Irene, and her husband, Simon.

Norma stopped taking the pill once they were all settled in, and when she became pregnant in November of 1994, Lawrence was ecstatic. He would call more frequently from the office just to check on her. Even the sex, which her gynecologist cautioned some expectant fathers can feel weird about, became freer and more adventurous. She was no longer the only one suggesting new things.

Almost every night he held her feet and calves in his lap and massaged them with peppermint oil. He loved to feel her stomach when the baby was kicking and to press his face close to Norma's stomach, talking to the baby. "Hurry up and come on out of there! Daddy can't wait to see you." Moxie gave them a couple's baby shower in June, and they took Lamaze birthing classes at Georgetown. They practiced the breathing exercises and spent many hours decorating the nursery.

Norma stayed home puffing through her labor as long as she could. Lawrence's mother and Moxie accompanied her to the hospital on the humid August day Norma's water broke. The hospital would only allow one other person, in addition to the father, in the room. Because her mother's abundant love often felt like a heavy, smothering quilt, Norma wanted it to be Moxie. Her mother would remain in the waiting-room area. "Go ahead," Doris told Moxie. "You're my third daughter any-way—the one I didn't give birth to," and she let out a vigorous laugh to assure them that she'd be okay.

While Norma grunted, cursed, and tried to breathe when Moxie told her to, Lawrence pressed on her back with his fist, as he'd learned in class. The nurse brought ice chips which Lawrence spoon-fed to her. She asked for juice, but then she vomited it back up. Lawrence cradled the basin under her chin, emptied her vomit, and wiped her face and neck with a washcloth. Moxie held her hand and counted through the contractions. An hour went by like this.

"She's in so much pain," Lawrence said to Moxie, without taking his eyes off Norma. "I feel helpless. What we learned in Lamaze class seems irrelevant now."

"You're doing great," Moxie said. "She just needs us to be here. Oh, here comes another contraction. C'mon, breathe through it, Norma. Try not to tense."

Lawrence tried to hold Norma's other hand, but she slapped his away. "My back, damn it! Get my back!"

While he rubbed her back, his eyes followed the monitor and the reams of graphlike paper it was spitting out. "Another one coming," he said softly.

"I can't help the way I'm acting," Norma told him between contractions.

"You're amazing," Lawrence said. She asked for her soft jazz cassettes, and he put the earphones around her head.

"Can you rub my legs, you know how you do?"

Lawrence brightened. "With the peppermint oil?" She nodded. He had stuck it in her hospital bag and began rubbing her legs and feet until the next contraction.

Dr. Gupta, an East Indian woman who always wore a child's plastic headband, ordered intravenous Pitocin to help strengthen the contractions, because several hours had passed and Norma was only at three centimeters. With the Pitocin the contractions grew stronger and close to unbearable. On the graph paper they looked like volcanoes, but Norma was firmly against an epidural, "I don't want anything to hurt the baby or slow down my contractions." Dr. Gupta said that the epidural would help her relax and perhaps encourage her cervix to open wider. Both Moxie and Lawrence had to work hard to convince Norma it was okay to request pain relief.

"I begged for it with my first contraction," said Moxie, smiling.

"You'll still retain your membership in the Strong Black Woman Club," Lawrence said, kissing her on the forehead. "I love you, and if you can feel better while you go through this, why not?"

When Norma finally requested the epidural, the nurse said she had to be at least five centimeters. Norma closed her eyes and bit her lips, as she felt another pyramid of pain rising from deep inside. Moxie walked around the bed and whispered to Lawrence, "Pitocin is a bitch." She passed him a damp facecloth to use again on Norma who was kicking the sheets from around her feet. She was able to fall asleep between contractions, and Moxie told Lawrence that would give her more strength when it came time to push.

Norma had been in labor for more than twenty hours, and she was exhausted. "Where's my doctor? I can't do this anymore. Can she check me now, please?" Her voice was strained. The nurse's shift was over, but she promised that the doctor would be in. When the doctor came, she pressed Norma's thighs apart to insert her gloved hand. Norma let out a piercing scream.

"Sorry. But you shouldn't scream like that. You'll be having a very sore throat tomorrow."

With each mountain of pain and valley of interlude she could feel the baby doing its part, working its way down. A calm took hold of her as she rested. Lawrence leaned across and kissed her cheek. But then the deep digging, tugging feelings between her thighs took over once again as she closed her eyes and breathed through each one. She clutched the hand Moxie offered to her. "Somebody, do something! This hurts too goddamn much."

"They paged the anesthesiologist. She'll be here soon," the next nurse responded placidly, adjusting the monitor belt.

The anesthesiologist's assistant arrived first. While Norma was contorted in pain, he asked for her medical history. "How old are you? Any allergies? Any surgeries?" Norma could barely answer. She held up her finger signaling him to wait. When the anesthesiologist appeared, he told Moxie and Lawrence to stay outside the room while they inserted the epidural. Norma was helped to an upright seated position. She stayed perfectly still, clenching her teeth through a contraction, while the anesthesiologist burrowed the long needle into her back, and the smooth numbing covered her from the waist down like a heavy blanket. "You'll be in love with me in a few seconds," the anesthesiologist said, checking the catheter the nurse had inserted.

When Moxie and Lawrence returned, Norma was flat on her back, with her eyes closed. "She's definitely feeling less," Moxie said.

"Can she still have contractions like that?" Lawrence asked.

"She's having one now." The nurse lifted the monitor paper to show him.

After an hour more, Dr. Gupta was summoned. "Okay, good, you're finally at ten now. The baby's ready to come out. When I tell you, take a deep breath and push. You'll see your baby soon." The doctor smiled widely at Norma, showing her gums. She brushed past Moxie. "Come here, husband," She beckoned to Lawrence. "Hold one leg like this. You'll see the baby good from here when it comes out. I'll let you cut the cord, okay?" Lawrence shifted one foot in front of the other and

placed his hand under Norma's thigh. When she stiffened at a contraction, he moved back. "No, stay here, husband; hold on to her. Here we
go. Okay, now push."

Norma pushed every time Dr. Gupta commanded, but she felt as if
she were pushing against an impenetrable wall. Once someone had
said that having a baby was like shitting a pumpkin and this image kept
crowding her mind. The nurse directed Dr. Gupta's attention to the
flashing digital numbers on the monitor machine. The baby's heart
rate had slowed.

"What's wrong?" Norma asked in a fragile voice.

Moxie and Lawrence both stared at Dr. Gupta. The doctor put her
hand inside Norma again, then said something to the nurse about the
head not being engaged. "We could put in an internal monitor but you
may have pelvic-cephalic incompatibility, Norma—baby's head might
be too big to squeeze down the canal. With baby's lowered heart rate,
we don't want to take any chances. I'm going to take this baby by
Cesarean section." Lawrence moved back from the bed, wiping his
hands on his trousers. Moxie stepped in to wipe Norma's face, pearls of
sweat dotting her forehead.

"Don't worry. Everything will be just fine," Moxie said to both
Norma and Lawrence. "Remember, I had a C with Zadi." She patted
Norma's trembling knees.

Dr. Gupta told the nurse to page the anesthesiologist again and have
him come to the operating room. Looking down her glasses at
Lawrence, she said, "Baby's father, we need you to get in scrubs."

Lawrence had backed up as far as he could go without leaving the
room. One hand gripped the metal sink. The nurse held out a package
of scrubs to him. He took them reluctantly, his eyes filling with tears,
"I didn't want them to have to cut her."

"She won't feel anything," Moxie said, approaching him. "It's for the
safety of the baby."

He stood near the door. "I didn't want them to have to cut you,
Norma," he pleaded, as if it were somehow his fault.

"Why don't you wait in the waiting room and let her girlfriend stay,"
the nurse said to Lawrence gently.

He looked toward Norma for assent. Norma was too tired and in too much pain to object. "Okay." Although she wanted him to remain, she knew that Moxie would be calmer.

Moxie put a hand on Lawrence's arm. "Lawrence, I don't know how to convince you, but everything is really going to be okay."

"I can't lose her, Moxie," he tried to whisper. Moxie would never have imagined seeing Lawrence this frightened. He always appeared so in control of things. "I've lost too many people already. I wouldn't know how to lose somebody else I love."

Moxie led him outside the room. Hospital personnel bustled past them. "You're not going to lose her. She's not going anywhere. You two are about to become parents." She wanted to wait until he was less anxious, but knew Norma needed her back inside. "You just take it easy. Go to the gift shop and buy some cigars."

He reached down and hugged her hard. "Thank you, Moxie. Don't know what we would have done without you. Thank you for being her friend."

"I'm yours, too, LL," she said, and meant it. She was impressed with all that Lawrence had overcome: the early death of his parents, working his way through college and law school, surrogate parent and sole support to his brother. And she loved his devotion to Norma. If Moxie couldn't have a thriving marriage, at least her best friend could.

As disappointed as Norma was about having a C-section, she wanted them to hurry up and do the operation. She was grateful to Moxie for handling things with Lawrence. Moxie returned to Norma's side, and the nurse directed her to go change into the scrubs. The nurse turned back to Norma and rubbed her shoulder. "You okay?"

"Yes. It's all right. My husband's just worried because in our Lamaze class they warned us about unnecessary C-sections."

"This isn't one of those," the nurse assured, as she unhooked the monitor belt.

Norma felt the wave of another contraction. With the epidural, though, she didn't even need to breathe through it.

The nurse and another assistant took Norma's bed down the hall and through double metal doors to the delivery room. It was a larger room with a black-and-white tiled floor. Big metal chests and tables lined the circular room. There were huge bright lamps hanging from the ceiling. A long metal table in a cross shape stood alone in the middle of the floor. They rolled her onto this table while she was in the midst of a contraction. The ripple of pain plucked at her, and she realized the epidural was wearing off. She cried out in panic, as she lay supine, hands taped to the table. A crucifixion scene briefly came to mind.

The anesthesiologist returned and added more medicine to her epidural catheter. Soon she could feel nothing below her waist. She sighed deeply. Where was Moxie? The room seemed crowded. Some-one put up a low curtain in front of her, and though she couldn't see, she could hear people moving about, their voices and the sharp clang of metal instruments and the running of water.

"Hey, Ms. About-to-be-a-Mother." Moxie came in quietly, wearing the scrubs. Her feet—Norma could tell by the sound—were covered with flat paper shoes. Moxie bent way over to give Norma a gentle hug. "How you doing?"

"I can't stop shaking. My whole body keeps shivering like it's zero below. Is it cold in here?"

"A little." Moxie sat on a low stool and moved it closer to Norma. She put one hand over Norma's palm that was taped to the bed. "You are doing such a fabulous job. And your baby will be here any minute now."

"You're lying. I'm not doing anything. I'm scared out of my mind. Did you see Lawrence when you went out there?"

"Yes, poor thing. You think you're scared. He's scared to death—doesn't want anything to happen to you. Your mother's talking to him. You know Doris; she's something else, already made friends with everyone who passed through the waiting room. And your dad's out there now, too."

Norma could see the doctors' masked faces looking down into her belly. She grimaced as they yanked at her insides. How much room can there be in me? she wondered, as their hands probed deeper and deeper. She stared at the tiny holes in the white ceiling and tried to think beyond the moment to what a baby would feel like in her arms. She closed her eyes, squeezing Moxie's hand, because her heart seemed to beat way up into her neck.

Just when she began to worry that it was taking too long and tears started dripping down to her ears, she heard a high-pitched wail. Dr. Gupta shouted, "A boy!" and held him up above the curtain for Norma to see. Still attached to the cord, screaming and covered with blood, his reddened face squinted at the light shining on him. Norma quickly noted that along with the mass of black hair, all the limbs and body parts were there.

"Oh, Norma, he's so beautiful," said Moxie, wiping at her eyes.

Norma spoke in tearful spurts, "Thank you, I love you so much. I couldn't have done it without you here."

"Yes, you could." Moxie dabbed at Norma's eyes with her fingertips. "I love you, too."

Norma tried to turn her head but couldn't see much from her position anymore, "What are they doing to him?"

Moxie reported what was going on to her. "They're putting him on the scale. He looks huge. No wonder you couldn't push him out! They're washing him now. Wrapping him up, putting a knit hat on his little head."

"How much does he weigh? Can I hold him?"

"Not yet, sweetie," a nurse answered. "We'll bring him over to you in a sec, though. He's nine pounds, seven ounces. We've got to take his footprint and get some mucus out of his air passages. We'll bring him before the pediatrician examines him."

Norma, startled, tried in vain to sit up. "Mucus where? Is he okay?"

"Oh, yes. This is all routine stuff."

Dr. Gupta and her crew continued to press on Norma's belly to expel the afterbirth. She groaned, but it wasn't as bad as the delivery. She had a son. Lawrence! He should know. "Would somebody please get my husband?"

They didn't have to go far. He told her he had been at the double doors the whole time, trying to peer through the thick-glassed window.

They named the baby Miles because Miles Davis was Lawrence's favorite jazz artist. Norma conceded despite Moxie's protestations: "He beat Cicely's ass and bragged about it, for God's sake!"

Norma liked Lawrence's rationalization, though: "Maybe if he's named after someone with flaws, he'll be okay."

She waved Moxie off with a smile. "We *know* that Miles's godmother won't let him grow up to be a woman beater."

Norma stayed in Georgetown Hospital for four days. Her parents came by twice; her sister, Irene, and her husband visited once. Moxie and Lawrence came every day. A couple of times Moxie stopped by during her lunch break, since the front desk nurses already thought she was Norma's sister. On her last night in the hospital, Lawrence's younger brother, Bernard, came to visit. A few months earlier, he had dropped out of college in New Orleans because, according to him, there were "too many city folks with country minds down there." He didn't seem at all disturbed that he forfeited the money Lawrence had already paid for his tuition. Recently, Lawrence learned from the school administration that the true cause of Bernard's expedited departure was an altercation with a young woman.

Norma was disturbed Lawrence hadn't sought more details from the school about Bernard, and she wasn't exactly overjoyed to see him or his date at the foot of her hospital bed. Even before this latest news, his constant expectation of handouts from Lawrence, the arrogant way he tilted his head and strutted about, as well as the steady flow of women in and out of his life, all exasperated her. Although she wouldn't want to admit it, Bernard also represented less refined next-of-kin, the poor relation she'd rather not have known about.

In the hospital room, he and Lawrence gave each other the one-armed hug black men often do. "Man, I never heard you sound as pumped as you did on the phone the other night! Maybe *I* need to become a daddy so I can crow like that!" Bernard shook his girlfriend's shoulder brusquely in his enthusiasm. Angel carried a single rose in a narrow plastic tube, 7-Eleven fashion, and didn't seem to know what to do with it.

"Thank you," Norma said when she handed it to her. "Why don't you stick it in one of the vases with the other flowers?" Lawrence offered the woman his chair, the only one in the room, but she declined. She seemed to prefer standing beside Norma's bed.

"We can't stay long," Bernard said, mostly to Lawrence, and focused his attention on the overhead TV screen.

"Did you all see the baby in the nursery?" Norma asked. They shook their heads, no. She tried to sit up a little more, but her stitches were still quite painful, and she cringed. Angel rearranged Norma's pillows behind her while Norma eased herself back against them. "They should be bringing him in soon. They took him for his bath."

When the nurse rolled the baby in, Lawrence carefully lifted him from his basinlike bed, rewrapping the blanket around his tiny form. Angel moved Norma's dinner tray to one side so Lawrence could lay Miles on the pillow Norma had placed over her lap. Bernard turned away from the TV and seemed mesmerized by Miles. He reached out with one finger and touched his puffed, still-reddened cheek. "Hey, little man." Norma frowned at Bernard's cigarette stench and wanted to ask whether he had washed his hands, but she held back. "Cute little guy. Head round as a balloon. He's awfully light-skinned, though," Bernard said, seemingly concerned.

"He'll get darker," Angel assured in a hushed tone, as if sharing a secret.

"Right. They say you can tell by the color of the ears." Lawrence pointed to the brown wrinkled skin at the tips of Miles's ears.

"Well, we gotta go, y'all." Bernard nudged Angel, who was stroking the baby's tight, almost transparent, fists.

"You want to hold him?" Norma said to her, ignoring Bernard. She nodded gratefully.

"Just for a minute," she pleaded to Bernard, who had inched nearer the door. Angel reached out gingerly toward Norma, clutching the baby, still bundled tightly in his blanket.

"Find anything yet?" Norma overheard Lawrence asking Bernard as they both stood beside the large metal door. They were the same height, and Lawrence had his arm around Bernard's shoulder. She was sure Bernard was poised to ask for a loan.

"Got an interview Monday, man. Construction company in Bowie. Looks good. Something to tide me over, you know, until I get my own business set up." He looked up, caught Norma's eye, and looked away.

Yeah, right, she thought, and turned back to the baby. Bernard and Lawrence slipped outside the door for a few moments.

Angel swayed back and forth on her feet, under Miles's spell. She instinctively rocked him tenderly in her arms, even though he wasn't fussing. "You're so lucky," she said to Norma.

"We gotta go." Bernard had reappeared, and his voice had an urgent edge to it.

"I'm getting ready to nurse him, anyway," Norma said in an effort to comfort Angel. She handed Miles to Norma, and she and Bernard left.

Lawrence came over to Norma and folded one arm around her, grazing the top of her pillow. They both stared in silent amazement at their creation.

After Miles's birth, Moxie was essentially the only friend Norma could fit into her full life. Moxie listened and never grew impatient with Norma's angst over her immediate future. Sometimes Moxie and Zadi would come over and just hang out while Norma plied Moxie with redundant questions. "Should I stop teaching?" "Should I work part-time?" "Will the baby hate me if I put him in day care?" "Will I ever have a life again?" Moxie hadn't had the luxury to choose with Zadi, so she encouraged Norma to stay home with Miles as long as possible. Norma stopped teaching at the arts center. She would return when he got older, she promised herself. She spent her days nursing him, sleeping beside him, and simply watching him—falling in love. Moxie was right. In October he turned two months old, and she understood the meaning of elation. He was healthy and thriving, and she was no longer in pain. Her stitches were out, and she had begun enjoying her husband fully, once again.

It was autumn, her favorite time of year. She took Miles out often in the stroller to look at the fall leaves. Their various colors reminded her of voices in a chorus. Alto, soprano, tenor—they all sounded different but blended together for one glorious sound. She tried to capture the intensity of her feelings with the camera lens. She had used a professional developer for color film, and when she retrieved the prints, she saw even more colors than she had through the lens.

She took countless photographs of Miles. Miles on his back, Miles on his side, Miles propped up with pillows. Lawrence was just as infatuated. He was determined to become an equity partner in the firm, but he did his best to get home to his family by a decent hour each night.

Sometimes he'd surprise her by stopping in briefly for lunch. In the evenings, no matter how tired he was, he wanted to do the things for Miles he had missed out on during the day. Norma welcomed the breaks. She'd go down to the basement and develop her photos in the makeshift darkroom.

By the time Miles was four months old, thanks to the breast pump, he could be left with Norma's parents while Norma and Moxie took in a movie or chatted over tea and latte until Norma's breasts were heavy with milk again.

This was Norma's life. She had everything she wanted: a happy baby, a beautiful home, caring friends and family, flexible and fulfilling work, and most of all, a loving husband. In March of 1996, when Miles was only seven months old, Norma became pregnant again. She had half hoped that the old wives' tale about not being able to get pregnant if you were nursing might have some truth to it. "Oh, come on, Norm," Moxie said. "You should have known that was a bunch of bull some man made up who didn't want to use birth control." Norma didn't mind. Her riches could only increase; and if the baby was a girl, their family would be her idea of perfect.

Lawrence immediately revived his role, massaging her feet and talking to the baby inside, while rocking the baby outside. One September night, not long after Miles's first birthday, Lawrence mentioned that Norma hadn't called him over, as she usually did, to feel the baby kicking. She told him it was just sleeping, although she couldn't remember feeling the baby kick during the day. Lawrence accepted what she told him and settled Miles down for the evening. Norma and Lawrence went to bed after practicing their Lamaze exercises, but Norma awoke in the middle of the night because the baby had formed such a hard, uncomfortable ball on one side of her stomach that she couldn't sleep. She shook Lawrence as hard as she could, bringing his snoring to an abrupt end.

"What's wrong?"

"The baby's not moving, and I'm scared." Her head ached, and she put her hands on her chest to slow the palpitations.

Lawrence rubbed at his eyes with his fist and sat all the way up. "Let's call the doctor." She nodded. Dr. Gupta told them to try not to worry, it was probably nothing, but she would check just to be safe. Lawrence held her hand in the car while they went to drop Miles at Norma's parents' house, and he held it all the way to Georgetown Hospital. Sometimes he patted it; sometimes he just rubbed it. "Don't worry. Stay calm," he said, over and over. She knew he was saying this for his own sake as much as for hers.

Dr. Gupta inserted an internal fetal monitor, a very painful procedure. Norma vise-gripped Lawrence's forearm until it was completed. The "bleep . . . bleep" on the monitor was the loudest sound she had ever heard. Dr. Gupta called another doctor in. They looked, listened, and talked in low voices in one corner of the room. The baby still hadn't moved. They would have to do an ultrasound. Norma looked at the clear plastic bassinet in the room, designed to put a newborn in after birth. It was empty, and somehow, she knew it would remain that way.

Lawrence bent over and whispered in her ear, his face close to hers. She couldn't make out exactly what he said, though. Something like, "Don't worry."

"I'm sorry," said Dr. Gupta. She hugged Norma and grasped Lawrence's hand. "Do you think you can get some rest tonight and in the morning we'll take the baby by C-section?"

Norma couldn't imagine trying to sleep with a dead baby inside. Lawrence read her face and asked if it could be done immediately. The doctors made arrangements and scrubbed up. This time Lawrence stayed in the room holding her hand.

When they were alone, she asked him whether he blamed her. He said no, but he didn't say much else. After some time in the recovery room, the nurses moved them into yet another room, away from mothers who had had live births. It was four in the morning. Norma wanted Lawrence to call Moxie. He held the phone to Norma's ear, and her fear and sadness were momentarily relieved by Moxie's simple words: "Everything will be fine. I love you." Dr. Gupta sent in a social worker, who encouraged them to talk about their feelings. She also urged them to name the baby.

After the social worker left, Lawrence said, "How about naming her Crystal?" It was his mother's middle name. All Norma could think was that both Crystals were dead.

Norma could still see Crystal's heart-shaped face that was tinged bluish gray because she choked on her own cord before she had a chance to breathe. Her parents kept Miles while she stayed in the hospital for those few days after she lost Crystal. When she woke up, Moxie was usually there to offer comfort and support. She brought inspirational books and healthy food. She'd sit beside Norma's bed in silence while Norma cried, or hold onto her if she wanted to be held. Lawrence was there every evening also, but he was usually typing into his laptop or talking on his cell phone.

As they prepared for the wake, though, the minister had to pry Crystal's still body from Lawrence's hands to place her into the casket. Norma had never seen one so tiny. When the funeral was over, she climbed back into bed and remained there for as many days as she could, trying to keep thirteen-month-old Miles in there with her. He had recently started walking and wouldn't hear of it, so she had to gather herself and get out of bed sooner than she desired. Friends called, but most didn't know what to say. For several weeks, Moxie visited daily after work or after picking Zadi up from ballet class. She tried to think of cheery things to bring each time besides food and flowers: a Whoopi Goldberg comedy tape, happy-face balloons, old photos from college.

Sometimes Norma's parents were there, but more often, just her mother. She and Moxie would water the plants, wash clothes, and straighten the house. Doris always hugged Moxie and told her what a precious friend she was. Irene called every few days and offered to come from Annapolis and help out, but Norma told her everything was taken care of. It was a half-hour ride, and Irene usually sounded tired. Norma and her sister, with five years between them, had never had much in common.

When Zadi came over with Moxie, she'd entertain Miles, who was too young to know how ravaged his parents' hearts were. Zadi would build towers with his Lego set and read him stories. Norma wondered if she'd ever stop crying. "You won't be sad forever," Zadi said, looking at Norma intently. Of all the things people said to her, it was the one that gave her the most hope. Sometimes Norma dozed off and would wake up with Moxie watching over her, just like in the hospital.

"Shouldn't I be doing better than this?" she asked Moxie after two weeks.

"You'll be over it when you're over it," Moxie said.

"It doesn't matter that I didn't have her for long. She was my baby, and I miss her so much," Norma cried into her friend's arms. Moxie cried along with her. Norma's grief racked her as if she and Norma shared a heart. She helped Norma locate someone to do light house-keeping and look after Miles so she wouldn't be so stressed. Moxie didn't know what to offer when Norma asked if she thought she'd ever get Lawrence back. "He's so withdrawn."

"Men grieve differently. They keep it all locked in; we let it out. It's a stereotype, but it's true. Who knows why? Of course, he'll be back. Don't worry." But Moxie was worried. She had noticed the changes in him, too.

Lawrence returned to work the day after the funeral and appeared to be getting on with his life. But Norma could tell things were off-kilter for him. He started working even longer hours, as well as bringing more work from the office. He'd still come home at dinnertime to be with Miles and tuck him in, but then he'd head back out. When she asked him about it, he said, "Since the other one left, I'm the only black part-ner now in an otherwise white firm. I have to work harder and longer than the white boys."

"But I need you here, too."

"Norma, my work keeps me from thinking about the things I have no control over."

She knew that he was still disturbed after what had happened the week before when he tried to negotiate a bank purchase for Norma's father and several other retired army officers. They had pooled their ample resources, and Lawrence's firm was delighted because a bank acquisition ensured additional legal work and clients who would continue to rely on the firm's services. When the negotiations came to a standstill because one of the sellers decided, after reflection, that he couldn't stomach a black bank president, the law firm blamed Lawrence and his clients. No one said so directly, but he heard the sec-ondhand and thirdhand comments about how the clients "lacked sophistication" and were "undereducated" and how Lawrence "hadn't thought things through to consummation."

Norma understood that the undoubtedly heavy weight of his law office's politics contributed to Lawrence's state of mind, but it shouldn't have been enough to drag her marriage down as far as it was headed. A month after Crystal's death, Norma began interviewing marriage counselors. Better to deal with it before all the thread comes off the spool, she thought. Lawrence didn't put up a huge fight but was late for each appointment. Norma would be on a roll with Dr. Matthews and then he'd saunter in, pulling his tie from around his neck as if it were a noose. Most often Lawrence's responses were cool and clipped, "No, I don't necessarily agree that we need help," or "Yes, I love my wife and child." Not infrequently, he'd be interrupted by his cell phone and have to excuse himself for a moment. But at the fourth and last meeting he attended, Lawrence said more than ever. Norma knew it was because he had been drinking before he came, something he rarely did.

Norma was in the rocker. He sat on the end of the floral loveseat, near Dr. Matthews's armchair. "My office has booby traps everywhere. Set just for me. I'm the last to find out about an important new corporate client or a major meeting, and if I complain, they act mystified. The response is, 'You're a partner and you didn't know?' I look the fool. Even though deals fall through every day, don't let one of mine fall through. They immediately start whispering about my overall competency, even though I've proven to be more than average time and time again. I just keep my head up and keep dog-paddling. But I can't close my eyes for a second around that place."

"That must be exhausting," said Dr. Matthews, her eyebrows raised in genuine, though distanced, sympathy.

Lawrence looked over at Norma. "And so my wife is right. I'm probably not the same man she married. I wouldn't know where to find him if I could. You know, Dr. Matthews, talking about this actually makes it worse."

Dr. Matthews spoke about the necessity of going through pain in order to heal. Lawrence didn't heed her words, though, because he refused to go back. "No, thanks. It's like we're her dish towels, and she's trying to wrench every last drop of despair she can get from us."

"To help us," Norma pleaded.

"Got to be another way."

For a while, he made an effort to at least be present in the house more. But that's all it was—his physical body. He'd work on his computer in the den or in the TV room while Miles watched videos. The house phone or his cell phone constantly rang with calls from his office or clients. He had little if any conversation for Norma. She feared he had crossed some invisible line to a place from which he might be unable to return. And though he didn't talk about Crystal, he'd refer to the "times before." Norma didn't know how to help him on her own. She kept seeing Dr. Matthews for several months because she didn't know how to stop the nightmares about Crystal.

She cried less, but less was still a lot. Sometimes it just came out of nowhere. She tried not to when he was around, because she could see it upset him. He'd leave the room abruptly, unable or unwilling to comfort her—she wasn't sure which. If she mentioned Crystal, he'd cut her off gently with, "She's gone and there's nothing we can do about it. Somehow we have to come to accept that." He wasn't cruel, but he wouldn't say more than that.

"Try to be patient. He's going through something. I'm sure it'll pass," Moxie insisted. "LL is a great guy, and remember, he still loves your dirty drawers." She hoped that would make Norma smile, but the smile was very weak. Norma knew Moxie thought Lawrence could do no wrong because she always pointed out his virtues ("He does the laundry, the dishes, *and* cooks!"), but she also knew her assessment was based on a comparison to James, Moxie's ex-husband.

Lawrence came up with an idea that they should buy another house, as if their sadness would be left behind on Aspen Street. Because, for the first time in a long while, he seemed excited about something, she went along with it. But the responsibility of finding a new place fell on her. She was physically drained and about to give up when the real estate agent finally found something she liked in the 1600 block of Holly Street, Northwest. It was located in a partial cul-de-sac, secluded and quaint, containing the pre-requisite large light-saturated rooms for her throng of plants. There were four bedrooms, two with real fireplaces, and a partially finished basement with a separate entrance. The two things she loved most about the house were the beautiful white-barked birch tree in the front yard and that the house looked out on a large woodland, allowing a visual reprieve from the typical city landscape. After all her searching, Lawrence only said, "If you like it, fine."

They moved into their new home in November 1997, with Norma hopeful things would return to the "before." When she brought up fashioning a darkroom in the basement, Lawrence suggested renting a separate studio space. The idea was appealing because she worried her photography was becoming stagnant. Miles had been on a waiting list to attend the Capitol Hill preschool recommended by his pediatrician, and she had just been notified he would begin next month. It made sense for Norma to rent a studio close to the preschool.

What she missed most was Lawrence's touch. He used to caress her body tenderly but urgently, as though he'd been thinking about it all through the day. After Crystal died, however, things became starkly different and remained so. In bed in the new house, just when she thought the pace of his breathing meant he was asleep, he would grip her shoulders and slip himself into her. His angry thrusts were often painful. She waited patiently for the previous tenderness to return. "It's okay," she'd say when he couldn't come or came too soon. He'd mutter some jumbled words under his breath and turn away, and then he'd try again the next night or so. It was something he forced himself to do. The times when he was able to achieve orgasm, in his shudders, she sometimes thought she heard him sniffing away tears, but it was always too dark to tell. She wished he'd just hold her, without the compulsion to perform a feat, but she didn't know how to talk to the husband with whom she now shared little more than a house and a bed.

Equally troubling, Norma found herself struggling with conflicting feelings toward Miles. He was more independent now, drinking his milk and juice from a covered cup and saying a few words. Since he had gotten bigger and more autonomous, he seemed harder to love. That made no sense to her, though. She told herself the negative feelings would diminish and she would once again feel the all-encompassing love she had when he was born and during the months she nursed him. He seemed to be uncontrollable at times, rendering her helpless and frustrated. She wondered if something was mentally wrong with him. Moxie thought maybe it was because things weren't right with Lawrence, but Norma was certain the two relationships weren't intertwined.

"Relax," Moxie would say. "Don't try to force it. It will come back naturally." Moxie was always saying things like that, and because her positive predictions hadn't come true with Lawrence, Norma felt doubtful.

One night when Lawrence was still at work, Miles became extremely wound up over a broken toy. He cried incessantly, pointing to the cabinet where she kept the glue and yelling, "Fix, fix." No matter how she tried to explain that it was beyond Krazy Glue, he kept screaming. Norma wanted to scream, too. Her parents and Irene had told her several times she needed to at least spank his hand, but she and Lawrence had agreed they wouldn't use physical punishment. Lawrence said he got whacked around too much as a child to do that to his own, and she had read enough books on childrearing to convince her that there must be another way.

But watching Miles's flailing legs and heaving chest as he stretched out on the rug, she began to think that if she hit him once, maybe he wouldn't act this way again. She bent over him and slapped at his legs and his arms and whatever part of his body she could make contact with as he rolled around. Something burst free inside of her and she kept slapping at him. He opened his eyes wide, startled and afraid. She had gone too far. She needed to make up for striking him, frightening him. She sat on the rug with him, opened her shirt, and drew him to her breasts, even though the milk was long gone. He kicked his feet and bit her nipple, but she felt she deserved the searing pain.

After he finally cried himself to sleep, she had an idea born out of desperation and overwhelming sadness. Since Crystal's death, she hadn't wanted to take any photos of Miles, even though he used to be her favorite subject. Maybe forcing herself to do so would help her previous feelings for him return. Norma stood at the foot of his bed with her camera. As she peered through the lens, she saw that his head was awkwardly turned to the left and the angle of his neck almost looked as if it were broken. The rest of his body coiled to the right, giving him a frightfully distorted appearance, and she wept as she took the picture. She knew whatever she felt at the moment would be evident on the resultant image. This time she was afraid of the very truth she ordinarily quested after.

Days later when she developed the print, Miles emerged, not like a sleeping child, but instead, still and lifeless. Norma destroyed the print and the negative, something she never did, because it was so frightening. Alarmed at the expanding indifference, almost coldness she felt toward her son, she was too ashamed to admit the depth of it to Dr. Matthews or even Moxie.

A Real Mother, an Authentic Mother, wouldn't feel such things. Bad things. Real Mothers, who are awakened in the middle of the night, give sleepy-eyed smiles to crying children, no matter how exhausted they are. They automatically know how to love their babies; no one has to teach them, and they never forget. Real Mothers always want to hug and kiss their children; they aren't ever repulsed by the thought. They want to get down on the floor and play, and they enjoy reading the same bedtime stories over and over night after night. They may get angry at their children and may feel like slapping or beating them, but they would never actually do it. And if they were to ever cross the line, they would know how to make it up to the child because of their Great Love. These are the basic tenets to enter the queendom of Real Motherhood. All the mothers she knows have these credentials.

When her own mother raised her and Irene, spanking was the norm. Back then if you didn't spank your children, they would've turned out "spoiled," like bad fruit. Even the experts thought it was okay.

Although Norma thinks her mother veered to the extreme of loving too much, she realizes it wasn't her mother's fault that her second daughter didn't know how to accept all that love. A Real Mother can't keep herself from caressing and heaping praise on her children. Maybe Norma was always inherently selfish. Maybe that's the crux of the problem. Somehow her mother is able to constantly give her whole self, like a sacrificial lamb, to her two girls, husband, and grandchildren. It's as if she doesn't need anything left over for herself or her self is swallowed up into her family and she doesn't mind.

Norma's sister, Irene, is also a Real Mother. She, like their mother, was content to stay home with her small children, reading and finger-painting and baking snickerdoodles. They didn't desperately seek baby-sitters or opportunities to escape from their homes, like Norma. Irene, practically a math genius, taught school before having children, and then quit until her children went to full-day kindergarten. She was satisfied updating math textbooks from her home office and never considered working outside the home. A Real Mother doesn't have anxiety attacks when she contemplates raising a child as her only career. A Real Mother doesn't sigh with relief when her children are at day care. When a Real Mother *has* to work, she is in agony because she would prefer to be home with her child. Like Moxie, who has told Norma stories of how she cried in her office after leaving Zadi with baby-sitters and at day care.

The other kind of mother is a Bad Mother, for there is no middle ground. Mothers who cannot love their children are to be shunned. And even though losing a child is a horrendous, difficult thing for any mother to absorb and move through, Real Mothers do it without losing love for the remaining child or children. During enslavement, black mothers had children ripped from their bellies and arms, often more than once, never to see them again. They grieved and then rose again to love and care for who was left. A Real Mother would not let the death of one child stand in the way of loving the live one.

The worrisome feelings continued to chew through her, as slowly and deliberately as a thick rope beginning to fray.

Thursday, Jan. 7th
GAP jeans
GAP black sweater
black Nikes

Dear Sistergirl:
We had a Diversity meeting today because it's almost black history month and some of the seniors thought there should at least be some kind of assembly. Last year Ms. Thompson told us Willow believes that black

history should be all year round, but like Beth Bathsheba said, we could roll with that if they actually did something all year round, but they don't. At the meeting, some of the white kids were saying stupid stuff like, we should have white history month. Please! So things got a little OC (out of control). Some of us black people tried to explain what it felt like to be in the minority at Willow. What rocked me is that Beth started crying and saying how she's the only black senior and how stressful that is, and then she went off like she was possessed or something. She yelled, you all don't know what it's like to have your daddies lynched and your mamas raped! Maia Simms whispered, neither do we. Part of me wanted to smack Beth back to her senses, but part of me agreed. I was scared that somebody was going to drape a towel around Beth and escort her out and we'd never see her again. But instead other black kids started crying, too. Tara Hicks said she had the feeling that none of her teachers expected her to succeed. Then some white girls started crying, too. One of the teachers Tara was probably talking about tried to defend himself, but it was a blower. I left the meeting feeling jive depressed and still not knowing if we'll have a black history assembly or not. Jemmi Stockholm with her flat-ass self said it seems like we're always doing things to make the black kids feel good. If I was a public school kid, I'd be figuring out where and how to beat her ass.

Allegra and I didn't even stop at CVS to look at magazines on the way home like we usually do. That's how stressed out we were after this morning.

Allegra says I'm lucky that my parents are divorced cause I get more clothes that way. She swears I have more clothes than her, but I don't think so. Dad will get me most of the stuff I ask for if I beg long and hard enough. I guess he starts feeling guilty about what happened with him and Ma, cause he'll go, Zadi, I know you wish your mother and I were together, but I have another family now and blah blah blah. Like I don't know that. I used to be really upset about their divorce. But I'm mostly over that now, on the real.

I think Ma might be convinced to let me get a pager. I told her she'd always be able to get in touch with me if I had one. Why didn't I think of that before? Allegra told me that's what worked for her. From there I can progress to a cell phone.

Friday, Jan. 8th
blk Lycra top
Express Classic Fit jeans
Tims

Dear Sistergirl:

Still do not have a boyfriend and I'm only seven months away from my sixteenth birthday. I don't plan on being a virgin past sixteen, so something's got to happen soon! This is an informed decision. I've heard all the talks about abstinence, peer pressure, teen pregnancy, AIDS, and STDs. We had two counselors come in and talk to the high school students. One was a lady who works in an AIDS clinic, and the other was a teenager who has AIDS. He did not look like it (actually, he was so fine!), and he gave a good talk, and I know I definitely do not want that situation. I have also watched the PBS tapes about sex Ma rented when I was in junior high. And I have read parts of the articles she cuts out of newspapers, photocopies at work, and leaves on my bed because I asked her to stop talking about all that stuff. What people don't realize is that this is a different day and age. Only nerds and religious freaks are going to wait until they get married to have sex. Be for real. Most normal people are going to have sex in high school or college. Some people will do it in junior high and elementary, but I personally think that is way too young.

Most of the time grownups don't want us to have sex when we're in high school because they don't want us to have fun. They know that sex is fun, and they want to keep it for themselves as long as they can because they also know that we are younger and in better shape than they are and will probably have more fun than they can. They want us to wait until we're all old and out of shape like they are. I don't even like thinking about any of my teachers or Ma and Dad having sex. I mean, that is so foul. It gives me a stomachache, for real. Last year my history teacher, Mr. Jones, married the eleventh-grade Spanish teacher, and we were talking about them doing it before they got married, and we laughed about it. But they were jive young looking, so it didn't make my stomach hurt. Ma doesn't even talk to any guys on the phone or anything, so I don't have to worry about her. Plus I should have gotten her the Tae Bo video for Kwanzaa because she needs to seriously work on her arms and her stomach. She's not fat, but she's got a lot of what she calls loose skin. She used to go to African dance class, but she says she's too tired and too busy now. I'm never going to be too busy to take care of my body.

During Thanksgiving weekend I was at Dad's, and one night I stayed up really late watching videos and went back downstairs to get something to eat. I went into the first floor bathroom, which is unfortunately next to Dad and Fawna's room. Their door was closed, but through the bathroom wall when I didn't have the water running I could hear Fawna making all these mew mew sounds like a damn kitten, and I could hear Dad moaning. I hate even thinking about it. I couldn't even eat my snack after that. I don't go downstairs late at night anymore when I'm over there.

Once you're in high school and college, you're more mature and can figure out better who's the right guy, and you can figure out how not to get pregnant. I mean, I know girls who got pregnant and they might as well be wiped from the face of the earth. Last summer I ran into this girl from sixth grade, Tawanika, at the Gap sale. She was in Gapkids buying clothes for her baby. I mean the baby was cute and everything, but it's like that book we read in sixth grade about the bag of flour. I forget the name of the book, but in the story this teacher wanted her class to know what it was like to have a baby when you're too young, so she made them carry this five-pound bag of flour around with them everywhere. But the thing was you had to treat it like it was a straight-up baby and not a bag of flour. Some of the guys tried to go play basketball, and they'd put the bag of flour on the concrete, and the other kids doing the experiment would be like, Hey you can't put the baby on the ground! So they found out it wasn't easy carrying a baby around all the time, and those bags of flour didn't even cry or need to be changed. I'm saying all this because reading about that experiment told me what I already knew—I do not want a baby any time soon! And I'd be too scared to have an abortion like I heard at least two white girls in my school did over the holidays.

Somebody just called into LoveTalk on WPGC and said she caught her boyfriend creeping and what should she do? They said, girlfriend, you need to go call Lorena Bobbitt. Damn, that was cold.

Ma got voice mail from the phone company, and now I have my own mailbox. You press 2 to get me. It took me twelve tries to make my message perfect. I had to write it down cause I kept messing up. Janet Jackson singing Go Deep is playing in the background while I say, This is Zadi. I'm out right now. Leave a message and I'll hit you back. A'ight. Peace. That's my message. I hope Octavius will call and hear it.

> *Saturday, Jan. 9th*
> *Nautica sweatpants*
> *white T-shirt*
> *white Nikes*

Dear Sistergirl:

  Allegra still has not done it either. She went to this guy's house last night, and they were going to do it when his mother was out walking the dog. But Allegra said the mother must have just turned around and come right back in, cause she caught them taking off their clothes before they had a chance to do anything. Allegra said the woman wanted to call Allegra's parents, but Allegra wouldn't give up the phone number (her parents thought she was over here). The woman said she better never catch Allegra over there again. Damn, she was lucky! So now they have to figure out some other place to do it.

  I think that is one of the hardest things for teenagers. A lot of white kids have cars, so they can do it in their cars, and sometimes they have two and three couples using the car at the same time (that is so trifling). I hear girls at school talking about it all the time. Most of the black kids don't have cars, so we have a harder time. Some kids do it when their parents are at work, and that makes us a little even with them because a lot of white kids' mothers don't work, so they're home during the day and when they get home from school. Most of the black kids' mothers do work, so they aren't home. But people like me have too many activities after school, so there is really no time to lose your virginity. Until you can figure it out, you kind of have to act like you aren't a virgin, though, even though you are. On Tuesdays, Wednesdays, and Thursdays when I don't have ballet, me and Allegra get off the bus near Wilson and hang out— when it's not too cold. We try to act like we go to that school, and we act like we're not virgins cause you don't want anyone calling you a virgin bitch. Some of the white girls at school say they're still virgins because all they do is blow guys. Watch on Monday, somebody will be talking about how they blew five or six guys over the weekend. They brag about that shit! I'm sorry but I think that is so foul.

Ma is about to get me in trouble for real. She was looking at my history notebook like she does every now and then, and she saw this list of pros and cons about colonization of African countries that Ms. Lewison gave out, and she went crazy. She was like, Zadi, do you understand how absurd this is? Do you understand that there was nothing positive about colonization? Africans had a complex educational system. They had their own religions. Intricate governmental structures—Give me a damn break! She totally kirked out and said this is what she was trying to tell Dad about the problems of going to private school. She says she is going to write a letter and fax it to Ms. Lewison Monday and she is going to send a copy to Ms. Thompson and blah blah blah. I'll probably get a F in history now for real. Why does she have to fight every cause? If she doesn't care about embarrassing herself, she should at least care about embarrassing me. That shit really irks me. I might have to call Norma to help chill her out.

I got my pager today after ballet! It's not fancy cause we had to get the cheapest kind. Ma put the initial payment on her credit card, but she says I'll have to pay the monthly fee. She acts like I have regular money. But I said okay, whatever. I can't believe I finally have it.

Octavius finally called, but then he said somebody else needed to use the phone or something and he'd call right back. I'm like, what? I didn't even get a chance to give him my pager number. I'm getting sleepy—it's my turn to call Allegra back and then I'll go to bed.

Four The café on Connecticut Avenue has dark walls covered with paintings by local artists. The metal tables and matching chairs have a quaint European look. Norma loves the way the windows are positioned so that sunlight has no choice but to lurch through them. The smell of ground coffee beans seems to leak from the wallpaper. Norma breathes it in like fresh air.

There are several customers eating, conversing, and reading the Sunday newspapers, more than Norma anticipated would be here this early. Some are part of a couple or a group, others are alone. A black woman with sagging cheeks and bosom sits on a stool by the window, reading the Bible. Norma watches as steam spirals up from the woman's mug and contemplates how striking a photograph the scene would make. *I'm seeing a man and he's white. No. I'm seeing somebody and he happens to be white.* She might shoot the photo standing behind and to the right, capturing the black woman unaware, with the light from the window nuzzled against the woman's face. If the woman was someplace more accessible, it would be a perfect shot for her zoom lens. She loves the intimacy a zoom provides. From quite a distance away, she can zero in without having to ask permission, without the subject posing and erasing the truth of the moment.

Norma has been standing near the doorway, where the chime sounds every time someone enters. She decides to hang her coat and uses the pay phone to leave Woody a message at his office. Several weeks ago, she impulsively looked up his home phone number and was both mesmerized and repelled at seeing it there. A reminder of his other life that she's not a part of. When his voice mail picks up now, she says, "It's Norma calling on Sunday. I know you're not there, just wanted to listen to your voice even if it's only a recording. Miss you." She knows he checks his messages on the weekends, anticipating hearing from her.

Norma selects a table against the wall to wait for Moxie. She sits and absently tucks her turtleneck into the waist of her pants. Looking up, she sees Moxie maneuvering toward the table. Her locks are wrapped with African fabric, and her cheeks appear rouged by the cold. Moxie shivers when she takes the seat across from Norma. "It's really chilly out there. Been here long?"

"Not long. A few minutes. It's more than chilly out," Norma says.

"Sorry I'm late. Fussing with Zadi." Moxie removes her coat and scarf and drapes them over the back of her chair.

"What now?"

"That girl makes me crazy sometimes. She doesn't get fired up enough about racial issues that come up at her school. Even though, mind you, I've exposed her since day one to cultural things. But she—I don't know why, just refuses to take a stand, so once again— I'll have to."

"I know how you agonize about her school, but you made a compromise with James, and you say you're satisfied with the academics. Think back—were you such an activist at her age? Sure she can't handle it without you getting involved?" Norma asks, cautiously. She scoots her chair closer to the table, allowing another patron to get by.

"Norma"—Moxie puts her hand up—"I don't even want to talk about it. You'll tell me you know what private school is like, meaning I don't; you'll side with Zadi and it'll just infuriate me again, so let's order." She turns in her seat and tries to read the posted menu. "What are you going to have?"

"Wait a minute. You just totally dismissed me in one sentence."

"Sorry. I get frustrated with that school on so many levels. I told you how I tried to organize a meeting of black parents, so we could check in with each other, compare notes on how the kids are doing. But I think only ten parents showed up out of the already paltry thirty-five or forty black families. Later I heard things like they thought it was going to be a gripe session or something divisive. From black people! Some of those folks act like they came to the school to get away from themselves. I swear—it's such a headache."

"I'm sure it's not easy for you," says Norma, opening her purse, somewhat annoyed. "But you have such strict standards." *Woody's a good man. He really is. He's white but he's a good man.*

"Like what?" Moxie listens intently.

"Oh, come on. You know how you are. No one's ever black enough to suit you," Norma says with a smile. "If it was up to you, you would have me, Zadi, and your dad running around tied up in kente cloth all the time, celebrating Kwanzaa every other month." Norma laughs, pleased with her half-serious joke, and then busies herself, taking several dollars from her wallet. "I think I'm going to have a vanilla latte. What kind of tea do you want? I'll get yours."

" 'Tied up in kente cloth.' Norma, you're crazy." Moxie laughs, too. It's Norma's customary way of digging at her.

"You know what I'm saying is true, Moxie. You know it's your life-long dream to someday be crowned Ms. African American."

Moxie waves her off. "Leave me alone." She squints at the sign displaying the coffee shop's offerings. Although she laughed, Moxie knows all too well what it's like to bear the brunt of a racial-Richter-scale judgment. She recalls feeling not black enough for some of the people at Zadi's African-centered preschool. Her gaze lingers on Norma's relaxed hair, cut in a bob with amber hair coloring to disguise the gray strands, a constant reminder of one of the differences they have silently agreed to sidestep for the sake of friendship.

"I was supposed to be ordering—What kind of tea do you want?" Norma asks. "Oh, I'll take that Gypsy Ginger Rose. Why'd they have to call it 'gypsy'? Why couldn't it be just plain 'ginger rose'? I mean, is that exoticism or racism?"

"See—you're the crazy one." Norma is still not as relaxed or ready as she had hoped. She leans forward and changes the subject. "So, Mox, it's a new year, any potential dates or mates on the horizon yet?"

Moxie clears her throat. "I told you. I'm not dealing with that. What—you don't believe me?"

"It was on your wish list *last* year."

"Yea, and where did it get me? Entanglements that stressed me out. I need to work on *me* before I can be involved with anyone. I'm tired of giving myself away to men and getting only half of them, or less, back in return. I don't even want them taking up space on my voice mail. I told the last guy I went out with to call me back after he'd had a year of therapy. He called and I said, Did you start therapy? And he laughed, and said he didn't think I was serious. I was *very* serious. He had 'issues,' as Zadi would say. This year I'm concentrating solely on my family. Understand?" Moxie raises her eyebrows for emphasis.

"Yes, but remember Phillip, the guy from the Eastern Market Gallery we ran into before the holidays?" She can see that Moxie doesn't remember. "The halfway cute one who had his dog with him? He's asked me twice about you. If you want, I could arrange a little dinner, nothing fancy, grilled vegetables, lamb or chicken. Could be a nice hookup . . . never know."

"No thanks. I barely remember him, but unless he's the reincarnation of Gandhi, Martin, or Malcolm, I don't want a thing to do with him. What is with you and my father constantly trying to play matchmaker?"

Norma removes her sunglasses from her turtleneck collar and places them low on her nose. She looks over them at Moxie and speaks in a mock baritone. "I understand what you're saying, Sister Moxie. But I have a dream today. I have a dream, my sister, that you will walk into the sunset with an upstanding brother who is not only my reincarnation but the others you mentioned, all rolled into one." They both laugh heartily, as Norma takes off the sunglasses.

"Norma. I'm serious, though," Moxie says, reaching across to touch Norma's arm. "This year I just want to be really happy with myself, by myself; I want to be closer to my dad and to Zadi; I want to make a difference in the lives of my clients. And of the utmost importance is keeping Zadi a virgin."

Norma puts her glasses back on her nose and deepens her voice once more. "I see, Sister Moxie. Let me understand, are you talking about for the rest of the girl's natural life?" They laugh again.

Moxie stops laughing, a little abruptly. "Well, at least until she's in college. I don't think that's too much to ask. Norma, I see so many parents knuckling under the pressure. They hand out condoms to their sons, take their daughters to get on the pill. To me, that's condoning it. And I'm not just being paranoid—I can tell Zadi's thinking about sowing her wild oats. Her body is blossoming like some damn springtime. She walks around with her boobs, bigger than mine, pushed out all the time and jiggling like Jell-O. Never mind that butt."

"Yeah. She's a brick house. So what? Are you jealous?" Norma's eyes brighten as she smiles impishly.

"I've had my brick-house moments," Moxie says, pushing her chest forward and placing her hands on her hips. "But she looks a bit too much like prime meat to me." She glances up at the menu again. "I thought you were going to order?"

"Just don't go overboard with my girl, Moxie, please. All right? Okay, I'm finally going to get the tea. Want anything else?"

Norma goes over to the counter while Moxie flips through the *New York Times* sections left at their table. Moxie looks up and notices a black man come in, locked in laughter with a tall red-haired white woman. His arm is hinged on her shoulder while she regards him as if he were the only person in the world. He glances around, Moxie thinks, to make sure all are taking note of their presence. She won't give him that satisfaction, though, and returns to perusing the newspaper. When Moxie looks up again, Norma is engaged in a conversation with a white woman who holds a small child's hand.

"You know so many white people," Moxie says to Norma when she returns carrying a tray with two steaming mugs on it.

"Oh, she's a parent from Miles's preschool," Norma says, ignoring the way Moxie's comment pricked through the surface. "I've run into her before. She's one of the few who recognize me outside of the center." Norma knows this statement will help put her back on track with Moxie. Moxie nods. Often when she encounters white people she knows through work or Zadi's school, they don't recognize her if the meeting takes place in a different context.

After Norma sits down, Moxie whispers, "Why does it feel worse when it's a brother?" She aims her eyes in the direction of the interracial couple.

Norma looks over her shoulder at the couple, then unwraps a muffin and puts a napkin in her lap. "Worse than what?"

"Worse than if it was a sister."

"Oh, no, are we going to be subjected to your where-have-all-the-brothers-gone speech again? You know it doesn't bother me. If they're happy together, then so be it," Norma says, feeling slightly piqued. "What is it—you think he should be dating you instead?"

"No, thank you," Moxie says, blowing onto a spoonful of tea before bringing it to her lips. "I just wonder if he rejects *all* black women, and what his mama thinks about that."

"His mama! I don't believe you. For all we know, she's happy as a clam thinking about those light-skinned, straight-haired grandkids she's going to have." Norma glances at Moxie slyly, while she swallows a piece of her muffin.

"On the other hand, she might be the type who'd be devastated," Moxie says without smiling.

"Devastated? Don't you think that's a little strong?"

"Not really." Moxie frowns as she contemplates her statement. Norma says nothing, but shifts around in her seat. The black half of the interracial couple approaches Moxie's chair from behind, holding her scarf. "Excuse me, Miss. Your scarf was on the floor."

Moxie turns and searches his face but receives only an empty smile. "Thanks," she says, as coldly as she can manage, wrapping the scarf around her neck. She watches him go back to the white girl. His narrow behind hardly moves beneath his leather bomber jacket.

"So, now did he redeem himself enough for you?" Norma says, leaning forward to playfully tug at Moxie's sweater.

"Just another lost brother." Moxie waves one hand, dismissively, and returns to her tea.

"That's not fair, Moxie. Remember, even your boy Malcolm X came to the conclusion that all white folks aren't devils."

Moxie adjusts her fabric hair wrap and peers at Norma. "And I never said they were. I just think it's important not to forget the history of who was the oppressor and who was the oppressed." She reaches across and tastes a piece of Norma's muffin. "Did I ever tell you what my old roommate used to call them?" she asks in an attempt to relax the conversation.

"Who? Brothers?"

"No, interracial couples."

"What?"

" 'IRCs.' " Moxie laughs. "Well, anyway, what's this big thing you want to talk to me about?"

Norma takes a sip of her latte, holding it in her mouth for a second before letting it slide down her throat. Moxie is the main one she has trusted with her secrets and feelings for more than ten years. *I'm having an affair with someone who's white.* "Moxie," Norma says slowly, not meeting Moxie's gaze, "I—I'm seeing somebody, a man I met." She can feel Moxie staring at her, but Moxie says nothing. "I put off telling you for a while because I know what you're going to say—that it's wrong. But you know I've been so unhappy for the past few years, and it's not like I haven't tried to work on my marriage." She gets it all out without taking a breath.

Moxie backs her seat away from the table. "'Seeing somebody,' does that translate into—'screwing somebody'?" Norma nods. "Well, I guess I don't have to say anything, since you already know what I'm going to say. Just hope you know what you're doing, that's all," Moxie says, feigning indifference. A bulky silence hangs between them.

Norma presses her fingers onto the leftover crumbs on her plate, then to her tongue. Moxie's words pierce the edges of her skin, making her feel nauseatingly warm and embarrassed, as if she were a scolded child. She looks at Moxie, and is not fooled. She sees the judgment shadowing her face, "It's not like I was out there looking for someone. This thing with Woody just happened." She covers her remaining crumbs with a napkin. "I told you because supposedly friends share things with each other."

Moxie drains the mug of tea. It's clear from Norma's unrelenting gaze that she longs for something Moxie can't give. Moxie looks away. She wishes she were somewhere else. Friendships change and grow over time, arching and aching along the way, but this one has been the sturdy monument that weathered anything. She thinks about the night she and Norma came into each other's life, how Norma's dormitory room, with Frankie Beverly crooning in the background, became her refuge. It disturbs her that, at this moment, she can think of absolutely nothing to say that won't be problematic.

Over the surrounding chatter, Norma notices that the coffee aroma seems even stronger than when she first entered. Moxie is drifting from her, and she fears she will be unable to reel her back in. "Things with Lawrence have been bad for a long time, and they're not getting better. You know this. I'm not justifying it, but Woody feels like a badly needed vacation. Maybe I am justifying it."

"What happened to working on your problems the way most married folk do?" Moxie lowers her voice when she realizes she's loud enough for others to hear. There is a long line of people at the counter. The black woman with the Bible, Norma's white friend and her child, and the interracial couple are gone, but they've been replaced. Almost every table is full.

"I've tried to work on my marriage for the past three years, but where has it gotten me?"

"Your marriage is made of gold compared to some of the ones I see and hear about. He's not beating your ass; he's not cussing you out; he's not trying to sell your children for drugs."

"Oh, come on. Moxie. You can cut the ghetto melodramas. James wasn't doing any of that to you either." Norma crosses her arms and holds her elbows, inching forward. "And you all split up."

"But I didn't start something else before the first thing was finished. And to this day I still have regrets, still wonder whether there wasn't something else I could have done to avoid divorce."

"My recollection, based on what you told me, is your situation boiled down to the suddenly-socially-conscious sista versus the money-instead-of-the-motherland material guy and never the twain could meet. Those weren't exactly insurmountable battered-wife, alcoholic-husband type issues." Norma's face is hot, tears threatening at the periphery of her eyes. She picks up her mug, but the latte is tepid and almost gone.

"You're missing my point, Norma. I'm saying yes, we had problems, but I wasn't sneaking around having an affair behind his back, smiling in his face at the same time. I spent my energy trying to salvage the marriage and then accepting when it couldn't be salvaged. I mean, how is this affair going to help you figure out your marriage? Have you thought about going back to counseling?"

Norma looks beyond Moxie for a moment, trying to collect her scattered feelings. "He wouldn't want to go. I wouldn't even ask him."

"No, I meant you."

"I don't know if I'm ready to listen to her questions and comments about me seeing Woody."

"Like you really don't want to hear mine." Moxie's tone softens. Some relief seeps through, loosening the conversation. "Norma, is it worth it? Is it that damn good?"

Norma rests her elbows on the table, hands under her chin. "Can't you just try for one minute to understand what I'm talking about? All this time I've been laying back, quietly tolerating Lawrence's indifferent lovemaking. Forgetting that I'm supposed to feel something, too. And no, it's not just about sex. Woody and I talk about our work, our children, our lives . . . Something I can't seem to do anymore with Lawrence."

"Well, I hope you think long and hard about what you're doing to your family. The more you continue, the more chances they have of finding out, Norma. With information like that, Lawrence could take Miles from you." A spiky-haired employee comes from behind the counter with a dishrag in his hand. He removes the tray and their empty cups and plates.

"Lawrence stopped letting me in on his feelings a long time ago," Norma sighs. "Maybe it doesn't sound like it, but I do care about Lawrence, Moxie. I never wanted us to end up like this. But I'm not in love the way I was, nose wide open, head all turned around like a broken Barbie doll. He blew it." An elderly man at the next table, with several medicine bottles lined up in front of him, leans over and asks to borrow the honey. Norma passes it to him. "Moxie, I feel like I'm stumbling around in the dark, trying to figure out my life, and here you come saying 'wrong move.' Makes me wish I hadn't told you. Can I please find out for myself whether it's the wrong move or not?"

"Sure," Moxie says. "Absolutely. You're right—this is your life. But don't you want to feel like you're doing your best? Isn't that what's supposed to happen as we get, supposedly, more mature and closer to dying? What about Miles? Have you thought about him?" Moxie refolds her napkin, so she doesn't have to look at Norma.

"Miles isn't even four years old yet—he doesn't know what's going on."

"You'd be surprised at what kids feel and remember."

"Oh, here we go. More expert advice from your probation-officer annals? I'm not Zadi, you know." Norma pushes her coffee cup to one side.

"Norma. I'm trying to help you see the whole picture. What you do affects everybody." Moxie presses at her temples out of habit. "I never told you this before, but I was in the pediatrician's office with my mother once, when I was around five or six. Dr. Luther, I think his name was, had already examined me, but we waited like two hours for him to finish with all the other patients, and then he gave us a ride home. Because it was raining, my mother said, and we had taken the bus there because she didn't like to drive in the rain. There was something about the way she and he talked and laughed together that struck me even at that young age. I remember he touched her shoulder when we got out of his car. I asked her if she liked him, and she said, 'Don't be silly.' But I never forgot how strange and a little scary it felt. Somehow I knew not to mention it to my father, even though she didn't tell me not to."

Norma stares at Moxie. "You never told me this."

"I haven't thought about it in a long time. I don't think she had an affair with him or anything, but I never forgot it."

"What happened when you went back to the doctor?"

"We switched pediatricians and never went to his office again. I thought about it several years later but didn't know how to verbalize what I wanted to ask. I never did mention it to my father because I didn't want to bring up something that would cause him more pain."

Norma nods and crosses her legs against the table. "The way your father talks about your mother, they must have really been in love, though. He makes it sound like they never even had arguments. My parents used to argue all the time, even though my father was in the service and away a lot; Irene and I were always afraid they were on the brink of divorce. But they stayed together, and now they seem very content."

Moxie takes her car keys from her purse and places them on the table. "It was different, I think, because, my mother was depressed so much of the time. She'd get mad at my father for little, absurd things, and he wouldn't react. I don't know how he did it," Moxie says. "Anyway, the point of my story is—Miles isn't too young to feel something, even though he might not be able to say what he's feeling."

They both know it's time to leave. Moxie removes her coat from the back of her chair. Norma stands and retrieves hers from the coatrack. Two white women weave their way purposefully toward the table Norma and Moxie are about to abandon. Moxie, irritated that the women can't even wait for them to move away, that white people always feel so entitled to everything, sits back down at the table and fumbles around in her purse, as if she's looking for something. This contrivance to hold up the two women embarrasses Norma, compelling her to tell them she and her friend are leaving, they're welcome to the table.

Outside the cafe, though, Norma embraces Moxie. Moxie hugs her back but is first to pull away. She stands still and watches Norma walk toward Dupont Circle. Partway down the street, Norma casts a brief glance over her shoulder at Moxie and waves vigorously. Moxie waves back, with less vigor.

Sunday, Jan. 10th
black jean skirt from Lerner
red & blk stretch top
black Banana Republic boots

Dear Sistergirl:
Spent the day doing homework and still didn't finish it all. When I took a break, Ma was watching Waiting to Exhale *on TV tonight and laughing like crazy. I like the way Ma laughs when she's really happy and not stressed; it's like a wave that starts out small and gets bigger, and it makes you start laughing with her even when you don't know what she's*

laughing about. I asked her if I could watch the movie with her, and she said only if I had finished my homework. (I'm probably the only teenager in the world who isn't allowed to have a television in their room.) The usual rule is no TV on school night. I reminded her that it was really still the weekend and that there's something I don't understand in math. I can get it done in study hall before class.

I saw Exhale when it first came out. My favorite part is when Robin is waiting for Troy and he comes over all late and all high and she says, You leather-wearing-in-the-summertime blah blah blah. That shit is so funny. Lela Rochon's hair is off the hook in that movie. I wish I could have my hair like that or like Aaliyah's—all straight. I wonder if she wraps it, like Allegra says she does.

Me and Ma sat under a comforter on the floor, and she made us popcorn. It was fun. I wasn't even bugging when she put her hands in my braids, which usually blows me. When it was over, Ma said her favorite part is the three of them dancing to TLC in Loretta Devine's house, drinking, and talking trash about men. She said it reminds her of when she and Norma were at Howard. They played old music and hand danced with each other once when they didn't have a date. I asked her if she used to drink and get high. She rocked me when she said, To tell you the truth, yes, which is why she hopes I never try it. She said even though at first she liked how she felt, later on she had bad experiences and kirked out and once even thought she was dying. She doesn't know about Norma cause Norma graduated way before her. Then she told me about a girl who drank so much she fell asleep on the toilet and they had to go in there and pull her panties back up and everything. That's so not mellow, like Janet says at the end of Free on the Velvet Rope CD.

Note: No call from Octavius.

Five Moxie cradles the phone and aimlessly scribbles on a yellow notepad while she waits to hear Octavius's tired excuse for missing his appointment this time. "Miss Dillar," he begins, "ain't tryin' to talk on this cheap pay phone, but trust me, can't make it over there today."

"Why not?" Moxie says. "And what are you doing on a pay phone anyway?"

"Home phone got cut off. And I ain't trying to run up my cell-phone bill. Last time you was mad when I didn't make it down there and didn't call you, so I'm callin'." He sounds as if he's trying to whisper without knowing how.

Moxie pulls herself upright from a slumped position in the chair. "I appreciate that, Octavius, although next time try to call earlier, okay? Now what's going on?"

"Miss Dillar, I know you won't believe me, but this for real. I just gotta lay low for a while. That's all."

Moxie waits for the sound of a siren on his end to fade out. "Did you go to school today?"

"Miss Dillar, I'm trying to tell you—I can't go nowhere right now."

Aware of the potentially grim consequences attached to retiring from the drug-selling business, Moxie still isn't sure whether to believe Octavius. "Tell you what, I'll come do a home visit, since you can't explain what's going on over the phone. Just have to finish up some things here. See you shortly."

"You ain't got to come over here, Miss Dillar."

"You were due a home visit soon anyway. I'll see you in about twenty minutes—four-fifteen or so."

Moxie was assigned Octavius's case about a year and a half ago when he was convicted of "simple possession" of crack cocaine and sentenced to one-year probation. He was fifteen at the time. Although Octavius never exactly admitted it, Moxie and his public defender pieced the story together. His mother, Lucy Johnson, sent him to pick up a package but he was stopped by police, who observed the transaction, before he could return home. Shortly after Octavius's arrest, he and his four-year-old siblings were removed from their mother's custody. One of the twins had been found, according to the abuse and neglect report, "in a neighboring alley, dirty and scrounging for food." Octavius was shifted around to different foster homes, separated from the twins. Moxie's first visit with him occurred at one of the foster placements. He barely spoke a word. In the meantime Ms. Johnson completed a ninety-day inpatient drug program, and after several supervised visits, the children were returned to her care. Six months later, Ms. Johnson, who, by then, was receiving outpatient care at a drug treatment clinic and participating in job-training through the Support Services unit of the same department Moxie works for, became pregnant again. She also obtained a job. Octavius had been going to school and doing reasonably well, but things fell apart when Ms. Johnson had the baby and subsequently lost the job. The same week, before going to school one morning, Octavius sold a cocaine rock to an undercover cop. Moxie went to court and recommended additional probation because she wanted him to have another chance. The judge sentenced him to another year's probation but with a few extra kicks this time—a 9:00 P.M. curfew during the week and 11:00 P.M. on weekends, regular urine testing, and warnings about the likelihood of detention should he be rearrested or violate probation.

In the courthouse after the hearing, Moxie demanded an explanation for Octavius's unnecessary predicament. Octavius tried to brush her off. "Why do my piss have to get tested? I don't use no drugs."

"If you take the route the system expects, Octavius, you'll find out it only goes to hell."

"I come from hell," he said. "I ain't scared of it."

She detected his bravado was erected on shaky ground. "Well then, you don't need my help," she said, ready to surrender him if she had to.

He stopped her from walking away, the hint she needed that he might be retrievable. "Man, Miss Dillar, I ain't tryin' to be no gangster, and I ain't tryin' to be greedy or nothin'. But it gets to me when the twins be saying they hungry." His mouth twisted to one side as he spoke. "And I don't want my mother to get depressed no more 'cause she don't know how to handle it. I just be tryin' to help." Moxie knew Octavius's story wasn't a fable, and although it gripped her, she told him he had to stop dealing drugs, no matter how humanistic his intentions were. If he got caught again, like the judge said, she'd have no choice but to recommend boot camp or detention. She promised to help him find a part-time job. He was skeptical. "I can't be working at no Popeyes."

That last conversation took place a month ago. She had gone by the home and spoken with Ms. Johnson, hoping to convey the importance of Octavius staying on track. The pouches of skin under Ms. Johnson's eyes made her appear older than her thirty-two years. She seemed worn and disconsolate, but she told Moxie she was determined not to return to drugs again. "For the sake of my children," she said, gazing at the tiny baby in her arms.

"And yourself," Moxie reminded her.

"Yes, ma'am. For myself."

Before leaving to visit Octavius, Moxie flips through her Rolodex. She makes another call to a job placement office for Antoine. "I'm just checking back on Antoine Sanders—I called you last week about part-time work. Yes, I took him myself to get his work permit. All right, please let me know if you hear of anything remotely possible." She frowns at the chaos on her desk and attempts to straighten it quickly: a collage of office memos, case reports, pens, yellow Post-it notes, and old telephone messages. Moxie shuffles everything into neater piles. She'll do a real clean up some other day. A framed photo, taken last year by Norma, of Zadi leaping across the stage and a recent school snapshot are precariously near the edge of the desk. She moves them over to the bookcase that holds pictures of Moxie's parents on their wedding day and of Aunt BeJean, her mother's now-deceased sister, cuddling a six-year-old Moxie.

She often loses herself in the fantasies and recollections these photographs arouse. Her parents, so wide-eyed, skinny, and youthful-looking, appear full of hope. Nothing in the picture foreshadows the web that would later entangle her mother's happiness, eventually shrouding it forever. She wonders whether her father had some clue or warning. Or whether her mother guarded her secret carefully, like a Pandora's box, tightly closed before marriage, gaping open soon after, spilling the contents. More likely, her mother didn't know what was to come either.

Moxie is haunted by the picture of her with Aunt BeJean in front of her father's azalea bush. It was Aunt BeJean who stepped in when her mother faltered, supplying structure, hearty meals, and plenty of hair grease. And although she never doubted her mother's love, Aunt BeJean supplied an additional brand of it. Moxie ardently hopes she truly forgave Moxie's naive cruelness before her death. She assured Moxie that she had, but she was very ill by then and there was no time for Moxie to make those years up to her.

Brenda, the receptionist, buzzes as she's putting on her coat, and says she has a return call from a Howard alum, now a DJ at a local radio station. Moxie called him last week asking about possible paying internships. DJ Ron D tells her the station has concerns about minors and insurance coverage, but, for a fellow alum, he'll check into what other arrangements might be feasible. He thinks they may be able to use someone to sort through the massive boxes of demos from hip-hop artist wannabes. She gives Octavius more credit than he actually deserves, convincing Ron D he'd be perfect for such a position despite his probation status. No promises from Ron D, though, other than he will get back to her. She tucks her trench coat under her arm and shuts the office door hard so it will lock, fluttering the Kwanzaa and Christmas cards taped to the door. Moxie looks forward to telling Octavius about the phone call; this could be just the incentive he needs. She stops in Von's office to let her know where she's going.

"If somebody's trying to shoot him, what makes you think it's safe for you to go over there? You know these young hard heads would think nothing of taking you out right along with him."

"Well, it's still light outside. I'll be home by the time it gets really dark. And if I'm turning myself into a sitting duck, then so are his mother and her three other kids."

Von turns from Moxie, back to her computer. "Skip the martyr speech, Moxie. See if Leland or somebody can go with you. I don't want you out there by yourself. And don't forget you still owe me some reports."

"The only one you don't have is Bruno. The others aren't due till Friday," Moxie reminds her, sliding her arms into her coat sleeves. "Don't worry, you'll get them all then. I'll see you tomorrow."

Von has a tendency to get maternalistic, but Moxie has no intention of asking anyone to go along with her. She walks past Von's computer-generated sign on the waiting-room bulletin board that reads: "To Our Clients—We lost one already this year. Don't let the same thing happen to you. Change your life now." Tacked up below it is a photograph of Reebok standing beside a cardboard Maserati, with a young lady. Moxie stops to look at it, unable to tell whether it's the same girl who had his baby. She remembers Reebok's refusals to sit when he first began coming in for his meetings ("I ain't got time; just go 'head and ask me my questions."), which later turned into her having to practically kick him out the office, his macho front, his corny and often inappropriate jokes ("Why does a hunter make a good lover? He aims before he shoots.") and his excitement over becoming a father ("Gonna name him Maurice, Jr., if it a boy, and Maurisa with a *s* if it a girl."). She had laughed and said she sure hoped it would be a boy. He frustrated her because he didn't believe that his life could be more than it was, and she didn't have enough time with him to help him believe. She hadn't realized, though, how much she would miss his presence in her life. Damn you, she mouths at the photo.

On the wall next to the elevator buttons, someone has drawn crude directional arrows with a black marker. Moxie appreciates the effort, since the original ones disappeared long ago. She presses the button for down, and the elevator opens instantly, startling her because it's usually a long wait. Norma steps off. "Leaving already?"

"On my way to see a client. What's up?" Moxie gets on the elevator, holding the door open with one hand.

"I was in the area, tried to call you from the car, but your line was busy. So I decided to stop in. Can I ride with you so we can talk?"

"Um, okay. I'll have to speak to my client alone though," Moxie says as they ride downstairs on the elevator. "Do you need to put money in your meter first?"

"No. You know me. I parked in a lot."

Moxie drives through downtown and out H Street to Benning Road, Northeast, and then over to Minnesota Avenue. She is burdened by the silence between them. "So what did you want to talk about?"

"I didn't like how it felt when we left each other yesterday. After I told you about Woody." Norma takes her camera out of its bag and clicks the lens into place. "You seemed . . . I don't know . . . really disturbed."

Moxie begins to feel anxious about Norma being with her and about Octavius's problems. She heads toward Jay Street and the stacks of red-brick apartment buildings that match the muddy clay they rise from. The buildings are similar in shape and design; she drives closer to make out the timeworn numbers. Octavius's building looks more like an institution than anyone's home. An apparently fire-ravaged apartment on the top floor of the building appears vacant. In one window a curtain, torn and charred at the edges, flaps in the empty window frame. Someone has stuck a piece of plywood in the other visible window.

A group of young men huddle at a nearby corner. One wears a bandanna around his head, another has on a heavy down parka with a fur-trimmed hood. Several are in leather coats. Moxie wonders whether they are drug dealers or workers on the late shift. She doesn't like it when she buys into stereotypes, but in this part of town folks seem to have less of everything including grass, trees, and decent jobs. While Moxie decides where to park, Norma rolls the window down and starts snapping pictures. "What are you doing?" Moxie asks, trying not to scream at her. "Did you even consider that those guys might not *want* you taking a picture of them and might not hesitate to do something about it?"

"I wasn't taking them," Norma says, with her face pressed against the camera, gripping its edges. "I was trying to get that building with the burnt curtain. But, no problem, I don't have to."

Moxie backs into a parking space. "That's my client's building."

"Oh. You don't come over here at night, do you?"

"Norma, this isn't the only part of town where bad things happen." Moxie is surprised at the ardor with which she defends a neighborhood that also alienates her. She recognizes that it has more to do with what she's feeling toward Norma than with the surroundings.

"I know that. But be honest; look at those guys. Would you want to walk past them alone, in the dark? Not me. You can't tell me you don't feel more comfortable in some places than others." She zips up her camera bag, puts it over her shoulder, and gets out of the car.

"Norma, I hope you're not planning to take pictures of my clients," Moxie says, locking the car door.

"No, I'm not. Why are you so edgy? Is this still about yesterday? If you're mad, why don't you just say so and let me know how long it's going to last?"

"Listen, I'm really not supposed to bring anyone with me who's not a lawyer or a PO. I said you could ride. If you want to come up, I'll have to ask my client's mother's permission."

"I don't have to stay. I can leave."

"You're here now. We can't have you wandering around in the ghetto, now can we?"

As they approach the doorless entranceway, they have to step over a discarded Christmas tree, its dry pine needles trailing a few pieces of tinsel like unrolled toilet paper. An old man wearing a bow tie and a long coat descends the stairs as Moxie and Norma wait by the elevator. His too-small hat sits forward on his head. "Elevator ain't workin' no mo'," he says through toothless gums. Something about the dignified way he's dressed despite his surroundings reminds Moxie of the stories her mother told her about the grandfather she never met. He cleaned white people's houses for a living, but he traveled back and forth by public transportation wearing a suit and tie, carrying his work clothes in a briefcase.

Moxie knocks at the apartment door, and after a few moments a child yells, "Who that?" Then Ms. Johnson partially opens the door and peers at them. She closes the door to remove the chain lock and then opens it again. Ms. Johnson holds a baby on her thin hip, and two small boys stand next to her, tugging on her bathrobe. "Go on back there," she says to the boys, flicking them from her robe. They scurry into the next room but peek at Moxie and Norma from the doorway.

Chinese restaurant and barbershop calendars are tacked to peeling wallpaper. An attractive but worn couch, two large chairs, and a coffee table crowd the middle of the room. Pushed against the back wall are four folding chairs and a card table strewn with books and papers. In the center of the room, an empty mechanical baby swing rocks back and forth emitting a weary ticking sound.

After greeting one another, Moxie asks Ms. Johnson's permission to have Norma wait while she talks to Octavius. "Sure, sure. It's all right. Tavius didn't tell me you all were coming by today. I would have fixed it up better in here. But come on in, have a seat." She pulls the sides of her bathrobe together. Norma notices how neatly everything is compacted into the small space. Even the children's toys are stacked tidily in one corner of the room.

"It looks just fine, Ms. Johnson. You should see my place," Moxie says. "I can't get over how the baby's grown! He's a cutie." She introduces Norma. "So where's Octavius?"

"He's in the back." Ms. Johnson rocks the baby, who is starting to fuss. "Thought I was gonna get my paper finished before he woke up, but . . ." She nods at the baby. "So I'm gonna feed him and see if I can't get him back to sleep. You all have a seat and make yourself at home. I'll call Tavius out here." The baby's surprisingly stern features give his tiny face the look of an elderly person's. He lies perfectly still, with only his eyes darting about.

Moxie and Norma slip off their coats while Ms. Johnson walks away with the baby. Moxie goes over and examines the stack of open library books turned facedown on the card table. She picks up two of the books: an anthology of black writers and a collection of British plays. Ms. Johnson returns with a bottle and sits down in one of the armchairs. "Tavius'll be right with you." She smiles proudly when she notices Moxie holding one of her books. "I'm writing a paper for my English class at UDC. I'm not full time or nothin', but I'm taking two classes. Got to finish my paper before Friday."

"You've been busy since I last saw you." Moxie is impressed.

"How do you do all that and take care of the kids?" Norma asks, sitting down on the couch.

"God is good. Found me a baby-sitter right here in the building. A nice lady who raised seven kids of her own. Real trustworthy. I do her hair for her every two weeks."

"That's great," Moxie says, coming over and sitting in the other chair. "How are the classes going?"

The baby makes little sucking noises, and his fists open and close repeatedly around the bottle. Ms. Johnson shifts him around on her lap. "They're going good. I take math, too. I really love the classes. I know that sounds crazy, but I do. My English teacher is a young thing, looks like she's still in high school. Didn't think she could teach me anything, but she's smart as I don't know what. And she says I'm a good writer. Can you believe that?" Her smile broadens.

"Yes, I can," Moxie says. "Congratulations."

One of Octavius's brothers comes from the other room, stands next to Ms. Johnson, and stares at the visitors. "Mommy, Raynard hit me."

"Raynard, come here!" Raynard, a shorter version of the first boy, comes in slowly with his chin pressed down on his chest. Ms. Johnson pulls him to her and smacks his butt. He holds his lips together tightly but doesn't cry. "How many times do I have to tell you, don't hit your brother? Now you and Damon say hi to these ladies and go on in the back. And no more hitting, okay?"

"Mommy, where they gonna take Tavius?" Damon asks, looking worried.

She comforts him. "Nowhere; they just came to visit him." The boys stare for another moment and then dash off. "Tavius is like a prince to them. Specially to Damon." Ms. Johnson adjusts the angle of the bottle as the baby's sucking noises increase. "Does Tavius listen to you, Miss Dillard?—'cause he sure doesn't listen to me. I know I hurt him bad when I was using, but I was weak and didn't know the Lord."

"He's been telling me how well you're doing," Moxie says quickly, almost interrupting. She doesn't want to get into a religious discussion.

Ms. Johnson puts the baby over her shoulder and burps him. "Oh, really?"

Norma moves along the couch closer to where Ms. Johnson sits and gestures toward the baby. "Would you mind if I held him?" Ms. Johnson passes the baby to her. Norma cradles it and says, "Hi, Poopie." She looks at Ms. Johnson. "It's a boy, right?"

She nods. "His name is Avon. I got me four boys now. I never wanted a girl. Boys get in trouble, but girls are nothing but trouble."

"I have a son," Norma interjects softly. She tries to get the baby to hold her finger as she rocks him in her lap.

"I don't know about girls being nothing but trouble, Ms. Johnson. You know I've got a girl," says Moxie, smiling. "I have to think positive."

"That's right; how is your daughter? What's her name again?"

"Zadi. She's doing fine."

"You're a big boy," Norma says, in the high-pitched way people talk to babies, getting close to his face. "Aren't you a big boy? Aren't you such a big boy?" He looks uncomfortable, like he's drowning. He is about to fuss. She adjusts his position in her arms and gently rubs his stomach.

"He likes you," Ms. Johnson says. "Maybe he'll let you hold him while I work on my bibliography. Just wish I had a computer so I could type it up."

The three women turn at the sound of Octavius's shoeless feet slapping against the linoleum. He appears, his long body folding over itself, his shirt unbuttoned revealing a tank undershirt and pants hanging so low you can see his underwear. He walks immediately to the dilapidated window blinds and closes them. "Aren't you going to speak?" Ms. Johnson glares at him.

"How ya doin'?" he mumbles, moving past them with his shoulders thrust forward, sinking his chest.

Ms. Johnson waves Moxie away. "If you can overlook the mess, why don't you go on back there. See if you can you talk some sense to that boy."

As Norma rocks little Avon, she thinks about Crystal and feels the familiar twinge of loss. Ms. Johnson goes to sit at the card table, opens a book, and begins writing on a pad of paper.

Moxie follows Octavius down the short narrow hallway, past the bathroom, where Damon sits on the toilet sucking his thumb, his pants around his ankles and his feet dangling above the floor.

"Man, you gotta close the door just a little bit. We got company, man," Octavius says, grinning at his brother. Damon squeals when Octavius touches the doorknob. "My bad." He doesn't close it. "He be scairt a lot," Octavius explains.

Octavius enters one of the two bedrooms. There is a double bed neatly made in the center of the room. Another foldaway bed covered with a tangle of sheets and blankets is crammed next to the window. A poster of a bandanna-wearing Tupac, giving what looks like the peace sign, is tacked up on one wall. Moxie searches for somewhere to sit. The only chair in the room is covered with abandoned clothes. She scoops them up, moves them to the bed, and settles in the chair. "Your mom looks well, Octavius."

He nods. Octavius is too big for the room. He remains standing between a chest of drawers and a closet and avoids her eyes. He begins folding the clothes from the heap, slowly and neatly, and putting them away in the drawers.

"My daughter had that same poster of Tupac."

"Yeah?" His eyes brighten and land on Moxie's face briefly.

"I think she has something else up there now, though. Don't tell me you think he's still alive, too?"

"Basically. Youngin just chillin' somewhere till the time is right. Look at all the music he keep making and the movies. Look at the one he did 'bout Biggie, and he supposed to have died before Biggie."

Moxie smiles knowingly. "Okay, okay. I've already traveled down this road with Zadi, so let's pretend I didn't even bring it up. Can we talk about what's going on with you?"

He walks back and forth in the small space with his clothes, frowning. "Ain't nothin'. For real, Miss Dillar."

"You can't afford to mess up in school," she says. He looks toward the door as if to make sure he has an escape route. She pats the bed. "You're making me nervous standing around like that. Why don't you sit down?"

Moxie thinks she has Octavius somewhat figured out. His personality is like soft, malleable clay at one moment and hardened stone at the next. She has to knead him enough now so he'll give her the information she seeks. Sometimes you have to play games with people—act disinterested and then they'll want to talk, especially the male species, Moxie acknowledges. "Well, okay, Octavius. I came over because I thought you had some things you wanted to discuss face-to-face rather than over the phone." She smoothes her hands against her skirt. "But, if I misunderstood, then I'll leave and go on to the next place."

"See, somebody told me somebody out there lookin' for me. That's all."

"Somebody like who?"

He shrugs.

"No idea?"

He shrugs again.

"How can I help you if you don't want to tell me anything?" She wonders fleetingly how Norma and Ms. Johnson are getting along.

Octavius smiles sheepishly, as if he'd been caught playing a practical joke on somebody. He looks up and his eyes meet Moxie's by mistake, graze her body quickly, and then land safely on the wall beyond her. He coughs a laugh. "I didn't ask for no help."

"Octavius."

"For real, Miss Dillar." His lips force themselves into a pout. "Ain't saying I wanna die, but I ain't goin' out like a punk neither. I ain't scairt of nothin'."

Moxie shakes her head. She stands and yanks his elbow through Octavius's flannel shirt. "Hey, you sound like you're ready to pack it all in. What happened to your dream about becoming a rap singer or a DJ?"

"Maybe I said that 'cause you kept buggin' me about what was my dream. But everybody don't get them kind of breaks." He folds his lanky arms in front of his chest and leans against the closet door. "And what if somebody's dream turns out to be a nightmare?"

Moxie feels drained. Octavius's dreams have already been abridged by his reality. The urgency of adolescence, which seems to lessen teenagers' capacity for listening to others, doesn't help either. "Octavius," she says, touching his arm again, "it's up to us to make our own dreams come true. It's our responsibility to honor and respect them. Yours is a good one. It doesn't mean you won't need help or time to achieve it. I heard from Ron D, the DJ at WPGC. He wants to arrange for you to come by and check out what they do. They might have a part-time position for you, assessing demos. Interested?"

"What you mean?"

"You would listen to the demo tapes and CDs people send in hoping the radio station will play them. And help decide which ones sound good enough. All I'm saying is you can decide to have a different life, Octavius. Your own mother's a role model for that, and you're just as strong as she is." Moxie moves toward the door and places her hand on the knob. "You don't have to travel on Reebok's route." Octavius doesn't speak. "I'll take you up to the radio station to meet with Ron. How about one day after school next week?" He nods. "Do you have a social security card?"

"Lost it."

"We'll have to get that taken care of first. Come in Wednesday with your birth certificate and school ID, okay?"

He plunges his hands in his pockets and walks slowly behind her to the door. "For real, though, you ain't got to worry 'bout finding me no job 'cause I might not be around that long."

Moxie turns her head up toward Octavius. He looks away. She stares at the sharp lines of his haircut above his cheekbones and the small gold ring in his left earlobe. A person so young shouldn't feel so hopeless. "If it's that serious, then what about staying at a friend or relative's place for a while? What about alerting the police?" She knows what kind of response to expect from her last statement, and sure enough, Octavius surveys her skeptically. But Moxie has no protection to offer him. She can't promise him that he won't get hurt or that the threats on his life are mere crowing by harmless gangster imitators. "I could see about transferring you to another high school. Anacostia wouldn't be too far."

He frowns. "Naw. Anacostia ain't no safety zone. That ain't gonna work. Not my mama's prayers neither. Ain't nothin' nobody can do. That's the just the way it is, like youngin said." He shifts his eyes to the poster of Tupac.

"I don't accept that, Octavius. If you need to take certain precautions, let's do it. I'm trying to work with you." He offers no further statement or expression. "Well, if I need to come pick you up

Wednesday to go the social security office, call me. *After* you go to school." On her way out of his room she notices some glossy pamphlets on Octavius's dresser. "What are those?"

Somewhat chagrined, he says, "Oh, just some of them funeral joints. They was passing them out near the metro."

"What would you want with funeral pamphlets?" She goes over and flips through one with annoyance.

"Don't know. In case. But them plots and tomb stones is jive expensive." He shakes his head and Moxie walks out the door.

When she returns to the living room, Norma has pulled a chair up to the card table, and she and Ms. Johnson are engrossed in one of the library books. The baby is asleep in the ticking swing with his head tilted to one side. Norma edges her chair slightly away when Moxie comes in, as if she has been caught doing something wrong. "Working on her paper," she says softly. Moxie nods and retrieves her coat from the couch. "Moxie, Ms. Johnson asked me to take a picture of her and the kids, but I didn't know . . . if . . . whether you'd want me to do that."

"It's okay," Moxie says, even though it's not. She feels a rumbling indignation at the apparent connection that has developed between Norma and Ms. Johnson in the short time she was with Octavius. A childish response, she knows, but she can't help it.

Norma opens her camera bag. "Ready when you are," she says to Ms. Johnson, who goes in the back.

Ms. Johnson returns, having changed from her robe to a blouse and skirt and added a little lipstick. She rounds up the small boys, wakes the baby for the photo, and even Octavius consents to a hard-looking pose. Moxie stands, watching, with her coat over her arm. She wonders if Norma's photograph will capture the competing forces of hope and tragedy on her subjects' faces.

Outside is dense with cold air and the sky appears gray and impenetrable. The street shines with fresh rain, which Moxie hopes doesn't turn to ice while she's driving. The same group of young men are still at the corner laughing forcefully, talking in loud voices, unfazed by the steady drizzle. Moxie unlocks the car door on Norma's side.

"Your client seems kind of lost. Did you have a good visit with him?" Norma adjusts her seat belt.

"It was fine." Moxie starts the car. It cuts off, and she has to start it again. "How about you—did you get all the pictures you wanted? What will you call this series—the Have Nots?"

"Moxie, why are you acting like this? Ms. Johnson asked me to take those pictures. I wasn't looking down on her at all. Actually I was really amazed by her. Her determination—grit, I guess you call it—in spite of it all. I realize it could be the other way around; I could be in her shoes. The piece I don't get, though, is why in the world would she have another baby with no job and no man in sight? You'd think it would just make everything harder, you know?"

"I'm not there to pass judgment on her life," says Moxie, turning her wipers to the intermittent mode.

"Oh, really? How come it's okay for you to pass judgment on mine, then?" Norma stares at Moxie, who looks straight ahead into the rain.

Monday, Jan. 11th
Express Classic Fit jeans
leopard print spandex shirt
Tims

Dear Sistergirl:

Octavius just paged me. Right in the middle of study hall. I turned the pager to vibrate because what if I was in class for real or something? He knows I'm in school. We aren't allowed to use the pay phones during study hall, so I'll have to wait. Why isn't he in school? Ma found the condoms that I got from the assembly we had for AIDS Awareness last week. I left them in my jeans. What was she doing snooping around in my pockets anyway? She says I left my jeans in the bathroom and when she was about to put them in the laundry basket, something made a crackling noise. She thought it was a gum wrapper. Yeah, right. She must think I'm really stupid. She kirked out, and then she went into her thing where she adds other stuff to what she's already mad about, like me not doing the dishes last night and telling me not to take a long shower this morning.

I'm like what are you talking about? All this unnecessary shit while I'm still in the bed.

I'm writing in my notebook at school because sometimes it's just too boring. I'm in study hall and I'm supposed to be reading Othello, *but it's getting on my nerves. Why couldn't Shakespeare just say what he means in plain English? He's so damn irritating. Why does he have to disguise everything so we have to wrack our brains trying to figure out what the hell he was saying? If he was a writer now, nobody would buy his stuff. Maybe he was wet then, but he's played now. Instead of tripping, you'd think he'd want to make sure people understood him for the next zillion years instead of leaving so much for people to figure out on their own. So anyway I'm reading* Lolita *on the down low. Humbert is a trip. I love this book. This is not my first time reading it, though. I also love Colette's writing, especially the* Claudine *series. My mother is always trying to get me to read books by black writers like Toni Morrison and Alice Walker. I give them props, but she doesn't understand that sometimes I want to read about something different from what I am. I did at least read all Terry McMillan's books and half of one of Bebe Moore Campbell's books. Windy likes to read Asian writers, and she says her mother is always pressing her to read Jewish writers, so I guess some stuff is the same when it comes to mothers who constantly try to sweat your business. I like to hear Windy talk about being Jewish. We don't really have a religion, and that trips Windy out. Allegra is Baptist and is in church almost all day Sunday. She and Windy always ask me if I pray. I do when I'm really worried, but I don't exactly understand it or who I'm praying to. For a while Ma was taking me to a lot of different churches, including a couple that were African, but we haven't been there in a long time.*

Six | After dropping Norma back at her car, Moxie listens to the hissing sound her car makes driving along rain-soaked Rhode Island Avenue toward her father's house. The car's noise is comforting after the cramped silence in which she rode with Norma. When they did speak to each other, it was strained and raw-edged. Their lives have been gratifyingly interwoven for so long that Moxie took for granted they would always be. But Norma has turned into someone she's unable to recognize—jeopardizing her family with another man and expecting Moxie to sanction it. Marriage is hard, labor-intensive. It's not supposed to be easy. Moxie's protective interior barricade will cast its scrutinizing shadow on whatever Norma says or does now. She misses the Norma she didn't need to judge.

At a red light, she watches small dark puddles form inside the sunken potholes and rain beads drip from a metrobus sign, resembling the last trickles of pee. She brushes the painful thoughts about Norma aside, feeling the familiar shade of sadness trying to shove its way in. She turns the radio to an oldies station in an effort to combat her deflating spirit. The Dells belt out, "I love you. Stay. I love you. Stay. I love *you!*" Other than her father, James is the last man who said those words to her and meant them, well over ten years ago. That fact alone is depressing. Moxie used to think having a man in her life could keep the melancholy moods at bay, but she knows now that was a delusion. She has to rely on her own inner monologue. *I am doing fine,* she affirms, wanting to believe. *I am happy, I am loved, I am loving.* She's

thankful James will pick Zadi up from dance tonight. She doesn't
always want Zadi to know when she's sliding mentally downhill.

Her mother suffered from sporadic bouts of depression and took a
fatal overdose of sleeping pills when Moxie was eleven. Moxie still lives
with the images of her mother, a tall and slender woman, looking very
small. She would huddle in her favorite armchair with a crocheted
blanket over her shoulders, eyelids swollen and red-rimmed from
hours of silent crying. As young as three, Moxie learned to recognize
the hollow eyes and trembling lips that meant her mother would stay
in the armchair all day, rising only to pour endless cups of tea and
gather more piles of old magazines to flip through. Moxie would bring
her little wooden chair, her dolls and crayons, and sit with her mother.
If she got hungry, she knew to eat whatever she could reach in the cabinets and in the refrigerator, usually stacks of saltines, cheese squares, or
spoonfuls of Jell-O. When her mother's really bad days collided with
the nights her father had evening patients, Aunt BeJean would come
over and cook dinner, wash clothes, and give Moxie extra long hugs.

After her mother's death, whenever Moxie felt anxious or saddened
by things like an unexpected bad grade, a boyfriend's rejection, or a
friend's prolonged teasing, she worried her feelings would lead to the
depressive illness her mother had. She didn't understand that when disturbing events occur, sadness is a natural, almost required, response. In
later years, Norma had to remind her often that she wasn't her mother
and that the bad feelings were temporary. Now when Moxie senses the
blues creeping up on her like a stain, she battles it as best she can, still
afraid each time that what haunted her mother is beckoning to her.
Fighting herself, though, saps her of energy to nurture the most important relationships in her life—with Zadi, her father, and, before yesterday, Norma. Before Moxie decided she needed to re-evaluate that relationship. If Norma is so important to her, why does everything out of
Norma's mouth seem so damn irritating now?

Moxie's drives up her father's street, slowly crunching over the remaining snow on his unplowed block. The ebbing rain has begun washing
it all away. Moxie watches as her father stands on his porch pouring

bird food into the plastic feeders that hang down from the roof. He wears only a sweater and a slightly battered felt hat. He lifts onto his toes to steady the feeder and keep the seeds from spilling back out because he usually adds too much. He almost loses his balance and catches himself with the aid of a porch pillar. The sight of him like this, vulnerable and intensely involved with nature in front of the only house she has ever known, makes her chest hurt and her eyes tear. At this moment he looks almost as old and decrepit as the house, which seems to have aged right along with him.

Her father goes back inside the house while Moxie squeezes her car into a small space further up the street. Some of the residents have used their large trash cans to claim spaces, making parking for others more difficult. She gets out and trudges through the slush around her tires.

Snow hides the gouged-out concrete step covered temporarily for a more than a year with wooden planks. When Moxie steps on the spot, it creaks under its snow covering. The tattered metal sign that proclaims, "Dr. Ponsey Dil ard (with the second *l* in *Dillard* missing), Podiatrist," is rusty and leans to one side. It was once a great house— the hangout spot for many of her grade-school friends. Her mother was home during the day when she wasn't helping in the back office. On good days, Moxie could bring playmates to a sparkling house filled with vases of hyacinths, tulips, and bougainvillea from the garden and the smells of baked bread and a potpourri of spices from the kitchen.

But now the white pillars are dull and peeling. Although you can't tell from the outside, Moxie knows the curtains hanging in the windows are heavy with dust. She carries fabric with her to make new curtains using her mother's old sewing machine. She turns the ring of her key chain, searching for the key to her father's house.

Before she can open the door, she hears someone approaching from behind. A man, wearing a mudcloth jacket and drinking something from a mug, negotiates the snow mounds washing onto the walkway. His smiling face is the color of wheat toast. He is hatless and his closely cropped hair has flecks of red and gray in it. "Hi," he says. "Moxie, right?"

Oh, great, she thinks, some other man her father must have told about his "available" daughter.

"Pardon my hot chocolate," he says, climbing the stairs and switching the drink to his left hand so his right is free to shake. "My name's Haleem. My son and I moved into the run-down place two houses down." He gives a lighthearted laugh. "We've been in there a little over two weeks. Your dad and my son met first and found out they have the game of dominoes in common. He's been a real old-fashioned neighbor. Mentioned you several times, so I'm glad to meet you."

Moxie turns the key and the doorknob and smiles briefly, "Well, it was nice meeting you, too."

He doesn't budge. "Real challenge living in a house and working on it at the same time. Especially during the winter. But I love challenges. I told your dad I'd help him fix up some things around his place, while I'm working on mine. I'll be happy to show you what I've done so far . . . sometime. Your father's seen it and given his seal of approval."

"Oh, sure. Sometime—that would be good." She nudges the door open and puts one foot on the threshold. A boy, maybe twelve or thirteen, comes to the fence at the beginning of the walkway and yells, "Come on, Dad. You said only a minute."

Haleem laughs, showing a gap in his teeth. "Kids. They're so impatient. That's my son, Jupiter."

"Jupiter?"

"Yeah. I'm kind of a space and solar system nut. Jupiter is one of the largest planets, plus it was the only one my ex-wife and I could agree on in terms of a name. You have a child, too, right?"

"Yes. A daughter."

"Your father told me. How old is she?"

From inside the house comes the faint wailing of the telephone. "She's fifteen. As a matter of fact, that might be her calling. Better go." She latches on to the timely excuse and escapes inside.

The hallway and staircase carpeting, worn out and replaced once, is worn out again. Some of the balusters from the wide staircase are missing, reminding Moxie of an old set of teeth. The house she grew up in is also burdened by weary furnishings, missing bathroom tiles, and a mildewed basement. Her father doesn't complain, though. He has created a chaotic museum by filling all available space with pictures, old newspapers, knickknacks, and mementos of the family's life together.

Most of Ponsey Dillard's savings were depleted by his wife's compulsive spending, her psychiatric treatments, medications and periodic hospitalizations, Moxie's college tuition, a trust fund for Zadi's education, and his own heart surgery, which forced him to end his practice earlier than he had intended. He has what he needs to live on but nothing extra to fix up the house. Moxie has assisted financially, when she could, with some of the smaller repairs like fixing the garbage disposal and sporadic plumbing problems.

Her father wants Moxie to live in this house when he's gone. But this is the house her mother died in. She can't even enter it without visualizing her mother, her caramel smooth skin and the all too infrequent smile like the end of a laugh. The memories are strong and able to wreak havoc with her psyche if she sits in the armchair her mother often cried in, or passes the corner where she sat in the dark for hours, or thinks about the lonely weeks her mother was hospitalized and Moxie couldn't visit because she was too young. Even if the house was miraculously restored, she still wouldn't live here because of her mother's absent presence. She would rather fix it up, sell it, and take her memories with her. She said that, yelled it in fact, the last time Ponsey mentioned bequeathing the house to her and Zadi. She hadn't wanted to hurt him, but she didn't know how to apologize. And why couldn't he understand she didn't want to think about losing him either?

She finds her father in the living room, where he has his feet up on an ottoman and is wading through a mound of old newspapers with a pair of scissors in his hand. His Siamese cat lies on the ottoman between his slippered feet. The cat narrows its eyes at Moxie, groans, and rises, dismounting from the ottoman as she approaches. "Hey, Daddy," she says, bending and burrowing her face in his neck, breathing in his ever-present scent of Old Spice.

His glasses slip down his nose as he looks up, releasing her. "Hello, there, Moxiegirl. You surprised me. Wasn't expecting you today. And where's my Zadigirl?"

"Left work early to see a client. James will bring her home from dance. I know you'd rather I brought her with me, but when I go home, I'm going to be in for the night." She slumps into the loveseat next to her father's chair. "What'd I miss on the freak shows this week?" she kids. This is a standing joke. Her father is a devotee of *Jerry Springer* and other kindred television shows. She, on the other hand, is repulsed by them; it's almost torture for her to watch the people writhing in their own sociopathic behavior. Her father can speak for hours on the subject, though, while she sits there without saying a word, appearing interested.

He launches into a recap of the day's most astounding shows: a man who confessed to his wife that he's been sleeping with her mother, a teenager who moonlights as a prostitute during recess, and a minister who wears a diaper under his robes. Ponsey skims the newspaper for political and world issues just enough to be informed, but he pores, enthralled, over the strange stories in the tabloids. He cuts out the most intriguing ones and keeps several boxes of file folders containing these articles. During the winter months when he can't work in his garden, this essentially becomes his work. Moxie used to try to dissuade him because she thought it would depress him, but most of the time he seems buoyed by the strangeness of the events he uncovers.

"Okay, why did I ask? I hear enough tragic stories at work. Don't tell me any more."

"Everything's not all bad. Some of the things are funny. Listen to this: a robber in Manassas got caught taking a shower in the house he had just burglarized." He laughs loudly. Her father continues relating highlights of the week's talk shows and newspaper articles with Moxie half listening. When her father falls asleep in his armchair, she busies herself straightening up. She puts some towels in the washing machine and unloads the dishwasher. Then she empties the cats' litter box, rinses it out, and adds new litter. Out of curiosity, she wanders into the back rooms, which housed her father's podiatry practice. She hasn't opened these rooms up since early summer when she aired them out. Three big aluminum foot tubs that look more like concrete-mixing vats are lined up under the windows. Beside them sit the old-fashioned speakers that used to pump Henry Mancini and Nat King Cole into the examination rooms. The high-backed, leather-look waiting room chairs pushed into one corner are outdated, yet stately. Everything is covered with dust and cobwebs again. Whenever Moxie comes into these rooms, she can still smell the peppermint foot lotion her father's nurse rubbed on patients' feet after their footbath. The dust makes her sneeze, and she closes the door. After things on the first floor look a little better, she rests for a moment on the couch next to her father's chair and dozes off as well, lulled by his raspy, steady breathing.

When she awakens a half hour later, the living room is basked in only the dim light from the droning television. She holds her watch close to her face to make out the time. Seven o'clock. Zadi's ballet class is over. She leaves a message for Zadi at home on the new phone company voice-mail system. She smiles as she listens to Zadi's greeting.

While her father snores, she prepares a meal for him from the smorgasbord of leftovers he has in his refrigerator—a casserole of sorts that he can heat up for the next day or so. Her father enters the kitchen, stretching. "Smells good. What you making?" He looks into the casserole dish, nodding approval. "You're a good woman, Moxie," he says, massaging her neck. "You know that?"

"Yes, Daddy, I do, but please stop thinking I'm lonely and in need of a man. I'm not. I met your neighbor, what's-his-name, outside. He said you told him about me." She fixes her father's plate, grabs silverware, and carries it into the dining room.

He follows her. "Oh, Moxiegirl. I didn't mean any harm by it. Just think Harlem's a nice young man. He don't mess around with drugs, works hard for a living, takes care of his child, and don't have women coming in and out of there." He holds up one hand and pulls his knotted fingers down one by one as he speaks.

"How do you know all this about him? Didn't he just move here?"

"I wasn't born last night, you know. And still got a mind sharp as a cat's claw. Met his boy first. Could tell he's being raised by someone who cares. Then I met him. I know these things by talking to him, observing him, watching him with his son. One good man can spot another."

"Fine. Just understand this—I do not want to date your 'Harlem.' And I believe he said his name is Haleem. Please don't start with that bachelor-number-one stuff. I'm not interested. Now sit and eat your dinner before it gets cold."

"Aren't you going to eat with me?" His facial expression melts into the gaze of a pleading child.

"I munched while I was cooking, so I'm not really hungry."

"Just sit down for a minute with your father." He taps the place next to him. "Why don't you take some of this home for Zadi?"

She sits at his end of the table. The dining room table, an elaborately carved antique, is long enough to seat ten people comfortably. When her mother was well, she loved to entertain, especially with large dinner parties. Ponsey takes her hand as always and bows his head. "Heavenly Father, I thank you for this meal. And for my beautiful daughter who prepared it and does not need a man. Amen." They both laugh. He scoops his food up as if it might disappear should he take too long. "Now, Moxie, you know your old father worries about you. I want you to experience true love, the kind that only comes from friendship and companionship. I'm not talking about all this sex and craziness they got on the movies and TV. I'm talking about the real thing, like your mama and I had. That's why I didn't need to marry again because they might not have lived up to Cerise. Even though I did have plenty of opportunities," he says, chuckling. "If I ate all those cakes and pies the church ladies baked over the years, I'd be big as this house!"

Her father has repeated this speech many times. She appreciates his sincerity and the way his face still lights up when he speaks of her mother. Especially when he tells how her mother discouraged his attentions at first, because he was ten years older. It astonishes her that he rarely mentions her mother's depression, only the good times. Even when Moxie was little, he'd say, "Your mother's in one of her moods. Leave her be till she comes around." As if she were merely having a bad day.

"Anyway," he continues, "it hurt me to my heart that things didn't work out with you and James. Don't plan to leave this earth until I know you've got a good mate." Moxie dislikes when he alludes to his own mortality. She has already lost her mother and Aunt BeJean, the others who shaped her. Her father is seventy-six now, which she tells herself is too young to die, mainly because she is not yet prepared to be an orphan.

"I have a full life, Daddy. Don't worry."

"I know you have Zadi and your friends to keep you company. Specially Norma, the sister you never had. But a life companion is a different thing."

She feels a twinge of exasperation at the mention of Norma's name, but ignores it. "I had one husband, Daddy, and I'm not convinced I'd be any happier if I had another one."

"All right," he says, feigning hurt, "I'll just mind my own business from now on."

"I wish I could count on that. Let's change the subject." She sips a glass of water. From the living room they can hear a television anchor announcing the evening news.

Her father wipes his mouth with his napkin and pats his slightly protruding stomach. "Are we having dessert?"

"No, Daddy, not tonight. I'll bring you some ice cream this week-end."

"Well, then, I think I'll fix myself a cup of tea, if I can find a tea bag."

They both go into the kitchen. Ponsey's cabinets above the stove are crowded with cans and jars that appear to have been around for years. All she finds, tucked between the ancient spice bottles, is a vintage box of peppermint tea. The tea bags inside it are hard and faded. She rustles through the box to find one that won't crumble in her fingers. Their frailty makes her think about her father's as well. "The only kind you have is peppermint."

"That's the kind I want then. You don't have to make it; I said I'd do it."

"I've got it. I cleaned a little down here, but Zadi and I will straighten upstairs when we come this weekend, okay?" She microwaves a cup of hot water and delivers his tea to him in the living room, then prepares to leave.

"Sit here for one more minute." He must be feeling lonely. "Tell me what my favorite granddaughter is up to." He drinks his tea from a spoon he dips into the cup, making soft slurping noises.

"Your only granddaughter. She's fine. Managing school and dancing. I'll find out more when I have my conference with her teachers. Found some condoms in her jeans this morning which she said they passed out at school. I don't know if I should believe her. When I say anything to her about sensitive subjects like that, she practically bites my head off. Hard-core parenting stuff doesn't work with her."

"Didn't work with you either. Remember?" His liquid eyes examine her from under their droopy lids.

"What are you talking about? You used to beat me all the time."

"That don't mean it worked. Zadi is the spitting image of you in almost every way. When I talk to her about not letting the boys get fresh with her, she'll say, 'Oh, Granddaddy, what you talking about that stuff for?' She says I'm old-fashioned. She don't understand boys are the same today as they were yesterday. They only want one thing and when they get it, they don't hardly even remember the girl's name that gave it to them. But if my granddaughter says she got them condoms at school, then I believe she got them at school."

Moxie sighs. "I know; she can do no wrong when it comes to you. Anyway, do me a favor and have one of your talks with her again, would you? So it's not just me on her case all the time."

"What about James? Doesn't he say anything to her?"

Moxie frowns. "Who knows? We haven't been communicating too well lately. He was late with a child support payment because he bought her a computer. Said she needed to have Internet access. His priorities are so off. . . ."

"Well, a computer's a good investment. It's the way of the future. His priorities might not be the same as yours, but that doesn't mean they're wrong. Plus he's her father for the rest of her life. Your mother had different views from me. But we still got along like a bird and its wings." He fishes his tea bag out of his cup and presses it onto the saucer with his spoon.

She doesn't want to discuss James or his priorities right now. "Was it hard on you when I was a teenager?"

"Good God." He almost spits the tea out of his mouth. Some dribbles onto his chin. "Was it hard? Some days I thought I might not live through it. I thought you wouldn't live through it. But you were just hardheaded. I wish I had a dollar for every beating I gave you."

"So you wouldn't beat me now if you had it to do all over again?"

"Didn't say that. All I know is, as much as I beat you, you were still hardheaded." He tips his teacup until the tea is gone.

"I spanked Zadi a couple of times when she was little," Moxie says, "but I don't know if it worked or not. It was mostly out of my own frustration."

The mantel above the fireplace is a shrine to Moxie's mother except for the framed photo of Martin Luther King, Jr. on the wall, a picture of Moxie at her high school graduation flanked by Aunt BeJean and her father, a progressive series of Zadi's school pictures, and an old, smoky-looking photo of Ponsey's parents. The other ten photographs are all of Cerise. In Moxie's favorite, her mother is sitting on a bench at the National Zoo. One hand rests atop Moxie's baby carriage. In her other hand, her mother holds a melting ice cream cone that is dripping down her arm. Moxie loves this photograph because her mother looks happy. Her hair is pulled back, and she's smiling pleasantly as if she's unaware of the melting ice cream. Moxie used to ask her mother about this picture all the time when she was little. "It was your father's ice cream cone," her mother told her. "I was just holding it while he took the picture. I didn't want a picture of me licking the cone."

"Your mother has standards, honey," Aunt BeJean was fond of saying when Moxie didn't understand why her mother wouldn't let her pierce her ears until she was ten and said she'd have to wait until she was twelve to wear pantyhose, and black clothes before thirteen were out of the question.

Once when Moxie was about eight, she went to the corner store and slipped a box of candy into her pocket. The proprietor, who knew the family, kept Moxie in the store while she called her mother. When Cerise arrived a little out of breath, wearing her blue housedress snapped in the front, Moxie realized how upset she was. Her mother never went outside in her housedress! Not even to empty the trash.

Moxie remembers how delicate her mother looked that day, as if she could be easily blown over, like a dandelion in the wind. Her mother apologized to the store owner and then stared at Moxie for a brief moment that seemed to last an eternity. Moxie felt the package of Boston Baked Beans candy in her hand, the corners of the box digging into her palm as her mother extracted it. Outside, in front of the store, she held Moxie tightly by her shoulder bones and said, "I go into that

store several times a week, Moxie. One day I went in there to get some
things we had run out of. Had them all on the counter and then I
looked in my purse and didn't have a dime. Do you know that they let
me take the milk and eggs or whatever it was home and bring the
money back later? They trusted me. How could you do this? This isn't
what I taught you. Just when I think I know who you are, you act like
somebody else. You're a stranger in my heart." She didn't say anything
more, but Moxie almost wished she had beat her with a belt instead.

Her father has settled down to watch one of the police shows he enjoys.
She walks upstairs with the bag of curtain fabric, listening for the pecu-
liar creaking sounds the fourth and sixth steps make. Moxie switches
on the light in her mother's sewing room. Although the door is slightly
ajar, the room still smells close, as though it has been without fresh air
for some time. After her mother's funeral Moxie slept in this room for
months, even though several people tried to coax her out of it. Her
mother's collection of dolls and favorite books fill the shelves against
the wall. The dolls are all white, dressed in costumes from different
countries. Her father's other cat, the mutt, lounges on the bed. It
stretches and saunters away, underneath the bed.

Her mother collected too many things, though. She went on major
weekly and, sometimes daily, shopping sprees. Sometimes she would
pick Moxie up from school and say, "Guess what. We're going shopping!" But instead of being excited, Moxie dreaded it. The embarrass-
ment of her mother buying her five pairs of sandals or twenty pairs of
socks at one time was too much. Cerise would do the same for herself
and Ponsey, no matter how many times he asked her to stop or told her
they didn't need all those things. Periodically when the laundry piled
up, she'd throw all the dirty items away and then say, "Nobody had any
clean clothes, so I had to buy some new ones." Her father tried taking
away the credit cards, but she'd become so upset and despondent that
he usually returned them and just paid the outrageous bills as best he
could. Moxie doesn't even own a credit card for fear she will abuse it.

The black Singer sewing machine, one of her mother's more well-
thought-out purchases, stands in a corner, mostly unused since her
mother's death. It is still surrounded by piles of fabric and boxes of

thread. Her mother made most of her own clothes and many of
Moxie's until she began fourth grade and started protesting about
wanting only to wear her store-bought items like the other kids at
school wore. She hurt her mother's feelings back then by refusing to
put on the lovingly stitched clothes. If she let herself now, she would
cry about it. Where are those clothes? She has opened the closets and
drawers many times, stifled by the scent of mothballs and cedar. But
there are too many boxes and suitcases, and whenever she starts going
through them, her chest begins to feel tight. She picks up a piece of
cloth to wipe this week's dust off the sewing machine.

The same year Moxie protested home-made clothes, her mother
decided to teach Moxie to sew and to purchase the new sewing
machine, after perusing several store catalogs. Moxie and her mother
drove downtown to Hecht's department store, where the black Singer
was the last one of the desired model. Gleaming with gold trim and lettering, it had buttonhole-making capability and several other func-
tions the old one didn't. It was the display model and no box could be
found for it, so the price was discounted.

Moxie's mother pulled the car up to the service entrance, and a
Hecht's employee carried it out to the trunk, tying the trunk down
with heavy rope. Her mother could be quite assertive with people she
deemed to be at her service. Moxie had witnessed Cerise direct the
butcher toward a particular cut of meat or complain about its price,
and Moxie had heard her upbraid the supermarket checkout worker
about the way her groceries were packed. It was no surprise, then,
when her mother requested extra roping from the Hecht's employee
and had him turn the sewing machine in several directions before she
was satisfied.

On their way home Cerise sang because she was so happy about the
purchase, and anytime her mother was happy, Moxie was delighted as
well. They sang together, nursery rhymes and unseasonable Christmas
carols, unable to recall all the verses of any of them. Slicing through
their revelry, Moxie heard a siren, and her mother immediately pulled
the car over. Cerise began to breathe heavily, and her hands trembled as
they clung to the steering wheel. The policeman approached. He was
very tall and leaned in through the window her mother had rolled

down. After her mother showed him her license and registration, he took them from her and said, "Where'd you get that sewing machine?" Moxie expected Cerise to dole out the same treatment she had given the Hecht's worker. Instead, she saw her mother cower and begin to frantically search in her purse, timidly repeating, "I have proof, I can show you, please, sir, I have it right here," until she retrieved the receipt. The policeman plucked it from her wobbly hand and returned to his patrol car. Moxie sat still, frightened and confused.

After the policeman reluctantly let them go, her mother plunged immediately into her abyss. Moxie didn't understand the way her mother had reacted to the policeman. The only difference she could discern was his white skin color. The other people she had watched her mother interact with were all black. Thinking about it made her stomach queasy, and as time went on, she began closely surveying other black people in situations with white people, wherever she happened to be: the grocery store, the bank, the museum. Unwittingly, she assessed the perceived levels of power the members of each race wielded. She watched to see whether the black people shrank, groveled, or transformed themselves in a belittling way. And it happened all too often for her. She developed such a revulsion toward it, she determined from a young age that she would never venture down that shameful path.

The sewing machine resides near the east window of the room. Moxie was always comforted to hear the crooning of the sewing machine when she came home from school because it meant her mother wasn't crying or despondent. And she loved it even more when she learned how to use it as well. Even now, the sound has the same effect on her. She won't begin making the curtains until the weekend, but she wants to hear the sound before she leaves. Sliding a small fabric remnant under the needle, she steps on the foot pedal and jumps when she hears the "ping" sound of the needle breaking. She fishes for more needles in the cabinet drawers. Painstakingly, she sits there for several minutes inserting a new needle. After finally inserting it correctly, though, the machine still doesn't work. She checks to make sure it's plugged in. "Daddy!" she calls, running down the stairs two at a time, "Something's wrong with Ma's sewing machine!"

"You sure? Didn't you use it a few days ago?" He leans forward in his chair.

"I put in another needle, but something else must be wrong. I was going to make some new curtains for the front hall—Oh no, Daddy, it can't be broken!" She slumps onto the couch.

"Calm down, honey. We'll take it to a repair shop, get somebody to look at it. They'll be able to fix it, baby." He pats her head and rubs her shoulders, trying to soothe her.

"But it's old, Daddy."

"Just means it's sturdier."

She hunts through the yellow pages in a frenzy and sees that there are several repair places listed. She contemplates taking the next day off to get it fixed but remembers she has a court appointment with Antoine. She usually takes a mental health day when she senses the blues shadow hovering over her, in an effort to stave off anything more severe. Those days seem to be needed once a month. Her therapy is to drink tea and listen to Frankie Beverly's "Joy and Pain," ever since that night at Howard when Norma played it to ease her discomfort. Norma has suggested professional counseling several times, but Moxie is fearful that a counselor will confirm she has inherited her mother's illness. Before leaving her father's, she is drawn again to the mantel, to the ice cream picture. She holds the frame tenderly in her hands. "Daddy, can I have this picture? You have so many."

He looks up from a newspaper article, hesitant. "Only if you promise not let nothing happen to it. You know how you and Zadi do—pictures all over the place."

"Only the ones we don't care about." She kisses her father's smooth forehead. The skin feels tight and slippery. She stares at the picture, now hers, and wonders whether her mother would be proud of her and the way she is attempting to raise Zadi. She remembers that when Zadi turned eleven, panic moved in with Moxie for the entire year. She knew it was irrational, but she became fearful she might die and leave Zadi motherless, as she had been left at that age. When she worries these days about not connecting with Zadi, she reminds herself that she made it through tougher periods, like that year. This is what is required of her: making it through, one event at a time. If she keeps that in mind, life is less overwhelming.

As Moxie opens the front door to leave, Luther, the Siamese cat runs up the steps and darts into the house, brushing Moxie's leg. The street lighting coupled with the remaining snow casts a reassuring brightness on the evening. Moxie decides to walk two houses down to observe the work Haleem has done on his house. From the sidewalk she can tell he has painted the porch and perhaps done some carpentry—she's not sure. He's also added a porch swing. She has to admit, it is a definite improvement.

Maybe she can talk to him about how much it might cost to work on her father's house. If they can pay in installments, the important repairs may be feasible. The idea of fixing up the house is linked in her mind with granting her father longer time on earth. The crisp air hovers at her neck and quickens her pace back to where her car is parked.

Monday, Jan. 11th (later)
Express Classic Fit jeans, etc.

Dear Sistergirl:
Dad picked me up from ballet. Mom went over Granddaddy's. When she got home, I was here chilling, doing my homework. Janet Jackson is off the hook. I pray someone gets me a ticket to her show. I could beg Norma, but she hasn't called here recently, I don't think. I just finished reading about Janet in a Rolling Stone *magazine that Windy let me borrow. Janet works out like six days a week. I'll be doing that as we get closer to recital time. Don't know if my stomach is ever going to look like hers, though. It's so flat it goes in. Somebody said she had six ribs cut out to make it so flat. I don't believe that. She's not crazy like Michael.*
I know the whole Odette/Odile dance by heart now, but I'm getting nervous about the audition. When I get nervous, the back of my neck starts to sweat. I still haven't told Ma what Miss Snow said about my hair because I'm waiting for the right time. With Ma that could actually be never.

Allegra got moved to A Math today. She was trying to act like it wasn't a thing, but it was. She's like that in math. I'm like that in English, but I don't throw it in her face like she does to me. I'll be trying to figure out an answer in study hall and she'll go, "Did you finish math yet? It was so easy!" when she can see I'm still doing it, so obviously I'm not finished and obviously it doesn't seem easy to me. That's when I start wondering if she's really my best friend. At least now we won't have the same homework anymore. Ma told me to let her know if they ever put me in another section where I'm the only black girl (I'm the only one in French) because she'll go talk to Ms. Thompson. Now with Allegra moving to A Math, I will essentially be the only black girl in B Math because even though Maia Simms is in there, you can't count on her being black. Lucy Parker is in C Math.

I have a pimple right in the middle of my nose. Allegra told me to put toothpaste on it. (She never gets pimples; she just read about using toothpaste in a magazine. It's not fair.) And Ma told me to rub a little soap on it (she used to get pimples).

No call from you know who.

Seven | After the stressful way she and Moxie parted from Moxie's client visit, Norma lies stomach-down on her bed, staring at the television without paying attention to the story line. It's late, but she doesn't feel tired. Miles has been bathed, read to, and tucked in, and Lawrence isn't home yet. When he comes in, though, she will pretend she's asleep in case he decides to touch her. Although the distance between them has grown vast and unmanageable, Lawrence occasionally rubs against her late at night and fumbles with her nightgown, without saying a word. Before she started making love with Woody, Lawrence's maneuvers aroused her enough to become a reluctant participant in listless sex, after which she always felt worse. Sometimes she would go into the bathroom, turn the faucet on so Lawrence couldn't hear, and cry. It wasn't love that he had to give her anymore. The thought of sleeping with two men, something she easily did in college, is now repulsive to her. Back then she didn't know the value of what she was giving away so freely.

Norma wonders what Woody's doing, visualizes him lying in bed anticipating her arrival. He called her on her cell phone before she put Miles to bed and referred to their time away from each other as "torturous." They will meet midweek, though, only a few days away. For Norma, too, the interval seems almost unbearable. Heavy into her daydream, she doesn't hear Lawrence come in and jumps when he says, "What are you watching?" Turning to respond, she can't remember when they last looked into each other's eyes. Even now, his hastily blink away from hers.

"Wasn't really watching. Just had it on." Too late to feign sleep. She scoots herself up to a sitting position and slides on her slippers from the rug beside the bed. "I promised to make some calls for the parent association," she says, on her way out, feeling his eyes on her back. "Good night."

She walks through the dark hallway to the stairs and down to the kitchen, where she pours a glass of wine. She sits at the table, tucking her legs under her, hugging her knees. Maybe it's her fault, maybe she gives too many mixed messages, that it's okay to be this ghost of a husband. It seems eons ago that she lived for the times when Lawrence reached for her late at night. When those moments first began to dissipate, she was desperate. "You do the bills more often than you try to do anything with me," she told him. But his fingers, which once caressed her tenderly, began to do so carelessly and with such detachment they came to feel like unwelcome intruders on her body.

She makes the calls that could have waited, so she won't be a liar. When Norma carries her wineglass upstairs, she can hear Lawrence snoring loudly. She goes past him into the bathroom and runs water into the Jacuzzi tub. She searches the cabinet for her aromatic candle and bath gels. Norma dangles her hand under the torrent of water and turns the faucet further toward "hot." She puts on a shower cap so she won't sweat out all her curls and eases herself into the warm water. The black-and-gold marble steps cut diagonally down to the bottom of the tub. On each step Norma has placed tiny arrangements of silk flowers and matching decorative soaps. A basket of floral potpourri rests on the high windowsill overlooking the tub next to a photograph she took of a sunset at the Eastern Shore.

She leans her shoulders back slowly, readying herself for the abrupt cold of the marble. Simultaneously, steam from the hot water rises as she reclines back, covering her, like a warm quilt, with perfumed bubbles. She leans forward to switch on the jets. The bathroom door is abruptly flung wide open. Miles stands in the doorway wearing only his pajama top. She crosses her arms in front of her to hide her breasts. "I peed in my bed, Mommy."

"Oh, Miles . . ."

"Can I take a bath with you?"

"No, Miles! Mommy needs privacy. I'll be right out to help you."

"Can I get in with you, please? I peed." He frowns and blinks at the light. He swings the door back and forth.

"No, honey, you can't. I'll be out in a minute. And please don't do that to the door. Where did you put your wet clothes?"

"On the floor."

"Okay, go and put them in your bathroom sink. Go on, please," she says, unable to keep the tone of her voice from ascending. "I'll be right out." He leaves after she coaxes him a few more times. The thought of Miles and his pee-splattered body in the bath with her is loathsome.

She hears a sharp sound, like something metal hitting the wall or floor repeatedly. Miles is obviously doing something other than what she directed. Norma sighs, knowing that Lawrence will sleep through all of this. She dries off and grabs her robe from the nearby hook, instructing herself to be patient with the child whose needs constantly interrupt her life.

Waking up next to the wall, in Miles's bed, her head feels as if she wore a tight hat all night long. She picks the sleep from her eyes and glances at the Big Bird clock on his wall. 6:55 A.M. She gingerly climbs over Miles's spread-eagled form and goes into her bedroom. Her legs and neck are stiff from the contorted sleeping position she was relegated to. While she dresses, Lawrence emerges from the bathroom with a towel wrapped around his waist and puffs of shaving cream on his face. "Morning," he says, clearing his throat. "Seen a package of razors? Bought some new ones the other day, and now I can't find them. Think Mrs. Coleman moved them?"

"She hasn't even been here this week. Not in the cabinet or under the sink?" she asks, her voice stuffed with annoyance.

"No, I looked." He goes over to his dresser, moves bottles around, and opens drawers.

This morning, partially because of her uncomfortable night in Miles's bed, she finds Lawrence's nonchalance more disturbing than usual. "Lawrence, excuse me, but how can you act like nothing is wrong here?"

He has moved over to the shelf of his closet, pushing aside clothes, but pivots sharply. In the undershirt he has slipped on, his body looks more fit than it actually is and his face is smooth and brown. There is no sag in the skin that draws tightly around his mouth. He opens and then closes it, as if rendered speechless. On the second attempt, he says, "What are you talking about? I shouldn't have asked you about the razors?"

"No. I'm talking about us. You just act like this is some normal relationship we have here. How much longer can we go on like this? You haven't even noticed I try to be either asleep or somewhere else when you get in the bed." She sits at her vanity, removing rollers from her hair.

"Norma, why would you start a conversation like this when I'm on my way to work?"

"Because I'm thinking about it right now!" Her anger feels reckless.

"Well, I'm sorry but I'm thinking about the structure of my deposition. That's where my head is. Can we talk about what's upsetting you a little later?"

"What's upsetting me! Later like when? You don't mean it, Lawrence. We never talk about anything of substance anymore."

"Norma, I don't think I have the vocabulary for what you want to hear. There's already enough pressure at the office. Home should be a place to relax." He finds his razors in a plastic drugstore bag and raises them in the air like bounty. He walks into the bathroom and then calls out to her, "I know you think that sounded insensitive, but it really wasn't meant to. How about if I let you know when things ease up a bit with this case and the merger discussions?"

"Right," she says. Always the same story, she thinks. That'll be another year from now. What Moxie doesn't understand is that she's tried, she's really tried. She stares down at the pile of plastic rollers in her lap. It dawns on her that neither called the other last night. They usually talk before going to bed, if only to report on their respective days.

She remains looking at herself in the vanity mirror while Lawrence shaves, dresses, and then finally touches his lips to her head. She listens for the creak of Miles's door across the hall as Lawrence looks in on him. After the *brush-brush* sound of Lawrence's shoes going down the steps, she can't hear much else. She knows he will retrieve the newspaper from the front porch and peruse it quickly while sipping the coffee automatically brewed by a timer. He'll review the front page first, then Metro, and he'll separate out the Business section to stuff into his briefcase. Bag in hand, he'll grab his trench coat from the hall closet, and if she listens closely and there are no other sounds, she will hear the double click of the front door being unlocked and then locked again. These are things she can count on. He's content like this, she thinks, incredulously.

Despite an overnight snow dusting, Norma can see tufts of grass patches in her yard when she goes outside to retrieve the newspaper Lawrence didn't bring in after all. It is a cloudless, bitterly cold day. At the kitchen table she looks through the paper and finishes the last of her coffee, regretting that it's gone but not enough to fix another cup.

Miles's attention is on the television in front of him. He lies on the couch and stares straight ahead while Norma tugs at his pajama bottoms until they slide down, revealing his bony hips and buttocks. "Okay, Miles, get dressed, please. Your clothes are right over here." She points to the edge of the couch. "If you need help, I'll help you. But I know you can put on your underwear yourself."

One of his hands absently picks at a scab on his elbow, but otherwise he doesn't move or respond.

"Miles!"

He frowns. "Mommy, I wanna see TV."

Norma leans forward and grabs his arm. "Miles, it's time to get dressed. Understand? If you don't do it, I'm turning the TV off."

"No, Mommy!" He moves distractedly toward the freshly ironed clothes she has laid out. His eyes remain on the television while he does this. Miles pouts and fingers the pants as if they carry germs. Then he drops them on the floor. "Don't want these pants. These are itchy pants. I want army pants like Uncle Bernie."

Patience, Norma mentally commands herself. "Miles, you don't have any army pants."

"I want pants like Uncle Bernie!" Miles folds his arms in front of him, mocking her stance.

"Miles, pick the pants up off the floor. If you don't want to wear those, you go get something else out of your drawer." She feels herself losing control, which she partially attributes to Miles mentioning Bernard, a man who brings out the worst in her. "Did Bernard call or something?"

"Yep. He said he's gonna come see me."

"When?"

"On Saturday," he says, spinning in wide circles on his way out of the room. Norma is well aware that "Saturday" is Miles's standard response whenever a day of the week is called for. A phone call from Bernard can only mean that he wants something.

"Miles." Norma raises her voice again. "It's time to go!" Norma picks up the remote from the coffee table and snaps off the television. Miles saunters back into the room, still undressed, with a pair of rumpled jeans in his arms, probably retrieved from the dirty clothes hamper. She says nothing.

"Mommy, turn the TV on!" he shouts.

"Let me see you getting dressed, and I'll turn it back on." She's failed as a mother again. He begins dressing with loud choking sobs. "I wanna see TV! I wanna see TV!" He sits on the carpet with one leg in the second pair of pants. His face contorts, and his cries climb the scales. He drops and rolls on the rug, dramatically waving his arms and kicking his legs, sending the pants flying. "I want Daddy, I want my daddy!" he screams.

She stares at him writhing on the floor and wonders if she has somehow mentally damaged him. The urge to hit him is insisting again, whispering in her mind that she'll feel better if she does so. She knows she'll only feel worse, so she walks over to the large window and stares out at her beloved birch tree, raw and white and stunning in its bareness. She counts to twenty and then tells him that if he gets dressed, she'll take him to McDonald's for breakfast. Bribing is in the failure column, too, but it has instant, albeit temporary, results. Miles sits up abruptly, wiping at his runny nose. The once-ironed shirt is beside him, rudely crumpled on the rug. He begins putting on his clothes. She may be ruining him for the rest of his life, but sometimes the future is just too far away.

Norma watches Miles dress. He doesn't really look like her or

Lawrence. His ears protrude, and his head seems out of proportion to his small body. Norma is relieved to finally drop him off at his preschool. It's an expensive outlay, but he's safe and stimulated in a way she wouldn't have the fortitude or inclination to try at home. She is grateful to yearn after him as he leaves her to hang his jacket in his cubby and join his friends at the Lego table. When she's away from him, she begins to feel loving and normal, at least for a few hours.

Wednesday, Jan. 13th
Nautica sweatpants
DKNY T-shirt (white/black trim)
white Nikes

Dear Sistergirl:

Dad surprised me and picked me up from school today. I really wanted to go with Allegra, though, cause Wednesdays is our day to hang out at the bus stop on Wisconsin or Metro Center. But he gave her a ride home, too. He used to pick me up more often, but now he doesn't have as much free time cause he teaches music at Ellington and does musical arrangements, production, and whatever for BET Jazz. He also has a CD of him playing his sax with some other musicians. I heard Ma tell Norma it figures that when he was with her, he only played gigs that didn't pay that much, and now that they're not together, he's got money coming in from everywhere.

Before he took me home, Dad said, Your sister, Tiffany, is in a play on Friday and she'd like you to come. (He can't say Tiffany's name without adding—your sister.) He said he'd come get me after ballet and take me to the play. This thing about Tiffany wanting me to come is b.s. cause I know Tiffany could probably care less if I come or not. He wants me and Tiffany to be close, and he's always trying to find fake ways to make that happen. I told him it's not happening, she isn't my sister, and I don't know if I want to sit through some boring little kid's play. He didn't like my attitude, he said. But I didn't say that I don't really like his attitude either. He always acts like Tiffany and I should instantly like each other and not have any problems (please!). But he has his own problems with her. Back when school first started, Dad said maybe Tiffany shouldn't watch TV during the week, and Fawna (who always spoils her) butted in and said Tiffany usually does her homework in the after-school program, so it's okay for her to watch TV. Dad said, well Zadi used to read a book if she had finished her homework. Even I knew that wasn't the right thing to say. Fawna was like, well, good for Zadi. I guess they think I can't hear them when they're going through their changes. I told Ma that Fawna and Dad had an argument, just to mess with her and kind of test her to see how nosy she'd be. She acted nonchalant like she didn't care, but I could tell she was hoping that I'd say more and I purposely didn't. So later on, she was like, so did your Dad and Fawna resolve their argument? I didn't answer her but I was like, yeah, I got her open. Ma is such a trip.

*Friday, Jan. 15th
blk Parasucos
blk/white checked top
blk Nikes*

Dear Sistergirl:
    Called and paged Octavius a couple of times from the phone booth at school, but he didn't call back, so I was like, whatever. Since Daddy was begging so much, I decided to go to Tiffany's stupid-ass play. She's in third grade in a charter school. It was about the civil rights movement, in celebration of Martin Luther King, Jr.'s birthday. It wasn't a real play, just characters giving speeches. A little boy with a really loud voice played Martin Luther King. He must have listened to a lot of King speeches because he was actually jive good. Somebody else did Malcolm X, etc. Tiffany was Rosa Parks. She was actually jive funny. For real. She had a little hat and glasses, and her hair was in a French roll, and she said something like: I worked long and hard today and, no, I don't think I feel like sitting in the back today. And she shook her finger in the invisible white man's face.
    I'm spending the night here at Dad's. It's a long weekend because of the King holiday, but I'm going back home after ballet class tomorrow. I've

*got a million projects to get an early start on. Science Fair coming up—I
hate science. Daddy has a gig tonight, and Fawna went with him, so me
and Tiffany are here by ourselves. She's not bugging me for once. She's in
her room watching TV. Here I am almost twice this girl's age and I still
don't have a TV in my room at home because Ma trips. Over here I sleep
in the guest room. I've never seen anyone else sleep in it, but that's what
Fawna calls it. She doesn't say, Zadi's room. Dad just says things like, I
put your suitcase in the room. Anyway at least there is a TV in here. I'm
getting ready to call Allegra, even though she got on my nerves today
cause she was like, how'd you get a pimple on your nose anyway? I didn't
even answer her. She never gets pimples—it's so trifling. I'm going to
watch BET videos, even though Fawna told me not to because she doesn't
want Tiffany to walk in here and see them cause she thinks they're
inappropriate for her. Not a problem, because if she comes in, I'll just tell
her to get the hell out.*

*Paged Octavius again. When he called back, he was mad cause he got
kicked off the basketball team cause of his grades.*

*Saturday, Jan. 16th
Old Navy flared jeans
DKNY shirt
new blk platform boots—
　　Steve Maddens—(Dad bought
　　cause I begged)*

Dear Sistergirl:
*Dad was gone before I woke up, and Fawna dropped me at the metro
so I could go to dance class. I was cold, so I stopped in McDonald's on
Georgia Avenue to get a small hot chocolate. This one guy was arguing
with the girl behind the counter about his hash browns. He said they
weren't hot enough. She told him they had just come out the grease. She
told him he was just trying to get more hash browns and if they weren't
hot, how come he had eaten half of them? Another lady was in there with
her little girl, and she was all loud like she was on crack or something. I
felt like I'd never forget that little girl's face. She had the biggest eyes and*

they looked so scared. I wondered if she hits that little girl. The mother started cussing at the people behind the counter. That's when I left without getting my hot chocolate. Plus I was about to be late. I'm glad Ma isn't foul-acting like that. Sometimes I feel embarrassed and ashamed about those kind of black people. They seem so different from me, even though we're all black. I think about how the white girls at school lump us together, especially when they talk about stuff they don't even know about, like all Southeast being a ghetto. Except for Windy and a few others who don't act like that.

Sunday, Jan. 17th
Tommy jeans
white Bebe shirt
Tims

Dear Sistergirl:
    Octavius called late last night when I was on the other line with Allegra. I told her I got to go, dog. I was supposed to call her back when I finished with him, but I forgot. He wants to know if we can go to the movies sometime. I said yes. Duh, what took him so long? He was using his neighbor's phone at eleven at night! He told me he is only sixteen!!! I told him I thought he was eighteen. He said he'd call back because his neighbor had to make a phone call. He said his cell phone wasn't charged up. I kept the phone near my pillow, but it didn't ring again and even though I turned the ringer down I know I would have heard it.
    Took me all day to finish my Lit paper about aspects of faith found in Othello. Plus I had to work on my history project. We have way too much homework. I mean, we got the history assignment last week, but none of the teachers cut back on the day-to-day homework even though they know we have a big project. They act like you're not supposed to have a life other than with your books. I did get to watch some Living Single *reruns that Allegra taped, but that was it. (Sunday doesn't count as a no-TV night.)*
    When I got finished with homework, we went over Grandpa's house and fixed dinner for him. I cooked rice with chicken broth and made the

salad. Ma made ginger chicken with tofu and vegetables. Grandpa was fake complaining and saying, how come you all can't just make regular food like meat and potatoes. He calls tofu, tafu, and makes a face, but he eats it. I get scared about him dying sometimes because he is so old. He says he's not lonely, but I don't see why he never got married again after Grandma killed herself. It makes me sad that nobody could help her and that I never got to meet her. I think it still freaks my mother out because sometimes she acts really funky for no reason and when I ask her what's wrong, she'll say, I was just thinking about your grandma. When she told me about it, I was eleven, the same age she was when her mother died. She said family secrets aren't good for kids and she didn't want me to have to carry that around. But how could I be carrying something on the down low if I didn't know about it? I wish Grandpa didn't have to live in that old house with only the TV and his newspapers to keep him company. I asked Ma if I could live there with him instead of with her, and she just laughed at me. I was being for real, though. Sometimes he gets tired and forgets to do the dishes, empty the trash, or clean the cat box, and we have to go over there and straighten stuff out for him. I don't mind. I'll do anything for him.

Eight | Norma's studio is only minutes away from Miles's preschool. She gets there shortly after ten. She nods to a man out front putting rock salt on the path. A crow flees a branch above her, gently powdering her head and shoulders with snow just as she pushes the downstairs door open.

The studio is quiet and dark. She opens the blinds, ushering in the sunlight, as if it's a salve. One relationship issue at a time should be enough. But life rarely deals out what she thinks is fair. Although Norma has left two messages for Moxie and Moxie returned one of them, they've been playing a semi-intentional phone tag. Norma left the messages at Moxie's office after hours, and Moxie's call was to her house during the day, when she knows Norma is usually at the studio. Norma tells herself they probably both need time away from the other to let go of what's bothering them. Moxie is the one who pulled back first. There's not a whole lot Norma can do.

This is not a good time to be deserted by her best friend, though. She didn't realize how Moxie-centered she was until she tried to count on one hand who else could stand in. She has lunched with a friend from art school, and one morning a white parent from daycare invited her to coffee. She enjoyed herself, but cultivating lifetime friends takes, well, almost a lifetime. She's also smarting from not being able to *share* the whole story about Woody with Moxie. And a week after Lawrence promised they would talk, he still hasn't ventured any attempts at a discussion. It is especially troubling that all the questions and mixed feelings she has about herself, Lawrence, and Woody can't be sifted through the person who knows her best. Whatever hope Norma harbored, that her friendship with Moxie was so strong it would work the kinks out of itself, is beginning to dissipate. She wonders whether Moxie will even show for her exhibit next month.

Norma keeps her coat on while she adjusts the heat and fills the coffeepot with water. Then she pops her Smokey Robinson CD into the boom box, sways from side to side, and sings in an exaggerated fashion, "I'm a choosy beggar, choosy beggar, and you're my choice, baby, you're my choice . . ." trying to pump up the volume of her spirits.

She is thankful that she can delve into preparing for her exhibit. It has been a long time in the works. In order to become an experienced photographer, she paid her dues with routine wedding assignments, photos for her mother's church and Miles's preschool. These days she can be more selective and only accept assignments that allow her to explore the art of photography, like the brochure she shot recently for the National Museum of African Art. Her solo exhibit is an opportunity to show what intrigues her and draws her in. One of her favorite photographs she took on a whim, one afternoon, while in Miles's school playground. In their exhilaration, the children had abandoned their jackets and coats in a heap beneath a bare-branched tree. The way the discarded coats seemed to hold the shape of the little bodies that deserted them stirred something in her. It has been agony, though, trying to narrow her work down to twenty-five pieces, the limit for the wall space. She must decide which represent her best work, her most authentic. The children's coats are definitely going in.

She drinks her coffee, gathers the film wheel and print paper, and turns on the enlarger. She'll spend a few hours in the darkroom printing what's on the last few rolls of film. It's doubtful, though, that she will use any of these new prints, but she wants to see them just in case there is something really compelling.

As she works, her thoughts amble easily to Woody. The memory of his fingers playing on her skin is starting to fade, the result of their being unable to mesh their schedules last week. When she met Woody during the summer, she had no idea she was even capable of such a liaison. She had been asked to photograph a community center tai chi class for a health newsletter. After the assignment, Norma enrolled in the class to help her relax and because it didn't seem too strenuous and the location was also convenient to her studio.

Norma noticed first that he was white, of course, but she also noticed in almost the same instant that he had a genuine smile on his face, not the stiff, frozen one presented by most white strangers. His eyes and the curl of his mouth seemed to say, "I want to know who you really are." He began conversing with her after the first class as they both walked toward their cars. "How did you just walk in and do that lunge thing so well?" he asked, badly imitating the move. "I've been trying to do it for a month."

"You mean the one she calls, 'grasping the peacock's tail'?" Norma asked.

"Yes, the good old peacock's tail. I can't believe you got it the first time!" Then after each class, he'd have something pleasant, complimentary to say to her about her performance. After a couple of weeks, she saw that he purposely lingered one day while she put on her shoes. "You're the Katherine Dunham of our class," he said, opening the glass doors for her.

He caught her off guard—a white man who rolled Katherine Dunham's name off his tongue as if he was comfortable with it. She perked up and smiled at him.

"What? You're surprised I know about Dunham?"

"No, no," she said too quickly.

"Yes, you were," he chided. "I've always been interested in learning beyond what was expected of me or what was given to me."

They talked for a few minutes about how they found the class and what its potential benefits were. His goal was "peace of mind." He explained that he taught literature at Catholic University and lived on the Hill. They decided to have lunch after the next class and were drawn into a discussion about their respective arts. She told him how she used to prefer shooting in color until she saw Roy DeCarava's black-and-white work and David Douglas Duncan's war photos. Duncan said that if his photos had been in color, people would be distracted by the blood. She doesn't want to be distracted by color.

"Do you consider yourself a preserver of images?" he asked. "I once read about a photographer who said that was what he did."

"No, I don't think so," Norma said. She thrilled at explaining her work. "I don't try to stop an image in motion. I try to capture the movement of it, if you understand the difference. I love what Roy DeCarava says, that he 'eavesdrops on life.' And that's what I hope my work is. That's why I hate posed shots, like traditional wedding photos. They're the worst. I prefer the truth of the situation: the bride and groom staring into each other's eyes oblivious to their guests. The uncle who's had too much to drink, making a fool of himself on the dance floor."

Woody leaned forward, captivated. "Do people, your subjects, want the truth?"

"Well, some do, some don't. Most don't. Once, after I had taken all the requisite shots of a wedding party, I went outside and saw the bride's mother discreetly crying by a rosebush. I thought the picture was one of the most beautiful I put in the album. But the mother didn't like it, so I kept it."

"Wow. I'd love to see it."

Listening to herself talk to Woody helped her realize how knowledgeable she was. She wasn't often asked to explain her pride in this passion. "What I try to do is capture and freeze an emotion. I want people to look at my photographs and say, yes, that's right, that's the way it was, or that's the way it probably was. They should be certain of it if I've done my job." She became self-conscious about having said so much. She hadn't meant to. "What about you? Do you like your work?"

He told her he enjoyed teaching—"reaching into the minds" of his students, he called it—but would rather be writing full-time. Writing "completes" him, he said. "I've been working on a novel for three years," he told her. When she asked what it was about, he added, "A man not unlike me—who worries far too much and is searching for something to make him happy forever." There was a wistful somberness to his jaw that reminded her of a puppy she had when she was a little girl. They were huddled over big bowls of Greek salad in a restaurant on Pennsylvania Avenue. The waiters bustled around them, arranging food on trays and preparing hot drinks and fountain sodas. "What do you worry about most?"

She thought it was a strange question, but it was an opportunity she seized without her usual concern about being judged negatively. "I think it's my relationship with my son. I worry that I don't love him enough. Do you have children?"

Woody's elbows rested on the table momentarily, and he brought his two hands together, folding them. She looked at him. "Yes," he said. "Two. Reuben is fourteen and Elena is seventeen. My mother used to constantly say raising us was the hardest work she ever had to do. I never understood until I had mine."

"I know."

"How old is your child?"

"Miles is three." Norma glanced down at her left hand curved in her lap and turned her wrist slightly to look at her watch. She had been talking to Woody for over an hour, but she was ready to leave.

He saw her look at the time and nodded. "It's getting late. Let's grab the check."

Outside, she walked somberly with her head down. He said, "Did my bringing up the kids and all that . . . did it disturb you? You seem kind of, I don't know, pensive."

Lifting her head, she said, "No, it's okay. I'm always thinking about my son and what I can do better."

They were standing at her car, and he touched her shoulder. "What do you think is the problem with you and your son, if you don't mind my asking?"

"It's me; it's not him. My friend, Moxie, says it's tied up with my relationship with his father, which isn't so great right now. And maybe that's it." That was all she wanted to say at that moment.

"I don't profess to have all the answers just because my kids are older. But I do know that as parents, we can only do our best. I'm constantly reviewing what I've said or done with them. If I messed up, then I go back and apologize and tell them I'll do better. Really, what else can we do? My advice—don't be too hard on yourself."

Two weeks later, they both dropped out of the tai chi class because of other commitments, but they exchanged work numbers so they could continue meeting for lunch, coffee, and later, each other.

As much as she hates to admit it (and she wouldn't to anyone), Woody's whiteness has turned into an added allure, and she is flattered that a white man finds her attractive. Even though she doesn't know where it's going, it feels good and she has felt bad for much too long.

She leaves the darkroom to pour more coffee into her mug, breathing in the steam and the aroma. She loves coffee's power to convert her from a wilted procrastinator to an energetic craftsman. She usually drinks two cups each morning and sometimes one in the afternoon. Norma puts her cup in the microwave even though the coffee is hot. She likes it to almost burn the skin of her tongue. The way Woody did the first time he kissed her.

Sometimes this thing with Woody feels like a potent drug. A lovely, seductive high, but perhaps, as Moxie has suggested, too costly in the long run, because she doesn't know where it will lead. In spite of these concerns, she doesn't want to wait one more day. She picks up the telephone on her desk and dials his office, expecting his voice mail. Instead, he answers. "Woody?" she says, almost out of breath with anticipation. "How long do we have to wait? Can't you spare some quality time for me today?"

Monday, Jan. 18th
black jean skirt
white sweater
tights/black
Banana Republic boots

Dear Sistergirl:
I'm about to do my homework, call Allegra, and listen to the 112 CD I borrowed from Desmond. We always run into him at the McDonald's near school. He goes to Wilson and is trying to talk to me. He must be

crazy. His front teeth are really gigantic and he always has spit in the corner of his mouth. But he does let me borrow his CDs. Ma wouldn't stop gabbing in the car, so I didn't get to listen to the whole thing.

Got a letter from Grandpa today. It says, in his scrunched-up handwriting, to the most beautiful dancing granddaughter in the universe from the most handsome grandfather on earth. He only lives about twenty blocks away and he writes me these crazy letters!!! I love him! He doesn't mind that I never write him back. He says in a few months it'll be time for me to help him work in his garden, which I didn't used to like, but now I do. When the snow's gone, we'll have to clean up the garden and pick up all the sticks and dead leaves that fell off the trees.

I got to ballet early and Miss Snow had me demonstrate chassé, pas de bourrée, and echappé to the intermediates. I had to write the words on the board for them, too, because Miss Snow wants you to know how to spell the words, not just dance them. Miss Snow yelled at them and told them to stop landing like truck drivers with their echappés. Everyone's nervous about auditions Saturday. Grandpa wants to come watch. I don't mind because he thinks that everything I do is great. I'm not telling Dad about it because he gets too nervous, and that makes me even more nervous. I don't need the extra stress. It's enough knowing you could mess up and Miss Snow will be watching. Even though it's not as bad as if you mess up during the actual recital. I'll never forget what happened to Angel Harrison that time we performed Giselle *and I was in the corps. We had to do bourrées for about five minutes. Miss Snow told us a thousand times not to come down off point before the cue or she would kill us. Angel came down early. When we got off stage, Miss Snow grabbed Angel by her arms and lifted her up, and Angel is a lot taller than Miss Snow. I'm not going to lie, I thought that girl was going to die that day. But Miss Snow just yelled all up in her face, spitting and everything, and shaking her like she was totally OC. Angel was crying saying her mother was going to sue Miss Snow, but we knew that was fake. Everybody's parents are scared of Miss Snow. Angel was back the next week and her mother didn't sue anybody.*

Wednesday, Jan. 20th
DKNY jeans
GAP black sweater
black platform boots

Dear Sistergirl:
   Norma called on the other line while I was talking to Allegra. Norma is so excited about Lauryn Hill being nominated for a whole rack of Grammys. I was like okay, okay, yes, Lauryn she is off the hook (even though O says her flow isn't as tight as Da Brat). I thought I was going to have to click over so she could talk to Ma, but Norma said she'd call back later. What's up with that? They must be having some kind of issues. O called, just to say good night, he said. That was sweet. He couldn't talk long. We're supposed to hook up tomorrow. He's going to page me. I didn't even bother with star six-nine.

Friday, Jan. 22nd
Tommy jeans (trying to front
   like Aaliyah)
black Lycra top
blk Nikes

Dear Sistergirl:
   Tonight while we were waiting for the younger kids' class to end, Toni asked me and Todd (we were standing outside the office practicing that step with all the arabesques) to go down to the supply closet in the basement and bring up some more paper towels, toilet paper, and air freshener. She knows damn well it's her job to get that shit. She tries to copy Miss Snow too much and act mean and authoritative, but Toni is just a fake with her long fake-ass acrylics. (She has her initials painted on each one. How ghetto is that?) I told her Miss Snow might need me to demonstrate a step to the younger kids and she said, You ain't the only star, girlfriend.
   When we got to the basement, it was all dark and I was reaching for

*the string to pull the light on and my arm touched Todd's and the next
thing I know we were kissing. For a second I was worried about my
braces, but his tongue was so far back in my mouth I almost choked.
When we got adjusted to each other, his lips felt all soft and wet but firm
at the same time, and he was holding me real tight. I was like, I don't
believe this and kind of lost my balance, and then I guess he got
embarrassed or something because he stopped all of a sudden and turned
on the light, and we got the toilet paper and paper towels and stuff for
Toni and went upstairs. I keep thinking about him and thinking about
whether we are going to hook up for real and trying to remember if I
actually felt his you-know-what when he was pressed against me (only
because when I called Allegra as soon as I got home, she said he probably
stopped cause he got hard; she swears she's so knowledgeable about these
things even though she's still a V). Ma kept yelling at me to get off the
phone. Her voice is so irritating when she does that.*

*Meanwhile I did not hear from O. My pager was on all day and
night. But tomorrow is the audition, so I need my rest anyway. I'm not
even going to think about O or Todd any more tonight. I wonder if what
happened with Todd is considered cheating on O when we haven't even
done anything.*

*Saturday, Jan. 23rd
gray sweatshirt
Nautica gray sweatpants
white Nikes*

Dear Sistergirl:
*I did it! I got the part of Odette-Odile!!! Well, I have to share it with
Sonya. I'll dance it the second night, and she'll dance it the first night. I
have to say my dancing was like that. I did my fouettés perfectly. I was on
time with the music, and I imagined that my arms were really swan
wings the way Miss Snow is always yelling at me to do. And you know
what? It actually worked and felt jive good! I'm serious, it did. I know it
made my dancing better because people were clapping and everything
when I got finished. Ma and Grandpa came to the audition. Ma said she*

was convinced I was a swan. She told me my dancing made Grandpa cry.

Miss Snow acted like it was the actual performance, talking in her fake French accent, calling the parents, "Dames and Messieurs." She had on a black dress that stuck out like a tent because of her big bosom. Her puffy feet were stuffed into her ballet slippers, but she can stand in a perfect first position. If it wasn't for that, it would be hard to believe she was ever a dancer because she's so short, but she weighs about as much as Biggie before he died. I'm not trying to jone on her, but it's the truth. Her short hair is stretched back so tight from her forehead it makes her eyebrows go up and she always looks surprised. When she gets dressed up, like today, she slaps this fake black bun on the top of her head that looks like a burnt pancake! Ma says Miss Snow looks exactly the same way she did when Ma took dance lessons from her like thirty years ago. Miss Snow is only a little bit younger than Grandpa—hey, maybe they should get married! That would be a real trip! Norma took dance from Miss Snow, too, but she and Ma didn't know each other back then. Norma says Miss Snow scared her with all her yelling, but now she regrets that she didn't stick with it. She says Miss Snow is a great icon; she just has her idiosyncracies (sp?). Ma told me that Miss Snow originally came from New York and studied with this woman, Doris Jones, who started one of the first black ballet schools right here in D.C., not far from Miss Snow's studio. Miss Snow was a fabulous dancer, but Ma said that in the 1950s it was very hard for black ballerinas, especially dark-skinned ones, to get good roles with major dance companies unless they went to Europe or something. Miss Snow had to change her dream around and open her own ballet school instead.

Nine | Because it's Sunday, Moxie isn't sure whether the library parking lot will be open, but as she turns left from H Street onto Ninth, she locates a vacant parking space. She lines her car up next to a mound of dirty snow and shifts into reverse. Before getting out, Moxie spots a group of teenagers huddled on one of the stone benches in front of the Martin Luther King Library. The sun is setting, and she squints because she can't tell whether Zadi is among the four girls and one guy. They're laughing, and one of the girls playfully hits the boy. When he jumps up, the girl jumps up, still hitting at him, like a kitten pawing a rubber ball. The boy backs up as the girl moves toward him. In the next moment he grabs her arms and wrestles with her, both laughing. The boy is tall, wearing a baseball cap and an oversized jacket. The girl is almost as tall, and as he spins her around, Moxie sees that it's Zadi.

Look at her, sticking her boobs and butt out as far as they can go, Moxie thinks. Moxie feels her breath quickening as she walks toward the group. And Norma wants to know why she is so concerned. Norma should know—that Zadi reminds Moxie of herself. Moxie has told her how she would have done anything for a boy's attention when she was Zadi's age. And did. She wants to spare her daughter that if it's not too late.

"Zadi!" She walks up on the kids, forcing herself to relax and smile. It is important that they like her and think Zadi has a cool mom, rather than an obsessive one. The best way to keep track of what your teenager is doing is to befriend their friends. Moxie's theory is that if the kids think you're cooler than their own parents, they'll let you be privy to more than your own child would ever consider.

The group of teenagers keep pushing against each other, giggling endlessly, and seem not to be at all bothered by the cold weather. There is one girl with an almost indecently short dress and leggings. Such extreme dressing leads Moxie to wonder whether the girl might have been molested as a child. She's had many clients who saw and clad themselves in the style of the sexual objects their abuser treated them as.

Zadi sidles away from the young man and comes toward her mother. "Hi, Ma. The library closes early on Sundays now. My friends stayed and waited for you so I wouldn't have to wait by myself." Zadi twirls one braid that has come loose from the French roll she fashioned. Moxie smiles at the other kids. One of the girls is fair-skinned, with a rather blank look on her face. She is pretty, but a bit too aware of it. The other two are, like Zadi, several shades darker. Moxie wonders what if any effect this has on their relationship, remembering how much more attention the light-skinned girls garnered when she was in high school.

"This is Mia, April, Peaches, and Devante." Up close Moxie notices the darkened, arched eyebrows and shimmery lipstick repeated on each girl's mouth. April and Peaches have short permed hair cut in pixie styles. Mia's long, straight hair touches the middle of her back. The girls are similarly dressed in leather jackets, tight jeans, and platform shoes or boots.

Devante looks no different, except for the book bag, from one of her clients, in his designer jacket and loose-fit jeans that cascade into a denim puddle around his expensive-looking sneakers.

"Hi," Moxie says, trying unsuccessfully to look each child in the eye. "Does anyone need a ride to the metro?"

"It's right across the street," Zadi says, as if her mother's question were the most absurd utterance she ever heard.

"Oh, right," Moxie says.

The teenagers walk off, smacking their gum.

"Why couldn't I take the metro home?" Zadi asks, lagging behind Moxie as they walk to the car.

"The original idea was I was going to meet you here and help with the research."

"That was your idea. You treat me like I'm a baby. I wanted to hang out with my friends."

Zadi glances in the direction of her friends, who are halfway across the street.

Moxie sighs. "I'm not trying to treat you like a baby, Zadi. You didn't mention that your friends would be here. I don't even know these new friends. If you provide me with a little more information sometimes, we might be able to compromise more."

Zadi catches up to Moxie and puts her arm through her mother's and leans her head on her shoulder. She has to bend a little to do this, since they are almost the same height. Moxie covers her daughter's hand with her own, rubbing it to make it warm. "So if I give you more information, then you'll say yes?" asks Zadi.

Moxie is always pleased when Zadi displays affection, even if it's because she wants something. "We can certainly talk about it. Where do you know those—friends from, anyway?"

"Mia and April go to NCS and they used to take dance from Miss Snow. I saw them again at the Saint Alban's gogo. You know Peaches. Don't you remember her? She used to go to my elementary school. I forget what school she goes to now. And Devante is April's cousin. He's only fourteen. Doesn't he look like he's seventeen or eighteen?"

"He sure does." She finds herself ironically comforted that two of the girls are private school kids. "I bet their parents don't know they're walking around with all that makeup on. Do you do that when I'm not around?"

"Not that much. Ma, do you think Devante's cute?" Zadi says in the little-girl voice Moxie knows she sometimes uses when testing her mother's patience.

"He's attractive. But you know, I hope, that surface looks aren't everything." Moxie jangles the keys in her coat pocket and turns to look at Zadi. They continue walking side by side.

"You always say that. Anyway, he's too young to be anybody's boyfriend. He's goes to public school, but he's in a pre-engineering program. We were teasing him 'cause he says he doesn't have time for a girlfriend." Zadi has, of late, acquired a flippant way of moving her head around and widening her eyes when repeating something she finds remarkable. She does this now as she talks. Moxie hates it.

"Sounds like a smart guy," Moxie says, unlocking Zadi's side of the car. "But with all those friends hanging out at the library, how much did you accomplish on your project?"

"Ma, I keep telling you I have plenty of time left to do it, and I can use the library at school, too. I can also get on the Internet. It's not that big a deal. I don't know why you're so pressed about it!" Zadi throws her book bag in the backseat.

"Watch how you respond, young lady. Don't start acting like those spoiled rich girls at your school." Without looking, she knows Zadi is rolling her eyes.

Moxie gives Zadi a sidelong glance after she enters the flow of traffic on Ninth Street. She blended so well with those girls at the library, who, from all appearances, could have been the "hoochie mamas" her clients are drawn to. At least Zadi has natural hair, unlike those girls, and Zadi has stopped asking her about straightening it. "Zadi," she says, "do you know how beautiful your brown skin and your natural hair are?" A rhetorical question, for sure, but she hopes what she has given Zadi is solid enough for her to become her own best self.

She tells Zadi about a newspaper article she read at work. A young woman from a southern state, North Carolina she thinks but isn't sure, wasn't allowed to become a debutante because she wore dreadlocks. "And it wasn't white people who told her she was unacceptable. It was her own people, other black folks."

"Well, maybe they voted and they all wanted a certain look and she was going to be the only one who looked different or something." Zadi fumbles around in her book bag. She takes out her Walkman, puts on the earphones, and starts rocking her head from side to side.

"Oh, Zadi, you're missing the point. The adults shouldn't have condoned any such thing! It's pure self hatred!" Moxie drives down to the traffic light at the intersection. The sky is layered with fog, making it seem later than it is. Someone cuts in front of her, and she honks, angered afresh over the debutante story and Zadi's unpiqued interest in it. She changes the subject. "So you've known those kids for a while, then?" She taps on Zadi's earphones with one finger.

Zadi frowns and moves the earphones down to her neck. "Huh?"

"I was asking about those kids back at the library—how long have you known them?"

"Can you change the radio station, if I can't listen to my earphones? You always have the news on."

Moxie reluctantly allows Zadi to change to the local hip-hop station.

"Thanks." Zadi starts moving her shoulders and head, singing the words: " 'It's all about the Benjamins, baby. . . .' "

"So you just met those kids recently?" Moxie tries again.

"Who? Mia and them?"

"Yes."

"I told you I been knowing them. Well, not Devante but the girls."

" 'Been knowing'?"

"Excuse me! I have known them for some time now," Zadi says with extremely crisp articulation. "I know how to talk, Ma. You're always talking about how you want to make sure I'm retaining my 'blackness' even though I'm at a white school. And then when I try to retain it, you don't like it. You'd prefer me to talk white."

"Oh, I see, speaking Ebonics or whatever you want to call it—that's black, huh? To achieve in this world, Zadi, you need to speak the language of currency. Ebonics won't fly in the job market," Moxie says definitively, as she contemplates whether to stop at the drugstore or go straight home.

"Don't worry. I speak both languages fluently."

Moxie knows that Zadi is right. She wishes she hadn't embarked on the language thing when that wasn't even the real issue. Sometimes she feels as though she's walking on a mine field with Zadi. Every sentence carries the ability to ruin all that preceded it.

"So did you know those kids would be at the library?"

"No, just ran into them. Why are you sweating me about this? I got some work done, okay?"

"I'll be curious to see how much you actually accomplished. You were acting as if you really like what's-his-name, Devante."

Zadi doesn't look at her mother. "'I can't stand the rain,'" she sings along with the radio.

"Zadi."

"Dang, Ma. I told you. Devante is cute, but he's too young. I'm not thinking about Devante. Why are you always so pressed? I don't sweat you about what guys you like or don't like."

Moxie decides to go straight home; her conversation with Zadi is becoming stressful. Zadi has no right to try and equate the two of them. What happened to the days when children were seen and not heard? She has to admit, those days disappeared even before she was a child.

"For real, Ma, how come you never want to meet the guys Granddaddy finds for you? It's not like you're finding any on your own."

Moxie is instantly angered. She screeches to a stop, having realized at the last moment that the light is red. "I'm not looking for a guy, Zadi. Please believe me—a woman does not need a man to be complete."

"Okay, Ma. Okay. I'm hearing you. But what about just to have fun?"

Zadi's statement penetrates Moxie's annoyance and shatters it into laughter. "That wouldn't be too bad. But I haven't met that guy yet, the one who only wants to have fun, without any strings attached."

Zadi nods, chewing her gum and moving her head to the rhythm. "Ma, we're almost home; why don't you let me drive? Daddy let's me drive sometimes when we're near his house."

"That's Daddy. You're not old enough. You can get your learner's permit when you're sixteen, and I'll be happy to discuss it then."

"Ma?"

"Yes?" They drive past Providence Hospital and wait while an ambulance exits with its siren and flashing lights going.

"Ma, did you ever love my dad?"

Moxie wonders where this question came from. "Uh, yes, I did. At one time. We both loved each other and you very much."

"And then what happened?"

"We've talked about this before, Zadi," Moxie says, shifting in her seat. "Both of us changed, and we realized we didn't love each other anymore and that it would be better for us and you if we separated. That's it."

"But who left who?"

"We both decided. Really. I know it's hard to understand, but that's the way it was."

"I guess you have to be a grown-up to really understand. I don't want to talk about it anymore anyway; it makes me nervous. I just wanted to see if you'd say the same thing Daddy says."

"Did I?"

"Kind of. Anyway, I want to talk to you about something else. Something totally different. Now, you know how Miss Snow is. You know how she has certain rules and her mind set on certain things. And you know how once she's made up her mind, she never changes it," Zadi begins.

"Zadi, what are you trying to tell me?"

"Well, she says I have to get my hair pressed or permed or I can't have the Odette/Odile part. Ma, I have to get that part! Please. I know how you feel about my hair, but I'm fifteen years old and most people I know started getting their hair straightened when there was only one number in their age. . . ." Zadi's words rush together as if her time to speak is about to elapse.

Moxie holds her exasperation in, feeling it chafing against her chest. "I'll get this settled once and for all with Philandra Snow because I'm about sick of her reign of tyranny. You won't lose the part, but we're not going to mutilate your hair for her precious recital either," she says, tightly closing her mouth after speaking. She turns onto Buchanan Street and parks close to their brick semidetached house. She sits for a few moments with the car running. "Miss Snow must be out of her damn mind!"

"Ma, you guarantee I won't lose the part? Miss Snow doesn't play. She said no nappy heads in her show, and she was looking right at me. Please, Ma, don't upset her. This is too important to me. Don't ruin my life, please." Zadi's desperate expression serves only to enrage Moxie more.

She turns off the ignition and dangles the keys between her fingers.

"Zadi, calm down. I promise you won't lose the part. What you don't understand is that this is about power, which Miss Snow is entitled to have—like deciding what costumes you'll wear and what hair*styles*. But she doesn't have the right to tell you to chemically alter the texture of your hair for her damn show!" She gets out of the car but sees Zadi hasn't budged. "Aren't you coming in the house?"

Zadi's eyes widen in an urgent plea. "I just can't handle losing this part, Ma. Then Sonya will have it both nights. Ma, please don't ruin my life." With the car's interior light still on, Moxie's sees the glistening of tears in her daughter's eyes. Then Zadi gathers her belongings and gets out.

"Zadi, I love you. I promise not to ruin your life." Moxie closes her car door. She feels simultaneously invigorated and terrorized by the thought of confronting Philandra Snow. After all, she's wanted to tell her off for years.

Sunday, Jan. 24th
Lycra jeans
white sweater
Tims

Dear Sistergirl:

Dad congratulated me on getting the Odette/Odile part when he called me tonight, but he was kind of perturbed that I didn't invite him to the audition. He was like, Zadi, why didn't you tell me, you know I want to be there for you, sweetie? Ma told me to invite him but I didn't, partly because he makes me nervous cause he gets so nervous for me and, to be honest, I didn't want him to bring his tagalongs: Fawna and Tiffany. I just saw them last weekend, and Tiffany is really a spoiled brat, so for real I don't need to see too much of her. Tiffany is on my last nerve. Dad lets her dance on his shoes when he plays his old songs, the way he used to do with me. I tried to get on his shoes once, but he told me I'm too big now. I guess I am.

Windy sent an E-mail asking if she can come to the recital. She said when she was little she never even thought about the existence of black ballerinas because there weren't any in her ballet class. But then her aunt or somebody took her to see Alvin Ailey. I was like, Windy, thank you for sharing.

Monday, Jan. 25th
gray miniskirt
leopard print shirt
black platform boots

Dear Sistergirl:

 It's only been three days since Todd kissed me in the basement, but tonight he acted like nothing ever happened between us. For real, he acted like we didn't even know each other! He was dancing weird too, stiff or something, even Miss Snow noticed. She said, Todd, I don't know what your problem is, but you'd better get over it quick. Unless you're terminally ill with only a week to live, and even that won't be a problem because I'll kill you first. She can be so cold.

 When I did my three pirouettes in a row, the part where he's supposed to hold my waist, he acted like he didn't want to touch me. I wasn't going to say anything, but I was starting to feel strange, too, like I was about to have my heart broken or something. I know that sounds stupid, but I was building this thing up after the kiss. I told Zora. She was like, Zadi, where have you been? Didn't you know that Todd is gay? I was like, he is? She was like, duh. So why did he kiss me? Zora said maybe he's confused, maybe Louie or somebody dared him. I'm like, what are you talking about? I mean, I have had a crush on this guy from even before I had breasts. That wasn't my first kiss or anything, but it definitely was the most promising of late.

 Then while I was over in the corner putting rosin on my toe shoes and Todd was stretching at the bar I thought about just asking him straight up, Whatsup, are you gay? But it was making me too stressed, so I didn't. Forget it, Zadi, I told myself. Forget him. Back to waiting for Octavius, I guess. He looks just as good as Todd, and I know he's not gay. I refuse to be devastated by what happened with Todd.

 Allegra likes this Puerto Rican guy she sees at the bus stop, and she has her phone number written down on a piece of paper ready to give him when the time comes. I don't want her to get off the V train before I do, but I refuse to be messed up about Todd.

Miss Snow announced again tonight that there will be no nappy heads in this performance. Then she said, "Understand, Zadi Lawson? That means you." Of course then everybody started staring at me. This is what Ma thinks—that straightening your hair means deep down inside you want to be white. And I was like—Ma, Winnie Mandela has her hair permed. Give me a break. Ma says that you get more respect when your hair is natural. When you walk down the street, guys say, hey, sister, instead of calling you hey, baby or whatever. But I'm not feeling her on that because personally I'd rather be called "hey, baby." I know she's going to talk to Miss Snow, but Miss Snow isn't going to change her mind. I can't take it if I lose this part.

Report cards came in the mail today. Passed everything but didn't do that great in science and math, which is no big surprise. Cs in both. In the comment portion, they said I need to speak up more in class, but how can I speak more if I don't know what the hell is going on. Mr. Higgins said I need to be more engaged. F- him. He needs to just get engaged (I think he's probably gay like Todd). Ma is going to get on my case about those comments cause she'll think I'm not paying attention. I am, but he is the most boring teacher in the world and Biology is the most boring subject in the world. Got A- in literature (Ms. Dana says I am a good writer, but I have to be consistent), B in world history, B+ in Spanish, and B- in French, and P for Pass in Art. Ma was perturbed about the Cs, but I was like, hello, they're not Ds! And I'm taking an extra language, you know.

Watched a little of Ally McBeal. I like how they play that Barry White theme music for Biscuit. I was thinking that my theme music would have to be Janet's Go Deep. I hear that in my head for real sometimes when I'm walking. Ma started screaming about no TV during the week. When she yells her voice is so unbelievably irritating.

Ten

Moxie lies in her sleeping bag on top of the stiff camp bunk bed. She has drifted, like a boat loosely tied to a dock, in and out of sleep the whole night. Something is amiss, but she doesn't know what yet. Then her counselor, Mary Elizabeth, stands over her, whispering, "Moxie, wake up, you have to leave quickly. Your mother needs you. You're the only one who can save her." Inside her sleeping bag she is fully dressed, as if she knew to be prepared. The cabin is flooded with a red light that Moxie follows, actually steps onto like a space saucer. It whisks her home. Her mother is in the sewing room, lying on the narrow bed, propped up with blankets and pillows. Her face shines with fever, and her hair is spread around her shoulders. One arm reaches out for Moxie. Moxie enters through the room's only window and grasps her mother's outstretched hand. Her mother smiles and nods, relieved. Other people—doctors, nurses, Moxie's father and aunt—are in the room, but they are all clueless. They shake their heads and look to Moxie for the solution. "I'm here, Mommy," she says. As she holds her mother's hand, her mother's fever is instantly gone. She kisses her and the pain is erased. She lays her head on Cerise's chest, and her once weak heartbeat becomes strong and vital. Moxie massages her mother's head, and all the sadness dissipates. She is happy forever after. Everyone starts clapping and cheering.

When she awakens from the dream, she is perspiring. She wipes her forehead with one hand and turns her clock radio around so she can see the time. 3:45 A.M.. She sits up and lets the tears come, heavy and choking. The dream was so vivid and real. But of course, that's not how her mother died. There was no fever to alleviate, no last chance to hold her hand.

The night before she left for camp, she tried to shrug off an uneasiness she could explain to no one. "I don't want to go," she pleaded to her parents, but they barely heard her. She couldn't sleep that night either, and during the entire car trip, the tightness remained, like a fist clenching inside her stomach. All week long, the camp staff didn't know what to make of Moxie, who had been a vigorous, extroverted camper the summer before. This time around, she had little to say to other campers and often wanted to wander alone instead of participating in scheduled activities. At the end of that first week, the worried staff allowed her to call home. "Is everything okay?" she asked her parents. "It feels like something's not right." They assured her that things were fine, that they loved her and would see her in three more weeks. Moxie felt better and returned to her cabin, more like her old self. But five days later, Mary Elizabeth awoke her, just as in the dream, to tell her that Aunt BeJean was coming to take her home. "What's wrong?" She clung to Mary Elizabeth frantically. The counselor had no answer for Moxie, who waited anxiously in front of the cabin with her bags.

When Aunt BeJean arrived, her eyes were red-streaked and the lids swollen. She held Moxie tightly but wouldn't say anything more than, "We have to get you home right away." The three-hour drive seemed endless. BeJean spoke infrequently, and when she did, it was only to point out the beauty of the mountains or the roadside. Moxie heard her sniffling several times, but BeJean claimed it wasn't time to tell Moxie what was wrong. Moxie knew it was her mother and remembers asking her aunt to drive faster, faster . . . but it was too late. It had been too late even before her aunt came to pick her up. She said that she couldn't bring herself to tell Moxie until they were in front of the house. "Her soul was weaker than any of us knew," Aunt BeJean said finally, holding Moxie by her arm to stop her from racing out of the car. "There's no other way to say this to you, precious. I know my sister's sin will be forgiven, but she took her own life."

Moxie pulled away from her aunt's attempts at comforting, and ran into the house looking for her mother, calling for her. She found only the arms of her father, who appeared gray in color, weak, and slightly bent over, which he hadn't been before she went to camp. Moxie remained enclosed in his arms while friends stopped by the house with food, flowers, and words of sympathy.

After a time, when she let go of her father, she wandered outside onto the porch. The heat stuck to her skin like plastic, and the sun was aloft in the cloud-free sky. Moxie could even hear the high-pitched ballad of the sparrows that congregated in her backyard. Their song blended in with the jump-rope tunes of Lisamarie and Linsey, the girls from down the block she sometimes played with. Mr. Brooks across the street was washing his mammoth Lincoln Continental with a hose that snaked from behind his house. Her own house was startlingly beautiful. Her father had it painted back in the spring in an effort to cheer her mother. It worked for a short while. Her mother had planted multicolored pansies and impatiens in window boxes that were fastened on to the porch railings. Her father's garden, which began in the front of the house and continued around to the rear, was alive with majestic flowers and bushes. But Moxie didn't understand how all this flourishing and normalcy could occur when her world had just been overturned.

After the funeral Moxie plied her father with questions about her mother's death, as if she had a lone, desperate mission to investigate it. "Which pills did she take? Who was home? Why was the whole bottle in her room?" Moxie knew that her mother's sleeping pills were usually kept in the bathroom because she didn't need to take them all the time. And Moxie learned that Aunt BeJean had stayed over the night before her mother died. Her car had a flat tire, and even though Moxie's father changed the tire, Cerise became hysterically afraid for BeJean to drive home, thinking it would happen again on some dark, lonely road. Accepting that her mother had killed herself meant accepting that her mother had made a conscious decision to leave Moxie behind. That was too much hurt to shoulder, so Moxie began to blame Aunt BeJean for her mother's death.

She concocted vivid scenes of BeJean crushing the mountain of pills with her father's hammer and dumping them into a drink she carried in to Cerise. Perhaps Aunt BeJean secretly wanted to marry her father and take over raising Moxie. After all, BeJean had been coming periodically for the past several years, as her mother descended further, to help with the cooking, cleaning, and Moxie. She was, after all, the one who combed Moxie's hair for school when her mother wasn't up to it. The pieces of the crime came together enough for Moxie's eleven-year-old grieving mind. Once Moxie started thinking along these lines, it wasn't hard to stop loving Aunt BeJean. For one thing, Moxie despised having Aunt BeJean touch her hair. Up until the age of six, Cerise just let her hair go wild. She'd gather the whole mass into a "bushball," as she called it, with a rubber band or a ribbon. Sometimes she'd make two bushballs, one on each side of Moxie's head. She'd stop combing out the tangles as soon as Moxie whimpered that it hurt.

It was different with Aunt BeJean. When she cried and tried to escape Aunt BeJean's harsh brush and comb, "she's just tender-headed," was all Aunt BeJean would say, dismissing her sister's tentative concerns. After Moxie turned seven, once every six weeks or so, BeJean would come over and take one look at Moxie's nappy head and heat up the straightening comb she tucked into her purse. She'd usually have to chase Moxie around the house until her mother yelled for them to stop it. "Just let her do your hair," her mother would sigh, surrendering her daughter. Moxie begged and told her mother how much it felt as though Aunt BeJean were combing her brains out and how sometimes she even burnt her with that comb.

"My mother doesn't straighten *her* hair. Why do you have to do mine?" Moxie would scream.

"Because your mother's got good hair and you got hair like me," Aunt BeJean always said.

"Look how pretty yours is when Auntie gets done," Cerise would say, touching Moxie's cheek, lamely trying to convince her. Moxie never thought it was pretty. All greased up and flat to her head. She didn't care that she looked "presentable," according to BeJean, or that all the other little black girls at Sunday school and in her second-grade class had similar curls, greasy and flat as ribbon candy.

Moxie didn't want to look like those other little girls. They were only imitations anyway, because none of them ever looked like the white girls on television and in the movies. No matter how hard someone worked to give the black girls straight hair, it didn't get wavy and stick to their heads when wet or fly about their shoulders, like a horse's tail, when they ran in the wind. The white hair didn't have to be worked at. It was the real thing. White girls could wash and blow-dry theirs and never be subjected to singed and crackling hair or the sharp stab of a burnt neckline, ear or forehead. But even better than white hair and what Moxie truly wished for was the "good hair" her mother had. It was the best of both, somewhere between nappy and straight. Good hair was more vivacious than white hair. Her mother's hair was like black ocean waves. Moxie loved to brush her mother's hair. As she brushed and brushed, she pretended hers was like that, too, and she would be comforted until the spell was broken when she looked at her own in the mirror.

If Moxie's hair couldn't be "good," too, then she didn't want a piss-poor imitation. She saw enough of that, from the grown women she was around to her own playmates. The girls with the shortest hair, straightened so hard they were bald around the edges, would long-ingly touch the tresses of the good-hair girls. Just as Moxie did with her mother. But Moxie never acted that way at school or church. Instead, she ignored the good-hair girls, refusing to pay them the compliments they were used to. For many of them were the same ones who had called her "African," pejoratively, when she wore the bush-balls. "Good! I'm glad!" she'd snap back. "I glad I'm African!" She didn't know any Africans, but she wouldn't allow these girls to hurt her with their words. She asked her father, and he showed her books and magazines with African people. "They're strong and beautiful, and we come from them," he said. If she was African, then she would love being African. She wanted to be special, anyway, the way her mother told her she was.

The weeks in between Aunt BeJean's straightening ordeals, when the new growth was coming in, Moxie felt free again, the way she did when she ran around with the bushballs. Her hair had a spongy bounce and fullness that disappeared with Aunt BeJean's hot comb and jar of grease. It was as if her aunt raised the smoldering comb and pro-claimed, *You will not be free, you will be who I tell you to be,* and her mother, the one who could have saved her, turned the other way. Moxie knew her mother would have saved her but was too weak during those sad-mood times, and Aunt BeJean knew it, too.

In Moxie's mind, Aunt BeJean became the one who must have killed her mother so she could control, not only Moxie's hair, but everything else around the house. Because Moxie figured she wanted to marry her father, Moxie effectively stopped speaking to her. BeJean, hurt and unable to do anything to alter Moxie's thinking, continued straightening her hair in near silence until a year or so later, when BeJean married somebody else, without ever trying to marry Moxie's father, and moved away.

Once she let go of her aunt as the culprit in her mother's death, blame fell back upon her. If only she had been more insistent about staying home from camp that summer, if only she had thrown one more tantrum, or run away until it was too late to go, then perhaps her mother wouldn't have died. If she had paid more attention to those strong feelings trying to tell her not to leave. The lesson she gleaned was that if you compromise your beliefs or your gut feelings, terrible results occur—like death. She vowed never again to veer from what she believed to be correct because any other path led straight to Fort Lincoln, the cemetery where her mother was buried. She begged her father to show her which bus to take, and when she was twelve, she went every week, taking the H2 or the H4 bus and catching one of the B buses or walking the remainder of the way. She drove with her father sometimes, as well, but when she was alone, she could talk to her mother in depth. Now she goes once a year on her mother's birthday, May 29, always leaving behind a long stem of gladiolus, Cerise's favorite flower.

She lies in her bed for a while, trying valiantly, but it's no use, she's not going back to sleep. Closing her eyes very tightly, she can almost feel her mother's arms around her shoulders and her mother's soft skin against her cheek, tearstained now, just as it was the day they left her at camp. Okay, breathe deeply, let your stomach expand, she instructs herself. Breathe deeply and then keep on going. She decides to take her shower and prepare for the day. It's just as well that she's up early. More time to mentally prepare for her visit with Philandra Snow.

How dare Miss Snow try to manipulate Zadi like this? Miss Snow does not know the full story of this hair. It begins with Moxie gently washing baby Zadi's frizzy halo in the kitchen sink. She would use a delicate orange blossom shampoo and conditioner specially made for infants. As Zadi grew bigger and her fine baby hair began to come into its own, Moxie could hardly contain her joy that the emerging grade was like Cerise's—wavy and naturally shiny—the hair Moxie always craved for herself. If she couldn't have it in actuality, she would have it *vicariously* through her daughter. It must be a gift from the grave, Moxie believed, and vowed to cherish it always. When Moxie would peek in on Zadi sleeping, sometimes she'd bury her nose in her hair, breathing in its richness, allowing the soft strong strands to graze her face. Miss Snow does not understand the years Moxie toiled, brushing out the webs of tangles, blow-drying them to a manageable fullness, caressing the scalp with mixtures of lavender, rosemary, and pepper-mint oils, and patiently braiding the rows of tiny tendrils that hang to Zadi's back. She wouldn't even share this sacred ritual with James, no matter how often he asked her to teach him, allow him to help out with all his daughter's needs. And now Zadi and Miss Snow want to destroy all that history and expect her to sit back and let it happen.

Moxie is achingly tired at work because of waking so early from the dream about her mother. Instead of writing case reports, she calls several sewing machine repair places, but they all seem disinterested. It's too old, they say, or probably needs another motor. "Bring it in; we take trades." That's not acceptable to her, but she doesn't let herself sink to the level of their disinterest. She'll call some other places tomorrow. For now, she needs to think about what she's going to say to Philandra Snow. Why is it making her so anxious? Ordinarily she would consult Norma before this kind of confrontation, or at least practice some opening lines over the phone with her. But she can't trust the relation-ship right now.

During her lunch hour, she drives up Seventh Street to Miss Snow's Studio Elegante on Georgia Avenue. Black-and-white photographs of Philandra Snow hang in the studio foyer. In these almost mystical pictures Miss Snow is young, slender, and appears to be dancing through the heavens. The pictures fascinate Moxie because try as she may, it is impossible to connect the stunningly graceful dancer in them with the stump-shaped woman who runs Studio Elegante. Even back when Moxie took dance lessons, Miss Snow looked nothing like those photos.

Toni, the receptionist, tells her that Miss Snow is preparing to teach her preballet class for toddlers. Moxie didn't even know she had such a class and is surprised that there are enough black stay-at-home moms to enroll their kids in it. Toni speaks to her in her usual disengaged tone and, although she has known Moxie for years, shows no sign of recognition.

"I just need one minute with her," Moxie says, trying to sound firm. Toni lets out a sigh too great for the situation and buzzes Miss Snow on the intercom, whispering Moxie's name. Moxie notices that every other one of Toni's fingernails is adorned with the letter *T* along with a minute rhinestone.

"She says she can only give you a minute."

Moxie walks behind Toni's desk, knocks on Miss Snow's door, and walks in. "Good morning, Miss Snow."

"Moxana, *bonjour*. How can I help you?" Miss Snow steadfastly refuses to call anyone by a nickname even if they want her to. A napkin tucked in the neck of her red dress, she completely fills a worn leather chair. She feasts from a takeout platter of slippery eggs, potatoes, bacon strips, and lumpy grits all sliding in grease. "Please excuse me, but I'm just finishing up my extremely late breakfast."

"Oh, go right ahead." As if she would stop eating for anybody, Moxie thinks. She glances around for a place to sit. All the chairs in the room are filled with satin-and-tulle strips and pieces of ballet costumes. Miss Snow doesn't suggest where to sit, and Moxie remains standing. "I came to discuss Zadi's hair with you. She said that you wanted it to be straightened for the performance, and I—"

Miss Snow's tiny unsmiling eyes flare at Moxie. "There's absolutely nothing to discuss, Moxana. I let it go in past years because she was younger and didn't have the significant role she does now. A role, I might add, that requires her to stand in the forefront representing Studio Elegante. Ballet demands a particular look: one of elegance, cultivated beauty, *à la mode*. These she cannot have with that nappy head. It's as simple as that, my dear." Her tongue protrudes from her round, pinched face to dab at traces of egg in the corners of her mouth. Then she pulls the napkin from her prodigious chest.

Moxie moves closer and puts her hands on the edges of Miss Snow's desk. "You happen to be talking about a parental decision I made quite some time ago. I am not about to put chemicals in Zadi's hair—for many reasons, one of which is to instill an appreciation of her natural African beauty. Why are you teaching these black girls that beauty comes from a European standard?"

"Oh, don't be ludicrous, Moxana. Are you aware how naive and preposterous you sound?" Miss Snow frowns as if struck with a terrible headache. She closes the takeout container and throws it in the trash can beside her. She takes a sip from a large plastic mug. "Have you ever been to the Continent, dear? African women are straightening their hair right and left, wearing geri-curls and weaves even. *They're* trying to be European while black people in this country are falling all over themselves to claim their so-called African roots." She expels a loud, raucous laugh as she rises abruptly from her seat, causing Moxie to step back a little. "Your daughter is very talented, Moxana, unlike you at her age. But she can be replaced. It's entirely up to your 'parental decision making,' as you say, of course." She walks from the room, her massive hips shaking like an overloaded washing machine.

Moxie follows her. "Miss Snow, I'm not going to let you threaten me."

Miss Snow lets her neck roll back and laughs again. " 'Threaten'? Wrong verb, Moxana. If *you* choose to wear your hair like some sort of ghetto Medusa in those dreadful dreadlocks, that's one thing, but to subject your daughter to ridicule during her pubescent years is tantamount to child abuse. Such a shame. And to cast the blame on African heritage—I shudder to think what other hypocrisy you are teaching that child!" She takes her ivory cane from the corner and heads toward the dance floor. *"Excusez-moi,* I must go to my babies. It's already five past one."

Moxie stays close behind her screaming at the back of Miss Snow's head. "Miss Snow, Zadi is *my* daughter! *My* daughter! Do you hear me?"

"*C'est la vie.* Life isn't fair, my dear. You must have learned that by now."

"I'm not finished talking to you, Miss Snow!"

"Yes, you are, Moxana. We are very much *fini!*" She disappears through the curtain that leads to the studio, leaving Moxie alone in her office. Miss Snow's voice bellows from the folds of the curtain. "All right, *mes enfants.* I gave you extra time to stretch. I hope you took full advantage of it. Let's begin, shall we? First position. *Plié.* What? No one remembers *plié?* Where are your brains—have you left them home? Ah—Leslie remembers *plié.* Yes, my dear, but remember, you simply cannot watch your feet and dance at the same time. Okay. Again, *plié.* Yes. That's right. Keep your backs straight. Everyone move up a little, you're jammed in the back. If the girl in front of you won't move, Keisha, then knock her down. Ballet is like life, *mes enfants!*"

Tuesday, Jan. 26th
Gap jeans
cinnamon sweater
black Banana Republic boots

Dear Sistergirl:
Allegra went to PG Plaza after school to meet the Puerto Rican guy. His name is Roberto. He thought she was Puerto Rican, too. She's medium dark, but she has straight hair. He's not mad at her, though.

I have some more projects to get done for school. You'd think we had done enough damn projects by now! I got a B on my last history reaction essay and a B+ on my literature paper about Othello. I don't understand why it couldn't have been an A, but Ms. Dana said I needed to stretch myself some more and dig a bit deeper and she knows I can do it. Stretch where, dig what? What the hell does that mean?

Next I have to interview one of my parents.

I'm thinking about the dying swan dance. We pretty much know all the choreography for the recital now. I told Allegra how Miss Snow choreographs without ever leaving her seat. She might point her foot or do a port de bras from there, but basically she just tells us the steps and we do them. Every now and then Miss Snow decides to change a step but not that often.

Octavius says we are going to the movies after school on one of the days I don't have rehearsal. Ballet makes a social life kind of hard, but I want this part too bad to miss a rehearsal. We rehearse three times a week right now. By April it'll be up to four times, and then for the last two weeks before the show, it'll be every day. Miss Snow says the only way we can miss rehearsal is if we're lying prone in a pine box! She's not playing either.

> *Wednesday, Jan. 27th*
> *Old Navy jeans*
> *white DKNY T-shirt*
> *white Nikes*

Dear Sistergirl:

Today I had to go see Mr. Higgins during study hall because he thought I didn't turn in a Biology assignment from last week. And I was like, Mr. Higgins, I turned it in, I swear I did. I started to panic for real because I didn't want to have to do it over, especially when I knew I did it already. Then he looks through his piles of papers again and finds it in with his eleventh-grade papers. And he goes, My bad, Zadi. Mr. Higgins is tripping. His bad, my ass. He does that shit all the time. Tries to act like he's down with the slang. Kind of reminds me of Norma. Except she at least asks how do you do this, how do you say that. She doesn't just try to act like that would be the natural thing for her to say. She used to always ask me what the latest dance was. She said, when she was a teenager, they had different dances they would learn like every month or something. I tried to explain that we just dance right now. I mean we had the butterfly and the percolator and all that stuff, but really we just dance. She always wants me to show her my clothes so she can see what the latest styles are. And she's crazy about Lauryn Hill!!! I'm like, you go, Norma. A little hip-hop will carry you a long way. Maybe she can help

Ma be a little more up-to-date—Ma likes Lauryn's hair, of course, but she's stuck on old-sounding music like Tina Turner and Luther Vandross. She stays in skirts and jackets for work, mostly, and sweatsuits on the weekends. She wears a lot of African stuff, too. Talk about boring.

Finally heard from Octavius. He called when I was already asleep. Luckily I had brought the phone into my room. I don't know what time it was, but I knew it was late. He said that he and one of his dogs were freestyling at a club over on Fourteenth Street. He sounded so pumped! He said if Ma had answered, he was going to hang up. It took me a couple of seconds to wake up, but we only talked for a few minutes.

Thursday, Jan. 28th
blk/white top
blk boot cut jeans from Limited
blk Nikes

Dear Sistergirl:

Allegra says Roberto's cousin is going to let them use his apartment one day after school so they can do it!! Now I know more girls who aren't virgins than who are. Windy gave it up before school even started. So did Peaches. Zora says she's going to be next. She's writing to this guy who's in boarding school, and they're going to do it during spring break. Octavius is my only realistic hope at this point, but then again, who knows.

I decided I'm not going on a diet, but I am going to try to eat less junk food so that by the recital I'll be maybe five to ten pounds smaller. You should see how small Sonya is. It's sickening. She has no breasts or ass whatsoever. I wouldn't even want to be that small. Actually I wish my breasts were a little bigger, but I'm glad I have a phat butt, even though Miss Snow says it's big enough to sit a glass of water on it. She doesn't understand that's what boys like. They're always talking about girls' asses right in front of our faces. Even Desmond (who only likes white girls!!!) says the problem with white girls is they don't have no ass. From now until the recital, I'm just going to eat one big meal a day, preferably a salad, and drink lots of water.

Octavius called at midnight. Good thing I had the ringer on low. I was like, I paged you and called your celly. (He keeps changing his message. Now it just says, leave a message, dog. I was like, I'm not your dog. I told him it should say, leave a message, boo. He was like, you ain't the only person who be calling me, boo. That was cute, wasn't it?) I was like, what happened to going to the movies? He said be cool, he wants to go someplace better for a first date, like someplace to eat. I was thinking, I hope this does not mean Taco Bell, like where Randy took Mia. (Even though he took her there in a limo!) I need to go someplace where the dishes aren't made of plastic or paper. He told me his mother has been sick and he has been taking care of his brothers. I guess he meant he hasn't been in school. I don't feel too good about that. He said he was watching OutKast's new video. I asked him who his favorite rapper was. He said Nas because of his flow and his lyrics. He wants to be in the rap game so bad. He said rap keeps him alive and helps him make it through rough times, like when his mother was on drugs. I tried not to trip, cause I did not know about that. He said he kept playing Tupac's Keep Your Head Up when all that was going on. I like that sensitive side of him. He asked me if I like gogos and said maybe we could go there for a date. I told him I've only been to the ones that private schools have. He was like, oh, man, those are so fake. He said I need to go to a real gogo with Backyard or Rare Essence playing, like the ones up on Georgia Avenue. I was like, whatever. I asked but he never did say where he was. After I finished talking to him, I did a star sixty-nine. It was a pay phone! He's tripping hard cause he's supposed to be on curfew.

Eleven | Before she's even inside the hotel room, Woody begins hugging and kissing Norma all over her face. "What happened to—hello, how are you?" she asks as she welcomes him into her. When he sighs, "I love you," against her cheek, she swallows hard and pretends not to hear. She can't tell if her own sentiment is love yet. If only it didn't feel so damn good, if only it didn't smudge so much of her pain, she wouldn't be so confused.

He wants to smoke afterwards and asks if she minds. As always, she says no. They sit naked at a round wooden table that faces the picture window on the fifth floor of the hotel but the drapes are closed. She eats the remainder of her salad while he smokes. "So how'd it go with Miles this week?" Woody asks. When they lunched the previous week, he had suggested she get more physical with Miles, roll around on the floor with him every now and then. His theory was that a forced closeness might help her actually cultivate that kind of affection, and Miles would eventually become less temperamental. Even though it was amateur analysis on his part and based on different circumstances with his own kids, Norma was grateful for the suggestion.

"I'm trying to do better," she says, shaking her head. "But it's real hard."

"You feel what you feel for a reason."

"More like what I don't feel. It's like I'm trying to take steps while wearing big concrete boots. What scares me is that I consciously think about how I should touch him more, but something stops me from carrying it out. Doesn't that sound terrible?"

"No, Norma. You know why? Because you're working on it. It would be a different matter if you were impervious to it. But you're so earnest." He smiles at her and rubs his foot against hers under the table.

"What about your kids? You said they were upset about the divorce."

"I guess I was naive or not dealing with reality when I thought Beth and I could continue living under one roof until the divorce is final, for the sake of the kids. She asked me to move out the other night. She listed the things that disgust her about me: things like how the veins in my eyelids look when I'm sleeping, that I often eat breakfast standing up, and that she constantly smells smoke even though I never smoke in there. So, it's definitely past time to go. Reuben will live with me; Elena will stay with her mother. Elena has sort of picked sides. My wife's. And so there's a kind of wall she's put up against me."

"What about Reuben?"

The lines in Woody's forehead deepens. "Reuben concerns me in a different way. I think he's depressed about all that's happening. His grades are slipping."

"It's hard for children," says Norma, "when their parents are unhappy."

"You don't say much about your marriage."

"There's not much to say. We just pass through each other's lives, trying not to get in the way," she says, feeling slightly uncomfortable.

"Sometimes my mind gets ahead of itself and I wonder what a life with you would be like." He takes a deep pull on the cigarette.

"And what do you think?" She says, momentarily empowered by his desire.

His eyes narrow to almost closed and then open wide again. This slight movement makes him appear vulnerable and endears him to her. "I think it would be lovely," he answers.

"How do you know? My son says I'm mean sometimes."

"I haven't seen your mean yet. It's probably lovely, too." He laughs. They watch the smoke from his cigarette curl above them. One of his hands taps ash into the ashtray, the other reaches across and rubs her arm, sprouting goose bumps. "I want to do other things with you, you know. Beyond coffee, lunches, and hotels. I want to know everything about you. Tell me your autobiography."

"Now?"

He laughs and coughs a bit from the cigarette. "Sure. I don't teach on Fridays."

"Well, good for you but I don't have the whole day to idle away." She smiles at him.

"Well, how about in installments, then?"

"I wouldn't know where to begin. From childhood?"

"Of course. That's the beginning."

"You're serious aren't you? I'm flattered but we'll have to postpone. Right now I have too much work to do."

"I know. Preparing for your exhibit. After it's all over, though, would you go apartment hunting with me? I asked Beth to give me thirty days at least."

His marriage moving toward a finale makes her contemplate the inertia of her own. She and Lawrence seem to circle around each other, never connecting, like timid pugilists. "Sure, I'll help you look," she tells Woody. "After my exhibit."

Woody mashes his cigarette butt and stands, pulling her up to him. He holds her so tightly it almost hurts. She lays her head against the hollow in his shoulder, which feels custom-made.

Woody follows Norma to her mechanic, where she drops off her car for brake repair. Before leaving her at a car rental office, he stares hard into her eyes making them water. Later that afternoon Norma goes to her parents' house for dinner and ice cream and cake. It is her mother's sixty-ninth birthday. Norma's parents have lived, for almost thirty years, in a spacious house on Blagden Terrace alongside Carter Barron Amphitheater. All the houses on the street are massive and stately, built to be around for a long while.

Norma opens the front door with her key. She goes through the foyer and enters what her father termed "the wreck room" because it was the only room she and Irene were allowed to wreck when they were small. Since those days, it has been updated with new carpeting and a big screen television. Norma greets her father and Irene's husband,

Simon, who are watching the news. She moves on to the dining room, where she sets down the cake she picked up at the bakery, and then follows the scent of roasted chicken and fixings into the kitchen. Her mother and Irene are here, surrounded by platters of already cooked food. Irene apparently brought over a turkey stuffed with wild rice. Her mother has prepared greens and sweet potatoes. Once they're assured she remembered the cake, they pretend, as usual, to ban Norma from the kitchen. "Lawrence can come in when he gets here but not you." At the family's weekly Sunday night dinners, she is often teased about her lack of interest in cooking. ("Sure you weren't adopted?")

Her mother makes a customary big fuss over Norma's arrival. She wipes her hands on her apron and opens her arms wide for Norma to reluctantly fuse into. From childhood Norma has dreaded her mother's hugs. She doesn't understand why, just that they are too much and too many. When she was small, she felt as if she couldn't breathe engulfed in Doris's embrace, so she'd hold her breath all the way through it. Dr. Matthews once asked Norma what effect her mother's overaffection had on her inability to show affection to Miles. The thought of a connection was too troubling for her to dwell on. How could she be angry at her mother for loving her too much? Doris shouldn't be held responsible for Norma's journeying to the other extreme. Now, within her mother's grasp, she is momentarily paralyzed until the hug ends. "Happy Birthday," she says when her mother releases her.

She tells her mother and sister that Lawrence and Miles will come after they attend the first half of a Wizards' basketball game. Lawrence's firm had box seats, so he wanted to make an appearance, but Miles's attention span isn't long enough to sit through the whole game. Norma leaves Doris and Irene arguing about whether to put mushrooms in the gravy. She wanders the house, stopping in the doorway of the den to speak to Irene's children, who appear to be doing their homework. Sometimes she's envious that her sister's kids are both good students and athletes and were never as rambunctious as Miles when they were little. She almost dreads Miles's arrival because she's sure Irene will be sitting in judgment upon her parenting abilities and choices.

In the empty living room she pulls the heavy strings to open the drapes, inviting in the waning sunlight. She conducts her usual inspection of her parents' walls, lined with photographs from her father's tours of duty when he was in the service to decades of family photographs, including many taken by her. There are several pictures of her parents, including their wedding photo. Her mother is luminous in a dress made by Norma's grandmother, which Irene also wore as a bride. Norma wanted to wear it, too, but Irene hadn't preserved it correctly and it developed yellow spots the cleaners could not remove. The last display of pictures is in the foyer near the front door. These are photos of Norma and Irene as toddlers as well as pictures of the three grandchildren.

Norma hears her mother calling Irene's children to set the dining room table and decides to help them. They enter the kitchen to collect silverware, glasses, and dishes. "Wait a minute; let's use the special dishes in the china cabinet," Norma's mother says.

Norma's father comes in the other side of the kitchen, from the family room, carrying an empty glass. He has a modest limp, but that and the increasing loss of hair on his head are the only discernible signs of his aging, Norma thinks. "Smells good in here. But is the birthday girl supposed to be working this hard?" Arnold gives his wife a squeeze around the waist then goes to the refrigerator and pours ginger ale into his glass.

Norma's mother laughs and hits at him with a dish towel. "Irene did most of it, and she actually offered to do the whole thing, but you know I love fixing for the family, and it's not as elaborate as a Sunday dinner." She smiles up at him. "Norma, don't you know what dishes I'm talking about? On the bottom of the china cabinet."

"What the devil do you want to drag those old dusty dishes out for?" Norma's father asks.

"Because we drag them out for special guests, so why shouldn't we use them for our family. We're just as special. And it's my birthday!" Norma's mother says.

"Keep telling her she should have been a lawyer. Am I right? Speaking of which, where's Lawrence?" Arnold looks around the kitchen.

"Wizard's game," Irene tells him.

"He'll be here, Dad," Norma adds.

Dinner is finished, and Lawrence and Miles still have not arrived. It is almost eight, and Norma can see from the way her mother's cheeks are sagging and the yawn she tries to stifle that she's growing weary. Norma overhears Irene muttering to Simon about their long drive and the children having soccer practice in the morning. "Why don't we go ahead and sing to you now, then?" Norma suggests. "That way we won't hold Irene and Simon up, and we'll sing again when Miles comes."

"All right, dear."

Just when Norma has placed candles on the cake, brought out the dessert dishes, and everyone is about to sing, the doorbell rings. Simon, Jr., answers it, and Miles runs into the room, as if someone's chasing him. "I gotta go peepee real bad. Daddy told me I had to hold it." He dashes past everyone. Lawrence follows carrying yellow roses, Doris's favorite. "Thank you, sweetheart," Norma's mother says. "You're always so thoughtful." Her eyes dart away from him and land on Norma.

Miles returns, drops to the floor and hugs his grandmother's knees. "Oh, my precious boy is here," she says, and tries to pull him up, but he flops around like a scarecrow and then lays flat out on the rug.

"Get up, Miles," Norma says impatiently, conscious of Irene's critical eye. When Lawrence bends and whispers something to him, Miles stands, and Norma's mother kisses him until he stops her, wiping his face.

"Can we sing now?" says Irene.

"Who won the game?" Simon, Jr., asks Lawrence.

Lawrence shrugs. "We were up by four when I left."

"We were about to sing 'Happy Birthday,'" Irene snaps. They all sing.

"Miles, come sit and help Grandmommy open these," Norma's mother says, presiding over her pile of wrapped gifts. Miles is spinning in circles. "Come here, sweetheart." Miles comes to her with his funny, quick-paced walk, hands straight down by his sides like a tin soldier.

He climbs up on his grandmother's lap. "Norma, do you have your camera, honey? This would be a good shot." No, it wouldn't, Norma thinks. Her mother is one of the people who usually dislikes the "truthful" candids Norma takes of them. She complains that she wasn't smiling or looking into the camera or something. Norma despises the orchestrated "happy family" shots her mother is after and, consequently, rarely brings her camera when she comes. Her father's precisely posed portraits will do just fine, she thinks. He takes aim with his camera as her mother begins opening the gifts.

Irene and her family move from the dining room and pack up the books and baking dishes they brought with them. Norma and her mother drink tea Norma has brewed while Lawrence and Norma's father clear the table. "You haven't said one word to your husband," Norma's mother whispers loudly. "I've been watching."

"Please. I'm not up to one of your speeches about acceptable marital conduct tonight."

"Norma, I just wish you would get it through your head that passion is not everything it's cracked up to be. There are other things that last longer and matter more in the long run. Why, your father and I—"

Norma cuts her off. "You've told me this a million times. You lost the passion years ago, but your friendship and similar goals and values have stood the test of time. Right?"

"Norma, you don't sound charitable. You need to be more appreciative of what you have. I know you're going to say it's old-fashioned, but some of these feminists could learn a thing or two from the old ways. Sometimes we women have to do a little more for our men. Fix him a special dinner every now and then, get out the candles and the massage oil . . ." She winks at Norma. "Thought your mother didn't know anything, huh? It would behoove you to listen to what I'm telling you, otherwise you might look up one day and it'll all be gone," her mother says, resignedly folding her arms.

"What will all be gone? You're speaking of the financial aspects now?"

"Not only that. But it would serve you well to remember that even if you never sell another photograph, you and your child do still have a roof over your heads."

"Thank you, Mom, for that vote of confidence."

"Oh, Norma, you always take what I say the wrong way. You know I think you're the best photographer in the world other than your father." Her mother sighs. The doorbell rings again. Norma starts to answer it but sees Irene headed down the hallway with her coat on, presumably intent on leaving. In a moment she hears Irene exclaim and then return through the archway with one arm each around Moxie and Zadi. Moxie, looking slightly startled, meets Norma's eye. They nod at each other.

Moxie embraces Norma's mother. "Sorry, we didn't mean to crash your party, Ma Simmons. I didn't even remember it was your birthday, so I'm empty-handed." Zadi lags behind until Norma's mother beckons to her.

"You're not empty-handed. You all are the present! I'm so happy to see you, and who's this gorgeous tall gal you've got with you?" she says, reaching for Zadi's hand, which she clasps tightly in hers. "Look how much you've grown! Neck and neck with your mother almost, aren't you?" Zadi nods. "I was just about to ask Norma about you, Moxie. You don't usually stay away this long! How's your sweet dad doing? I keep saying I'm going to call him."

"He's fine. He'd love to hear from you, I'm sure."

Before stopping by, Moxie had scanned the street for Norma's car, but didn't see it because Norma is driving a rental. She wouldn't have come in had she known Norma was here. Things are so awkward between them. She feels as if she owes Norma an explanation for her presence. "Zadi had to pick something up at a girlfriend's not far from here and she said, aren't we near the Simmonses' house, so here we are," she says to Doris but intends it for Norma. Doris pats a seat near her, and Moxie sits down at the dining room table.

"Come here, sistergirl," Norma says, and stands to give Zadi a long hug. "Open your coat—let me see what the fashion of the day is. Oh, you are just the bomb!" They both burst out laughing.

"We don't say 'the bomb' anymore."

"Really?" Norma looks crushed. "What do you all say now?"

"'Off the hook' or 'like that,' or if it's really like that, we might say 'vicious' or 'wet.' You have to know when to use which, though."

"Too complex. I'll never get it right." Norma laughs. Zadi confides in Norma's ear that she needs to talk to her in private.

Moxie compliments Norma on the pin she's wearing, a silver dove from Woody. "Oh, thanks. A gift," she says self-consciously. Norma's mother shows her birthday presents to Moxie, explaining who gave what. Irene sits down again without removing her coat. While her mother and Irene talk to Moxie, Norma takes Zadi out into the hallway.

"What's up, girl?" Norma says, nudging Zadi playfully.

"Can you please talk my mom into letting me straighten my hair?"

Norma eyes Zadi as if she's insane. "What? Zadi, I hope you know I would do just about anything for you. That, however, is a real tough request." Zadi explains the dilemma about Miss Snow's recital requirements. Maybe if she and Moxie hadn't been at odds, she might have agreed to at least discuss the subject and present Zadi's side to her mother. But with the current state of affairs, Norma can only pat Zadi's shoulder sympathetically and say, "I would do anything for you, except that. Maybe it'd be better to talk to Miss Snow and tell *her* what the deal is. If she understands where your mother's coming from, she might make an exception for you."

Zadi shakes her head somberly and looks on the verge of tears. "Norma, you know how Miss Snow is."

Norma wishes she could do something more than hug her. "You're right. That would never work. Don't give up, sistergirl. I'll keep thinking about it, too."

When Norma returns to the dining room, Lawrence enters from the kitchen to gather the remaining dishes. He brightens as soon as he notices Moxie. "Hello, stranger. How's it going?" He rubs his hand along her shoulder.

She stands to embrace him. "I'm hanging in, Lawrence. How about you?"

"Doing fine. No use in complaining anyway, is there? So good to see you."

"Good to see you, too." She wishes she could sit down with him, demand that he tell her what the hell is wrong, and then impress upon him the urgent need to save his marriage. The thought of him finding out about Norma's affair and experiencing more pain, which he doesn't seem to know how to handle very well, is extremely disturbing to Moxie. Moxie watches him pick up the empty cups and saucers.

"I'll bid you all good night, now," Lawrence says. "Got to go back to the office for a little bit." He turns slightly to Norma. "See you and Miles at home. I promised Miles he could stay up, since it's Friday. I'll put him to bed when I come in."

"Back to the office, so late?" says Norma's mother, looking at the grandfather clock in the room. "Don't work too hard. We worry about you, you know." She stares at Norma, who doesn't look up until Lawrence leaves the room. "Norma, Moxie was just telling us what Miss Snow is trying to do with Zadi's hair. Tell Norma, Moxie."

"Zadi just told me," Norma says, then wishes she hadn't.

"Philandra Snow should be ashamed of herself! Totally disregarding you, the child's own mother. Typical Philandra. Well, why don't you get her a wig, Moxie?"

"She said it has to be a bun, Ma," Irene says agitated, helping herself to a second piece of birthday cake.

"I heard her, Irene. But I've seen them in those Korean places. They have wigs you can comb into buns. You comb your own hair into the front part. For all I know, they might have some already made into buns. You know what I'm talking about, don't you, Moxie?" She looks at Moxie for confirmation.

"I know what you're talking about, Ma. But will Miss Snow go for it?" says Norma, clearly doubting.

"Oh, to blank with Miss Snow!" says Norma's mother, emphatically. They all laugh. "I'm still mad at her for making Irene dance in her underwear. Remember that Irene?"

"Here we go," Irene groans. "Of course I remember it, Ma; you never let me forget it."

"It was the meanest thing." Norma's mother leans forward to Moxie. "Irene was just a little thing then, six or seven at the most, and she had forgotten her leotard and tights. So what did you say to Miss Snow, Irene?"

"I don't remember the exact words."

"Something like, 'I can't dance today. I forgot my tights.' Anyhow, Philandra Snow says, 'Well, you've got underwear on, haven't you?' and made the poor child dance in her underwear. Can you imagine?"

"I can't say I'm surprised," says Moxie. "You should tell that to Zadi."

"I had a hole in my panties, too," Irene said. "I just wanted to die. All the kids laughed, especially the two boys in the class. I really wanted to die."

"You didn't have a hole in your panties, Irene. I would never have sent you out with—"

"Yes I *did*, Ma. Maybe you didn't know it, but that much I do remember!"

Norma's mother shakes her head in disbelief.

"So, Ma Simmons, what did you do? We parents allow ourselves to be so intimidated by her," Moxie says, still assessing her own performance challenging Miss Snow.

"Not me! The next day I confronted her. But she just brushed me off and said it was Irene's responsibility to have the appropriate attire and, you know, all that bull she gives you. That woman is something! That's why I never pushed Norma when she didn't want to continue. Now, to Miss Snow's credit, she *has* done some very good things for the children she brings in from the projects and the shows she puts on at the schools, but she can definitely try the patience of Job. Anyway, do like I said and check on the wig for Zadi."

Moxie excuses herself to find Zadi so they can leave. Only Irene's daughter, Gina, and Miles are left in the family room. Moxie delights in seeing Miles and kneels down because he's on the floor. He reminds her of a little Einstein, so small, yet he seems as if he's been in the world before. "How you doing, Miles?" She holds him close, and he lays his head against her. When she looks up, Norma is watching them from the doorway.

Moxie feels slightly anxious as she walks around, unable to locate Zadi. She knows she's in a safe place and that it's absurd for her to feel this way. Irene suggests that Zadi and Simon Jr. are probably in the basement, where Norma's father, a jazz devotee, keeps his state-of-the-art stereo system. It turns out that's where they are, listening to one of Simon Jr.'s CDs with the earphones on.

• • •

In the car, Moxie says, "So you had a good time?"

"It was all right."

Moxie realizes she is careening across Sixteenth Street and slows herself down. "You seemed like you were having a good time."

"I said it was all right."

"What were you and Norma talking about when you left the room together?"

"Nothing."

"Whose idea was it for you and Simon Jr. to go down in the basement?"

"His, I guess. I don't know. Why are you asking me all these questions?"

"Did you have a good time talking to him?"

"It was all right, Ma. Dag."

Moxie glances over at her. "You don't have your seat belt on. Put it on, please. I'm just curious how you ended up down the basement, away from everyone else, that's all."

"Okay—if you must know, here's everything that happened." Zadi, exasperated, starts talking very fast. "I went in the room to say hi to Miles, and him and Gina were watching Nickelodeon, and that was like kind of boring. And Simon Jr. started talking to me. I haven't seen him in a long time, and he wasn't all shy and nerdy anymore like he used to be, and he told me he can sing just like SisQo from Dru Hill. I said I didn't believe him. He said he had the CD, did I want to go downstairs and listen to him sing? So I'm like, whatever. So we went downstairs to listen, and he sang along with the CD and turned the volume down. He sounded jive good, so I pumped him up a little and said it sounded off the hook. So he said he wants to be a singer. So I was like, well, you should go for it, then. And then he said what school do you go to? and I told him, and then you came looking for us like we were on the ten most wanted list."

"That's all? You just listened to a CD? He said let's go down to the basement to listen to a CD?" Moxie asks. Zadi stares out the car window. Moxie travels down Kennedy Street and over to Missouri Avenue.

Zadi lets out a long, loud breath. "Oh, my goodness. He—yes, I listened to the CD and I listened to him sing. He sang while the CD was playing. I listened. Whatever. He's younger than me. He's not some-body I'd be interested in. Dag. Why are you always sweating me? You ask too many damn questions." Zadi frowns and glares straight ahead.

"What did you say?" Moxie whips her head to the side.

"My bad."

She keeps her eye on the car in front but grabs a fistful of Zadi's braids and tugs hard. "Don't ever forget who you're talking to, young lady. Do you understand?"

Zadi pouts and doesn't answer.

"I said do you understand?" Moxie pulls harder on her hair.

Zadi blinks back tears. "Okay. All right. Yes. I understand."

Friday, Jan. 29th
jean dress from $7 store
opaques
Nine West platforms (belong to
    Allegra, might trade)

Dear Sistergirl:

Ma is always asking me stupid-ass questions! She gets on my nerves with that shit. And it hurt like hell when she pulled my hair. Child abuse.

Allegra's boyfriend, Roberto, shut their relationship down. He called her and said his moms only wants him to go out with Puerto Rican girls. They didn't even get a chance to do it. Allegra was crying on the phone. I was going to stay on the phone with her till she felt better, but she said she wanted to hang up and go listen to some R. Kelly songs.

It was Oprah's birthday today; they said so on the radio when I woke up. She's forty-five now. She better hurry up and marry Steadman before she turns into a prune.

I have a rack of homework for the weekend. We're reading Jane Eyre *now in English Lit. I thought I wouldn't like it, but I love it! Ms. Dana described it as dense and thick like cream soup. I like that description and wrote it down in my notebook. I'm reading Françoise Sagan on my own because I finished all the Colette books I could find. I love* Bonjour

Tristesse. *I like the way these French people talk about love. Here's a line from* Cheri: *"Then, still on his knees, he clasped Lea in his arms, offering her a forehead shadowed under tousled hair, a trembling mouth moist with tears, and eyes bright with weeping and happiness. She was so lost in contemplating him, so perfectly oblivious of everything. . . . She twined her arms round his neck and gently hugged him to her, rocking him to the rhythm of murmured words." I want to feel that kind of love. But sometimes I wonder if writers just make it all up because I don't know any real life people who have it. Grandpa sounds like maybe he did with Grandma, but then again, she killed herself. Daddy and Fawna used to be so mushy all the time it got on my nerves, but they're not like that anymore. They might hug or kiss every now and then but nothing like they used to. So I don't know any grown-ups in deep love. Isn't that just dreadful? as Jane Eyre would say.*

Windy swears she had deep love for the guy she met last summer when she was in Ireland on vacation with her family. They didn't have sex until the night before she was leaving. She cried the whole plane ride home, however many hours that was. Her parents were tripping because they didn't know what was wrong. I was like, it's better to have that sweet memory because if she stayed in Ireland or something, it probably wouldn't have lasted. Windy's a trip, but she's my girl. She was home-schooled until this year. She says her theme song would be something by Beck, who to me sounds like he's just copying off of the Artist. Actually, I thought she was going to say something by Jewel.

Saturday, Jan. 30th
blk leggings
gray sweatshirt
drop socks with white Nikes

Dear Sistergirl:
  I need new toe shoes soon because the ones I have now are all worn around the point and I have to stuff the mess out of them with lamb's wool. I need time to break them in before the recital. Ma says I have to

use my own money. I wish she would be for real. The only money she gives me is $18 a week, which includes lunch ($1.50 per day) but not metro. She says I should be saving some every week. But I have to buy lipstick, lip liner, nail polish, and sometimes VIBE or Seventeen or Teen People, depending on who's on the cover, CDs of course, Big Red gum, Evian water, and hair scrunchies. I don't have time to baby-sit anymore, so I can't get that money. Sometimes I braid other people's hair, but that takes time, too. Dad is better than Ma when it comes to giving up funds. Ma is just plain cheap. With Dad, if I come over right after he finished playing his sax somewhere and he just got a whole rack of money, he'll give me some without me even asking. And he won't say, this has to last until next week, like Ma does. Once he gave me a $50 bill. I didn't tell Ma though. I hear her talking on the phone to him getting mad if he's late paying child support. (Which does not happen that much.) If she finds out I'm listening, she'll get upset and say, Zadi, this is between your father and me and has nothing to do with you. Pretend you didn't hear it. Yeah, right.

I'm over here at Dad's until tomorrow, so I have to write this in my notebook. He took me out driving tonight. Ma doesn't like him to because I don't have my learner's yet, but we only go in empty parking lots. Most of the time he says I do really great, but I went up on the curb when I was turning. This way when I get my learner's, I can sign up for the road test right away. Dad doesn't get all stressed out like Ma probably would if she did ever let me drive her car.

Tonight, Fawna and Daddy told me and Tiffany that Fawna is pregnant. They made a whole big thing of it. We had to sit on the living room couch, and Fawna sat in the big armchair, and then Daddy stood behind her rubbing her shoulders. I acted really surprised and told them congratulations, even though I overheard them talking about it earlier. They said, Zadi, you and Tiffany can baby-sit. I was like, yes, but you are going to have to pay me double because Tiffany really can't baby-sit by herself for a newborn. Tiffany was acting like she really didn't care one way or another. She was like, well, can I still get my room painted peach? and can I still have a friend sleep over even if the baby's sleeping? and blah blah blah. You know, spoiled little kid stuff.

Fortunately, Tiffany just left to spend the night at a friend's. I'm glad because she is such a pain in the ass sometimes. Always wanting me to do her hair and calling me her sister. I told her, look, this is not a sitcom! She and her girlfriends are into Barbie hard. Tiffany has Barbie's dream house, her car, her minivan, and her beauty shop. She also has a white Baywatch *Barbie. I was like, Tiffany, what are you doing with a white Barbie? She goes, I have tons of black Barbies, I have Asian Barbie and two white Barbies.*

Ma would never let me have a white doll when I was into dolls. To her that is like one of the worst crimes in the world. I remember someone gave me one once. One of my grandfather's friends from church, I think. Ma let me play with it while the lady was there, but when we got home I couldn't find the doll anywhere. I kept asking her and she'd say she didn't know where it was. Later I heard her telling Norma how she couldn't believe that a black person would give a black child a white doll and how she threw it in my grandfather's trash can. She said white people don't go around giving white children black dolls. I said, Ma, why did you throw my doll away? and she said because you need dolls that look like you. She acted like I was going to turn white by having a white doll. When I have kids, if I have kids, and have a daughter, I'll let her have all kinds of dolls because I think it's kind of racist to let your kid only have one kind of doll, but I would make the kid have more black dolls so she would know the black ones were more important. I'd let my boys play with dolls, too, if they wanted. I probably wouldn't let them take the dolls outside where other kids could jone on them, but I'd let them play with them at home. One time, when I used to baby-sit Miles, he was watching TV, and he saw a little mermaid doll. He said, I want that doll but I can't get it cause it's for girls. I said, who told you that? He said, my Mommy. I got on Norma's case, but she didn't switch up. So after that whenever I baby-sat him, I tried to remember to bring one of my old dolls over and let him play with it. All he wanted to do was comb the doll's hair and take the clothes off.

Fawna is bugging me to make salad for dinner. She is such a pain now that she's officially pregnant.

Sunday, Jan. 31st
blk jean skirt
Allegra's Eddie Bauer T-shirt
blk Nikes

Dear Sistergirl:

I need to get something pierced or tattooed. Janet Jackson has the velvet rope symbol tattooed on her back, her nipple pierced, and a tattoo or a piercing down near her coochie. Octavius has his name in Japanese letters on his chest, but I haven't seen it yet. Boy, do I want to see it. Windy says she's getting a tattoo that says, "Jewel rules" or something related to Jewel. I'm like, Windy, what if you don't like Jewel when you get older? She looked at me like what I said was really foul. If I didn't have anything better to do, I would try to get her on MTV's Fanatic show so she could meet Jewel. When I get my tattoo, I'm going to get either a pair of toe shoes or Scorpio '83 (my sign and birth year), and I'll put it on my right upper arm, I think.

Paged Octavius and he called me back right away. I was psyched. I forget sometimes that O is Ma's client until he reminds me by saying stuff about how he went out after his curfew check. He says he didn't go to his last appointment cause he knows she's going to get on his case cause he hasn't been going to school either. He says it's too boring. So I asked him, what have you been doing? His mother was still sick. She's okay now. I was like, so you're going to resume going to school. He was like, yeah, I'm thinking about it. I'm like, Octavius, I hope you're not doing any illegal shit. I cussed and everything so he would know I was serious. I told him I can't be down with that cause it's not going to lead anywhere but jail or the cemetery. He said he used to be into that, but he's not anymore. I don't think he would lie to me. I said, don't you dream about what it's going to be like in the future when you're all grown, doing what you want? He said, oh, man, you sure are your mother's daughter. I'm like, don't say that. He's like, you are, for real. That kind of hurt my feelings, but I didn't tell him. He said he already told me about his dream of getting into the rap game. I was like, yeah, you did. He asked me about mine. I told him I'm going to be a famous ballerina. He kind of laughed, like I was joking or something. He said he never heard of anybody wanting to be that. He thought I just did it for exercise. I was like, what are you doing about trying to be a rapper? I asked him, have you made a demo? Have you sent anything to any record companies? He said no. He said his boys was gonna hook him up. I'm like, what boys? and why you waiting on them, anyway, when you can do it yourself? Octavius was like, keep talking boo, you sound strong. And then I hit him with I'm not interested in guys who aren't going to be about something. You can't be no scrub and be with me, too. He got a little mad, I could tell. Guys always get mad when you mention No Scrubs. That's why they had to make that stupid No Pigeons song. Whatever.

Gotta go, Dad is about to take me home.

Twelve | On Monday, Moxie walks a few blocks to her bank's automatic teller machine. She takes out forty dollars just in case, hoping she won't have to spend it all. Then she crosses H Street to the Korean beauty supply store, Hair to Go. She has been in here several times before to purchase hair oil and shampoo, but the two shopkeepers greet her with the smile one gives a stranger. "Hi," Moxie instinctively speaks loudly and slowly, as if that will make them understand her better. "I'm trying to find a wig that can be combed up into a bun." She gestures with her hands as if forming a ball on the top of her head.

The women speak what she assumes is Korean to each other. "You buy wig?" says the one who comes from behind the counter and points at the wig section.

"Yes." Moxie nods. "Do you have any that are shaped like a bun or can be rolled into one?"

"Bun?" The woman repeats and looks at the other woman. They say something else Moxie can't understand.

Moxie redoes the ball motion at the back of her head, wondering if they'll be confused by her dreadlocks.

"Ah," says the woman behind the counter. Her face lights up. "French loll. You want make French loll?"

"*Ummm.* No. Well, sort of. Show me." The woman from the counter comes down a short step, and the other woman takes her place. Moxie notices that she has on butterfly earrings. She beckons Moxie with one finger and takes her over to another section near the back where there are more wigs on stands. Some are shaped like French rolls, and she points them out. Moxie thanks her and looks at the wigs, removing some from their stands. The woman waits there with her hands behind her back. One wig that looks as if it might work catches Moxie's eye. It is made to fit the scalp closely, looks like "bone straight" hair and it can be pulled back into a bun. It is only $19.99. She buys it and returns to the office humming the Janet Jackson song Zadi was playing on her boom box this morning.

Moxie rescheduled her file review meeting with Von for this afternoon. She makes a stack of the files they will discuss and is preparing to leave her office when the temporary receptionist buzzes to announce a phone call. "Do you know who it is?"

"Oh. Hold on. I'll find out."

Moxie has told the temp about this at least three times today. "Never mind," she says, and picks up the blinking line.

"Hi. This is Haleem Remington. We met several weeks ago—I'm your dad's neighbor. . . ."

"I remember. How can I help you?" She intentionally tries to sound rushed.

"You sound busy. I'll just take a second of your time." She can hear the disappointment in his voice. She's sure her father is the mastermind behind this phone call. "I'm about to go into a meeting."

"Should I call back later, then?"

"No. Go ahead." Let's get this over with, she thinks.

"Well, I was speaking to your dad and mentioned that I'd like to find an African-centered school for Jupiter. Your father said you had Zadi in one some years ago. I was just wondering if you could give me the name of the school, if it wouldn't be too much trouble." His voice was warm but uneven, like smooth pebbles being rubbed together.

Relieved, Moxie says, "Oh, sure. There are a few of them around. I'll give you the names, and they're all listed." She gives him the names and spellings of the schools.

"Great," he says. "There was one other thing." Here it comes, she thinks, knowing he's going to ask her out now. "I really like your locks and been thinking about locking myself for the last year or so. Do you do your own or do you have somebody? Sorry to be asking you for all this info."

"It's all right. I go to somebody. Here's her number."

"Oh, thanks." She hangs the phone up quickly. He wants to lock his hair! How lame can he get? He's just laying a foundation. She's going to have to be firmer with her father.

When Moxie enters Von's office, Von chastises her for being a few minutes late. She moves her glasses from her eyes to the top of her short natural. "I'm supposed to keep you waiting, not the other way around."

"I got a phone call, and the temp can't remember to find out who's calling. If she had, I would've skipped that one." Moxie sits with her files on her lap.

"Yeah, the elevator definitely doesn't go all the way up with that young lady. If Brenda's still sick tomorrow, I'm going to tell the agency not to send that chick again. As my son would say, she's so dumb she'd sneak on the bus and pay to get off."

Moxie laughs. "That's cold, Von."

"All right, let's get started. If I act like more of a bitch than usual, please excuse me. I gave up smoking over the weekend, and it's kicking my ass." She presses her finger against her forehead.

"Well, congratulations! Now you won't have to go outside twenty times a day," Moxie says, handing her the top case file. "All right, this is Antoine Sanders. Got him into treatment, but he left the program. Don't know where he is right now."

"Let me put that to the side," Von says, holding out her hand for the next file. "Next is Sean Foster. Pleaded to misdemeanor assault. Says here 'extenuating family circumstances'?"

Moxie pulls her chair forward. "That's the one where I suspected the mother had an abusive boyfriend." Von's eyes search the file report. "It's on the third page. Wouldn't talk when he was locked up. When I did the home visit, I knew something was up. The mother was scary, didn't want me to speak with him alone. I was able to, for a short time only, but he wouldn't open up. He seemed to panic when I mentioned the mother's boyfriend."

"So he attacked the boyfriend while he was sleeping?"

"Correct. A desperate, self-protection kind of thing."

"Did we refer to Social Services? Oh, yes, it says so right here. Any follow-up?"

"I have a call in but no return call yet. I hope they placed him."

"All right. Keep on it 'cause they're short-staffed over there and shit can fall through the cracks. Next. Octavius Johnson. Missed two appointments. Missed two urines. Where's he been?"

"If Octavius doesn't want to be reached, then he is unreachable. His home phone is off, so I've had to send the special unit out a couple of times to verify that he's in by curfew and so far so good. But I've lined up a potential part-time for him and haven't been able to get in touch. Left messages at his neighbor's place, paged him, and called his cell phone. Hope he doesn't lose out on this because I can't reach him."

"Let's make one last-ditch effort to get him in here and read him the riot act. Again. For the last time, okay? Who's next—Lucas Bruno?"

"Another probable abuse situation. I need to set up a home V for him, and he's due in next week."

Moxie spends half an hour with Von talking through each case. When she returns to her office, Octavius is waiting outside the door. "Well, we must have talked you up. But your appointment was last week, Octavius, not today."

"My moms been sick, Miss Dillar. I ain't lyin'." He gazes at the linoleum floor while she unlocks her door.

"What kind of sick?"

He waves his hand dismissively. "Not like before. Had some infection or something. She went to the hospital and everything. Had to baby-sit and take care of things. That's why I didn't make it last time."

"Sit down, Octavius. I thought she told me she had a baby-sitter in the building."

"She do, but I mean I had to take them over there and pick them up and all that."

"So you've been going to school?"

He doesn't answer at first. Then he says, "Sometimes. But I had to be cleanin' and cookin' and all. She back home now, though, so I'ma go tomorrow."

"Look, Octavius. I've been trying to reach you for almost three weeks. Why didn't you call and tell me what was going on? Did you forget about meeting with Ron D? I thought you were so interested. We were supposed to get your social security card, remember?"

"Can we do it today?"

"I'm not here at your beck and call, Octavius." She says, annoyed. "Let me check my appointment list. Go down the hall and take your urine. You better be clean 'cause you've already messed up on this end, and if you mess up over there, I won't be able to help."

While Octavius is gone, Moxie makes a new appointment for him at the radio station. She checks with Social Services and learns that Ms. Johnson was, in fact, recently hospitalized for several days. When he returns, she drives him over to M Street to apply for a social security card. The line extends to the waiting area. Most of the people waiting are older than Octavius, and several appear fed up with the process. A clerk calls, "Next in line," in a nonchalant, nasal tone. Moxie helps Octavius fill out the paperwork, then she leaves him in the line. "Last chance, Octavius," she says. She means it; she's let him slide through more than enough times. She's cautiously encouraged, though, because his earnestness seemed heartfelt as he was working on the application. Not his usual disengaged attitude. Moxie uses a street pay phone to check back in at the office. The temp transfers her to Von, who relates that Antoine is in lockup again for unauthorized use of a vehicle and she'll have to appear in court the next morning. She shakes her head. Antoine's going to jail this time.

Moxie pulls into the Willow School parking lot and locates a space right away. As she locks her car door, someone honks at her. It's James, driving a shiny black Explorer. Moxie wishes they could have separate conferences with Zadi's teachers, but the school says it would take too much time to accommodate all the divorced couples. James parks two spaces away, gets out, and hits the remote lock in his hand. The Explorer's horn sounds again. "New car?" she says, beginning to walk before he can catch up with her.

He takes two steps to her four. Moxie can smell his cologne as he gets closer. The scent is dramatic and forceful, the way James has always tried to be. "Just test-driving. See the dealer tags? If I decide to get it, though, I was thinking I can give the Cherokee to Zadi when she turns sixteen. Girlfriend is a pretty good little driver," he says proudly.

"A car? For Zadi? James, are you out of your mind? Zadi needs a car like a hole in the head. And you have a lot of nerve talking to me about a new car when you still owe me from last month. I haven't been able to pay her orthodontist yet."

"Don't start, Moxie, I'm not in the mood. I'm only behind because of Christmas. You'll get the money. You always eventually get the money." James holds the heavy wooden door open for Moxie. They enter through Willow's large vestibule, regal at first glance but comfortable, with three massive couches, several armchairs, ficus trees in each corner, and a pot of freshly brewed coffee on the table. Surprisingly, there are no other parents waiting.

"Don't play with the money, James. I have a tight budget with no room for improvisation."

James prepares a cup of coffee for himself. "Why are you so daggone evil all the time? And so bent on making my and Zadi's life miserable?"

"What are you talking about? Somebody's got to set limits for her!" Moxie tries to yell softly so the whole school doesn't have to know their business. James carries his cup through the windowed doors and pokes his head in the front office to alert them, she supposes, that he and Moxie have arrived.

"They'll be right with us," he says, pulling up the thigh part of his slacks before he sits down across from her. "You were saying? Oh . . . setting limits. Setting limits doesn't have to mean putting up damn barricades. Like all this grief about her hair. Why don't you cut her some slack instead of trying to make her feel like a freak?"

"A freak? Because I want to keep her hair natural? Oh, come on, James." Moxie looks at the wall clock. Their appointment was for five minutes ago.

"*You* come on. Can't you lighten up? It's not a crime for the girl to want to wear her hair straight, you know. She did your thing all these years, and she said she might lose the ballet part. You wouldn't go that far, would you?" He slides his chair closer to her, "Don't get an attitude now, Moxie. We should be able to have a civilized conversation, right?

Think about it—most of her friends have straight hair. In school, in ballet. She comes crying to me, begging me to talk to you. I don't know why she thinks you would listen to the likes of me. But seriously, don't you think it's time to give some of that Africa stuff a rest?" He stands up and paces around the room. "It's tired, Moxie, played out."

"And don't *you* think it's time to give some of that internalized oppression a rest? Against my better judgment I went along with putting her in this school where racism is practically embedded in the hallowed halls!" She jabs one finger against her chest. "I'm the one who has to fortify her daily to do battle here, and I'm not about to fry her hair for you or Miss Snow or anyone else with a twisted agenda!" Moxie has arrived at the point of not caring who hears her.

Quick-paced footsteps clicking down the far corridor interrupt their conversation. It is the tenth-grade counselor. "Good afternoon, Ms. Dillard, Mr. Lawson. Follow me, won't you? I do apologize—we're a little behind schedule." She guides them to the rooms where the various subject teachers are located. Other parents pass them, going in and out of the various rooms. Each set of parents is to spend ten minutes with each subject teacher. During several of their sessions, Moxie and James hear that while Zadi is bright and personable, her work has been inconsistent, particularly in the subjects that don't come as easily to her—math and science. The teachers recommend that she participate more in class. This irks Moxie because she knows Zadi is the only black student in at least one of her classes and possibly another. She offers this factor as an explanation for why Zadi may be hesitant to speak up. James hastily adds that they will speak to Zadi about it.

By the time they are on their way back to the parking lot, Moxie has lost the energy to continue sparring with James. Instead, she wonders why he isn't as concerned about the issues Zadi faces at Willow. "I just wish they had a black teacher, counselor, or somebody there. I don't think that's too much to ask."

"They have a black lacrosse coach," he reminds her. "I know what you're going to say—we do the sports thing well. But they did have that history teacher last year, remember? It nobody's fault she got married and moved away. Clearly the situation is not perfect, but Zadi's getting a damn good education. I went along with you when you wanted her in the African preschool. As you recall, that wasn't the smoothest ride either, but, I admit, she got a lot out of it. And you were the one the year before last complaining about her not being challenged in public school. You're never satisfied." His voice trails off.

"I don't know anymore. They could find more black teachers if they wanted more black teachers. Our girls in that school need role models." She can tell James has tuned her out. Moxie's head hurts, and she senses the familiar heavy sadness approaching. Maybe she'll stay home tomorrow to stave it off. She reviews tomorrow's schedule in her mind, contemplating taking a mental health day.

"I can get Zadi from ballet," James says when they get to her car. She is appreciative but feels depleted by their conversation, as she so often does. Her opinion no longer matters to him. It's like knocking at a door where loud music is being played on the other side. No one hears.

When she arrives at home, she turns on all the lights, even the one in Zadi's room. Since childhood the simple act of changing darkness to light has comforted her. Her father used to joke that he should have purchased stock in the electric company. It's as if the lighting will illuminate and draw out the shadows of melancholy lurking in the corners of her mind. She flips on the radio in the living room and tries to find something soothing and soulful—not easy listening, not rap, and definitely not country. It's too early for *The Quiet Storm,* which actually hasn't been the same since the departure of Melvin Lindsey, that unmatched slow-drag DJ. She settles for the oldies station.

More than one of Zadi's teachers calling her distracted bothers Moxie. Distracted by what? The recital and the hair issue? The boys she's trying to impress? Moxie wants so much for Zadi to achieve all that she can. After fixing herself a cup of tea and heating leftovers, she checks her messages, half hoping Norma has called. Norma used to be the calm, cooling waters Moxie needed when turmoil was swirling around her. Norma knows Zadi well enough to help Moxie through her maze of issues, but she is afraid to talk further to Norma about Zadi's hair. After all, Norma's hair is fried, too. Look how long Moxie has tolerated that. They both sported afros and braids in college. But when they resumed their friendship after graduation and Norma had permed her hair, Moxie stayed silent at first. Then, because it nagged at her, she confronted Norma. "Remember what you said about regretting never learning to swim in high school because you didn't want the white girls to see your hair get nappy?" (Norma had finally learned to swim in college and attributed it to her hair's natural state.) "So what happened?" Norma had just shrugged and said natural wasn't really her anymore. It was one of those troublesome obstacles that Moxie consciously side-stepped to preserve the friendship.

When James brings Zadi from ballet, he comes inside with her. The house is small enough to see into the dining room, living room, and kitchen from the hallway. Moxie nods to him from the dining room but doesn't invite him to have a seat. The weight of their earlier conversation keeps her from relaxing her resentment. Usually he just drops Zadi off when he brings her home and waits out front for Zadi when he picks her up. Maybe Zadi wants to show him her history report, Moxie thinks, because she was very pleased with how it turned out.

James scratches his head beneath a baseball cap that has "Southeast" printed on it, though he no longer lives in Washington. He stands near Moxie's cherished photograph of her mother and Aunt BeJean as teenagers, which hangs in the hallway. He looks as out of place as his cap. This is her home, hers and Zadi's now. It contains what she has acquired without him. Maybe he's trying to remember how it felt to live here with them. She was the one who wanted the divorce and recalls how awkward she felt when he broke down in tears at the court hearing.

Zadi comes in and checks the caller ID on the desk after she dumps her book bag on a chair. "Did the phone ring or anything?" she asks.

"Hello, Mother, how are you?" Moxie says, reminding Zadi of her omission.

"Sorry. Hello, Ma. Did anyone call?" Moxie tells her no.

Zadi has pinned her braids on top of her head. "Your hair looks cute up like that. See how many options you have?" Moxie says.

James moves from where he was initially standing over to what Moxie refers to as "Zadi's gallery" on the living room wall unit. Zadi at age one, naked in the tub wearing a startled expression and stuffed cheeks, at five doing pliés in Miss Snow's studio, a little older Zadi in an African outfit at her African school, and the same photo Moxie has in her office that Norma took of Zadi dancing. The only pictures without Zadi in them are the one Moxie got from her father of her mother with the ice cream, two pictures of Miles, and another photo by Norma of Ponsey in his garden.

After a minute or so of picture-gazing, James comes into the kitchen. "Pretty flowers," he says, acknowledging the vase of gladioli Moxie bought herself earlier in the day. "I thought we could talk to Zadi together about the conference we just had," he says. "You know, for the sake of continuity."

Moxie fixes Zadi a plate of food and heats it up in the microwave. While Zadi eats, her parents inform her of the teacher comments. "Why are you two ganging up on me?" Zadi puts her plate in the sink and starts to storm off.

"We're not ganging up on you, baby," says James, blocking her getaway by briefly massaging her shoulders.

"We just know you could be doing better in some of your classes. Don't ignore your history, Zadi," Moxie says, leaning across the kitchen counter. She looks intently at her daughter. "You've been given an opportunity some of your not-so-distant ancestors never had. Your father's father worked under cars all day so that his younger siblings, and later his children, could go to college. He had to scrub his fingers for hours each day to get all the dirt out. Don't let his sacrifice be in vain."

Zadi and James meet each other's eyes and burst out laughing.

"What's so funny?"

James takes a breath, clutching his stomach. "You always lay it on so thick, Moxie. It's just funny."

Moxie is not amused. She's tired and wants to get comfortable. She's ready for James to leave. Zadi announces that she's going to do her homework. Moxie hears the door to her room close and begins moving toward the living room, closer to the front door. "Okay, James, we talked to her. It's late now. I'm getting ready to turn in."

"I'm going to leave in a minute," James says, sitting on the edge of her couch. "But I want to talk to *you* for a second."

She doesn't sit but stands near the wall unit with her arms folded tightly across her. "Not about the hair again?"

His eyes fasten on hers, and he stretches his wiry legs out, crossing them at the ankles. "Naw. I'll leave that alone." He leans in and speaks in a low voice. "You think Zadi's okay?"

Moxie stares at him. "What do you mean?"

"I mean, maybe there are some other things keeping her from doing her best in school." Moxie can't recall James wanting to talk in depth about Zadi with her since they've been divorced. She hesitates to kick him out, as she would like to. She is concerned, though, about Zadi's overhearing them speaking about her, which she knows could be enough to set her off. She puts a finger to her mouth and then points to the door. "I'll walk you outside."

James goes down the hall to say good night to Zadi while Moxie puts on her coat. They walk outside, and Moxie holds her coat together instead of buttoning it.

"She recently asked me if I ever wish I was married to you again. But who knows if that has anything to do with . . ." James doesn't finish the sentence.

Moxie stops where her patch of grass meets the sidewalk and tries to look anywhere except at him. The stars are spread out across the sky, some sparkling like silver jewelry, some satisfied with giving off only a slight shimmer. It bothers her that Zadi apparently feels that she can't say this to her. She thought Zadi was finished harboring those kinds of hopes. "And you said what?"

"I said no and reminded her that I'm happily married. Told her that we (you and I) both love her and our breakup had nothing to do with her. She doesn't really talk to me, though. Does she talk to you, I mean really talk?"

"Sometimes." Moxie nods, slowly tasting her words. "Not about everything and not as much as I'd like. But she is obviously talking to you. She hasn't asked me how I'd feel about being married to you again."

"I just don't want her to hate me. You don't seem to worry about that."

"I don't want her to hate me either, but if I think I'm doing what's right for her, I can't worry about that. I'm sure she doesn't hate you. Maybe if you talked to her more about how guys think and act at her age. That's what she's interested in."

James adjusts his baseball cap. "Bet. Good idea. All right. Glad we had this little chat." We were talking on too serious a level, Moxie thinks, so he has to trivialize it. He puts one hand to his head as if saluting and walks in the direction of his car.

"Hey," she cups her hands over her mouth and calls out, "Zadi needs fifty dollars for her costume deposit. Add that to the check, please." She doesn't wait for him to answer.

Inside, Moxie goes to Zadi's room and knocks on the door. She hears only the low hum of the radio. The door creaks gently as Moxie peers in. Zadi is on her side still in her clothes, surrounded by her books. One arm is slung across her face as if she's hiding. Her breathing rises and falls steadily, and her mouth is slightly open, stuck in a pout.

Tuesday morning, Zadi is ready to leave the house earlier than usual. "I had a good sleep, Ma. Now I know why you're always telling me to get more sleep. I sort of vaguely remember you waking me up to take my clothes off."

"You were really out—snoring, mouth all open." Moxie laughs.

Zadi laughs, too. "No, it wasn't, and I don't snore." At the dining room table she inserts her history report into the transparent plastic cover her mother bought and begins flipping through it, admiring it. "Doesn't my report look good?"

"Yes, it looks great."

"Ma! You're not even looking at the report."

"Sorry." She puts down her tea mug and opens the report. "I looked at it last night, though. I think you did a very good job. Any more projects on the horizon? Something you can plan ahead, so it won't get done at the last minute."

"This wasn't last-minute," Zadi says, looking disturbed. "Anyway, we have to interview one of our parents about how they achieved their dream, so I'm going to talk to Dad about becoming a musician." She pulls her short black boots on and zips them. She returns the report to her book bag. "I know you're going to say how come I didn't ask you, but you haven't really achieved a dream."

"Of course I have." Moxie sits down at the table and glares at her. "I've achieved the dream of working to help people, of having a self-sufficient life, of raising a daughter who will achieve her dreams, and I've achieved the dream of not relying on someone else to be happy!" She tries to mask how perturbed she is that Zadi has written her off.

"But you're not *always* happy, and anyway, those are kind of, you know, vague things. I probably wouldn't be able to make it turn out that good. Dad's easier to write about, okay? Nothing personal. I'll do you next time." She takes her jacket from the hall closet. "Well, since I'm ready, I'm just going to go ahead and take the bus. I want to get there early because I left one book at school," Zadi says, strapping on her book bag. "Um, Allegra and I were going to go by the mall after school and then to her house. I'll start my homework there. Can you pick me up from her house?"

"Well, that wasn't in my plans, but all right. Call when you get there, and don't make it late. I'm talking no later than eight. Have a great day. Hey, I was thinking maybe we could see *Shakespeare in Love* Saturday after dance class, you know, before the Academy Awards," Moxie says as she scans the headlines of the day's newspaper.

"Well, I was going to spend the weekend at Dad's."

"You spent last weekend there."

"This way you'll be free to go on a date or something."

"A date? I'm not interested in going on a date. Where'd you get that idea from?" Moxie looks up from the paper.

"Daddy. He said if you went out on more dates, you would relax and not be so pressed about me."

"Oh, is that what he said? Well, he doesn't know what he's talking about. Listen, Zadi, if you were really troubled or having some . . . problems at school, you'd tell us, wouldn't you?"

"Yeah. Please don't start getting on my case again about what the teachers said. I wasn't focused before; I am now. You'll see. Can this be the end of the discussion, okay?" She kisses her mother on the cheek.

Moxie watches her walk out the front door, the way her jeans hug her rounded hips. They're a little bit tighter than necessary. She should call her back in and make her take them off but, mostly in the interest of time, thinks better of it.

Tuesday, Feb. 2nd
black lycra jeans
red/black top
Banana Republic boots

Dear Sistergirl:

   Octavius met me at Metro Center today after school. I told Ma I was going to the mall with Allegra and over Allegra's house after that, so it wasn't a total lie. I told Allegra to make sure she answers the phone until I get there, in case my mother calls or whatever. Octavius and I went to Union Station, but Scream 2 *wasn't showing there anymore, so we just walked around. We went in Footlocker cause he wanted to see if they had the new black-and-red Jordans. I wanted to go into Express and Claire's. We went in there, but he was acting all bored, so I hardly got to look at anything. We ate at Sbarro's downstairs in the food court. He put his arm around my shoulder when we were waiting for the pizza. He got pepperoni, and I had veggie. I told myself I wasn't going to eat pizza during rehearsal, but I love pizza! I'll just have to work it off. O says when he writes his raps, he tapes himself with an instrumental music track playing behind him. He says he has to do it over and over until it comes out right. He talks real ghetto. There's something sexy about it, though.*

He asked me if I dared him to show me his tattoo right there in Union Station. I was like, okay, I dare you. He pulled his T-shirt up real quick, and I saw it. It looks like his skin is raised up a little. It looks wet, though. We didn't do anything except walk around. I asked him when were we going to get together for real, by ourselves. And he acted crazy, saying, yeah, I got me a ho! I was like, I am not a ho. I just want to know. (Hey, that rhymes.)

I got to Takoma Park metro by 7:15, and Allegra was there waiting for me. She got her license last week the minute she turned sixteen. She says her parents are going to get her a used car soon. Tonight she had her mom's car. She said Ma hadn't even called looking for me. I started my homework over there, and Ma came to pick me up at eight on the dot. Everything was mellow.

Wednesday, Feb. 3rd
Tommy jeans
CK sweatshirt
blk Nikes

Dear Sistergirl:

Just came home from dance and checked my messages. Allegra. Mia. No Octavius. Why do I have to be last one off the V train?—They keep teasing me. Mia finally got her sex on. (I figured that's why she called me; she doesn't usually call me.) Allegra and me are trying to see who's going to be the first between us. She says her theme song would be something by Eve, like, What Y'all Really Want.

Sometimes O seems like he doesn't want to do it. It's like I'm always the one talking about it. I told him I'm tired of just talking on the phone. When I paged him tonight, he said he wants me to come over his house because his mother goes to some classes in the morning and his brothers go to Headstart. I'm a little worried. I definitely don't want to get caught by his moms like Allegra did. At first he was asking me to meet him someplace at night. I definitely couldn't hook that up, so I'm contemplating leaving school early to do it.

Called, then paged O, and for once, he called back right away. He sounded strange. I kept asking him if he was high, but he said he wasn't. Tonight was the first time we talked sexy. He asked me if anybody ever did stuff to me like put their tongue in my ear or suck on my fingers, stuff like that. I said, maybe, cause I didn't want him to know I'm a virgin, although he might already know cause every one of my friends who is not a virgin anymore says that you automatically change. Guys can always tell unless they're virgins, too. They say you definitely don't want to have sex with a guy who is a virgin. Look at what happened with Mia. The first time she tried it, the guy couldn't find the right place to stick it. She was too embarrassed to say anything, and it was a whole big mess. She told April he had the nerve to try and act like he did something special.

Octavius is so crazy. He wants me to listen to a rap song whenever he calls. Check out the flow, Zadi, he always says. Tonight he was like, Jigga what? Jigga who? I was like, do it when, do it how?

> *Friday, Feb. 5th (notebook)*
> *black boot-cut jeans*
> *Versace top Fawna gave me cause she*
>   *can't fit it anymore (she can dress*
>   *sometimes)*
> *blk Banana Republic boots*

Dear Sistergirl:

I have to remember to copy these notebook pages to my journal. There's a couple now I keep forgetting about. I came up with a plan about my hair today cause I can't take the stress anymore. Miss Snow didn't say anything out of her mouth today, but her expression was like, Zadi, you must not want this part, since your hair still looks the same! I talked my plan over with Allegra before I left school and with Zora after class tonight. Allegra says it's bad but not that bad because I don't have any other choice. Zora said, you know you're going to get in big trouble and things will be rough for a while, but then it'll all be behind you. They're both right. Ma left me with no choice, and I'll just have to deal with the consequences.

Dad, Fawna, and Tiffany came to get me from ballet. This was my plan: I told them Ma said she doesn't want me to straighten my hair, but she also doesn't want me to lose the part and that if I want to straighten it just for the part only, it's okay. I said I had to promise to take the perm out after the recital. And I said that she told me I have to find someplace on my own to get it done, she's not going to have anything to do with it. My heart was beating like crazy cause I thought Dad wasn't going to believe me or say he had to talk to Ma first or something. But he didn't. He just said maybe what he told her the other day finally sank in. Fawna said something about how you can't just take a perm out once you've put it in and wondered if Ma meant hot comb. No, I said, she meant perm, she just wants me to gradually let it grow out after the show. Damn, that was close, I almost messed up.

They really blew me! It was that simple. Fawna said she would make me an appointment with her hairdresser, and Dad said he would pay for it! I like Fawna's hair right now. It's dyed red and styled kind of like T-Boz used to have, with the back cut short and the sides hanging down long so she's always pushing it away from her eyes. Fawna called the beauty salon from her cell phone cause I was bugging about getting it done this weekend while I'm over there. Somebody had canceled, so I have an appointment for tomorrow!! Fawna was like, girl, you sure are lucky, that hardly ever happens. (I might learn to love her after all. . . .) I know I'm not going to be able to fall asleep until then. I can't decide if I should tell Allegra the plan worked or just surprise her, but I'll have to wait all the way until Monday.

When we got in the house, Dad said I'm going to have to tell your mother I'm proud of her. He said, her problem is that she does want the best for you, but sometimes she gets confused and doesn't realize that what's best for her isn't always what's best for you. You dig? He always uses that old-time fake expression. I definitely don't want him calling her to tell her anything before I get this done, so I said that she's probably not going to want to talk about it because she told me if I keep talking about it, she'll change her mind. He seemed like he was thinking about something else, anyway. Long time ago when I was a little kid and lied about finding some money that I actually took out of Ma's purse, she told me that you can't just tell one lie. Once you start you have to keep lying. I didn't know what she was talking about then, but I do now. But I'll get depressed if I think about that. If Ma wasn't so pressed about my hair staying natural, I wouldn't have to do this.

I'm going to stay up for a while taking all my braids out. Fawna and Dad said they'll help me. I can't believe I'm actually going to do this—finally!!!!! I'm halfway there—hair first, then V train.

> *Saturday, Feb. 6th*
> *DKNY jeans*
> *DKNY white sweater*
> *black platform boots*

Dear Sistergirl:

We just got back from the hairdresser. My hair looks off the hook!! Here's the whole story: Today was the first time just the two of us (me and Fawna) went anywhere together. Fawna picked me up from the studio and took me to her beauty salon. It's only a few blocks from the ballet studio, so when I need a touch-up, I know how to get there!! Everyone knows her in there, so they were all like, who is this, Fawna, your niece, your sister? I was like, whatever. They teased her about being pregnant and touched her stomach, which sticks out only a little and is only noticeable if you look real hard. Then they concentrated on me. When they saw how much hair I had and that it was all natural, everybody was shocked. The one who was going to do my hair, Vicky, was like, girl! Look at all this thick hair. You ain't never had no chemicals in your hair all this time? I said, no, never. Good lord, she said. The other beauticians came over and touched it. They were like, good luck, girl; you'll be doing her hair all night. They said they didn't know if the perm was going to take. But Vicky said it'll take cause her hair is thick, but it's not nappy. They couldn't get over that I never had a perm my whole life. They said, girl, don't you know this is almost the millennium. What you trying to do, be like Whoopi Goldberg or somebody? They laughed a lot, and I didn't feel too embarrassed cause all that was getting ready to be behind me. One hairdresser named Gladys said, girl, don't worry, your nightmare about to end. I was thinking, dag, it hasn't been that bad. Then the other girl, I think her name was Shondra, said, Vicky is going to hook you up. Chile, your hair gonna be down your back when Vicky get through with you.

She was right! My hair is down my back. She parted it on one side and gave it a loose curl and made it all shiny and STRAIGHT!!!! I can't believe it. I keep touching it and looking in the mirror. Vicky told me to sleep on a satin pillow case (Fawna says she has an extra one) and showed me what kind of rollers and wrap lotion (if I ever want to wrap it) I needed. Shondra told Vicky she better write instructions down for me cause I never had straight hair before. It's all Greek to her, she said. They had a good time messing with me. Vicky wrote down what kind of shampoo, hair oil, and conditioner, etc. I should buy. (Fawna bought me this stuff later). Fawna said, your hair is stunning. That's got to be the first compliment she ever gave me. When we got back to the house, Dad stared at me and didn't say anything. I had to keep going, Daddy, Daddy, do you like it? I was getting a little worried. Then he goes, maybe it was a mistake. Now you're really going to be a heartbreaker. I laughed, and he hugged me. Tiffany was like, you should have done that a long time ago. (She's had one of those Just for Me perms since she was six.)

I can't wait to show Norma, even though she wouldn't help me. I don't hear her and Ma talking that much on the phone lately. I asked Ma if everything was all right with them, and she just acted like she didn't know what I was talking about.

I thanked Fawna and Dad a million times.

Ma is going to kirk out.

Thirteen | Sunday morning Moxie is at her kitchen counter working on files from the office. Her reports have piled up, and at home she can work on them without as many distractions. Even here though, she has trouble concentrating. Lately, she has found herself calling old acquaintances and friends she's hasn't seen in months, all in an effort to fill the void left by Norma. It's not the same with other folks, though. Talk with Norma was loose and easy, like strolling along the beach. Nothing had to be kept in check or held on to until later, as she finds herself doing these days with other friends who aren't Norma.

She called Norma after the night of Ma Simmons's birthday celebration, but the conversation was guarded on both their parts. She wonders whether such a long friendship really has to end because neither of them seems to know how to retrieve the comfort and ease of the past. And the truth is there are things about Norma that have always pestered her, but she brushed them aside because preserving what they had was more important. Moxie's impatience with Norma's selfish ways and elitism has pushed its way to the surface, though, with the revelation about Woody. Trying to stuff it all back in again, like a broken jack-in-the-box, doesn't work. On the phone she wanted to ask Norma, are you finished with your tantrum yet? Have you dropped the guy? But she didn't even mention Woody. They hung up after a few minutes. Several days later Norma left a message reminding Moxie about tonight's opening of her first solo exhibit.

Moxie doesn't really want to go because she thinks it will be uncomfortable. But this exhibit is something Norma has dreamed of and worked toward for the last few years. Moxie decides to attend out of a nettling sense of obligation. If she doesn't go, she will be pursued by guilt and that could be worse than whatever discomfort she might experience at the reception. She has learned that moments of complete comfort in life are only temporary anyway. Perhaps she'll take her father along. He would enjoy it and Norma would love to see him.

She contemplates the pleasurable aspects she can expect at the exhibit despite the strained relationship. Seeing and being embraced by Norma's family and, of course, the work itself. The truth is she loves the vibrancy of Norma's photography. Norma has found a way to bare her feelings and expose herself without compromise, and Moxie is proud of her for that. For pursuing it even. The exhibit promises to be a celebration of the essence of Norma on display, the beloved photos Moxie has admired over the years and the new works she hasn't yet been privy to. Who knows, her attendance may be the catalyst they both need to rectify their friendship.

Market Five Gallery, where Norma's premier exhibit takes place, has a steady flow of patrons. Norma's mostly black-and-white photographs of varying sizes cover the clapboard walls. The light jazz sounds of Neena Freelon and others from Lawrence's formidable CD collection filter through the chatter of the art seekers. Wine, cheese, diced fruit, and vegetables are attractively arranged on two tables at either end of the room. Purple, fuchsia, and gold balloons graze the ceiling, their curled ribbons dangling above the guests' heads.

Her work will remain on display for one month. Guests are enthusiastic, and in the first hour she has already sold two photos. One from the hot-air-balloon series, even though she would have preferred to sell them as a set; and a photo of Zadi in an arabesque pose. Norma's parents mingle in the crowd, as well as Irene, Simon, and the children. Several colleagues, from art school, the center where she taught, and Miles's preschool, have also come. As they compliment her on the depth of her photos, her composition, and expert use of natural light, she notices that neither Moxie, Woody, nor Lawrence are in the room yet.

She stands near the guest book answering questions posed by an older gentleman, who introduces himself the way James Bond does,

"Covington. John Covington." He asks her whether she ever does posed portraits. She hesitates, and he continues, "I'd like you to photograph my family. In the photos you have of people, you seem to capture so much more than merely what the person looks like. It's almost as if you get inside their heads and hearts as well. Our family takes a multigenerational photo every two years, and I'd like you to do it this time."

Norma hands him a card from the stack on the table with the guest book. "Thank you. Please call me. We'll talk," she tells him. Two people who have been waiting to ask her questions about particular photos approach just as Moxie and her father come through the door. "Thanks so much for coming," Norma blurts out to her, immediately relieved. "Just sold a photo of Zadi!" Ponsey gives her a bear hug and Moxie smiles, touches Norma's arm, and they leave her with the throng of admirers that has quickly formed.

An abundance of white people, par for the course, Moxie thinks, eager to get to the displayed photographs. The one of her father's hands captivates her because although she was there when Norma took the picture, she hadn't yet seen it. She recalls Norma saying she was intrigued by how the light "encountered" her father's hands. She and her father couldn't see whatever it was Norma saw. The memory of the closeness the three of them shared that day and the picture's seraphic quality has Moxie dabbing at her eyes. She looks at her father, who is rubbing his as well. Moxie is once again awed by Norma's passion for her work and somewhat envious. There's a pureness to having a vocation that comes from a deep place in your soul, one that patiently waited to be discovered since birth. A South African writer she admires once said, "Babies are born with their hands clenched in tight fists holding the gifts God gave them. It is our job to help them discover those gifts during their lifetime so that when they die with open hands, their work has been completed." Norma has discovered the gift in her hands, Moxie thinks.

There is now a sizable crowd viewing Norma's work, and Moxie is pleased for her. She and her father have a mini-reunion with Norma's parents and Irene. Moxie leaves her father with the Simmonses and makes her way to the hors d'oeuvres table. She looks down, feeling a slight tugging on her coat, which she has draped over one arm. "Hi, Aunt Moxie."

"Oh, hello, Miles, sweetie pie."

"Daddy brought me so I can see my mommy's pictures."

"I came to see them, too." She glances around and sees Lawrence following behind him. "Juice, please," Miles says, holding out an empty paper cup to Moxie. She uses the ladle to pour him some punch, and then he waddles away, satisfied. Lawrence hugs Moxie. They joke about seeing each other twice this month, when prior to that they hadn't in quite a while. They converse sincerely for a few minutes, touching on job and child-stress and the beauty of Norma's photos. Seeing Lawrence this time and the last, she can't help but feel angry all over again. Here he is supporting her art, watching over their child so she can converse with her patrons, while she's running around screwing her brains out with somebody else. Try as she might, Moxie cannot get past this knowledge.

Lawrence moves on, while Moxie fills two plates with vegetables and dip. A white woman with a husky voice asks if she's a relative of Norma's. "No," she responds, uninterested in why the woman made the assumption.

"Oh." The woman sounds disappointed. "She said her sister lived in Annapolis, and I'm trying to remember the name of this wonderful restaurant I went to out there." As the woman walks away, Moxie swallows her irritation at the proverbial "they all look alike" syndrome. She sees her father and Norma's father talking and laughing together. She takes him a plate of food and thinks about going back over to Norma's mother or Lawrence, whom she glimpses unsuccessfully trying to keep Miles from popping one of the balloons. The loud "pop" sound makes Miles squeal in delight but startles the guests. Afterwards, Lawrence looks embarrassed and a bit dejected. Moxie aches again for him, because it's as if in his own way he's trying and failing and Norma is oblivious. Moxie has an urge to say something reassuring and all-encompassing to him, something to provide solace for everything he's going through without being aware of. Just as she decides to go speak to him again, someone bumps her, and she spills her plate of partially eaten vegetables on her dress.

"Oops, sorry." It's a white girl about Zadi's age. The girl keeps on going, doesn't even have the decency to offer her a napkin. Moxie returns to the food and drink table, gets a napkin, dips it into her cup of spring water, and begins wiping at the spot on her dress.

"Had a mishap?"

She looks up to the origin of the voice. A smiling white man pouring himself punch. What is this? she thinks, peevishly. Am I wearing a sign saying I want to be bugged by white folks tonight? "Oh, someone just bumped into me," she snaps at him.

"Oh. That's too bad." He bends and wipes up the water she has dripped the floor. She thanks him. "It looks like you've got most of the stain off," he says. "Other than that, have you been enjoying the exhibit?"

"Yes, I have." She relaxes a little, since he has been helpful to her. "I like Norma's work very much."

"Oh, so you've seen it before?" the man asks.

Moxie begins fixing herself another plate of food. "Yes, well, I've known Norma since college."

"Are you Moxie?" His eyebrows lift and he appears very excited.

"Yes, I'm Moxie," she says with surprise in her tone.

"Norma's talked a lot about you. I'm . . . a friend of hers, too. Isaac Woodruff. People call me Woody." He rests his drink on the table and reaches out a hand.

Moxie takes it but freezes in her space. *"You're* Woody?"

"Yes, has she mentioned me?"

"Ah, excuse me, Woody. I've—I've got to go." Moxie walks away quickly and looks around in a blur for her coat. She laid it down somewhere. As she searches, she notices Lawrence holding Miles in his arms. Miles tips his cup to his father's lips, sharing some of the juice with his dad. She looks over to another corner, where Norma, wineglass in hand, is surrounded by her many guests, laughing and talking, in her element. Moxie finds her coat and then goes over to let her father know it's time to leave. There's no need to say anything to Norma.

Sunday, Feb. 7th
Dad's T-shirt until 4 o'clock
blk Parasuco jeans
cinnamon sweater
Tims

Dear Sistergirl:

I stalled as long as I could about going home. It's dark now, and I know Ma's wondering what's up. I haven't been this scared in a long time. I spent the morning typing up the interview I did with Dad on the computer, but I kept looking in the mirror. I was here by myself cause they all went to look at baby furniture. Ma called in the afternoon, and when I saw the number on the caller ID, I got so nervous I started not to pick up. But I was like, no, that's crazy stupid, she can't see through the phone.

I must be acting strange cause Dad asked me if anything was wrong. What's wrong is, I'm really glad that I did this because it looks good and I can keep the recital part, but I'm also worried. I know that I shouldn't have lied to Dad and Fawna. I don't know if I believe in God or not, but there might be some punishment out there for what I did. I just hope whoever or whatever decides the punishment for people tries to understand that I only did it because Ma wouldn't listen to me. That's the only reason. And I guess the punishment will be that somebody will tell me a lie and I just hope I'm not too upset about it. Okay. I can't avoid going home anymore. Damn. Here I go.

Fourteen | From outside, Moxie realizes Zadi hasn't returned yet—there are no lights on. Zadi inherited her mother's habit of illuminating the whole house when she's alone. It's almost eight-thirty, she should be back by now. When Moxie called James's yesterday, Zadi sounded preoccupied and distant. Moxie catches herself from wondering whether Zadi has a better time with James and Fawna. She often doesn't even call home when she's over there. Moxie bends to pick up the Sunday paper, still rolled up inside a plastic bag, and goes inside the house.

She hangs up her coat, makes a mug of tea, and sits in the living room rocker. She thinks about Norma and how she flaunted white damn Woody in everyone's face and grows angry again. And how cowardly of her not to have mentioned his skin color or lack thereof.

When she hears Zadi's key in the lock, Moxie realizes she dozed off on the couch. The half-finished cup of tea and partially read sections of the newspaper are on the floor beside her. Her watch tells her it's only been twenty minutes, but it seems longer. Moxie rises to a sitting position, wipes at her eyes, and folds up the newspaper, not wanting to appear as disoriented as she feels.

Zadi walks through the door and into the hallway, wearing a scarf on her head and the tight kind of jeans Moxie doesn't care for. She waves to Moxie with one hand but goes straight down the hall to her room. Moxie hopes she's not in a bad mood. She needs to interact with Zadi to help take her mind off Norma. From the couch, she calls out,

"Finally, you're back. You stayed longer than usual; must have had a real good time. I missed you."

Zadi has closed her door, though, and music is blasting. Moxie gets up and knocks on the door several times. She can't tell if it's Eve's, L'il Kim's, or Foxy Brown's raucous lyrics coming from her daughter's room. Those hard girls all sound the same to her.

"Yes?" Zadi shouts back.

"I haven't seen you since Friday. I've been waiting to talk to you," Moxie yells to the poster of a scantily clad Janet Jackson, taped on Zadi's door.

"About what?"

"Nothing in particular." Moxie yells again, growing frustrated.

"I'm on the phone," Zadi calls over the music. Moxie looks down and notices the phone cord pulled taut from the living room into Zadi's room.

Moxie remembers she never finished eating at the exhibit. Maybe she should prepare something for both her and Zadi to eat in a little while. As she stands at the counter cutting up an onion and tomatoes for a salad, gloom grips her by the shoulders. I won't give in, she tells herself. She wonders if Norma even noticed that she left. When her father asked shouldn't they say good-bye to Norma, Moxie said she didn't want to pull her away from her fans. Her father had looked at her strangely, but made no further comment. She flinches when she accidentally nicks her finger and rinses the blood under the faucet. She finds a small adhesive bandage in one of the kitchen drawers and continues slicing vegetables. Then she boils transparent rice noodles that she'll mix with the steamed vegetables. She is careful to only cook the noodles for exactly four minutes. By the time she is finished, Zadi still has not come out of her room.

She wants to be patient but is incapable. She walks back to Zadi's closed door. "Zadi, I thought you were coming out. We haven't seen each other all weekend, honey. I went to Aunt Norma's photography exhibit today. Want to tell you all about it." She tries not to reveal the desperation in her tone. There is no response. "Zadi? Did you eat over there? I fixed something if you're hungry."

"I ate at Daddy's. I'm on the phone, Ma."

"Could you get off, please? I'd *like* to talk to you. Now." Still no response. "Zadi!"

The door opens a crack, and one of Zadi's arms thrusts the phone out onto the rug. Her voice says, "Norma's on the phone for you. And Allegra's still on the other line." Norma's call catches her off guard. She will deal with Zadi when she finishes. She tries to sound unruffled when she picks up the receiver.

"Hey. Moxie. Just checking—you left without saying good-bye or anything. Is everything okay with your dad?" There is a tightness to Norma's voice indicating she's concerned but on the verge of being perturbed.

Moxie returns to the living room and sits on the couch, clutching the phone firmly. "My father's fine. I didn't want to interrupt you, in case you were busy entertaining Woody!"

"What are you talking about?"

"Norma, you could have warned me!"

"Warned you? That he was coming? I wasn't sure he would. And why would I want to tell you anything? That day I tried to pour my heart out to you about him, you didn't want to hear it. All you wanted to do was tell me what a bad person I am."

Moxie stands abruptly and walks around the edges of the rug. "Norma, you could have warned me that Woody was white!"

"That's it? That's why you left with your ass in the air? Don't you think I knew you'd react this way—why would I warn you, as you put it? Don't you think I wanted to tell you that day at the cafe, but I knew you'd act . . . just like this." Norma's words come out sounding brittle as cracked glass. "Instead of like a friend."

"And then you—you parade him around the place in front of all of us, including your damn husband and child!" Moxie is shouting.

"Moxie, there's no point in continuing this conversation. I just called to make sure you and your father were okay."

"Make sure *I'm* okay? You don't need to worry about me. You better check yourself because you're the one who's losing it!"

"I'm going to hang up, Moxie."

"That's right. That's the way you always operate. You don't want to hear anything from me unless it's—oh, yes, Norma, everything's fine. You're justified in screwing your little white boy because you have all those big problems with your marriage. Give me a break, Norma! When are you going to grow the hell up?" She catches her breath and listens for a response. She hears nothing back from Norma. Moxie waits a second and then tests the phone connection. There is a dial tone. Norma must have hung up. Moxie stands in her living room doorway, feeling slapped, replaying the conversation. Why'd she have to call and push it to this? Her breath comes hard, as though she's been jogging. She puts a hand to her chest as if that will slow it all down: the breathing as well as what just happened between her and Norma. Maybe if she sits, she'll feel less battered. She sits down on the couch, leans back, and closes her eyes. She has no idea how everything will ever become all right again.

"Ma," Zadi calls out. "Are you finished yet? I told you Allegra's on the other line!"

"Well, she must have hung up!" she shouts, looking down at the phone on the floor. She walks out into the hall to Zadi's room. The door closes as she approaches. "Zadi, open the damn door! I'm out of patience!"

The door jerks open, and Zadi jumps back onto her bed. She has changed into sweatpants and a T-shirt. Piles of open magazines surround her on the bed. Moxie is puzzled by the print scarf tied on her head and tucked under in the back. She hasn't ever seen Zadi wearing a scarf, and her head seems oddly flat. "Why were you yelling at Norma?" Zadi asks.

"We . . . I don't know. It's something we haven't worked out."

"What did you want to talk to me about?"

"Nothing. I missed you. Just wanted to get a hug," Moxie says. Zadi slides up against her pillows and eyes Moxie cautiously. Moxie leans over the bed and they put their arms around each other. Zadi releases before Moxie is ready. "Whose scarf is that? Fawna's?"

Zadi nods, without looking at Moxie.

Moxie dislikes this frequent feeling of disconnection from Zadi. It twists inside her, like a cavity, knocking away her controls, broadening the disconnection rather than narrowing it. "So you had a pretty good time?" She knows the question will reduce Zadi's answers to monosyllables.

Zadi turns away and starts to unpack her overnight bag on the bed. "It was all right."

"What did you do besides drive around parking lots with your Dad?" She reaches for whatever is available, a ledge, a jagged cranny, anything to hold on to the conversation.

"Nothing. Hung around the house mostly."

"Finish the interview?"

"Yes."

"Oh. Well. Glad you had a good time. I missed you."

"You said that, Ma. I'm kind of tired. I'm going to get ready for bed early."

Moxie returns to the living room, unsettled about both Norma and Zadi. She turns on the television, pressing the remote every few seconds. Moxie remembers always wanting her mother near. Would that have changed if she had been alive when Moxie was a teenager? She wants to believe she wouldn't have shut her out of her life. Her estrangement from Zadi happens most often when Zadi returns from a visit to James. It's as if she has to deprogram from the experience over there before she can live comfortably with Moxie again. When Moxie married James, she knew nothing about who they both were in the depths of their souls. Instead, the decision was based on their enjoyment of each other's company, sexual passion, and the fact that Moxie was pregnant and didn't want to be a single parent or have an abortion. Now she knows those reasons weren't enough.

She wants to try again to reach Zadi; a different approach. She'll tell her about Norma's selling a photo of her. Moxie doesn't want to tell Zadi about what's happened with Norma, but she does yearn to be comforted. She wishes Zadi would give her her full attention. Moxie doesn't know how to ask for it, though.

She knocks, doesn't wait, and turns the knob this time. It's locked. What is she doing locking the door? Moxie bangs hard. "Zadi?"

"I'm on the phone, Ma."

"Again?"

"Yes, Ma." Moxie stands in front of the door, remembering Aunt

BeJean telling her that Moxie's grandfather wouldn't allow her or
Moxie's mother to lock the bedroom door they shared. Once when
they disobeyed him, he took out his tools and removed the lock. "No
locked doors in here unless I lock them," he said. Moxie wonders if
Zadi's talking to Allegra again or someone else. Someone she doesn't
know. She doesn't know her own daughter. As she stands, absently listening to the sounds blaring from the radio and staring into Janet's
cleavage, Zadi snatches the door open. "Ma, why are you bugging?
What do you want?"

"What's with that scarf on your head?" Moxie asks, stepping into the
room.

"I just feel like wearing a scarf. What is your problem?" Zadi
responds with an attitude, clutching the phone.

Moxie moves toward her. "Listen, young lady, I am not going to tolerate you speaking to me like that. I haven't done anything to you." As
she gets closer she notices again how flat the scarf is on Zadi's head.
"Zadi!" Moxie pulls on the scarf. "What did you do? What did you do
to your hair?"

"I gotta go." Zadi hangs up the phone and puts her hands tight over
her head, backing away from Moxie, closer to her headboard.

"Zadi, let me see!" Moxie practically runs after her. Zadi jumps to
the other side of her bed, hands still holding on to the scarf. Moxie follows. Then Zadi climbs back across the bed and starts to dart into the
hallway. Moxie climbs across, too, reaching for the scarf. Zadi forcefully tries to push her away and hold on to the scarf, but she can't do
both. They tussle a little, pushing and tugging at each other until
Moxie yanks the scarf off. They both stand against the wall in the hallway outside Zadi's room, Moxie trying to catch her breath. Her mouth
gapes open until she covers it with her hand. "Your hair!"

Zadi starts to cry and backs into her room. "I didn't want to lose the
part. You were going to make me lose the part!" She lies facedown on
the bed, her head resting on one hand. With the other hand she rubs at
her eyes, warily peeking out at her mother. Moxie is unable to move.
The shiny, newly straight hair cascades over Zadi's shoulders. The hair
Moxie loved to caress and run her fingers through, lifting the soft, full

braids one by one, is gone. No matter how tightly Moxie closes her eyes, when she opens them, the hair, Zadi's hair, Moxie's hair, is no longer.

Moxie sinks to her knees, expelling a wail from deep within her. She weeps for Zadi's hair and for far more than that. She weeps for herself, for all that was tied up in Zadi's hair and all that is lost with it. She cries for the memories of Aunt BeJean's hot comb, for the smell of greased hair, singed and crackling, for the sharp stab of her burnt neckline, ear, or forehead. For the hair that, though shiny and flat, never looked like white girls' hair and never looked like her mother's hair. Since the hot-greased days of Aunt BeJean wielding the straightening comb, Moxie has denied the truth even to herself. Even though she proudly wears her locks, the truth in her heart is that some unprocessed black hair is better than others. Zadi's hair, part kinky, part curly with its soft nappiness is better than the coarse thickness of her own. She always wished and perhaps pretended Zadi's hair was her own, just as she had wished with her mother's. And now it is all ruined. Zadi's hair is no longer virgin hair. Zadi's hair is dead and gone, like Cerise. Moxie cries for the truth of her own lingering demons. She cries for the motherless child she is and the mother without a child she feels as if she has become.

In the morning Moxie's head is heavy, and her eyes sting as if she spent hours in a smoke-filled room. She slept very little and cried most of the night. She lies in bed on her back and brings the covers over her face, blocking out the sun's attempt to reach her from the window. She hears faint knocking on her door but doesn't answer.

"Mommy? It's like almost seven-thirty." Zadi's voice is soft and tentative.

Moxie says nothing.

"Aren't you going to work?" Zadi whispers, pushing the door open slightly with her elbow. From under her comforter, Moxie sees that Zadi's relaxed hair is pulled back into a ponytail holder. Zadi stares at her mother bundled in her blankets. "I made you some tea." She places the cup and saucer on the night table and waits a few moments. Moxie hears the door creak as Zadi closes it behind her.

Ten minutes later, Zadi is back in her mother's room. She stands next to the bed and talks to her mother's form beneath the blankets. "Mommy, I'm leaving now. I'll see you later, I guess. I just want to tell you, I didn't do it to—upset you. . . ."

Moxie doesn't want to look at Zadi or her dead hair anymore. She rolls onto her stomach, wishing she could sleep a sleep that would wipe away everything that has happened. But she is unable to rest. When she closes her eyes, she sees images of Fawna and James, holding hands with Zadi, who is between them, all skipping off to the beauty parlor.

About eleven A.M. she manages to lean up onto her elbows and call the office. She tells Brenda that she won't be in. She hangs up and lies back against her pillows, pulling the comforter up to her neck. She listens intently to the sounds of the sadness lodged in her chest. The room is quiet; all she hears is a car going by outside and the bathroom toilet midway in its cycle of running before it shuts off. She tries to fight off the question, but there's no denying it. Do I feel bad enough to die? she asks herself. Do I feel as bad as my mother did?

There were many days when Moxie's mother stayed in bed from the morning until the night. A year or so before she died, Cerise remained in the sewing room bed for several days in a row. She wouldn't allow any light to come into the room, not even sunlight through the blinds. She snapped at Moxie when Moxie tried to open them. That was the one other time Moxie didn't want to leave her mother. She asked if she could stay home from school, but her father reminded her that he would be right there, working in his office, and he would check in on her. Moxie hurried back from school each day and did her homework in the darkened room holding her books on her knees, sitting close to the window, straining toward its one tiny arc of light. The room developed a gray hue after Moxie had sat in there for an hour or so. Moxie's eyes stung from staring so hard at her books. She remembers hearing no sounds in the house, only her mother's breathing and intermittent sobbing. She'd do her fractions and her reading comprehension sheet while peeking up at her mother every few minutes. Moxie moved her chair closer when she couldn't hear her mother breathing, because she looked as if she were dead. Cerise's hair sprayed across the pillow, glorious as black velvet, as she lay on her side with one arm shielding her face.

Even though Moxie was often chilly in the somewhat drafty room, and frightened about her mother's despair, she wouldn't leave Cerise during those worrisome days except to attend school. Her father let her eat dinner and sleep there, crammed beside her mother on the small, hard bed. She didn't mind so much because the dolls and books her mother had collected over the years also lived in that room and gave history and comfort to Moxie, even though she never once contemplated playing with them.

One morning, after the cluster of days without rising, Cerise got up, without explanation or acknowledgement, as if it were a new morning and she had only climbed into the sewing room bed the night before. Later in the evening, she resumed sleeping with Moxie's father in their master bedroom, and Moxie went back to her room. The worrisome days had ended for the time being.

Moxie remains in her bed for five days, an entire workweek. Zadi goes back and forth to school, looks in on her mother but doesn't bother her. Zadi's anxiety-streaked face reminds Moxie of her own years ago, but she cannot yet offer comfort. There is a bent and mangled tree on the grassy lot directly across from Moxie's window. She measures how she's feeling by that tree because on the days she feels depressed, the tree resembles a man hanging.

Each day she is able to do a little more for herself. Though she continues to test her progress by questioning whether she feels bad enough to die. The answer varies from "probably not" to "no." At least it's no longer "maybe." The first two days she only eats crackers and drinks water. On the third day she rises and makes tea and chicken noodle soup from a can. The fourth day, Moxie takes a long bath and lets the tears roll onto her bare skin. She listens to the messages on her voice mail. One from her father asking whether she's too busy for her old dad and one from Von leaving the phone number of a therapist. She returns her father's calls but doesn't discuss Zadi or acknowledge her own sense of despair. It is only on the fifth day that she notices the churning in her chest has slowed and she has the strength to prepare tuna salad. From her bed, she returns a few of the other phone calls she could not bring herself to respond to earlier.

She dials the number Von left for the therapist but hangs up after the first ring. Her justifications: She's doing much better than a few days ago, and she doesn't really have extra money to pay a therapist. That night, for the first time, she is able to look at Zadi and her hair without dissolving. Even the appearance of the tree outside her window has shifted. Now, instead of a hanging man, it resembles a figure with a parachute on his or her back. She stashes the phone number for the therapist in her purse.

Sunday, Feb. 7th
blk Parasuco jeans
cinnamon sweater
Tims

Dear Sistergirl:
Ma did kirk out about my hair. I knew she would, but I didn't think she'd be as bad as this. All sad and depressed, psycho shit. I don't know what to do cause she is not even talking to me. She started screaming and looking at me all crazy. I was like, is she going to hit me or what? I know she wanted to; I could see it in her eyes. She ended up crying in the living room. To be honest, I'm a little scared that she's going to disown me or something. I sort of feel like I should go in her room and say, okay, I'll take the perm out, but I don't want to do that, so I'm not going in there.

I thought about calling Norma to help me figure out what to do, but something happened with Ma and Norma today, too. I heard Ma cussing her out on the phone. Ma never uses really bad cuss words, so for her to say hell and damn means she's pretty upset. She's said those a couple of times when she was really mad at me or Dad about something. I heard her say, what the hell, or something with hell in it, to Norma.

They're best friends, so it must be really bad. I didn't start listening until the end so I don't know what it was all about. Anyway, that shuts my idea down.

Monday, Feb. 8th
Gap black sweater
Tommy jeans
Tims

Dear Sistergirl:
  I don't think Ma went to work. She's in her room, in the bed. Not talking. Not answering the phone. I don't even think she's been eating. Everybody else except her thinks my hair is off the hook cute!! I mean, I got so many compliments at school and at dance class that I thought my head would explode. People at school told me I look much prettier now, and when Allegra and I were around the bus stop, guys kept trying to touch it. One guy we see sometimes said, I didn't know you had good hair under all them braids. The one I was waiting on was Octavius. He met me at Metro Center. We got on the red and then the green line, and he rode the bus up Georgia Avenue with me to the dance studio. He thinks I'm even finer than before, or so he said. When we were walking along, he kind of grabbed my backpack and pulled me behind the ATM machine across the street from the ballet studio. We kissed. He can kiss his ass off. None of that sloppy, wet stuff I got from Todd. It was the kind of kiss you read about. It was nice and slow and filled my entire mouth up and made my legs shake. Damn. He said he was worried my braces would stab him or something. He's stupid. He never knew any black girls with braces before. He told me I was his bun-bun in my ear, and I felt like I was turning into liquid or something. I guess he's my boyfriend now. I told him I'm a virgin for real, and he didn't believe me at first. Then he kept looking at me real funny. Before he left me at the dance studio he said, I ain't never been with no virgin before. He seemed kind of mad about it.

Wednesday, Feb. 10th
Express Classic Fit Jeans
white Bebe shirt
white Nikes

Dear Sistergirl:

Ma is really tripping. It's like I took away her world or something. I'm sorry she feels bad, but I'm not sorry about how damn good my hair looks. The flowers I brought her Monday are still in the vase starting to get wilted. I was thinking, what if she dies from this? What if she kills herself like her own mother? When she first told me about Grandma, I asked her why Grandma did that. Ma said it was because she was really, really sad. Too sad for anyone to help her.

I don't hate Ma all the time. Sometimes she can be a jive good mom. Better than Fawna will ever be. I mean Fawna took me to get my hair done and that was all good, but it didn't make me forget that most of the time Fawna is a pain. She thinks I'm her slave off the real, though. She'll be like, Zadi, would you get me a glass of spring water, dear. Zadi, did you empty out the dishwasher? I'll be like, hello, what about your own lazy trifling-ass child Tiffany? And she'll go, well, Tiffany, has her chores and you're older than her, so you have more responsibilities. Blah blah blah. She's always saying, a lady doesn't chew gum with her mouth open like that, or doesn't sit with her legs crossed like that or walk with her behind sticking out like that. Blah blah blah with all that shit. She's just jealous cause her ass is so flat. At least my mother does have a butt, that she says shrunk after she had me. That doesn't make any sense—you're supposed to gain weight when you have a kid.

Octavius just called. He said Ma was supposed to take him to meet with a DJ, but she didn't go to work again. He wanted me to ask her to call the guy, but I told him basically she's not communicating with me right now. He wants me to call tomorrow for him and act like some secretary or something. I said, why don't you just call yourself? He said, cause you know how to talk proper and I don't. I told him he should write down what he wants to say, and I still had to help him out with that. Dang, he should know this shit.

I'm going to sleep. Unlike some people, namely Octavius, I have to go to school in the morning. He says he tries, but most of the time, school is just too boring.

Fifteen | "Are you brushing your teeth, Miles?" Norma calls while she decides what to pack for his lunch. No juice boxes left; he'll have to drink water. She searches the bottom rack of the refrigerator for the bottled water. His teacher has requested that she not send anything with sugar in it; Miles, especially, gets too "hyper" in the afternoons, she said. Norma resented her statement, doled out as if Norma didn't know what was best for her own child. As if Norma were some low-income, uneducated teenage mother or something. It's not as though she puts Twinkies or Snickers bars in there. At the most, a yogurt or a Jell-O, maybe three or four chocolate chip cookies.

Norma is running late this morning, and the class is going on a field trip to the Air and Space Museum. I've got to do better and make his lunch at night, she promises herself once again. She makes him a peanut butter sandwich on potato bread, with saltines, mini carrots, and a Golden Delicious apple. That should meet the teacher's approval.

Miles comes into the kitchen with his toothbrush dangling from his mouth, a foam cloud of toothpaste encircling it, and tries to hug her. She sends him back to the bathroom to rinse his mouth out. The phone rings as she is zipping Miles's lunch bag into his backpack. She grabs the cordless phone in the kitchen. "Zadi? Hi, sweetie. I'd love to talk to you, sistergirl, but I'm rushing."

"Norma, I'm in a pay phone at school. Can you please call my mom? I'm worried about her. Fawna took me to get a perm on the weekend, so I mean I knew she would be upset. But it's like she's dying or something. She hasn't gotten out of bed or been to work for three days. She won't even hardly talk. Can you help? Please?"

"Oh, Zadi, I don't know what to say. You're going to have to let things take their course. You took a big chance, and you have to be patient and deal with the repercussions of that. It'll take time for her to get over it. Eventually everything will be all right. Trust me," Norma says, unsure whether she believes it herself. "I can't really help more than that because, suffice it to say, she and I are having our own problems."

"I'm scared, though."

"You just concentrate on school, sweetie; do everything you're supposed to do from now on. I mean it! Call me if you need me. Maybe we can have lunch or dinner real soon."

When Norma hangs up, she can almost feel Moxie's pain weighing on her. And Zadi's apprehension. She makes a mental note to spend some time with Zadi soon. As much as she cherishes Zadi, she is definitely not calling Moxie. Moxie would have to make that move, and she's not expecting that anytime soon. She doesn't allow herself to think about whether they will ever talk again or what would make it possible for them to do so. Right now, she's still very angry. It hurts, though, that she can't call Moxie, that she has to hold on to all the things she used to talk to her about. There is no one else, however, with whom she can be her whole self, although Woody is coming close. Ironically she realizes that her "whole self" is what Moxie has a problem with.

The phone rings again. "Norma?" her mother's shrill voice vibrates through the phone. "Shouldn't you be gone by now?"

"We're about to leave, Ma."

"Thought I was going to get your answering machine and just leave you a message. Just wanted to tell you again how proud your father and I are of your photography. It was just a beautiful, beautiful show Sunday. You are so talented. Your father was reminiscing about when he gave you and Irene each a Polaroid and how you were the only one interested. He feels like he had some small role in the development of your immense talent." Her mother always translates and transmits her father's feelings about her. They never come directly from him. Norma resents his distance and wonders if in picking Lawrence, she subconsciously selected her father's understudy.

Her mother's compliments prevent Norma from vocalizing the impatience waiting on her tongue. "Miles, come on," she yells, moving her mouth away from the phone. "Thanks a lot, Ma. We've got to leave now or we'll be late. Talk to you later, okay?"

"All right. But call me back because Mrs. Logan—remember Mrs. Logan from my book club?—her daughter's getting married for the second time and she needs a photographer."

"Mother, remember? I'm not trying to do weddings anymore. They're a headache. Most people don't want you to be artistic on their big day."

"Well, it must be nice to have the luxury to turn down jobs." Her mother sounds a little hurt.

Norma sighs. "I've got to get Miles to school. I'll talk to you later." She hangs up and heads toward the stairs just as Miles descends bouncing a mini basketball. "Miles, didn't you hear me calling you?"

"I was coming," he says, his eyes remaining on the ball he's trying to dribble.

"When I call you, you shouldn't just be 'coming.' You need to come immediately, understand? Okay, get your jacket on. We're out of here."

At Miles's preschool, she watches a mother and her little girl rubbing noses in the coatroom. As Miles runs off, she aches for what that mother seems to be feeling. When she's about to leave through the heavy red doors, Miles darts out of the classroom and grabs her skirt. Norma bends over him and presses his little body closer to hers. "Love you," she whispers, letting the words spill out quickly, unable to say "I." Moxie always tells her to just make herself say the words, pretend she feels them, and one day she will. The words don't sound wrong, just awkward. Like learning to speak a foreign language.

She takes a deep breath and feels gratitude for such warm weather in February. It is almost fifty degrees. Spring, confused, seems anxious to show itself. Small purple flowering weeds have sprouted around the front of Miles's day-care center. The relief she feels now about her photography show is palpable. No more second-guessing herself. It's all done until the next one.

Norma spends the remainder of the morning viewing Roy DeCarava's exhibit at the Corcoran Museum. She considers him one of her mentors, even though they've never met. He works predominantly in black and white, like her, and what he produces is electrifying. Insightful yet gentle, what she strives for in her work. She can look at his photographs and see her own potential. Her favorite is of a woman in a white ballgown walking through a run-down neighborhood. Norma stands before it again, mesmerized by the contradictions in the picture. The sadness and decay of the woman's surroundings, mixed with her beauty, her dress, and the proud steps she takes. It makes her think about Ms. Johnson, the mother of Moxie's client, and how Moxie misunderstood and thought Norma was looking down on her. Did she and Moxie ever understand each other?

She leaves the museum replenished and stops by her studio to check messages and set up an appointment with John Covington, whom she met at her exhibit. She will photograph his family portrait before the month is over. She should clean up around the studio because she tore through it preparing for the exhibit, but instead, she remains sitting at her desk flipping through a photography magazine. It's all right if I do nothing today, she tells herself. Then Woody calls. He says he can bring lunch if she'd like.

Woody arrives with grilled-chicken-and-red-pepper sandwiches on thick focaccia bread. She can't even eat all of hers. They sit at her small desk and Woody tells her about an essay he's cowriting with another professor about the responsibilities and benefits of mentoring. "A few years ago, I would never have imagined writing this with Thomas. I couldn't stand the guy, and he couldn't stand me. We both thought the other arrogant and maybe we both were. He's a poet; I write prose. We'd subtlety try to outshine each other at faculty meetings with our literary knowledge." Norma laughs. She can't imagine Woody the way he's describing. "Then last year when Thomas announced his plans to retire this year, I couldn't comprehend my feelings of loss. I humbled myself, told him I would miss him, and we started really talking. We discovered how much we had in common. As an offshoot of that conversation, we came up with a joint poetry/prose course and offered it last semester and this. It's been great. There's a waiting list to get in it. And now we're writing this piece together, which also grew out of our discussions about mentoring our students and who we consider to be our mentors."

"That's really amazing." His story encourages her to talk about Moxie. She doesn't want him to feel responsible for what happened, though, so she gives him a little history about Moxie. It's a conundrum because she finds herself trying to justify Moxie's general distrust of white people, not wanting him to think her a racist.

"So that's why she practically ran away from me at your exhibit," he says. "I was wondering." He gets up from the folding chair Norma pulled up to her desk and comes behind her to rub her back. "You told me she was your dearest friend. It must hurt a lot." She doesn't mean to, but she begins to cry. He lowers himself to his knees in front of her chair and holds her.

"I'm sorry," she says, through her tears.

"It's all right."

After a minute or so, she straightens and wipes at her eyes. He leaves her and returns with a tissue and a cup of water. "Whew—I guess I needed to do that. I haven't cried about it before," she says, sipping the water.

"She'll come around."

"I don't know," says Norma. "It keeps happening to me. When I love people too much, they go away." Her eyes fill again.

"Not everyone, Norma. Your parents haven't gone anywhere, your sister. Miles . . . and I'm here. If you decide to love me, I promise not to disappear."

At the end of the week, on Saturday, Norma drops Miles at her parents' house so that she can meet Woody to look at apartments. Lawrence is in Philadelphia overnight on business. She ignored her mother when she asked where Norma was going so early.

At a red light just past the zoo on Connecticut Avenue, she checks the address again, scrawled in pencil by Woody on lined yellow paper. Why would he even consider living this far from everything? she wonders. His daughter, his job, and her.

The apartment building is vintage red brick. Ivy ropes travel up one side and brush against some of the windows. She is buzzed in and stops at the front desk. "Number four-oh-four," she says.

"That's the open unit. Go on up, he's waiting on you," a deeply wrinkled white man doing a crossword puzzle tells her. Has he mistaken her for someone else? Would Woody have described her enough for this man to recognize her?

When she steps from the elevator, the door to 404 is partially open. From the apartment's foyer, she notices spotless beige wall-to-wall carpeting and intricately carved woodwork. Woody's back is to her. He wears his favorite tweed jacket. A tall white man with a tan and a bow tie stands in front of Woody, examining a long sheet of paper.

"Excuse me one moment, Mr. Woodruff." The man aims a tight smile at Norma. "Oh, good, glad you got here quickly. It's the toilet; thank goodness we were able to turn the water off," the man says briskly to Norma before she has barely crossed the threshold. "Where's the mop? Go back down to the front desk. See if Joe knows where a mop is and get a plunger, too. The bathroom's down the hall on the right between the bedrooms. Mop all that water up, and see if you can figure out what's wrong with the toilet. . . ."

"Excuse me?" she says, puzzled.

Woody turns and his face brightens. "Norma."

"Aren't you from janitorial services?" The man pivots from Norma to Woody, obviously flustered. "You know her?"

"No, I'm not here from janitorial services!"

Woody interrupts temperately, "Norma, why don't you have a look around. Mr. . . . uh . . . ?"

"Stanley."

"Mr. Stanley is just going over my application and filling me in on which utilities are included in the rent."

Norma moves off to one side. She purposely doesn't acknowledge Mr. Stanley any further and walks through the spacious apartment, which has two fireplaces and two bathrooms. Considering its close proximity to Connecticut and Wisconsin Avenues, she's sure it's very expensive.

She looks out a window and sees a white woman walking a dog and two white men on in-line skates. Woody approaches her from behind, puts one hand on her waist, and murmurs in her ear. "Hey. You look stunning."

"Thanks. Are you actually going to rent this apartment?" She faces him with intense eyes.

"I don't know," he says, raising one of his eyebrows. "Think I should?"

"Not if you have to deal with good ol' Mr. Stanley."

"Too stuffy?"

"Too racist."

"Racist?" Woody says.

"Didn't you see how he assumed I was here to clean up the toilet, mop up the floor, or whatever he said. Didn't you hear him say he thought I was from a janitorial service?"

"Well, I think . . . I don't think it was necessarily racist. I mean he and I were engaged in a conversation, and he probably wasn't even really thinking—probably just said the first thing that came to him."

"Please, don't defend him, Woody. Why was janitorial service the first thing that came to his mind? Am I dressed like I'm here to do janitorial work, or is my skin color the only uniform I need? He didn't even apologize."

"No?"

"No! You were right there." She moves back a little toward one of the fireplaces, which, on closer inspection, she realizes is artificial.

"Do you want me to ask him to apologize to you?" Woody's neck reddens as he questions her.

"No. It wouldn't be genuine, so it wouldn't mean anything."

"Norma, maybe you're being a little sensitive?" He touches her shoulder.

"You don't have to go through this, so you don't see it. Black people go through this all the time." Norma turns from him and hears voices coming from the front of the apartment.

"Sorry. That's it. I just won't rent it, then."

"Woody, I'm not saying that. I'm trying to point something out to you." Norma sighs. "I want you to understand why I'm upset."

"Let's get out of here. It's inconveniently located anyway. I've got another place for us to look at." He reaches for her hand. They walk back out to the foyer, where Mr. Stanley is speaking to a white couple. "Mr. Stanley, could I have a word with you for a moment?" Woody says.

Mr. Stanley hesitates and then excuses himself from the couple. He comes over to Woody and Norma. "Yes, what can I do for you, sir?"

"This is my friend, Ms. Simmons-Greer. When she came into the apartment, you made an erroneous assumption about her. I'm willing to give you the benefit of the doubt and assume it wasn't racial, but, in any case, I think you owe her an apology."

"Well . . . I'm sorry, Miss . . . uh. I didn't . . ." Mr. Stanley turns beet red and makes no attempt to meet her gaze.

"Is that okay?" Woody asks Norma. She nods.

"You surprised me," Norma says once they're out by the elevators.

"I guess it could have been racial, but maybe it was gender motivated. Maybe not. Who knows? In any case, defining him as a racist, I think might be a leap. I guess I wish we didn't always have to think in terms of skin color." He looks at her intently.

"Only a handful of people *don't* think in terms of color. Most think in racial terms first, whether they admit it or not. That's just the way it is."

They get on the elevator, and he looks hurt. "You think what I said is naive or idealistic, don't you?"

They ride down to the lobby in silence.

"This next place is supposed to have a breakfast nook," Woody says outside in front of the apartment building. "Do you want to come with me, or are you thoroughly disgusted with this white man, too?"

Norma can't help but smile. "No, I'm not 'thoroughly disgusted' with you. Just don't take my color for granted. That's all."

"Jesus." He smacks his hand to his forehead. "How can I? You're apparently not going to let me."

"Yes, I want to see the other place with you. Where is it?"

"Adams Morgan."

"That's more like it. A diverse neighborhood."

They decide to travel together in Woody's car and come back for hers afterwards. "Do you mind if I smoke?" Woody asks after starting the ignition.

"You always ask me that. It's your car."

"I'm so used to people minding."

She shakes her head, no, she doesn't mind. He opens the window slightly, then maneuvers the cigarette smoothly with one hand, reaching for the car lighter and easily pressing it onto the cigarette, without taking his eyes from the road. His slim lips curl backwards over the cigarette as if he's Humphrey Bogart. He pulls the ashtray out from between them and taps ashes into it.

There is rarely parking in Adams Morgan, even on the winding side streets. The neighborhood is lively with street vendors hawking everything from fake-fur car seats to children's polyester-and-satin church clothes. Throngs of people are out, enjoying the unseasonably warm weather. They end up driving around for a while without any luck. Woody finally turns down a street that reveals a small parking space. "Can you fit?" Norma asks, doubtful

"It'll be tight, but I think I can." He turns the steering wheel repeatedly, maneuvering forward and back until they're in. They walk several blocks to the apartment building. The street is crowded with trees and townhouses nestled over the narrow sidewalk.

"Since today is apparently our day for heavy discussions, I want to tell you what's on my mind." Woody smokes another cigarette as he talks. They walk past a man washing his car and have to step over the hose. The man smiles at them.

"Which is?"

"As you know, my marriage is coming to end. I know no such thing about yours, and I'm feeling some qualms. If . . . there's a chance you and your husband might get back together, I don't want to complicate that."

Norma puts her hands in the pockets of her trench coat in an effort to control the rush of panic she feels. She doesn't want to discuss her marriage with him. That's what feels like cheating. "Like I tried to say before, Woody, something got lost between me and Lawrence a few years back and neither one of us seems to know how to do anything but be in the marriage."

"And, you know what? From my experience it'll remain that way until one or both of you can't stand to be in it any longer or something makes you realize you *do* want to be in it after all." He stops walking to compare the address on the paper with the building they are in front of.

"To be honest, it feels strange talking to you about it, Woody. He and I used to share so much; now we share so little it could fit in the palm of my hand."

He holds on to both her arms and turns her to face him. "That night at your exhibit—I knew he was there and I felt some semblance of guilt or something. I care a lot for you, and so I guess I'm asking myself, what am I doing here? Something I'm not exactly proud of, something I wouldn't have wanted anyone to do with my wife when we were still trying to work things out. These are the things I've been contemplating, you know?"

Norma nods. A ribbon of ache winds through her. "I think about all that, too, but don't know what to do about it. I've spent so much time being a responsible person. I just want to be irresponsible for a moment."

From the outside, the building appears older than the first one they visited. Some of the taupe-colored bricks are chipped away or missing. In place of the other building's climbing ivy there are merely untrimmed evergreen bushes lining the short walkway. Two stone lion heads stand guard at either side of the staircase. One is missing a nose.

The apartment itself turns out to be several square feet smaller than the earlier one, but there are two fair-sized bedrooms and a small den as well as a living room and dining room. Norma likes the arched doorways and the sliding doors between the living room and dining room. When they discover there is also a half-bath beside the kitchen, Woody decides he wants it. He talks to the building manager for several minutes and fills out an application form while Norma explores further. From the living room window she watches a cardinal dance across the branches of a tree. There is not one unstressful relationship in her life right now. This was supposed to be the one, but Woody's asking questions, having misgivings. This is an affair, damnit. An affair should equal a stress-free zone.

After a protracted wait for the elevator, they take the stairs, since the apartment is only on the fourth floor. The stairwell is dark and narrow. Woody descends first and reaches for her hand. Partway down he stops so suddenly she walks directly into the back of him. He turns to face her without breaking their contact. He puts his arms around her shoulders and kisses her. She puts her hands around his waist, under his jacket, and tells him her fantasy. He wants to make it come true. First, they have to go pick up her car, though.

He presses his fingers onto her neck, kneading it while she unlocks the door to her studio. Inside, he moves her back against the door. Fiercely, all at once, he nibbles at her neck, her ears, and washes her lips with his long tongue. She can hardly breathe.

"Which way to that lumpy couch?" he groans into her ear.

She laughs against his chest, remembering the much earlier time when they were so new and shy with each other. "The darkroom, I said." She motions behind her.

"Right. I've never done this before or even thought about it. Have you?"

"Thought about it, yes, but I don't even usually let people up here. Never mind in the darkroom. You and Moxie are the only people who have even been. My husband and Miles came when we first rented it, and that was it." They take pillows from the lumpy couch and put them on the darkroom floor. Norma covers the pillows with a comforter from the closet. It has a musty smell, but it's clean.

"How come we didn't do this the first time?" he asks.

" 'Cause you were nervous."

"Oh, I was nervous. I see."

She closes the door, and they are sheathed by the orange-red glow. They stand together against the sink. His hands are on her thighs, rubbing, groping under her skirt, inside her tights.

"Woody."

"Yes, sweetheart. What's this? What on earth do you have on under here?"

Beneath her skirt and the tights she is wearing a teddy that snaps at the crotch. She wasn't expecting to be making love today—just apartment hunting. She reaches down and unsnaps it for him. They abandon their clothes, and he puts on a condom while she watches. He stops her as she is about to sink back into the pillows. "Don't lie down. I want you to sit on me."

He gathers each breast in his hands and mouth, as best he can, and then roams back and forth between them. She closes her eyes and sucks on his shoulder as she eases herself down onto him. "Ride me," he says. "Ride me away." After a while she collapses onto his chest. "I love you, Norma," he says, burying his head in her hair.

"I love you, too," she says, not knowing or caring whether it's true.

She walks him downstairs to the front door. He holds her hand as if he doesn't want to leave. When he looks at her and says good-bye, he seems so exposed. It reminds her of the scene in *Last Tango in Paris* when Marlon Brando finally tells his lover what his name is. She tells him hers, too, and then shoots him dead.

Saturday, Feb. 13th
gray mini-skirt
white T-shirt
blk platform boots

Dear Sistergirl:
Had tryouts today at Duke Ellington for Dance Theatre of Harlem's summer program. Miss Snow let us come late to rehearsal. The dance instructors put us into different groups. I couldn't tell what the categories were based on. There were girls and guys from all over. Black, white, and two Asian-American girls. Some of those people could really dance. I was a little worried. They gave us combinations to do in our groups and kept making the groups smaller and smaller until there were only a few people left. They kept me in there until the end. So then I was psyched as a mug. But all they said was, Thank you very much. You'll hear from us one way or another. I was nervous, but I remembered to straighten my knee with my extensions and to point my toe all the way through. All the things

Miss Snow has hammered into my brain over the years. When they asked us to do sixteen fouettés, I was like that because I have been practicing those like crazy. I hope and pray I make it.

Sunday, Feb. 14th
DKNY jeans
leopard-print sweater
Tims

Dear Sistergirl:
   It takes more time to keep my hair like this on the real. I'm not complaining, though! I have to roll it up if I want curls, and I have to tie it with a scarf regardless. And do all the wrap lotion stuff if I want that look. I'll have to get a touch-up in six weeks. Ma is still flicked off, like it's her hair or something. Allegra and Norma both said she'll get over it eventually. I don't know if I can make it to eventually. At least she's out of the bed now. That was like a whole damn week. Still she's always staring at me, and that drives me crazy. Like if I'm sitting at the table doing my homework or something and she's in the kitchen, I'll look up and she'll be like staring at me and then she'll look away quick. Psycho shit again, but I'm not panicking.
   O called to wish me happy Valentine's Day. That was so sweet. I got him a little white teddy bear from CVS that says Be Mine, but I'm not going to give it to him unless he gives me something. He said he has something for me, but the way he said it, it might not be something he bought—know what I mean?

Sixteen | During the week that Moxie stayed home depressed about Zadi's hair, she realized it was possible for a thick sadness to claim her the way it had her mother, and she was prepared to accept that. Except it didn't. Instead, just when she thought she couldn't plunge any lower, she noticed that she felt hungry again and she observed the sun straining at her window. Little by little, she clawed her way back enough to return to work and it feels good to be there. With Zadi, though, things still feel very raw; one wrong move by either one and things could fall apart again.

It is Monday and she is grateful that when she checks in, Von doesn't mention the therapist or ask for details about what kept her away from the office all week. She has a stack of phone calls to return, which she prioritizes. Later in the afternoon, she sees several clients. Moxie's office seems to shrink when Belle Bruno, a beet-faced white woman with a drinking problem, enters, accompanied by her acne-prone, very decent, biracial fourteen-year-old son, Luke. Luke pled guilty to shoplifting two packages of cinnamon rolls and three bottles of Yoo-Hoo, but it was his third shoplifting offense, so he got six months probation. At their first meeting, Ms. Bruno told Moxie she didn't want to talk to "no black girl," but Moxie calmly told her there weren't any white probation officers in her department. She wondered how such sentiments translated to Mr. Bruno's feelings about her half-black child as she scowled her way through the remainder of the session.

Ms. Bruno is braless under a stained smock dress and carries a sweater in one swollen fist. The weather is getting warmer now, but Moxie realizes Ms. Bruno hasn't worn a coat all winter. When she sits down heavily, her loose breasts settle in a small heap on top of her stomach. "How many more of these meetings we gotta be at? Luke could be at work right now. Gas station man ready to pay him minimum wage, but he need him full-time."

"Does the man know Luke's only fourteen and still in school?" Moxie can feel her patience evaporating as she looks at Luke's tear-streaked face. She has never seen a child his age cry so much. She told Von her gut feeling that there is abuse in the home, and she has referred his file to the Social Services division.

Ms. Bruno crosses her arms and rolls her eyes as if Moxie has made the most absurd utterance imaginable. "I don't know what the man knows or don't know."

Luke slumps down in his chair. Several buttons are missing on his shirt and the sleeves don't quite reach his wrists. He fingers the metal buttons of a dingy jean jacket draped across his knees.

"Listen, Ms. Bruno, it's kind of hard for Luke to find a job at his age. What about if he just concentrates on school, right now. You wouldn't want him to violate his probation, would you?"

Belle Bruno mumbles something low and unintelligible. Luke's floating eyes are full of fading trust and broken promises. This is the part that hurts, knowing that a child may be suffering. "I'm sending your file upstairs so they can help me try to help you," Moxie says, preparing herself for Ms. Bruno's expected animus. "They'll call you to set up a home visit." Ms. Bruno doesn't say anything, just sucks her teeth.

After they leave, Moxie jots down notes in the Bruno file. While she scribbles, Brenda buzzes her intercom with a call from Octavius. He tells her he made a new appointment himself with Ron D for this afternoon. An hour away. While it means she won't be able to catch up on as much as she planned, she's pleased he took the initiative and followed through while she was out of the office.

She meets him downstairs in front of her office building, and he assures her he has come from school. She surveys his low-slung jeans and skull cap. "Lose the cap and tighten your belt," she says. It's not as though he was going to wear a suit, she tells herself. They ride up Connecticut Avenue and cut over to Nebraska without much conversation. "I'm proud of you for taking the steps to make a new appointment, Octavius," Moxie says as they pull into a "visitor" parking space. He nods, but seems somewhat agitated. He repeatedly clicks the top of a pen he holds in his hand.

"Don't know why I came up here," he murmurs. "Wasted your time. They ain't gonna give me no job."

"How do you know?" Moxie says, removing her seat belt.

"I don't know nothing 'bout being no DJ."

"They're not going to put you on the air, Octavius. Maybe some day in the future. But right now they want to talk to you because you say that you know something about rap music, right?"

"I guess."

"You guess? Come on. Be a little bit more confident. You represent other kids who might be in their audience market. You can help them figure out what kids your age want to listen to. You'll be very good at that." She gives him a slight nudge, and he opens the car door. Being back at work, concentrating on other people's problems has helped her stop dwelling on her losses.

She sits in a bustling waiting room while Octavius is interviewed. There are two televisions positioned slightly below the ceiling and tuned to BET music videos. Four speakers also blare music from the afternoon radio show. She hears, over the speakers, a DJ she's not familiar with offering cash and concert tickets to the sixteenth caller. People come and go through the waiting room. Some stop to ask if she wants a soft drink or coffee. Everyone seems very young, dressed-up and made-up, as if perpetually ready for a fashion shoot.

When Octavius returns, he's accompanied by Ron D, who shakes Moxie's hand and then, as an afterthought, hugs her. Walking back to the car, Octavius reports very little other than, "It was a'right" and that they promised to get back to him. He thanks her for making the initial arrangements, and she drops him at the Gallery Place metro, near her office. She buys a container of miso soup from the nearby health food restaurant, deciding to stay at work until it's time to get Zadi from ballet. She transfers her handwritten notes to the computer. After an hour of this, her eyes feel jumpy and her legs need a stretch. She walks through the hallway to the ladies' room, stops to talk to coworkers she passes, and then returns to her office via the lunchroom, where Brenda must have brewed coffee just before leaving for the day. The aroma makes her think of Norma, and how much she loves good coffee. A few years ago they took a road trip to North Carolina for a friend's wedding. Norma brought her own thermos of coffee because she didn't trust what they would find along the highway. Moxie catches herself before she thinks about Norma any further. Files completed, Moxie locks up her office.

She waits in her car behind other parents parked in front of the studio, engines still running. She stays in her car while some of them get out and chat with each other. It's a little chilly; she's tired and not quite up to small talk. Several wave to her, and she waves back. As the girls burst out the rear door of the dance studio, she studies everyone's hair. There is enough light from the streetlamp and the studio porch light for her to see. All straightened and curled, wrapped or pulled into ponytails or buns. No natural anything; Zadi was the only one. She knew this, yet she had determined Zadi could rise above it. Maybe it was a lot to ask. But isn't Zadi special, more special than any other girl in the world, and why then shouldn't Moxie have expected more from her? She wonders briefly if she can return the wig, never seen by Zadi, and still in the trunk of her car.

When Zadi comes out the studio door, her hair is now like the others'—bouncing behind her, rising easily off her shoulders. Each time seeing her hair, loose, straight, and flat, partially opens Moxie's wound again. Zadi, on the other hand, shows no signs of missing her old hair.

Zadi settles into the front seat of the car, one vertebrae at a time. "My arms are *so* sore."

"Seat belt, Zadi."

"It's going to hurt my shoulder, Ma. Miss Snow said my arms weren't swanlike enough, so I had to do the port de bras stuff over and over."

"You still need your seat belt on. It'll hurt a lot worse if you go through the windshield."

Zadi puts the seat belt on, cringing as she does. "Mom! Guess what?" Zadi yells breathlessly.

"What?"

"Miss Snow announced the names of people who got accepted into the summer Dance Theatre of Harlem program. Guess who was one of them?" Zadi speaks so fast, her words run together.

"Who?" Moxie is glad Zadi is excited about telling her something. She's anxious to have her back.

"Me, Sonya, Zora, James, and Todd. Almost all of the advanced class."

"Oh, congratulations! See how talented you are!" She wishes her own mother could have seen Zadi dance.

"I know it was 'cause of the *fouettés*. 'Cause I was off the hook with those. Sonya was, too."

"Which turns are the *fouettés?* I forget."

"You know, those turns when you bring your leg out sharp and then snap it right back in as you're turning. Miss Snow says the word *fouetté* means to whip. It's kind of like a *rond de jambe.*" She demonstrates by holding her hand in her mother's line of vision and jutting it in and out. "They're jive hard, but I like doing them. I like turns best, anyway. I remember when I when I was little, I didn't know how to spot. I used to get so dizzy, and you'd take me to see ballets at the Kennedy Center, and I was like how do they do it? Then one day I could do it, just like that."

"I never learned how to spot," Moxie says, regretfully.

"But how'd you turn without getting dizzy?"

"Pretended I knew how to spot and got dizzy."

"Ma. I don't know how you could stand that."

"Me either. I guess that's one reason I never became as good a dancer as you."

Moxie's car rumbles across a big pothole as she turns onto her father's street. "I wished they'd fix these like they keep promising," Moxie says. "I told Grandpa we'd stop in. I know you want to get home, do your homework, and soak, but we won't stay long."

She and Zadi notice right away that the front steps do not creak anymore. The plywood boards are gone. The steps are completely covered with new gray concrete. "They look really good. When did these get fixed?" asks Zadi.

"We didn't come over all last week. They look brand new," Moxie says, feeling bad about not visiting for the whole week.

"Look at these," Zadi says, touching one of the pillars. No more cracked paint; they can see by the porch light the pillars have been repainted. Zadi runs to the front door. "Hurry up and open the door, Ma. Let's see if the inside is new, too."

Moxie and Zadi walk in, looking around as if they are part of an official inspection team. Everything inside is the same, however, and Moxie is disappointed, as if she hoped a magic wand had been waved over the house.

"Granddaddy, where are you?" Zadi calls.

"In here, baby doll." Ponsey and Haleem are seated at the dining room table, bent over a small stack of paperwork. They both look up. Jupiter is at the far end of the table, apparently doing his homework.

"Grandpa, you practically have a new front porch," Zadi says, excitedly.

"Thanks to this young man here." He gently slaps Haleem on the back. Haleem looks up and smiles. He catches Moxie's eye briefly and then shifts his glance away.

"It really looks great," Moxie says, hesitantly approaching the table. "And it's only been a week or so since I was last here. You've done so much. . . ."

"Yes, sir, sure did help an old man out. And he won't let me even talk about money," says her father, shaking his head, as if expressing both disbelief and appreciation at his good fortune.

"That's right. Not a word," says Haleem, taking a sip from the mug in front of him. "After all, you're my Jerry Springer partner and Jupiter's domino partner." They both laugh heartily.

"Come sit down, you two." Ponsey taps the tall-backed chair beside him.

Moxie sits down, keeping her coat on her shoulders. "Don't tell me you watch that Jerry Springer junk, too?"

Jupiter pokes his head up. "He does. He won't let me, but he does."

"Grandpa finally found someone to watch Jerry with," Zadi announces.

"You did all that to the porch in a week?" Moxie asks, still a bit astonished.

"Well, it's not really that much," Haleem says, seemingly slightly embarrassed. "Want to do some spot-painting next, and the banister needs some balusters replaced." He expresses himself with his hands as he talks. When he finishes, he puts his hands in his lap quickly as if they went too far.

"Thank you for doing all that," Moxie says, turning to Haleem.

"Friends help friends," Haleem says. His eyes slide off her onto Zadi, who walks over to examine Jupiter's homework. "So this must be Zadi."

"Oh, you all never met?" Ponsey seems surprised. "Yes, this is my beautiful, brilliant, prima ballerina granddaughter!"

Zadi laughs. "Grandpa . . ."

"Nice to meet you, Zadi. You've got quite a fan club in your grand-dad. This is my son, Jupiter."

Jupiter looks up from his books. "She looks different from her pictures."

Zadi smoothes her hair back with one hand. She looks at her mother quickly. "Probably 'cause of my hair. My . . . dance teacher wanted it straightened for my recital. Do you like my hair, Granddaddy?"

Ponsey regards Zadi over his glasses. "Well, you know I think you always look beautiful." He gives Moxie a cautious examination. "I know your mother doesn't like it, though." Moxie says nothing. "But like I said—you were beautiful before. You're still beautiful now."

Zadi hugs her grandfather and sits down across from him. "Grandpa, I'm going to New York this summer! I got into the Dance Theatre of Harlem's summer program!"

Moxie's father looks straight at her. "Well, that's great news, isn't it? You'll go with her, won't you?" He sits forward in his chair.

"No, Daddy, I can't take six weeks off. I'll visit, but it's a whole organized program that's been around for . . . years. Very safe, they don't leave them on their own," says Moxie trying to convince herself.

Moxie's father appears concerned. He turns to Haleem, who has slid his chair over to Jupiter, and is crouched over his workbook. "Haleem, what do you think about all this? A girl not yet sixteen going off to New York alone! In my day we wouldn't even be discussing this."

"Grandpa, I'm not going to be alone. Come on, don't you trust me?"

Haleem has one hand resting at the back of Jupiter's neck. "If it were this guy, I'd have some apprehension, too, but you have to let kids go. Congratulations, Zadi. Sounds like a great opportunity." He shakes Zadi's hand, as she passes behind his chair.

"Thank you," Zadi says.

She leans over Jupiter and shows him how to solve a math problem.

Haleem marvels aloud that Zadi solved it before he did and says that he and Jupiter are going to leave and let Ponsey enjoy his family.

"Daddy, actually we're leaving, too, unless you need me to fix you something for dinner."

"Y'all act like I can't cook for myself. I've been cooking long before you were born. No, thanks. Got a dinner at the church last night I'm gonna heat up. Not hungry yet, anyhow. Hand me that *TV Guide,* will you, Haleem? Let me see what's coming on. Turned on what I thought was my cop show and it was a hospital show. Had the wrong night." He calls to Haleem, who has gone to look around in the living room, "See it over there next to the footstool?"

"Come on, Jupiter," Haleem says, returning with the magazine. "Time to go. Listen, Ponsey, don't try to move those paint cans before I get back. I know you. Good night, Zadi. Moxie." Jupiter gathers up his books, thanks Zadi, and follows his father out of the dining room, waving good-bye.

"Aren't we leaving, too, Ma?" Zadi asks Moxie.

"Just a sec. Be right back." Moxie walks to the front door behind Haleem and Jupiter. She goes onto the porch. The air has become heavy outside, a cottony mist, as if it might rain. "Excuse me, Haleem, could I speak to you a minute?"

"Sure," he says, looking at her with one raised eyebrow.

Jupiter swings his book bag onto his shoulder and shifts from one foot to another.

"It seems like an awful lot of work you've done. I'd like to discuss a payment plan."

He waves her off. "When we first got here, Jupiter was so down about leaving his friends behind, and I didn't have the energy to deal with it. Your father saw him moping around throwing snowballs one day and invited him for a game of dominoes. He came back to ask permission first—you know, stranger and everything—and he was excited! Might sound like a small thing, but Jupiter didn't know how to play and your father taught him. Now dominoes is Jupiter's game. Your dad didn't have to give a damn about some lonely kid he didn't know. So no, I don't want payment. Anyway, nice seeing you. Good night." He takes a jackknife out of his jeans pocket and cuts a few branches of thick green leaves from the bush in front of the house.

She's curious. "What do you do with those?"

"I put them on my altar. I'm a Buddhist."

"Oh." Moxie crosses her arms across her sweater and watches him finish cutting the evergreen and then walk with Jupiter toward their own house. He walks tilted forward, headfirst, body following. He doesn't look to either side or back at her.

Zadi is slumped in her father's armchair when Moxie goes inside.

"Take Zadi girl home, she needs her beauty sleep. Right, baby doll?"

Zadi flutters her eyes. "Oh, Grandpa."

"Who am I gonna have to mess with if you go off to New York? You better call me every night from that pitiful place."

"It's not a pitiful place. It's an exciting place. You can come up to visit with Ma."

"You still going to at least help me get the garden cleaned up and ready? Another few weeks and we'll get going—clean up the old leaves and all."

"Sure, Grandpa. Just remember, Saturdays is dance. So Sundays will be better."

Moxie goes up to the sewing room. She has forgotten everything dealing with Zadi's hair, even about repairing the sewing machine. She tries it again, hoping that she was mistaken last time, that it is really working. But it isn't, and she berates herself for neglecting it. She wipes a cloth across the dust that has collected and closes the door. Downstairs, Moxie helps Zadi up out of the chair. "C'mon, child." She puts her arm around Zadi's waist. Zadi doesn't resist, and they each kiss Ponsey good-bye.

They walk down the new steps, Zadi moving very slowly. "So, Ma, you like this guy Haleem now, don't you?" Zadi looks at Moxie slyly.

"No, Zadi. I just like that he's being so nice to Grandpa."

"Yeah, right."

"Seriously. When I first met him, I didn't know what kind of a person he was. Now, I think he's a good person." Moxie unlocks Zadi's side of the car. "That's all."

"And you went out on the porch to talk in private, I noticed. What was that about?"

"Zadi, please. Let me hurry up and get you home. You really must be very tired." Moxie turns the steering wheel, backs up and out of the parking space.

"So, does this interrogation sound a little familiar?"

"No, not at all."

Monday, Feb. 15th
Nautica sweat pants
gray sweatshirt
Tims

Dear Sistergirl:

Becky Sherwood set up an appointment for me, Allegra, and Windy to get birth control pills from her uncle (a gynecologist) after school today. We had early dismissal because of teacher planning meetings. Windy told us all we'd have to do was say we were eighteen and he wouldn't questions us. She didn't lie either. We each had to pay $50 in cash, student rate (Windy and Allegra each lent me $25 until I can get it from Dad). We went in one at a time. It was a quick examination, thank goodness. It's so embarrassing and weird to have somebody doing that stuff to you and telling you to relax at the same time. Ma said she is going to take me to a gynecologist when I turn sixteen; now I know what it'll be like. I basically held my breath and stared at the ceiling. We all got three months' worth of teeny pills to start with. I'm going to leave them in my locker. I wouldn't want to forget and leave them out at home or something. I started taking them so I'll be ready when the time comes.

I was a little worried that I'd be late for rehearsal, but Becky drove us and dropped us all off, so it was all good. Miss Snow was in a bad mood today. She usually starts getting stressed out the closer we get to the

performance, but we're not that close yet. She yelled at us like crazy. She
was going: You have two feet, you know. I'm sorry that you do, but you
do. Then she'd turn right around and say, You cannot watch your feet
and dance at the same time. Glissade. Rond de jambe. Sissone. We all
have problems, don't bring yours in here. You all look like you're old and
sick. Nobody better miss another practice. Zadi Lawson, I'm talking to
you. I was like, Miss Snow, I haven't missed a rehearsal. She said, Just
make sure you don't. Then Mishon raised her hand about having to go to
a wedding next weekend. Me and Zora just looked at each other like,
how could Mishon say something so dumb? Miss Snow said to Mishon,
Are you the bride? If you're not the bride, they won't miss you. And Miss
Snow wasn't joking. We didn't dare laugh, but we wanted to.

Me and Ma went by Grandpa's. That guy Haleem, who has a crush
on Ma, was over there with his kid.

Wednesday, Feb. 17th
red/blk stretch top
black jean skirt
black Banana Republic boots

Dear Sistergirl:
Miss Snow took some of the senior dancers to the Kennedy Center to
see Bill T. Jones tonight. It was off the hook good. Miss Snow said that
even though his work is nontraditional and modern, his foundation is in
the ballet, and she wanted us to experience what he does. I felt like I was
being lifted out of my seat and carried into Bill T. Jones's own, really
different world. He has all shapes, sizes, and colors of dancers in his
company. There were actually three heavyset people who nonetheless
could dance their asses off. And the choreography was like that—hip-hop
moves to Stravinsky music! The costumes were off the hook, too. Some of
the men had skirts on; some of the women had on baggy men's pants and
little bras or see-through slips. One Hispanic-looking woman had on
what looked like a bathing suit bottom and a corset top. In another scene
the women wore these little baby-doll dresses that would be vicious for
the spring.

The whole time I wished I was one of the dancers in that show. I didn't want it to be over. I cried when it was about to end cause it got way under my skin; I hope no one saw me. It took me to a place I wanted to stay. I never saw dancing that pushed things beyond their limitations. Bill T. Jones came out and took his bows. He's short and strong with a bald head and glasses. He doesn't look like he has AIDS. Miss Snow asked us what we were most impressed with. I said, everything, especially the fact that all the dancers were like prima ballerinas. No one was mediocre. Miss Snow said, yes, emblazon that in your minds. Toni drove the van that took us back to the studio. Our parents met us there. Ma looked like she fell asleep in the car.

Thursday, Feb. 18th
Gap jeans
blk lycra top
Timberlands

Dear Sistergirl:
   Got my braces tightened after school today, so my mouth is hurting off the hook.
   Today two girls in eleventh grade got caught smoking on school grounds. That is so ridiculously stupid. Willow sent home notices about it. Ma said they must have wanted to get caught, since you don't have to go that far to be off school grounds. Ma asked me if they were black or white. Her favorite question. She should know most black girls don't smoke—cigarettes anyway. It makes your nails and your hair and your breath stink. It makes you cough, too. I wouldn't smoke because it could mess with my body and interfere with my dancing. That's why I don't smoke weed either. I tried it once with Allegra, but it made me feel too psycho. Like I was walking through tall grass but couldn't step high enough. I can't really explain it. Allegra doesn't smoke weed anymore either cause she said one time she was smoking with Alton, her brother, when he was home from college, and she started feeling paranoid like she was about to die and that got her scared. She doesn't know if it had something in it. (Probably did.)

Octavius says he solves most of the problems in his life when he's high, but he keeps saying he doesn't get high that much. I told him something I heard on the radio—It's hard to succeed if you're smoking weed. He told me I'm crazy. I can't always tell when he's high like I could with Allegra. He says he likes to be high when he's getting cozy with a young lady. He told me I make him want to hold me forever. (I was psyched as shit!) He played this rap he wrote for me over the phone. Then I had him repeat the words a million times so I could write them down:

Chorus:
I wanna be your man
I wanna hold your hand
I want you to understand
That I do got a plan

Verses:
Girl, I wanna be your man
Wanna show you that I can
Be all that you demand
'Cause I'm your greatest fan

I wanna travel with you
Go to the farthest land
Lay in the softest sand
Get a tan in Iran

I wanna dine with you
Drink wine with you
Ain't no kind like you
If there is, they ain't as fine as you

I wanna buy you things
Like big diamond rings
And nice necklaces
Top it off with shiny Lexuses

I wanna please you
And I need you
'Cause me without you
Is like the ocean with no blue.

For real I didn't even know he could write that good. He rhymes better
than he talks. On the tape he has background music playing from a
sample he got from the DJ interview Ma hooked up. I told him it
sounded tight. But can you really get a tan in Iran? Usually I prefer
R&B, but I do like Missy, Eve, sometimes Puffy, and Mase. (O thinks
Puffy and Mase are played and not real rappers. Mase is supposed to be
switching to gospel or something I heard.) Lil' Kim and Foxy Brown are
a little too nasty for me. Although I am looking forward to finding out
about the hot spot for myself. But they talk about doing the oral thing
and I can't get with that. O says it doesn't matter that they're nasty, their
rap flows. I read an interview with Lil' Kim and she said whoever
becomes her husband will have to understand that Biggie is always going
to be her number one love and she's going to be with him when she dies.
What if Faith thinks the same thing? Ma showed me an article from the
New York Times *about Foxy Brown driving around in Harlem looking*
for someplace to eat late at night. And how she got out the car to look at
a poster of herself up close and said, Hi, me! Tripping. She's only a couple
of years older than me!!!! Ma must be feeling better cause she's back to
giving me articles all the time.

Friday, Feb. 19th
Old Navy flared jeans
blk/white checked top
blk Nikes

Dear Sistergirl:
    Met Allegra after ballet. Hung out at City Place. O came over there,
too, and Roberto. (She's back with Roberto; I guess he thinks it's okay
now to be with a black girl, but I don't think his mother knows.) We had

something like a double date. Roberto and O didn't talk that much. They just did a handshake and said, whatsup, playa, to each other. We walked around and went in the CD store, got some ice cream, and then Roberto and O wanted to go in the arcade. Me and Allegra were like, what? So we had to wait for them to play those dumb games, but that seemed to help them bond cause they were laughing and talking when they finally came out. Then Ma picked me and Allegra up around the front at ten o'clock. O and R disappeared quick.

On MTV FANatic *tonight they had a girl who was dying to meet Brandy. When she came into the room where Brandy was sitting, the girl went right back out and then came in again like she couldn't believe it. She was nervous and crying and everything. Then Brandy hugged her. She told Brandy how this was her dream come true and that her mother died of cancer and that Brandy's song "Missing You" (that was in* Set It Off *and made with some other singers) helped her get through it. Brandy held her hand the whole time. I was like, Brandy is really nice, although she did still trip a little bit. She told the girl that she acted that same way when she met Whitney Houston for the first time. I'm not playa-hatin, but Whitney Houston is played out. (Everybody thinks she uses drugs.) I wish my friends would get together and get me on* FANnatic *to meet Janet. Miss Jackson if you're nasty. I love her video with Busta Rhymes. She can't really be doing it with him, can she?*

Seventeen   Earlier today, Norma saw people jogging near the Capitol with shorts on. It is only the last full week of February and it's fifty degrees outside. She is glad that winter seems to be limping to its end earlier than usual. The meteorologists predict record-breaking temperatures before official spring. "Because of global warming," Zadi told her last year when there were several remarkably warm days, "the world is going to burn up by the time I'm grown."

"No, sweetie, it won't," Norma tried to reassure her, vaguely wondering herself about the scientific explanation.

She glances at the clock on her dashboard and looks forward to extended days when there will still be natural light until eight P.M. and when the days will stretch out lazily ahead of her instead of rushing into night. As she pulls into the driveway, she is surprised to see Lawrence's car already parked there. Before she can get out, her cell phone rings. It's Woody. She sends Miles on into the house to greet his dad. She and Woody briefly discuss planning a real date, rather than just holing up in hotel rooms.

When she enters the kitchen from the garage, she is surprised to find turkey burgers sizzling on the stove and Lawrence mixing salad ingredients at the counter. Miles hovers near his father, hopping around on one leg. He wriggles out of his jacket and lets it fall on the floor along with his woolen hat. He grabs Lawrence's pants' leg, giggling. Lawrence puts down the knife and reaches for his son, lifting him up, away from the stove and the counter. "Hey, buddy, did you miss Daddy? I sure did miss you! How was your day?"

Norma and Lawrence move mechanically toward each other, barely brushing lips. "Home early," she remarks. Norma drapes her coat and purse over her arm, carrying them to the hall closet. "Miles, pick up your jacket and hat, please, and put them where they belong."

"I know! In-the-closet-so-Daddy-and-Mommy-won't-get-mad," Miles sings the words like a nursery rhyme.

"That's right."

"Thought I'd get dinner started," Lawrence says. "Bernard called me at the office today. Said he wanted to drop by tonight." Lawrence stands near an assortment of copper pots and pans hanging from an overhead rafter. He reaches for a frying pan and then turns the burgers over with a spatula.

"Yay! Uncle Bernie's coming!" Miles skips around the room singing. He finds his colored markers and construction paper on a shelf and carries them to the table.

Norma sifts through the day's mail, which is stacked in a neat pile on a ledge next to the refrigerator. "So that's why you're home cooking dinner. How much does he want to borrow now?"

"Norma. Please. He didn't say anything about money. He just said he wanted to stop by and see us." Lawrence adds some cooking oil to the second frying pan. "That he hadn't been over in a while."

"Right," she says, hoping to anger him. "Name one time he's come over here without wanting something. Miles, watch out with those markers. You're about to write on the table."

Lawrence opens a plastic package of hamburger buns, spreads them apart, and places them inside the toaster oven attached to the stove. "I came home early so we could eat before he arrived. I didn't think you'd want to eat with him. Did I guess right?" He looks at her, his eyes deep black and unyielding. She used to love those eyes, back when they brought his face to life and welcomed her. Now his face appears as dull and off limits as his briefcase. "French fries or baked potato?" he says to Miles.

"French fries," Miles answers, opening the refrigerator door to get a juice box. "Make them like McDonald's, okay, Daddy?"

"I guessed right. French fries it is. Don't know if I can make them like McDonald's, but I'll try my best, okay?" Lawrence retrieves a bag of frozen French fries from the freezer.

"Miles, you still haven't put your jacket away, and you didn't ask if you could have juice. Lawrence, he had French fries last night." Norma knows she gives Miles a harder time when Lawrence is around because now Miles is the one who gets all of Lawrence's love. In some convoluted way, she hopes to strike at Lawrence through Miles, and although she recognizes the absurdity, control of her actions spirals away from her. She feels like an insolent child who reluctantly realizes she is having no fun and it is her own fault. Miles dashes from the kitchen, clutching the juice box close to him.

Lawrence sets the table, removing Miles's art supplies. Norma turns down the burner on the French fries and pours herself a glass of spring water from the cooler, bringing the condiments and napkins over to the table.

By the time the doorbell rings at around nine, Miles has fallen asleep on the family-room couch, even though he fought valiantly against it. He begged not to be made to go in his bedroom because he didn't want to miss "Uncle Bernie." Norma is in the bathroom when she hears the doorbell. From half a room away she can smell Bernard, the ever-present scent of cigarettes and the dank and repugnant cologne he overuses. Curiously, Lawrence and Miles never seem to notice the odors attached to Bernard.

When she returns to the room, Bernard sits on the couch, stroking Miles's head, which rests on his lap. Lawrence is in the recliner with his shirt unbuttoned and absent his tie. "Nobody tagging along tonight?" Norma says, standing in the doorway, with her arms folded.

"Hey, Norma. Naw, sorry. Just me." He shifts his weight, raising his hips, and fishing in his pants pockets. He retrieves a crushed package of Marlboros and starts tapping on the bottom of it. Then, he meets her disapproving gaze and puts the pack back in his pocket.

Lawrence sits with his socked feet crossed at the ankles and smiles at his brother, gesturing toward Miles. "You see your buddy tried to hang. Wanted to see his Uncle Bernie. Couldn't make it, though."

Bernard laughs. "They must wear them out in day care. Brought him a little car I've been working on for him." Bernard produces it from another pocket, a sand-colored creation carved from a small block of wood. Miles has a collection of three or four such items Bernard has made him. Even Norma has to admit they are clever and enchanting. Bernard lets the toy rest momentarily on Miles's chest, rising and falling with the short breaths he takes in his sleep.

Lawrence puts his arms behind his head and leans back in the recliner. "Norma, do you want to sit?"

"No, that's all right. I'm going to let you all do your male-bonding thing."

Bernard clears his throat a couple of times and sits forward, moving Miles's head slightly. "I wanted to talk to you both. You all have been really good to me over the years." Norma braces herself. With this kind of introduction, he must want big money. Bernard clears his throat one more time and rubs his thighs nervously. Miles stretches beside him, and Bernard strokes his head gently until he settles himself again. Norma can barely contain herself, wanting him to get to the point. She uncrosses and crosses her arms. "As you all know I had a few setbacks in the last few months in terms of my employment. What you don't know is I ended up getting evicted. Been staying with a couple of friends."

"Why didn't you tell me? I could have . . ." Lawrence leans toward Bernard, visibly disturbed.

"Because, like I said, you been too good to me, man, and I hate like hell to disappoint you."

Norma can't believe Lawrence is falling for Bernard's nonsense. How many times is he going to be taken in by him?

"Thought I could take care of it," Bernard continues. "But then when I got laid off, I realized too late, I guess, that I couldn't. Want you all to know I'm . . . really going to get myself together this time. Just started a new job, and in a minute, I'll be on my feet again." He lowers the decibel of his voice. "But I can't stay with my partner any more. Need a place to stay for"—his eyes dart toward Norma—"a couple of months. Put in an application for some apartments. Should be hearing something soon."

"Stay *here?* You can't be serious!" Norma steps all the way into the room and looks at Bernard, then at Lawrence, then back to Bernard. How could Bernard propose something so outrageous? She is certain Lawrence knows better.

"Believe me, I wouldn't be asking if I had any other choice. Didn't want to ask you all for any more help, and to be honest, I guess I didn't think it was really gonna happen. But they don't play with evictions in D.C."

In the midst of tuning Bernard out, Norma hears Lawrence saying, "You sure? Couple of months is all you need?"

Bernard nods his head like a puppet. "I'm thinking what . . . no more than three months at the very most."

"Three months?" Norma is virtually screaming.

"Norma, hold on." Lawrence glances her way only for a moment. "Bernard, you say you've got an apartment lined up?"

"He did not say that!" Norma is incredulous. "Lawrence, have you lost your mind? I can't believe you're even considering this." Her escalated pitch causes Miles to fidget and rub at his eyes.

"Norma, you're waking him up. Can you relax for a minute? This is a serious situation affecting my brother's livelihood." He looks back to Bernard, "And, Bernard, I do have to think about my family's comfort, too, so Norma and I will discuss it and I'll get back to you. All right, man?"

Miles is awake now, fussing and disoriented. Bernard cups his head and pulls him upright, hugging him close. "It's okay, little bud. Uncle Bernie's here. I brought you something. Come on, I'll put you in the bed." He stands and then lifts Miles into his arms and walks past Norma, who is seething. "Be right back," he says.

Norma takes a seat on the couch Bernard abandoned. "Lawrence, what in the world are you trying to do? It's not as if we don't have enough tension in this house already."

"For one moment, would you stop being so selfish. You've got family galore. Parents still living, sister, aunts, uncles, cousins. Bernard is all I have. I know he's got his problems. But he's all I have, understand? I have to help him. It's not that I'm ignoring your needs or the fact that you and he aren't exactly the best of friends. Can we talk about a compromise—what if we limit it to two months instead of three?"

If Lawrence does this against her wishes, any chances of resurrecting communication between them will dissolve for good, she tells herself. "What can I say? You've made up your mind." She stands. "I can't believe you."

"Norma, I'm not trying to make you any unhappier than you are, but how can I turn him down?" Lawrence stands up, too, but doesn't move closer to her. "I don't know how to. Two months, I'm saying. Try to think what good might come of this. He can probably give you a hand with Miles. If he stays in the basement, you won't see him that much, since it's got a separate entrance. He won't have to use the bathroom or anything up here."

"What about eating?"

"Well, we can work that out. Last time I checked, that stove down there worked. Maybe we can give him some pots and pans and get one of those small refrigerators. We're talking sixty days, Norma. That's it. And I'll be firm with him about that."

She walks out of the room, tears pressing against the corners of her eyes.

Bernard moved in on March first. On March second, while she was at the studio, he tried to hard-boil some eggs and forgot about them, burning the bottom of her pot to a crisp and permeating the first floor with the charred odor. "Don't cook up here," she told him. "I thought we made that clear." He said that he couldn't get the downstairs burners to ignite and that he was only trying to thank them by making macaroni salad for dinner. "You have to turn the knobs sharply all the way to the right or they won't come on. And don't worry about fixing dinner for us. The best thanks will be for you to get your job and get your place just as soon as you can."

A week after the burned-pot incident, he overloaded the washing machine, bringing it to a halt mid-cycle. Norma had to call a repairperson, who was unable to come until the next day. She spoke to Bernard through tight jaws, "Take your clothes to the Laundromat from now on, Bernard. I have a child who goes through two, sometimes three outfits a day. I can't afford to have my machine out of commission because you can't follow simple instructions."

• • •

As much as she detests having Bernard in the house, she achieves a warped comfort from his dependence on them and her resultant ability to chastise him. She is glad she remembered to mention his presence to Mrs. Coleman, the housekeeper, so she wouldn't be startled on her days there. Bernard is like a bat, sleeping during most of the day and staying out late at night. She can't imagine how he can find a job with this pattern. To keep from an unpleasant confrontation, she mostly avoids conversing with him. When she asks Lawrence to check on the progress of his job search, Lawrence waves her off with, "Be patient. He'll be out of here soon enough, as agreed."

At the beginning of Bernard's third week, on a Sunday morning, Norma lays out dress clothes for Miles and crams his backpack with his favorite small toys, a coloring book, crayons, and play clothes to change into later. She knows Miles likes the idea of taking the backpack somewhere other than preschool. He sits on his parents' bed, swinging his legs and waiting while Lawrence adjusts his tie in the mirror on his closet door. She's happy the two of them are about to leave her alone, but then remembers Bernard is there, inhabiting the basement. Norma wonders what Moxie would say about Bernard living with them, having been privy to Norma's many complaints about him over the years. She wishes she could share her discomfort with Moxie, but she doesn't want to think of her this morning. She doesn't want to miss her so.

Lawrence is taking Miles to church and then to the park for bike-riding practice. Downstairs, Norma prepares mugs of coffee while Lawrence rolls Miles's miniature turbo bike with training wheels out through the garage. Miles follows closely behind Lawrence as if monitoring the situation. Norma has not pushed Lawrence for the conversation she requested several weeks ago. Instead they maneuver delicately around each other's life, steering clear of conflict or emotional outbursts. For now, this arrangement is tolerable, particularly with Bernard underfoot. After a few minutes, Miles and Lawrence return to the kitchen, ready to leave. Lawrence carries Miles on his shoulders. They walk over to Norma and Miles bends, pushing his lips out for a kiss. She tiptoes to reach him. "Mommy, how come you don't go to church with me and Daddy?" he asks.

Norma reaches for her coffee. "I guess because I think you can do the things they talk about in church without going to church." She doesn't look at Lawrence, who she is sure disapproves of this answer.

"You can't listen to the choir or put money in the basket."

She smiles. "That's true. I'll see you at Grandma and Grandpa's for dinner, okay?"

She sifts through the Sunday newspaper for the movie section, to select something to see with Woody. A half hour later Norma, freshly showered, stands in front of her closet, deciding what to wear. She settles on a knee-length black dress and puts on opaque stockings with flat shoes so she won't look too dressed up.

In the vanity mirror, her complexion doesn't look bad today. She fails to understand why, when she's almost forty, her skin still occasionally insists on sprouting pimples. But, thankfully, there are no new blemishes. She slides a bronze glaze across her lips and smacks them inward. She dumps the curlers out and lifts her fingers through her hair instead of combing it, giving it the tussled look she likes but can't always achieve. She makes a decision to embrace the moment she's in rather than constantly agonize about where she's going or where her relationships are going. It's worth a try at least.

Before leaving the house, she transfers the few dishes in the sink to the dishwasher. She is excited about having a real date with Woody. As she rinses out a cup, she pictures Woody eagerly anticipating their meeting, as well. But the crude smell of smoke reaches her as she stands at the sink. She yanks open the basement door. "Bernard. Bernard!"

"Yo, what's up?" he yells back.

"I smell smoke. You better not be smoking down there!" Her face has turned hot, and she rubs her hand across her forehead.

"I'm not!"

She knows he's lying.

Norma and Woody meet at Fresh Fields in Tenley Circle for a light snack before walking down the street to the movie theater to see *Saving Private Ryan*. It wasn't her first choice, but it's been nominated for an Academy Award, and Woody is very anxious to see it. And she is always interested in analyzing the choices cinematographers make. Woody

tells her he and Reuben are all moved into the Adams Morgan apartment now, and it's starting to feel like a home. He's a bit wistful, but
calmer, she thinks, than when they first met. Before they enter the theater, he squeezes her close to him. The embrace feels to her at once loving, sexual, and endearing. He moves her to a bricked-in corner of the
building that houses the theater and kisses her so deeply she holds her
breath. She wonders fleetingly about someone seeing them, but the
kiss demands her full attention.

The movie has already begun, so it's pitch black inside the theater.
They find seats, share a box of popcorn, and sit, arms entwined, for the
duration. The movie is long and draining and leaves both without
many words. They stand slowly, stretching their legs, while the list of
credits roll along with the soundtrack. Woody helps Norma with her
coat and encircles her shoulder with his arm as they walk up the ramp.
In the lobby, a line of ticket holders has formed for the next showing.
Woody turns up the collar of Norma's coat in preparation for the fickle
weather, which has become cold again. He caresses her face briefly with
one hand and then holds the door open for her, pushing her gently by
the waist. Someone waiting in line calls out, "Hey, Norma!" The unde-
niable voice immobilizes her like a pair of steel shoes. She knows without looking that it belongs to Bernard.

Norma spends most of the following morning volunteering at a bookfair for Miles's day-care center. She throws herself into sorting the
books into categories and setting aside a growing heap of purchases for
Miles. When her mind isn't fully occupied, it continues to sketch
Bernard's sinister smirk at the movie theater. Thankfully, she didn't see
him again last night or this morning. She is glad she has the bookfair
to distract her. Norma enjoys the way her fingers glide across the
smooth, colorful book covers and the fresh scent, almost like the
ocean, of new pages.

The preschool is using the lunchroom for the bookfair. Another
mother has created and placed signs on all the tables, indicating age
and subject categories. Norma dutifully carries piles of books to the
appropriate tables. When Miles's class arrives for their turn viewing the
displayed books, she notices him lingering beside his teacher and

attaching himself to her arm. The teacher doesn't seem to mind, but Norma feels embarrassed. Is he seeking the teacher's affection because he gets too little from Norma? He lurches from the lively but orderly line of three- and four-year-olds and runs to her, folding himself into her skirt. She shows him the books she has selected for him, and he expresses his agreement or disinterest in her choices. A blond boy with a cartoon smile and pudgy fingers stained with finger paint comes over, dragging his mother, and they introduce themselves. "Prentice talks about Miles nonstop," the mother says. Norma smiles. She's unfamiliar with the name, but maybe he's the new boy Miles has mentioned. Miles doesn't want her to leave when the allotted time for his class ends, so she returns with him to his room and sits beside him in a tiny chair while he eats lunch. "Now is it okay for me to go to work?" she asks. He nods his head, yes. When he presses his head down onto her lap, she puts one hand on his back and rubs along his spine, somewhat mechanically. As she continues to rub, though, she is comforted by the warmth she draws from the small form across her knee.

When she arrives at the studio, propped against the upstairs doorjamb is a bouquet of vibrant multicolored mini carnations. She lifts the bouquet and reads the attached note: "Even these lovely flowers can't match your natural fragrance or beauty. Missing and wanting. W." Norma smiles, puts the flowers in a large vase on her desk, and tucks the note into her bra so it will be near her heart. The rest of the day, she gives herself completely to her work.

At home later, she carries Miles upstairs from the den, where he has drifted off to sleep watching a children's video after his bath. He is heavy, and carrying him makes her chest hurt and her breath come out in snatches. I won't be able to do this much longer, she thinks. She accidentally bumps one of his legs against the wall as she rounds the corner to his bedroom, but he doesn't stir.

Norma tucks Miles in the bed, touching her lips to his forehead. He turns on his side, sighing softly and making a sucking movement with his lips. As she switches on his night-light, there is a loud banging sound from below. When she gets downstairs, the noise is even louder. She opens the basement door, yanks the light on, and yells to Bernard.

"What the hell are you doing down there?" He's been there for three weeks and now the basement reeks of his tangy cologne.

His head appears at the base of the banister, and he grins murkily up at her. "Didn't realize you were home yet. Just fixing this broken chair you got here. Thought I'd help out a little, since you all are helping me," he calls up the stairs to her.

"Well, Miles is asleep, and it's a little late for all that noise. That stuff is down there for a reason, okay? It's going to be thrown out."

Bernard comes partially up the stairs. "You know what they say— what's trash to some folks is treasure to other folks." His wide smile ends abruptly. "Like you got that white dude conned into thinking you're some kind of treasure."

"Bernard," she says, swallowing hard. "You can have the chair, all right? Just please fix it at another time." He continues up the stairs and follows her into the kitchen. She notices he's wearing a silk shirt she gave Lawrence several birthdays ago. The strong cigarette odor emanating from his clothes nauseates her.

He stands next to her as she opens the refrigerator. "Oh, you don't want to talk about it, huh? You want to act like nothing's going on. Well, I'm here to tell you, I'm not blind. Now you need to treat me right if you don't want me to spill your dirty-ass secret. You're not going to play me the way you play my brother!" She's forgotten what she wanted from the refrigerator but removes a bottle of juice. He follows her over to the counter where she pours the juice into a glass trying to keep her hand steady. "The first thing I want you to do is tell Lawrence it's all right for me to stay here as long as I need to, 'cause I just might need me a little more than two months. Understand?"

She walks away and out of the kitchen. In the doorway, she turns around. He's in the middle of the kitchen, still watching her. "Fuck you," she hears herself say, and goes back upstairs, forgetting her glass of juice.

She's frustrated that she has no plan devised. When she saw Bernard in the theater lobby yesterday, she knew he might tell Lawrence. She should have known he'd tried to use the information to his advantage. What will Lawrence do? She has no idea because she's no longer connected to his thoughts or feelings. Maybe she should just tell Lawrence herself, first.

She enters the bedroom, turns out the light, and lies down across the bed. Several places on her body ache, although she can't figure out from what. She'll close her eyes until Lawrence comes in, and then she'll decide whether to talk to him. Just as she begins to doze off, she hears Lawrence stumbling up the steps. He trips over something or bumps into it. "Shit," he says. She wonders what his problem is and clicks off the night-table lamp. She hears him enter their bedroom, opening the sliding closet doors with too much force so they resound against each other. Then he staggers past the bed and goes into the adjoining bathroom. Piercing light from the partly open door stabs at her eyes, and she protectively folds her head into the pillow. Lawrence makes gargling and spitting sounds. She hears him fart and then pee. From his actions and the sound of his forceful stream, he's been drinking quite a bit. How in the world did he drive home? The bathroom light goes off. She waits anxiously, arms wrapped around herself. He comes over to her, but he loses his balance and has to catch himself with the wall, sinking heavily onto the bed.

"Lawrence, what's the matter with you?" She smells the liquor as soon as he collapses beside her, arms reaching for her clumsily like he's blind. He peels the blankets off of her and licks at her face the way a dog might. She tries to turn away. He keeps her from moving by holding on to her shoulders. He kneels above her and inches forward until his penis brushes her chin, calling to mind a giant slug. He works it up and down to hardness. "Lawrence." She inches away from him as best she can. "Stop it. What are you doing?" He tries to stick it in her mouth, but she is able to twist her head to one side so it merely grazes her ear. "I said stop it." He keeps trying. She clenches her teeth against him.

"Please," he begs. "Please suck it." She won't.

Finally, he rolls off her wheezing, making the bed shake. She closes her eyes, thankful. She just wants to sleep and make it all go away. "How come I'm not good enough for you anymore, Norma?" he says in a barely recognizable voice.

"What?" she asks into the dark.

"You're probably sucking that white man's dick, why won't you suck mine?" His words linger as he trips on his way out of the room, "Bernard told me about the movies, and I saw the damn flowers today."

It is impossible for Norma to rest. She closes her eyes and puts a pillow over her head, trying to grab at sleep that eludes her the way bubbles do when you try to snatch them from the air. For hours she lies punishing herself with her thoughts until the digital glow of the alarm clock flashes three o'clock in the morning. She rises and puts on a bathrobe, deciding to make sure Lawrence is not passed out in the hall or something. She looks in the guestroom, Miles's room, and the upstairs office. She finds him eating ice cream down in the family room with Bernard. Lawrence sits in the recliner, his back to her. Bernard is stretched out on the couch. Lawrence holds the remote control and pauses at a scene in which a man and woman can't seem to get out of their clothes fast enough. Bernard makes a grunting noise.

"Lawrence," Norma says, entering the room, startling both of them. "Don't you think it's kind of late to be watching TV?"

"Don't wanna sleep," he explains without looking at her. His words slur more than earlier. He must have had more to drink.

"Good movie, though. Called *Saving Ryan's Privates,*" Bernard hoots, and winks at Norma. "Might as well go on back to bed. We got everything covered."

"Can't you see he's drunk, Bernard?" Norma then addresses Lawrence, almost desperately, as though she's playing a game of tug-of-war she didn't agree to. "Lawrence, you need your rest. You have to go in to the office tomorrow."

"Yep, sure do." Lawrence presses the remote again. "So no point in going to bed now, is there?"

"We *were* engaged in a much needed man-to-man, brother-to-brother talk," Bernard interjects, sitting up. "Before we were interrupted. So if you don't mind." Bernard twists the top from a beer bottle he takes out of a six-pack that she hadn't noticed on the rug.

"Yeah. Go back to bed, Norma." Lawrence fumbles and drops the remote, and when he leans forward to pick it up, he almost slides off his chair.

"Whatever," Norma says, disgusted with both of them. She returns to the bedroom and lies on her back, breathing deeply and counting silently on the exhaled breath, as her old tai chi teacher suggested for relaxation. She tenses her muscles and releases them, beginning with her toes and ending with the muscles in her face. A welcome yawn emerges, but sleep remains unattainable.

Monday, March 15th
Tommy jeans
gray Tommy T-shirt
  (Allegra loaned me)
blk Nikes

Dear Sistergirl:

  Damn! Allegra beat me to it. She and Roberto got their freak on today after school. She was tripping hard. She said, girl, there is no way to describe it, you just have to experience it. I'm like, come on. You're never at a loss for words. She was just like, it's vicious, it's straight up vicious.

  That's it. I'm the last one to go, but I'm next, damn it.

  We got measured for costumes tonight. I'll have one white tutu with silver trim and one black with gold trim. Miss Snow added some new choreography to my Odile section. Four fouetté turns and a grand jeté. The dance is more difficult, but it's wet, I must admit. And after sixteen, four fouettés are nothing. Sonya's fouettés did not look as good as mine tonight. I'm sorry, they just didn't. They looked better at the DTH tryouts. I don't know what happened after that. Miss Snow got on her case today and said, Sonya, you look like you're trying to make a cake with your foot. Miss Snow could write a whole book of ballet snaps.

  I paged Octavius at nine. He called me back at eleven-fifteen. I thought Ma was in bed, but she started yelling for me to get off the phone, practically in her damn sleep. Forgot to turn the ringer down. I talked to him for about twenty more minutes. He kept putting his Walkman to the phone. He wanted me to hear this rapper named Juvenile. I said, Are you crazy? He said, crazy about you. He said he's not going to call me unless I page him first because he doesn't want Ma to know he's talking to me (which I don't either, for real). Then he said, When you gonna let me slide? I said, I don't know, who said I was? Who said I like you anyway? I like playing that game. He liked it too, I could tell. Oh shit, he says, first you was Miss I Can't Wait now you Miss Hard to Get. He asked me could I make up an excuse to get out of school early on Friday. I said I would try. (You know I will.) We hung up but it took me forever to get back to sleep trying to work out this plan in my head: Allegra can copy my mother's handwriting. Ma is always writing me messages and hanging them on the refrigerator. I'll stick one of those in my book bag for Allegra to see. Once Allegra wrote a note and signed it from her mom saying she couldn't go to Lacrosse practice cause she had her period (but she really just didn't feel like it) and you would never know her mother didn't write that daggone note.

Wednesday, March 17th
black jean skirt
black/white checked top
white Nikes

Dear Sistergirl:

Me and Allegra have had to figure this sex stuff out all on our own with the help of some novels, two school assemblies, Allegra's brother Alton's nasty magazines, and our friends. This is where my white school friends come in very handy because most of them have already done it. A couple of them have even had abortions. Most parents can't help with decisions about sex, even though they might try to act like they can. (I could probably talk to Norma, but since she and Ma are going through their changes, I don't think I should bother her.) Allegra's mom gave her some library books about teenage girls and their bodies, but the girls on the cover looked so weird that we didn't even read them. They had on old-fashioned sweaters with bras that made their breasts stick out like ice cream cones. It was probably written in caveman days. All Allegra's father said was, if she gets pregnant, she can't live there anymore. Allegra says her parents never figured out that Alton used to sneak girls in his room on the weekends, before he went away to Morehouse.

Ma is always giving me books that she thinks will answer my questions. Sometimes I read them; sometimes I don't. There were only three I liked: Finding Our Way (more informational than the other two), Sugar in the Raw (essays by girls my age), and Am I the Last Virgin? (a novel which was off the hook good). Every couple of weeks Ma will try to talk to me about sex, but she does it in such a weird way. It's always when we're in the car. I guess cause that's where we spend most of our time. I never say anything when she wants to have those talks, and I always know when she's about to start one. She does this fake cough thing first. Then she pretends she's not uncomfortable when she really is, and that makes me uncomfortable. I don't want to talk to her about that stuff anyway, so I just sit there and think about something else, like my dance steps, or how I want my tattoo to look. Dad is weird in a different way. He does stuff like he'll put his arm around my shoulders or my waist and say, Any youngbloods try this with you yet? What makes parents think those kind of approaches will teach their teenagers anything except to avoid talking to them at all costs?

Friday, March 19th
blk Parasuco jeans
gray sweater shirt
blk platform boots

Dear Sistergirl:
I can't believe what I did today. This is the whole thing from the beginning:
Allegra wrote the note, it looked pretty good but not perfect. I made her do it like five times, until I guess I got on her nerves and she was like, no, this is the last time. The note said I had to leave school early to go to

the doctor. There is a new person in the front office. Thank goodness for that! I got a little nervous when she stared at it for so long. Anyway it worked, and I got an early dismissal. O met me in front of Starbucks. I thought he was going to take the bus up there. He was late, but he finally pulled up in a Chevy Blazer. I said, is this your car? He said it was his cousin's. He said he got lost because he doesn't usually go that far up into white people's town. We drove around Wisconsin Avenue, and he let me drive one block! We parked and walked around in Mazza Gallerie— and white people followed us around in the stores and shit. (Just like when I go in stores near school with Windy and they watch me, never her.) Anyway, Octavius said, I wish they would do something, I wish they would make me take off my Eddie Bauer coat so I could sue them for discrimination and win me and you some funds. But nothing happened except for us getting mad. We got back in the Blazer and drove down the street and got some pizza from Armand's and ate it in the car. He paid like he was supposed to. I told him I didn't think I was ready to do it today. I kept thinking about him telling me he ain't never been with no virgin before.

This is what he had on: A gray sweatshirt with a hood on it like the kind they sell in the Gap, but I couldn't tell (later on when it was lying on his bed, I saw the tag and it was from the Gap), and black Levi's jeans with black Timberlands. He said he liked what I had on and that we kind of matched. I spilled some pizza on my pants right when he said that.

His cell phone kept ringing but he didn't answer except once when he checked the caller ID. He was like, whassup, dog? Yeah, a'ight. Yeah. Yeah. I'm a be out of commission for a little while. Then he hung up and turned it off. That meant a lot to me cause I knew he was going to concentrate on me.

He told me he's going to give me funds to get a full set of acrylic nails cause I was talking about this new place in the mini-mall near Allegra's off Chillum Road. Roberto paid for her to get hers done there. I felt so good driving around in that nice car, and O was acting like I was his bun for real. I was getting nervous even though I'd been acting on the phone like us doing it was no big thing. But in person, face-to-face, it felt different. He said, how are you going to show me your appreciation when I get your nails done? I said, I don't know. How do you want me to show

*it? He said, how do you usually show people you like their gifts? I said,
sometimes I hug them or kiss them. We got to a red light. So I leaned over
and closed my eyes. He leaned over too, and we kissed. It was just a short
kiss, closed mouth, but I like how his lips felt pressing against mine. His
top lip is shaped like a heart that's been stretched out. Then he said, that
kiss seemed like you just liked it a little. So at the next red light, I was
like, okay, and leaned over again. This time he pulled me over closer to
him, but I bumped into the steering wheel, so he had to lean the other
way, and he put his right arm around my shoulders. And we tongue-
kissed until somebody honked. Afterwards, he said, You sure do taste
good. Do you taste that good all over? I didn't know what to say. (When
I told this to Allegra a few minutes ago, she said, Oh my God, he is so
advanced.)*

*Everything was cool until I asked him if he had condoms. It was hard
enough asking the question, but then he got all stupid. He said, girl, I
don't have no diseases or nothin'. Do I look like I have somethin'? Then
he put his hands out to the side like he was saying, look me over. He even
lifted up his shirt while he was driving, and he unzipped his pants a
little, probably just showing off his Versace underwear. (Which he says
costs $80, but he bought them wholesale.) Anyway, he's so crazy. I was
laughing when he was doing that stuff. But then I told him all I learned
about AIDS. I asked him if he knew who all the girls he did it with had
done it with. He acted like I was kirking out and said he didn't know
how to put them joints on. (I didn't tell him I do, since me and Allegra
have practiced a million times on bananas.)*

*I noticed that outside was kind of gloomy looking. You know, gray
with no clouds showing. I was thinking, this is a big day for me. It
should be sunny and bright, with birds chirping all over the place. But I
didn't take it as a bad sign or anything.*

*We drove past a 7-Eleven, and I reminded him again about the
condoms. He told me to stop tripping. I said, you stop tripping. He said,
how come you don't want no babies? How come you don't want no baby
by me? I was like, do you have a baby? He was like, not that I know of,
but I wouldn't mind. Then he goes, you lucky I like you. He went in the
store with an attitude. I didn't care. I wanted to do it with him and
everything, but I'm not going to be stupid. I didn't go inside with him.*

He was still a little mad when he came out. He said, I'm a use it this time, but that shit don't feel the same. You wouldn't know cause you a virgin. I looked at him to see if he was really mad cause if he was, I was about to tell him to take me back to the metro. (He wasn't.) He started laughing and said I was a trip. Then he put his face next to mine. It felt hot and soft at the same time.

When we got out the car, he put his arm around me all of a sudden and gave me a bear hug, pulling me way over so I almost tripped. Something like Alton, Allegra's brother, would do to us. Then he started laughing. I took my backpack off my arm and hit him with it, or tried to hit him with it, but he jumped out the way too quick. Then I started chasing him until I got out of breath. I thought you was in shape, he said, and he was laughing again. I was thinking, hello, I am in shape. Better shape than you.

We got to the yard in front of his apartment building. It had little patches of grass sticking up and a rusty swing set at the side of the building. Some broken-up plastic toys were on the ground. He kicked them when we were walking. I knew Octavius was kind of poor, I guess, but I didn't exactly know how poor he was. There were broken windows all over the place, and trash on the steps inside the front door and along the hallway. I started to wish I had listened to Allegra, who told me I should put some sheets in my book bag in case the sheets weren't clean. She's a trip, though. I'm like, how are you going to embarrass somebody and say boo, I got my own clean sheets with me in case yours are dirty. That would be so foul. I just figure he turns out the light and I don't look at the sheets. I could hear people talking, laughing, and playing music through the doors of the other apartments when we were walking up the steps. I was thinking, why aren't they at work? Are they all on welfare or what? He passed somebody he knew on the steps, another guy, who looked at my breasts. They just nodded at each other and said, Whassup, son.

He has three locks on his apartment door. I stayed near the door when we first walked in. It smelled like someone had been cooking pancakes in there. Then he told me to come with him. From the outside I didn't expect it to be so neat on the inside. No dishes left in the kitchen sink, like at my house. I mean the place still had kind of a poor look because the furniture was like the kind you see in those Rent-A-Center stores. I

stood there with my backpack on and started feeling like I had to go to
the bathroom. He showed me where it was, and that was real clean, too,
but of course I still put the tissue down on the seat. Part of the bathroom
tile was ripped back and the pipes and wood floor underneath looked like
you'd get a million splinters if you stepped on it. I could hear the heat
coming up through the pipes. It sounded like a high-pitch baby
screaming. I was thinking, man, I'm finally really about to do this thing.
I'm here and there aren't any parents or anything to hold me back. I
looked in the mirror and asked myself, Zadi, is this really what you want
to do? Yes, I answered myself. I'm ready. I stayed in the bathroom a
minute or two longer going over everything I liked about him, trying to
reassure myself, I guess, that I couldn't wait for someone better.

I turned on the faucet so he wouldn't hear me flush the toilet.

When I came out, I was trying to just act chill. I put my backpack
down on the floor and sat in a chair. He had a lot of posters and stuff on
the walls. Tupac, of course, his idol and mentor. Magazine pictures of
Master P, Nas, and Method Man. Even though there were all those
posters on the walls, they didn't cover up the cracks and holes in the
plaster. He turned on the CD boom box that was on top of his dresser,
and started blasting rap music. Damn, it was so loud my ears were
throbbing. I said, you're going to play rap NOW? So then he put on some
R. Kelly. That was better. I walked across the room and looked out the
window cause I didn't know what else to do. I could just see down into
the back of his complex. He closed the blinds even though there wasn't
any sun or anything coming in. He sat down on the bed, which looked
flat and bumpy at the same time, and smoothed it out with his hands.

Octavius took his shoes off and his shirt. That was when I saw all the
muscles in his chest and his tattoo, which was sexy and wet as hell. He
looked at me and said, you know what, you look like a dark-skinned
Aaliyah with your hair like that. Then he said, what you gonna do—
stand over there all day holding up the wall? For real, I was just standing
there, like I didn't know what to do. Which I didn't. No, I said, and sat
down next to him but with a little space left in between us. I took off
my boots.

We sat there for a few more minutes. I looked at my watch a couple of
times and thought about how if I was in school I would be just getting

out of fourth period Spanish. Then he lay back on the bed. What you gonna do—just sit there with your sweater on? I took my sweatshirt off and threw it onto the chair. Come here, he said. It sounded pretty sexy, but I was thinking why couldn't he come to me? But I lay back on the bed beside him. I felt a little cold lying there in just my bra and my Parasuco jeans. He leaned up and reached around me, took my right hand, which was by my side, and put it around him. Then he slid a little closer to me and said, for real, you never did this before?

I felt like I could have started crying, but I didn't. I didn't know why he didn't believe me, but I didn't say anything. Then he said, for real? He was like, oh, shit. Then he kind of laughed and told me about some friend of his who said there ain't no virgins in D.C. He said, I'm a tell him there is one, but by that time you ain't gonna be one no more, right? I'm a show you everything so you'll be a old pro after this. I'm not gonna hurt you. He sounded so grown I had to remind myself that he is only a year older than me. He'll be seventeen in July. R. Kelly was singing, Like a hotel room I'm checking into you. It was off the hook perfect.

He kissed my neck and stuck his tongue in my ear. It was kind of cold at first, like when the doctor checks your ears with that instrument, but then it got warmer and started feeling good! He kissed me again and sucked my tongue real hard. At the same time he was trying to move my legs apart with his leg. I could feel his thing pressing through his jeans. I kept my eyes closed because I didn't want to look at him and even though he shut the blinds, there was still a lot of light in that room. Move around the other way, he said in a different voice. Like he was the director for real. I didn't know what he meant. So he helped me move around until he was on top of me. My cheeks hurt from him sucking my tongue so hard. Then he started rubbing my breasts real fast like he was washing them. I tried to get into another position so it wouldn't hurt so much, but he was trying to unsnap my bra. I reached behind and did it for him. He was panting real hard by then. He put his head down and started kissing and sucking on my breasts. He kept doing it, and breathing loud. He did everything too hard, and I couldn't help saying, ow. He said, did that hurt? and he sounded surprised.

From then on, he did things softer, and it felt pretty good. He kissed all the way down my stomach and started to open up my jeans. Why y'all

*got to wear these tight joints all the time? he said. I sat up on my elbows
and helped him pull them off. We didn't look each other in the face,
though. His pants were already off; he just had his drawers on, but I
couldn't figure out when that happened. Maybe when he was kissing my
breasts? I don't know. Damn, he said. Your body is vicious as shit.*

*I felt good when he said that because I work hard to have a nice body.
Next thing I know he was on top of me trying to push himself into me
even though we both still had on our underwear. I didn't want him to
forget about the condom. He was kissing my neck (or I should say
practically biting it), and he told me to kiss his neck. So I did, and it was
nice, us both doing that together. Then I could feel him pulling my
panties down. Here we go, I told myself. He got them down to my knees
almost and couldn't get them off cause our legs were mixed together and
he was trying to get his off, too. I had to reach one hand over and pull
them down. Then I ran one foot up my leg to pull the panties off.*

*I could feel him in between me then. I don't know how to describe it
because it's not like anything I've ever felt before. He was breathing
extremely hard, like he was lifting heavy furniture. Condom, I forced
myself to say, keeping my eyes clenched.*

*He said, Shit, Zadi! You keep trippin'! But he got up. I opened my
eyes. I saw his butt!! It was hard and round and small. He looked like he
was kind of mad fumbling around in his pants pockets, and then I heard
him tearing the package. He fumbled around some more. I didn't look,
just waited. Then he came back and got on top of me again. He was a
little heavy, but it wasn't unbearable. He leaned over and started kissing
my breasts again. I took a deep breath in case he was going to do it all
hard like before, but he didn't. I was looking down into the top of his
head. When he moved his body up, I could feel his stuff. He stopped
kissing my breasts and started touching me down there. I closed my eyes,
then I opened them. I was kind of scared about seeing his eyes, though,
but he was looking down. He licked one finger and then he put that
finger in me, kind of like how Miss Zoe, the school librarian, does when
she turns the page of a book. I arched my back cause I wasn't expecting
him to do that. Next he started pushing himself into me. I kept my eyes
closed. He kept jerking himself forward, but it seemed like it wasn't going
in at first. He kept pushing, making all these animal type noises, and I*

was making sounds, too, cause it was hurting at first. He stopped for a second and then he tried again. That time it went in. It still hurt, but I held my breath and after a while it felt kind of nice and different all at the same time. With one of those pushes, it felt like he went in all the way up to my stomach. I guess I screamed, and he said, shh, girl, *and covered my mouth. I was too scared to open my eyes then.*

He moved back and forth inside me, rocking like a rocking chair. I didn't know what I was supposed to do, so I tried to move my pelvis around the way people do when they have sex in the movies. I guess that was right because it made him breathe harder, but we were both moving at different times. I didn't say anything. I sure wasn't going to make those cat noises like Fawna. When we seemed like we were moving together, he had this spasm thing and I was wondering, did he come? He kind of collapsed after that. All out of breath, he told me I learned quick. After a few minutes we did it a couple more times. And, yes, he used all the condoms in the pack!!! After like the third time, I was tired and sore and he was tired, so we just lay there on the bed. He kept his arms around me, but we had to adjust ourselves a little cause he said I was crushing his leg. He asked if I wanted to smoke some weed, but I reminded him that I don't do that. So he put his underwear back on, got up, and was messing with the boom box. R. Kelly had already gone off. He ended up just turning on 95.5 and got a joint out of his drawer. He smoked it while he was lying there beside me. This some crucial shit, *he said to me, and then started coughing.* Sure you don't want none? That's all right, *I said, and turned my face away so I wouldn't get a contact. He was coughing and choking and everything.*

She Got Skills came on the radio, and he said, that's you, boo. You do better than some girls who ain't no virgins. *That made me feel good. All of a sudden I was cold, so he pulled the covers up over us. I wanted to go to the bathroom, but I didn't want to get up all naked and walk out in front of him. Holding the blanket up over my breasts, I looked around and found my sweatshirt on the floor all balled up. I put it back on. It almost covered my butt, and I kept pulling it down in the back when I got up and went to the bathroom. He laughed at me and said,* I already seen your ass, Shorty. Who you calling Shorty? *I asked him. I went into the bathroom and looked around for a clean*

washcloth. There was a whole pile of towels and washcloths on top of
the radiator, so I took one and put some water on it and washed myself
carefully. There was some blood, but I was expecting that. I was so sore
and it stung so much when I peed that it made my eyes water. I
wondered if there was blood on Octavius's bed, but I never did see any.
I also wondered if I came, you know that is supposed to be the big
thing. Allegra says it usually doesn't happen the first time. She is still
waiting for it. Me, too, I guess.

When I came back from the bathroom, O got up and went. He looked
kind of skinny walking away. He came back, and I asked him how old
he was when he first did it. He told me he was about ten. I didn't believe
him at first. He said he was with Reebok, the one whose funeral we met
at. He used to live somewhere nearby and they had a clubhouse in the
laundry room in Reebok's apartment building. They used to hang out
there, smoking weed and stuff. There were these girls who he said would
give it up to anybody. All you had to do was promise to take them
shopping or buy them some Pampers for their little kids. They were like
fourteen or fifteen, and Octavius did it with both of them. I was
wondering wasn't his thing too small to fit in anybody, but I didn't
ask him.

We had one of our best conversations ever. I can see how having sex
can really bring you closer to the person. I can remember most of it.

Him: Before I did it with them girls I was scared as shit, man. I
thought it was like a snap turtle up there or something. I thought it was
gonna snap my shit off.

But Reebok did it first, and O watched him and saw that he got it
back. While he was telling me the story, he started looking sad. You can
tell he probably never cries because he started acting mad instead.

Me: Was Reebok your best friend? (Kind of a dumb question, I guess.)

Him: I don't be calling nobody my "best friend" and shit, but I don't
have nobody like him now. But, yeah, he was my dog, for real. We could
talk about anything really. And he taught me so much shit. Reebok had
dreams, man. Believe me. But he didn't have a chance. Both his folks was
on crack. His mother was tricking with niggas in the stairwell in his
building. It was like that. He was always picking her ass up, dragging
her in the house. My mother been on that shit, too. My old man's on

lockdown and he's crazy as fuck—I don't even go visit his raggedy ass no more. See—Reebok's life, my life—they ain't no PG rated movies.

Me: If Reebok's mother used crack, then how come he was selling it?

Him: What else he gonna do? He didn't smoke it hisself, but shit, if some nigga wants to do it, somebody got to be there to sell it to him. Why not him? He didn't sell to no kids or nothin' like that.

Me: But if he saw what it did to his parents, why would he want to do that to somebody else's?

Him: Man, that soft thinking. That's how girls think. You can't be thinkin' like that out here, man. Can't afford it. You can't be worrying about this one over here and that one over there. You just worry about yourself, you know what I'm sayin'?

We were lying back on the bed. I leaned up on my elbow to look at him. I asked him what I had been dying to know for a long time—did he still sell drugs? I mean, all those times when he didn't call me back what was he doing? He didn't answer right away, and then he said he's trying to get out of it. He told me that I don't know what it's like. He was just like Reebok, trying to save his family by working for Brotherman. Reebok got set up by Brotherman because Reebok's mother stole some of his cocaine and Brotherman didn't want to hear that sob story. Reebok tried to get the money back by selling what he had left, but in smaller portions so he could make more money from less. He ran into some crooked cops, though, who hooked him and told him to sell it all and give them the money. O said they told Reebok, We your pimp now. So Reebok didn't have the money to pay Brotherman back. That's how he knows Brotherman is the one who took Reebok out. That's when O made up his mind to get out, but he got arrested and the police took his drugs, too, which meant he owed Brotherman $500. I guess that's when Ma came back into the picture. He told me he thought Brotherman was going to kill him, too. I think he's still worried about that. I asked him if he has a gun. He got an expression like he wasn't sure if he should tell me the truth or not.

Him: You not gonna tell your mother, right?

That scared me, but I wanted to see it. He opened one of his drawers and showed it to me. He said Reebok gave it to him and that Reebok said it was a .25 caliber piece of crap. Brotherman is the one with all the

guns. He was supposed to give O something better, before O stopped
hanging with him. I said, so now you're back on the right track going to
school and whatnot? He said, you sound like your mother. Then he said,
but what difference do it really make? If I go to school, or if I go to jail?
If I keep my appointments, or if I don't? If I work for the DJ, or if I
don't? He said he has to keep working for Brotherman part-time till he
makes back what he owes or for real Brotherman's going to take him out.
He says he's usually home by his curfew, but then he goes back out again.
That's why sometimes he can't always call me and why he's too tired to go
to school sometimes.

I told him: I'm sorry, I don't believe your life has to be like this.
Especially if you're going to be my boyfriend for real. I know you had it
hard, but there's other people who had it hard too. Maybe I haven't had it
that bad, but I do know you can't just give up cause it's hard. At that
moment I felt really good cause we had screwed (to use Norma's word) and
we were talking like she said wouldn't happen if a guy just liked your body.
But this isn't something I can discuss with her, at least not right away.

Then he started tripping. He goes: Boo, (I love when he calls me boo
or his bun) you sound good and I know you a smart girl and all. You go
to that white girl school and everything. But you got a soft life. That's
what you got to understand. You messin with me cause you want to see
what it like on the other side, but you ain't gonna stay with nobody like
me. You can't even tell your mother you seeing me. I ain't stupid. I know
you just here for a field trip or some science project type shit.

I don't know if he's right or not. He sounded a little sad and he was
holding me with one arm around my shoulder. I told him, you never
know what the radio station job might lead to. He was like, yeah, but it
ain't much money, but he said he knows he can probably slip his own
demo in there. And then he kind of cheered up. He said somebody might
discover him and then he'll blow up and I'll be a famous ballerina. Who
knows, we might just end up chilling together when we're old and gray. I
asked him what his theme song would be. He was like, what are you
talking about? He's never even seen Ally McBeal before. (All he watches is
RapCity, Oz, Real World, and stuff like that—one of his neighbors
hooked their cable up for only forty dollars.) He said his theme song
would be Gangstarr's Moment of Truth cause it talks about life for real.

After all that talking he started messing with my breasts again and looking like he wanted to do it again. But we were out of condoms and I realized I was close to being late for ballet, and you know I can't play that with Miss Snow, so I told Octavius I had to leave. He said, okay, but when was I gonna let him slide again? I said that takes planning. He said, well, start making some plans then. Then he said, Zadi, how you get to stay a virgin so long, phat as you are? I kind of laughed and said, I don't know. He said, well, I'm glad you waited for me. You glad? He surprised me when he said that. I told him, yeah. (And that was true.) Then he said something about how he doesn't usually mess around with dark-skin girls. He said I'm dark as midnight but fine as wine. I guess it was a compliment.

I thought about telling Zora when I got to dance class, but I didn't cause we were never by ourselves. I was still sore and it hurt to lift my legs, but you know I had to. When I got home I couldn't wait to close my door and call Allegra. Ma kept telling me to get off the phone and do my homework. Allegra said, well, finally, dog! Welcome to the real world.

All right, so that's my whole story. To be honest, it was jive different from what I thought. I could have used some more hugging and kissing, though. That and the talking afterward was the best part.

Eighteen | Thoughts about Woody, and his increasing significance in her life, as well as the disturbing episode with Lawrence earlier in the week eddy through Norma's mind. On Saturday morning, she travels Interstate 95 south toward Richmond to photograph several generations of the Covington family. Lawrence's behavior exposed his distress about her affair, but after that night they both returned to their previous stances. Surface conversations only, no tackling of the issues. It bothers her that she's been just as cowardly as he, but it hasn't bothered her enough to recast herself. Woody, on the other hand, has been loving and responsive. He told her how worried he was after Bernard saw them together, but she assured him nothing had come of it. She saw no reason to tell Woody about all that drama.

Norma glances down at John Covington III's directions lying on the passenger seat. Her Richmond exit is the next one. When she first contemplated the four-hour round-trip drive, she wasn't enthused. But the opportunity to photograph one of Richmond's premier black families eventually outweighed the travel time. Once in Richmond she makes a wrong turn but can't figure out her mistake. She pulls into an Exxon station and gives the street address to an older black man smoking a cigar beside the soda machine. "You must be going to the Covington estate." He squints at her, sizing her up as if evaluating her presentability. He seems respectful and in awe of the Covington family as he dispenses new directions. "Give my regards to Big Mary when you get there!" he shouts. "My nephew went to Duke with one of her grandsons, but she don't know me from Adam." He laughs heartily and continues puffing on his cigar, his shoulder wedged against the vending machine.

According to the old man, she doesn't have much further to travel. Sure enough, half a mile down the main stretch is a small street sign that reads, "Covington Lane." Norma wonders what it must do for your self-esteem to live on a street that intentionally bears your family name. The road is gravel at first and then, as it narrows, smooth black tar. It is tree-lined and curved. Some of the trees are beginning to show signs of leaves again. This drive will be heavenly in a few weeks, she thinks, noting the varied shapes and sizes of the sparse trees and bushes against the sky with its whipped-cream clouds. Another sign, done in calligraphy and mounted on a pole in the ground, announces, "Covington Manor and Estates." She continues slowly around the bend at less than five miles per hour past additional signs indicating the stables, the bathhouse, the servant quarters, the rose garden, and the greenhouse. Narrower roads radiate from the curved one she is on, apparently leading to those places. She wonders what the acreage is of this place, but she can't see the land boundaries and is still cruising along the curved road. A cluster of small white cottages emerge on her right. Another more elaborate sign: Covington Manor. At last.

She checks her time. An hour and a half before the appointed time. She had hoped to have two hours to set up, but this will have to do. A large wrought-iron gate stops her from driving any further. Turning to the second page of directions, she reads that she must use the phone attached to the gate. The voice on the phone gives further instructions, and the gate parts magically for her. She would have liked Miles to see it.

Although she knows this is a family of considerable wealth, she is unprepared for the massive stone structure that confronts her at the end of the driveway. It sits on a hill of sorts, like an enormous crown. Norma counts twenty widely spaced windows and three doors in the front of the house alone. Huge rocks or boulders are embedded in the solid gray mortar of the house and those boulders are in turn encrusted with smaller rocks and pebbles. She puts the car in park and takes out her camera to photograph the house, the afternoon sun highlighting the texture of the stones.

A man in a three-piece suit holding a walkie-talkie to his mouth walks up to the car while she's shooting the house. "Miss Simmons-Greer? We'll park the car for you. Do you have anything to carry inside?" She can't remember the last time she saw someone wearing a three-piece suit.

"Yes," she says, pointing to the backseat that holds her fold-up cart, camera bags, and equipment. He opens the car door for her and takes her keys, directing her to the front entrance. Another man, taller and younger than the first and dressed in a sports jacket without a tie, opens the intricately carved middle door for her before she has climbed all the front steps. "Good afternoon, Ms. Simmons-Greer. Mr. Covington is expecting you." She is still admiring the thickness of the wood and the designs in the door when he asks to take her coat. Norma feels proud that black people are at the helm of this kind of fortune. The ceiling above her is two stories high and covered with a hand-painted floral pattern. A shimmering double chandelier dangles between the foyer and the vast swirl of a liberally carpeted staircase. Several elaborately framed watercolors of oceans, boats, and fruit-and-flower still lifes line the walls of the stairway.

"Just one minute. Let me check to see if the room is ready." The man disappears with her coat slung across one of his arms. She is glad he has left her for a moment. She can admire everything more fully, without seeming like such an awed tourist. The decor is definitely rooted in the sentiments of another generation, from the large painted roses on the floor tiles to the heavy brocade valances above the rows of lace-draped windows. But some of the antiques are exquisite, she has to admit, even if she wouldn't put them in her own home. There are two oversized oriental vases on either side of a large chest. Behind her a stained-glass window graces the area above the front door. It depicts the classical masks of tragedy and comedy. In each corner of the enormous foyer are oak and marble tables supporting arrangements of fresh-cut roses in several shades of red. The exquisite size and fragrance of the roses make Norma want to visit the garden before she departs. Dazzled by the visual stimulation of the place, Norma is startled when the man in the sports jacket returns and informs her the room is now ready. She decides he must be the butler.

She follows him through a long hall maze of richly draped walls until they arrive at the designated room. Over the phone, Norma told Mr. Covington she needed a room that received plenty of natural afternoon light, and this one is in the west wing of the house. The room, four times the size of her living room, contains four evenly spaced pillars toward the center. Each pillar has a circular, cushioned loveseat attached to it. A long couch and two armchairs have been set up near the windows. There are three rows of benches arranged like steps behind the couch and chairs. Her equipment has been stacked near one of the chairs. The wooden floor is so highly polished it bears the shimmer of an ice rink. Bright sunlight peeks through the lavishly laced windows. She asks the butler to pull the curtains back and to move some of the furniture around so that the light will shine where she wants. He begins to accommodate her as Mr. Covington enters, revealing widely spaced teeth when he smiles. He grasps both her hands and shakes vigorously. All she knows about him is that he is in his late sixties and is a physician, as were his father and grandfather. His grandfather, the family patriarch, was one of the first black doctors in Richmond.

"This is the cotillion room. Does it meet with your approval?" Mr. Covington is a squat, stockily built man who flings his arms out to his sides when he speaks, as if gathering in the entire room.

"Oh, yes," she says. "I've never seen anything as breathtaking. You've had cotillions here?"

"Every year since, I think, 1924 the Negro debutantes of Richmond have held cotillions here. It can hold one thousand people standing and eight hundred with chairs. Although we've had fewer requests the last few years." He shakes his head with emphasis. "People don't think it's important to teach kids etiquette and the finer things in life nowadays, but, I tell you, it might eliminate some of the problems we're seeing."

"Do you live here?"

"No, this was my grandfather's house. His only living child is my aunt, Big Mary. Mary Covington Davis. She was the baby and the only girl. His sons, including my father, moved out when they grew up, but

Mary never did. Even when she married. She's eighty-two now, a widow, and lives here with her two daughters. We call her Big Mary. You'll meet them all very soon." He watches as she sets up the tripod and begins to take readings with the light meter. She holds her hand up, flipping it front and back like a fan, to gauge the shadows. Mr. Covington excuses himself, after making sure Norma doesn't need anything else. She continues setting up her artificial lighting in accordance with her readings.

When Norma is almost ready for them, a few people begin noisily drifting into the room. Some saunter in and others walk painfully with canes. Mr. Covington brings two large-boned women over to Norma. Norma is relatively short in stature, but these women, at nearly six feet, tower over her. Although they have finger-waved blue-gray hair and wrinkled necks, they wear identical purple chiffon dresses and matching bow-toed shoes. With their height and very small breasts, they both remind Norma of Olive Oyl. "Ms. Simmons-Greer, these are my cousins, the twins, Big Mary's daughters: Valencia Covington Douglas and Vonecia Covington Jacobs."

Norma shakes their hands, "A pleasure to meet you." The two women purse their lips into a strained smile and then walk over to the arrangement of chairs and benches.

Mr. Covington whispers, "They were both widowed within a year of each other, and neither of them had any children."

"That's quite something," Norma says. She wonders if they always dress alike, as well, but doesn't ask, because he is ushering others over to meet her.

A young man in a military uniform holding the hands of two small children is introduced as John III's great-nephew. When the children squirm, he calls them to attention and they immediately salute. Norma laughs as she thinks of attempting that with Miles but stops herself when she notices, by the expressions of Mr. Covington and his nephew, that the salute was not meant to amuse. She is introduced to more people than she can possibly keep track of. John, Sr., had five children who all had children, and most of them had children. Apparently everyone still lives in and around Richmond, except for the nephew who travels with the military. The photo shoot was planned around his schedule.

The family members mill about and seem to be arranging their own seating. She hears one of the aunts say to one of the cousins, "Don't you remember where you're supposed to be?"

"Excuse me," Norma says, walking over to the expansive group. "Don't worry about where you're sitting or standing right now. I'm designing that as we speak, according to the colors you're wearing, your height and age, where the light falls, those kinds of considerations. No need for you to be concerned at all with the seating arrangement, okay?" As she addresses them, she notices that they eye one another almost incredulously. Mr. Covington's brother, Richard Convington, explains, "Didn't John tell you? We usually sit in a certain order. Big Mary won't want to change that." Everyone nods and mumbles in agreement. She senses they are disturbed by her suggestion of a change. Alarmed even.

Big Mary has not arrived as yet, although it is almost three-fifteen and they had agreed to a three o'clock shoot. Norma opens the back of her camera and loads the film. She will, of course, respect Big Mary as an elder, but she will not allow her to direct the photography shoot. After all, that is why they hired her, isn't it? Her "particular artistic talent," what she can "uniquely bring to this year's family portrait," were the words Mr. Covington used. And he said something at the exhibit about her ability to capture what was in their "hearts and heads."

A boy, perhaps nine or ten, with licorice eyes, dressed in a navy blue, gold-buttoned suit, politely excuses himself and asks, "What do you have to study in school to be a photographer?"

"What a great question!" she says. "You have to study everything— you have to study very hard, too. Because a photographer needs to be able to notice details and be aware of all kinds of things: most important of all, you have to understand light and how it works. So science is a good thing to study and art and math and reading, so you can learn about photography. . . ."

"Oh, boy!" her young interviewer smacks his own head, dramatically. "I thought it would be easier than being a doctor. Everybody wants me to be a doctor like my great-great-grandfather and my great-grandfather and my grandfather and my father."

"My goodness!" Norma looks at him with real concern. "It will be easier than being a doctor only if you love it. What's your name?"

"John Covington the Fifth."

She wants to roll her eyes. "Johnny, you don't stand a chance do you?" She didn't realize how entrenched the Covington medical legacy is. The boy casts his eyes to the gleaming hardwood floor. "I mean, you have to really want to be a photographer, John. It shouldn't just be a hobby. If you continue to want to, as you get older, then just be determined. Nobody can make you do what you don't want. Your dad and grandpa would probably be mad at me for telling you this, but if you still want to be a photographer when you get to high school or college, give me a call." She takes a business card from her purse and hands it to him. He smiles again, and she lets him peer through the lens of her medium-format camera, one which allows for the larger negative she wants from this shoot. John Covington V skips off happily when he is called by one of the adults. Poor thing, she thinks. She takes out her pad and, contemplating the composition she wants to create, begins jotting down where to position each person, referring to them on paper by what they are wearing.

Someone announces in a boisterous whisper, "Big Mary," followed by *shhhh* and the buzzing chatter in the room grows faint. Big Mary makes her entrance in a motorized wheelchair, and Norma is surprised that she is not big at all. Her long legs, shapeless as boards, dangle past the wheelchair and almost drag the floor, suggesting she is a tall woman like her twin daughters. She is so slight, however, that possibly two of her could fit into the wheelchair. Her attendant attempts to maneuver the chair, but Big Mary waves her off to the side. She navigates herself through the doorway and across the floor to the gathering of relatives. Big Mary's stiff organza dress billows around her like sheets in the wind. Her hair is full and white in a long braid coiled cobralike on the top of her head. A silver-and-diamond brooch winks from her deflated chest.

"Big Mary's here now," she says in a startlingly loud but jagged voice, as if things were in disarray and she would now order them. Norma feels a little intimidated but decides to attack it head on. She will assert herself and let them know who's boss. She wonders whether Big Mary can be photographed out of the wheelchair.

Norma walks over to her and offers her hand, which Big Mary does not take. "Hello, I'm Norma Simmons-Greer, the photographer, and I'm glad you're here so we can get started. I was just about to tell everyone where I want them. I'd like you right in the center of the couch, surrounded by the children. Can someone help you out of the chair?" Norma is proud of herself for sounding firm and in charge with this woman everyone else seems petrified of.

Big Mary contorts her face, deepening the columns of wrinkles. She turns her chair away from Norma. "See why I didn't want to deal with a new one?" she confides, without lowering her voice, to no one in particular. "But the old fella went off and died on me." Big Mary wheels back around to speak directly to Norma. "Everybody knows their places, miss. You don't have to tell them anything. And my chair and I go in *front* of the couch!" Her southern drawl is spiked with agitation. She snaps her head around and says to her flock, "Why didn't you all tell her?"

Richard Covington is directly behind Big Mary, and he moves even further back. "We tried to," he says, looking toward Norma as if it's all her fault.

"Get in your places now, then!" demands Big Mary, raising her voice a notch. She wheels herself away from Norma.

"What is she talking about?" Norma wonders aloud. She walks over to Mr. Covington, who remains on the outskirts of the group and no longer appears as approachable as earlier. "Mr. Covington?"

"Big Mary likes us to put the light-skin ones in the front and the dark ones fill in the back." He slowly lifts his hooded eyes to meet hers. His solemn expression cautions her not to interfere.

"What?" Norma is unable to penetrate the mask firmly in place on his countenance. "You can't be serious." She looks to Big Mary, now with her wheelchair planted in front of the couch, who is, Norma realizes, the fairest complexioned of them all. Except for the size and shape of her nose and lips, she could probably "pass." Norma looks at her closely. Big Mary's rodent-gray eyes stare back so hard, Norma's eyes water and she has to focus elsewhere. Seated slightly behind her are the twins, just a swatch darker than their mother, the color of ginger tea heavy on the cream. They offer no solace. "This is really what all of you want?" Norma asks the question into the wind. Listening to herself, she thinks she must sound desperate. Most of them nod in subdued agreement, from the latte-colored descendants of Richard Covington, standing to the left of the twins, to Mr. Covington's uncle Donald and his terra-cotta-toned wife and children on the right side and to Big Mary's cocoa-hued second cousins relegated to the outer fringes of the assemblage.

"This is the way we want it," Mr. Covington says to her from his designated honey-colored position toward the middle of the group.

Norma sees it all now, the gradations of color in their precise arrangement: the very light, damn-near-white, of Big Mary, the ivory tinge of the twins and their cousins, and so on. Norma visibly traces the route of color seepage on through to the mocha aunts and walnut uncles bringing up the rear.

Although the significance of their choice curdles her stomach, Norma is reluctantly intrigued by how this arrangement will translate to an image, and by the outrageous brazenness of it all. Squinting through the camera's eye, Norma hears heels on the floor behind her. An attractive and very dark young woman dragging a little girl with matching skin-coloring comes into the room a bit breathless. "Sorry I'm late," she says. Norma watches, frozen, as the relatives in the back part for the woman and child, who know their places. Why didn't Big Mary just marry white and tell them all to do the same, or was it always understood that these darker relations would be welcome as long as they knew where to stand? The latecomers settle in, and the group shifts attention back to Norma, apparently ready to say "cheese." Some of the children squirm and have to be reprimanded by their elders, but for the most part, everyone is in position. All twenty-one of them.

It's their picture, not hers. They commissioned her to do this. It will not be hanging in any exhibit, just on their walls, she rationalizes. It's not as if she's selling her soul. Right? She walks around her subjects, with the light meter, making some adjustments with the lighting in the back row. "Okay," she tells them. "On the count of three, I want your best smile."

The butler leads her to a different door from the one by which she entered the mansion. She'll be closer to her car, he says. Another employee follows with her equipment. They pass through a long corridor adorned with portraits of family members. At the end of the hall are several large photographs of the family taken by previous photographers. Sure enough, everyone is in their colorized pecking order. And the photos span many years, even back to when Big Mary was still Little Mary. But always the color coding. She hurries past the portraits, unable to look at them any further.

She sits in her car without starting it. She feels compromised, betrayed by herself. What happened to all those things she told Woody about wanting the truth to prevail in her work. She told him that she wrenches truth from its hiding place if she has to. Was that all lies? No, she shakes her head, as if she's not alone. Today she photographed the truth, as uncomfortable as it was. The truth shouldn't have to cause pain down through the generations, but it does. It wasn't her job to put it to rest. She could have been stronger, though. She could have said, look, this is wrong, unacceptable. I will not do it. What had she been afraid of? It's like Glorie Dickson, the girl who threatened to beat her up for having hair ribbons that matched her dresses and socks. She'd cower each time and surrender cookies, pencils, barrettes, a Mickey Mouse change purse, whatever would stave off Glorie. Many years later, she heard that Glorie had given herself over to drugs and prostitution, which didn't make Norma feel any better about her cowardice.

Moxie would have stormed out of there after she told them all how sick they were. Damn it, what bothers her most is that the artist in her wants to see how the photograph will turn out. Mr. Covington shook her hand extra hard and pressed an envelope into her palm before she left. "Threw in a little something extra for your trouble," he had said. She pulls the envelope out now and looks at the check. He added three hundred dollars to the agreed-upon fee. Guilt money, she thinks. Norma rips the check into shreds, envelope and all, and stuffs the torn bits into a plastic bag she keeps in the car for Miles's trash.

She drives around in circles, asking directions several times, until she locates Monument Row and the statue of Arthur Ashe. It is almost dusk by the time she gets there. She parks her car and walks up close, sharing the view with a young family. Ashe stands, magnificently sculpted with a book in one hand, tennis racket in the other, talking to a group of children. The statute was controversial from the beginning. Die-hard Confederates and others didn't want Ashe to be included in this row of heretofore white Virginia leaders of various stripes. She stays there in front of the statute for a very long time. Several groups of viewers come and go. After the last of the people admiring the statute leaves, she returns to her car and calls Miles at her mother's house. Lawrence has just picked him up, her mother tells her, adding that they said something about going to get ice cream. She doesn't call Lawrence's cell phone.

As she approaches the highway to leave Richmond, she is glad that night has fallen, although she usually dreads a long drive in the dark. Night can erase the day. She is alone with the thoughts that crowd her mind, like an impatient mob. Where would she and her family have been relegated to if they had been part of the Covington portrait? All in the back. She laughs aloud. Moxie would be closer to the front than she, and Woody—where would he stand? In front of Big Mary, most likely. And if she were married to Woody instead of Lawrence, and if they had a child together, that child would stand in front of her. Why should one color weigh so much more than another? Even in her own life. She tells herself, it's merely a fact that a white man happens to satisfy the needs her black man is unwilling to fulfill. She wishes it wasn't so much more complex.

Washington, D.C., ninety miles, the sign says. A mile a minute, she always calculates. Ninety minutes left. Driving alone in the dark, she looks ahead and sees nothing but the lights from the other cars and the vast ocean of blackness with a scattering of stars. She's not exactly sure how, but she vows to be stronger in the weak areas of her life. And she is going to sort out her own truth, so she won't be in danger of letting herself down. Because, quite possibly, that is the very worse thing a person can do.

Saturday, March 20th
Gap jeans
white Bebe T-shirt
Nine West Mary Janes

Dear Sistergirl:
    After ballet I took the bus over to Fawna's hairdresser. There was a kirked out lady on the bus with headphones dancing like she was in somebody's video. It was kind of funny, but everybody was trying not to laugh. She didn't care that everybody was looking at her. I guess if you're kirked out, you don't get as stressed as everybody else. Dad paid for me to get my touch-up. (Yes it's been that long!!!) A new girl did my hair cause Vicki had an emergency or something. I had to wait a long time for the other beautician, though. They were watching Ricki Lake *tapes in there and listening to Chuck Brown.*
    Allegra is in big trouble. I haven't talked to her yet, but she paged me 911 and left a message saying her parents found her birth control pills and her father is threatening to end Becky's uncle's medical career. I just tried to call again, and they wouldn't let me talk to her. I'm sorry for her, but I also want to make sure she didn't tell her parents that I got some, too. I'm trying not to stress.
    I'm watching Planet Groove while I eat dinner. I like this video with Brandy and Monica except doesn't Brandy ever get tired of those damn braids? On the sides it looks like her hair is falling out. Now they're showing an old Aaliyah video. She is so pretty. I'm going to copy her hairstyle tomorrow, but it's time for her to shut down that Tommy Hilfiger cropped top, baggy camouflage thing and do something else.
    Can you believe I finally did this? I have a real boyfriend, and I'm finally not a virgin anymore. I guess I didn't know what it would feel like, but I thought it would feel better than it does. More exciting, but it doesn't. Not yet, at least. It was weird, though. Kind of messy and just . . . weird. There aren't any other words for it. Allegra says it gets better the more you do it. I think if you're really in love, it'll be off the hook. I don't think I'm in love, but maybe I should try to be so I can see if it makes a difference.
    Octavius called me back finally. He forgot that I'm on spring break

*next week. Public schools are out the week after. That is so outrageous.
Ma told me my choice is to go to Florida with Dad to visit his sister or go
to work all week with her. She won't say why, but she doesn't trust me to
be home by myself all week. I just knew I was going to be lying up in O's
house at least a couple of those days. So I'm going to Florida. A lot of kids
from ballet will be out of town, so Miss Snow was not that mad when I
told her I would be, too. She just said we better stretch and practice on
our own or our bodies will pay for it when we get back.*

*Sunday, March 21st
DKNY jeans
Alvin Ailey T-shirt
   (finally found in closet)
white Nikes*

Dear Sistergirl:

*I'm so tired. My body still hurts from yesterday's class. Miss Snow is
seriously trying to kill us. I'm too tired to even soak. At least I finished my
French essay, and I've finally got enough money to buy new toe shoes. I
would also like to get TLC's FanMail CD, but I can't if I get the toe shoes,
so TLC will have to wait. Ma's always talking about learning to save and
budget. But how many times do you have to learn it? You don't always
have to experience things to learn about them—isn't that what she says?*

*O just called, talking about how he wants to hook up his clothes for
tomorrow so he can look like R. Kelly did on the Soul Train Awards with
that "wife-beater" undershirt and big plaid shirt over it. I told him I don't
like that name for those undershirts, and he was like, girl, you are always
tripping about something. I asked him if he was going to miss me when I go
to Florida, but he wouldn't answer, just kept asking me what did I think.*

*Allegra's still messed up with her parents. They're driving to Atlanta to
visit her brother, and she says it's going to be torture—eighteen hours or
something crazy like that. At least me and Dad (no tagalongs!) are flying,
and he's not mad at me about anything so far.*

My new theme song is I'm Good at Being Bad from that Fan Mail CD.

Nineteen	By Monday, Norma hasn't yet erased the bad taste left over from the Covington photo shoot. She's been frustrated with her work all day. At almost

four-thirty in the afternoon, she begins poring through her stacks of photography books. It is exhilarating to appreciate all VanDerZee accomplished within the limitations of his times and equipment, and of course DeCarava's soul-touching work, as well as the haunting and sometimes depressing achievements of Nan Goldin and Salgado. Instead of her own work, she decides to spend the next few days immersed in the work of other photographers, observing what they saw or at least what their lenses captured, pondering what they were trying to create and assessing whether they succeeded. She gives herself an assignment to study the textures in more depth because she'd like to experiment with textures a bit more in the development phase. At a gathering of local photographers, she saw exquisite work by an artist whose nature shots had a blurry, grainy quality because of the speed of the film he used.

She closes a photo book, feeling in a better place, and decides to leave the studio a little early; start fresh tomorrow. As she begins switching off the lights, the doorbell rings. She hopes it's Woody, because although she's left several messages today, they haven't talked. She feels fidgety when she hasn't spoken with him during the day. Now that she's without Moxie, she leans and relies on him much more. She presses the intercom and is startled to hear Lawrence's voice echo back to her, not Woody's. Lawrence hasn't come here in years, yet this will make the second time in two weeks. She waits for him to come up the stairs.

"Hi, I wasn't sure whether you'd still be here," he says, one hand tucked in the pocket of his pants, pushing back his suit jacket. "Thought maybe we could pick up Miles together."

She doesn't get it. This is the man she once loved so much she would literally start shivering at the thought of him and his love for her. It had seemed so easy in the beginning; they needed no rules or road maps to follow. He was her first real love. The others before him were just men to practice on. And then he turned to stone on her. She can't deny, though, that something about him still pulls at her, after all this time, after all this Woody. Yes, she will go with him to get their child. She takes her jacket from its hook, puts her camera bag on her shoulder, and grabs a folder of prints she wants to take home. "Do you want me to carry something?" Lawrence asks. She hands him the prints and lets him out the door so she can lock up with her key.

Lawrence goes downstairs and holds open the outside door for her. As Norma descends, she sees Woody on the sidewalk approaching the front steps. He is carrying daffodils wrapped in transparent paper. "Hi," says Woody. "Leaving?" He looks at Norma, at Lawrence, then back to Norma. He places one foot onto the next step but doesn't move.

"Yes. Going to get my son. Uh, Lawrence Greer this is Isaac Woodruff." She frowns as Lawrence steps down to shake hands. He smiles the way she imagines he would greeting a new client.

"So you're the one who brings the flowers," Lawrence says. Norma feels chilly. She pushes her camera strap further up on her shoulder, although it wasn't slipping down, and wraps her arms around herself.

Woody nods, yes, he is the one. He shifts awkwardly, tucking the daffodils under his arm. "You're Lawrence," he says.

"Yes. Still the husband."

"She wasn't expecting me. I just . . . wanted to see some of her work." His eyes light on Norma and plead with her for something, and she smiles helplessly, weakly. Cowardly.

"I bet," Lawrence says smugly. He continues down the walkway without looking at her or Woody. "I'll be in the car, Norma."

Woody's cheeks puff out as he sighs. The daffodils get partially crushed under his arm when he reaches for his cigarettes. "I'm sorry." He looks so uneasy she has an urge to gather him to her and hold him close until he feels better.

"I think it's really all right," she says. "Can I call you later?"

"Yes, please. Would you?"

Her eyes reach past him, locating Lawrence's car parked less than a block away, next to a lamppost. Woody lights the cigarette and draws hard, like it's a straw. "You sure you'll be able to call?" He shifts the flowers to his other arm.

"I'm sure."

Norma is anxious to talk to Lawrence, understand what he's feeling. She wonders if he'll even express it. She hurries to the car, looks at him through the window, and then climbs in beside him. Lawrence sits with one hand on the steering wheel, the other in his lap. The key is in the ignition, but he hasn't started the car. "I know that was uncomfortable. I'm sorry . . ." she begins.

He stops her. "You weren't even worried."

"What do you mean?"

"You weren't worried that I'd try to kick his ass or anything. Am I right?"

She stares at the side of his face, what she can see of it in the light from the streetlamp. She doesn't understand what point he's making. "No, I guess I wasn't. That's not generally the way you behave."

"How many times have I met one of your lovers?"

She looks away as he turns to question her. She doesn't answer.

"Does he bring you flowers every damn day?"

"No." She clenches her camera and purse on her lap.

"How long have you been . . . seeing him?"

She is unprepared. Vagueness will be better than truth, she thinks. "A couple of months."

"Do you love him?"

"Lawrence . . ."

"A simple question, Norma." He hits the steering wheel with the heel of his palm. By accident, the horn sounds softly. "Do you love him?"

"I'm confused about my feelings. . . ."

"Damn it! What do you want? Do you love him? Do you want to be with him?"

She puts one hand on her knee to stop its trembling. "I'm not saying it's an excuse, Lawrence, but you cut me out of your life. I kept trying to get back in, but all the doors were closed. I was lonely and empty, that's why I did it."

Lawrence lets out a short, painful laugh. "You know, I felt that guy's existence long before Bernard told me anything. And you don't even like war movies, Norma!" He sighs. "All the things I put in place to shroud me from pain, and none of them helped. You were so nonchalant back there. I don't know if that means you're completely gone already or what." He looks at the clock on the dashboard. "Right now, I'm going to go get Miles."

"I thought we were going together."

"No, I'll just go. Where's your car?"

She points. He drives her further up the street, and she gets out.

Will he bring Miles straight home, or will he take him away from her forever, as Moxie once predicted? She drives aimlessly through the streets away from her studio and through parts of Northeast, delaying her return home. It is almost dark now. Driving down H Street toward North Capitol, she selects people she would photograph if the lighting were better, if she wasn't so troubled: two teenage girls in huge platform heels waiting at a bus stop next to an older woman in sensible shoes; and an overweight man jogging slowly, trailing a small dog on a leash. Moxie flashes across her mind. I need a friend, damn it, she thinks. The street is sprinkled with people getting on with the minutiae of their lives. She must get on with hers.

Lawrence and Miles are home when she arrives, making tuna sandwiches. There is no sign or sound of Bernard. She tells Lawrence that Mrs. Coleman left a couple of dinners in the freezer. "This is what Miles wanted," he says.

"Yeah," says Miles. "I wanted a sandwich." They sit at the kitchen table eating the sandwiches. Miles seems to be less finicky when Lawrence has prepared the meal, maybe because Lawrence has a knack for turning something plain into something elaborate. In the short time he's been home, he toasted sourdough bread and added tomatoes, relish, onions, and Dijon mustard to the tuna and garnished each plate with red leaf lettuce, dill pickles, and olive oil potato chips. Lawrence's cell phone rings while they're eating. It is not lost on Norma that he reaches onto the counter for the phone, glances at the displayed number, and turns it off.

"Daddy makes good sandwiches," Miles says. After eating, he wants to paint. She sets up the paints at the artist's easel in his room and pours a tall cup of water for him to clean the paintbrush in. She lets him know it will be time to get ready for bed soon. He makes big swirls of color on the paper.

She finds Lawrence straightening things in the kitchen. He wipes down the countertops and the table with a sponge. She can't read him. He doesn't say anything to her, but she can tell it isn't an angry silence. It's a soft, pondering one, and she can't bear it. "About tonight," she starts, one hand holding on to the counter he has just cleaned. "I want you to know I didn't mean for that to happen . . . for Woody to come by the studio."

Lawrence shrugs without looking up.

"Okay. Well. I'll go run Miles's bath."

As she watches the tub fill, adding bubble bath and toys, she predicts what will happen. Lawrence will throw himself into work even deeper than before. Tonight's incident will bother him for a while, but he'll manage it by continuing to keep his feelings and Norma at bay. She can tell by the way he's reverted back to not wanting to talk.

After Miles's bath, Lawrence reads him a story, and they both tuck him in. Miles seems overjoyed to have the two of them attending to him. He begs to kiss them both over and over. They remain in his room until his breathing smoothes into a rhythmic pattern that means he's asleep. Norma goes into their bedroom, thinking that a bath will help calm her, as well. She sits on the side of the bed, removing her shoes. She can feel Lawrence in the doorway.

"I've decided for now it's better for me to sleep in the guestroom," he says.

"Okay," she says, lying back on the bed, covering her eyes with one arm. She listens as he gathers some of his things and leaves the room. Tears build, although she doesn't understand why his statement makes her want to cry. They haven't been doing anything but sleeping on opposite edges of their bed, anyway. She had imagined it would be she rather than Lawrence who would move into the guestroom one of these days.

During the following two weeks, Lawrence surprises her in a myriad of ways. He either calls her at the studio and says he will pick Miles up or is already at home preparing dinner when she and Miles come in. Although he still seems reluctant to talk to her, he is in the house nightly to participate in the bath-and-bedtime-story routine. One night there's even an unexpected outing for the three of them to the circus at the Armory. Over a weekend he and Bernard install a swing set in the backyard, to Miles's delight. Norma doesn't comment because she keeps waiting for things to relapse, for Lawrence's presence to disappear again. As much as she wants to rely and sink into it like a comfortable chair, she doesn't trust its staying power. She doesn't admit to herself how much this reminds her of the old days before Crystal or how the tension, that courses through her body daily like current, has begun to melt away.

During the second week of Lawrence's behavioral change, on the Friday night before Easter, Miles falls asleep on the rug. He had been watching *Space Jam* for possibly the hundredth time. As Lawrence lifts him to his shoulder, Norma reminds him to take Miles to the bathroom first. He's been doing well, but occasionally he still wets the bed.

She stretches out on the couch in the family room. "I Believe I Can Fly" blares sickeningly from the movie's soundtrack, and she snaps the television off with the remote. It dawns on her that she hasn't heard Bernard moving about tonight. In fact, for the last several days, he's been like a recluse. Thank goodness, she thinks, because overall, since seeing her with Woody at the movies, Bernard has gotten worse. What modicum of respect he had for her previously has dwindled to dust between his fingers. The house always smells of cigarette smoke, no matter how much she rants. And even more disturbing, several times she has found perfume bottles and jewelry oddly rearranged on her dresser and her drawers rifled through. Nothing appears to be missing, just tossed around. Any other time, she would have leapt at telling

Lawrence and pressuring him to force Bernard to leave. But Lawrence's model behavior has even softened her responses to Bernard. She tells herself he's only doing these things to cause an eruption between her and Lawrence, and she won't give him the satisfaction. Only one more month, she tells herself.

After putting Miles to bed, Lawrence returns with two glasses of wine. She sits up and takes a glass, giving him an inquiring glance.

"Don't worry. I won't get drunk, like that other night." That wasn't what she was thinking. She doesn't know what he's doing or even who he is. He sips his wine and sinks into the couch but leaves enough space for another person between them.

She adjusts herself to observe him better. His expression is sincere; she is not sure how to react. "It's been nice for Miles to have you home more these past two weeks."

"Only for Miles?"

"Well, no, not just for Miles. But, to tell you the truth, Lawrence, I don't know what to think. I'm wondering if something's wrong at the office." She reaches for her wine, which she placed on the coffee table in front of them.

"Nothing's wrong. Just been doing a lot of thinking, that's all. About what I want to change in my life. Been talking with partners from another firm. I don't know whether you remember me discussing an entertainment-law firm, quite some time ago. Anyway, I've thought about it long and hard, and I'm really considering making a move, Norma. I'd be more appreciated and wouldn't have to bust my butt quite as hard for it. A hell of a lot less stress."

"Would you walk right in and be a partner?"

"They know that's the only way I'd go in there."

The wine settles her down inside. She closes her eyes and thinks about how she hasn't called Woody since he came by the studio and how he's left messages wondering if everything is "okay." She needs to and wants to call him. But to say what? The script of her daily life has changed so dramatically, she no longer recognizes her part. She wants Lawrence to continue talking and is awed when he does.

"You know, you get to be forty, approaching fifty and you start thinking about what the most important things in your life are and how do you give those things their due." Before he says more, Miles yells out something unintelligible.

"Probably a nightmare," she surmises. She puts her glass down and starts to rise.

"I'll go," Lawrence says.

She wants him to hurry back so she won't think too hard about what all this means or where it will take them. When he returns, he tells her that Miles had already drifted back to sleep. "Norma," he says, retrieving their conversation, "I know you've been suffering for a long time, but I didn't know how to help you relieve it. Guess I was worried I'd go back to feeling bad, too. I told myself that if I didn't think about what was difficult or confront it, I wouldn't feel it."

"Why did you shut me out in the first place, though? I didn't do anything to you." She finishes her wine.

"Want more?" he asks. She shakes her head no. "It wasn't that you did or didn't do anything," he continues. "When my parents died, I thought nothing worse could happen to me. It was so damn hard. I don't think I ever even talked to you about that because to acknowledge it made it hurt again. Then when Crystal died, I couldn't accept it. At all. Wouldn't let it take hold. In retrospect, that probably made things worse. It just about tore through me, sucking up my essence and leaving me without energy, without desire, without very much at all. It had nothing to do with you, except that you needed something from me I couldn't give."

She struggles to understand. "Couldn't you have said, 'Norma, I'm having a hard time getting over Crystal' or something?"

"No, I couldn't. I didn't have the words or the life force. I didn't want to live, really. I just pushed myself to keep going, keep living for your sake and Miles's, but I knew I was failing you both miserably. Which made everything worse, and juxtaposed with all the crap going on at the office, I felt like there was nowhere I could breathe. Some of me died with Crystal, you know. It's taken all this time but little by little, I'm crawling back to life."

She looks at him now. "You're saying that was how you dealt with it? By secluding yourself? What about what I needed? Lawrence, I needed to share my pain with you. It hurt so much, losing two people I loved."

"Norma, you have to believe me when I say I honestly want to be the one you share things with again, but this thing with Woody, I can't get past it. I'm not blaming you for doing what you did. I've tried, but I just can't get past it. I'm thinking about getting a place, temporarily, until I figure it all out. Someplace close, so Miles can go back and forth without too much disruption."

Tuesday, April 6th
jean dress
Nine West Mary Janes

Dear Sistergirl:
    I'm back! Got a little out of the writing habit when I was in Florida.
I left my diary home cause I was scared I would lose it down there.
Nothing much happened, anyway. Dad said it was going to be a time for
me and him to hang out by ourselves because Fawna and Tiffany weren't
coming. (Tiffany's charter school follows the public school vacation
schedule.) On the plane he told me that he hadn't had a real chance to
talk to me, but that he was really upset that I lied to him and Fawna
about Ma saying I could get my hair permed. I started crying and told
him I didn't know what else to do because I didn't want to lose the part.
He ended up putting his arm around me and saying something like, But
you can't lie to get your way, babe. It's not right, okay? I told him I was
sorry, and then he fell asleep and snored for the rest of the ride. He hates
for me to cry. When we got to Aunt Jolie's, he had to go straight to
rehearsal for the club he was playing at. We went to the show one night.
Aunt Jolie is so proud of him and was real happy to see us. She's older
than him, and it's funny to hear her telling him what to do. She has some
kind of consulting business that she does out of her house but no kids or

man. She's a little boring but nice. I went to the pool in her complex, and we also went to the beach a couple of times. (I think I did a good job washing and drying my hair afterwards, but I might have to go back to Vicki sooner than planned, we'll see.) Once we went fishing with some friends of Aunt Jolie's. It was all right, but there weren't any kids around cause Florida schools have a different school vacation, too. Had to go to church on Palm Sunday even though I didn't bring any church clothes. I was missing O and Allegra, but I couldn't call anyone except Ma. I told Dad I need my own calling card, for real.

Found a ballet boutique near the mall and bought toe shoes!!! I'm sewing the ribbons in my new toe shoes now. Miss Snow told me to get the Gambas, but when I was in the boutique, the salesperson told me to try the Freeds, which she said were exotic and a little more flexible. I love them, and both cost $65, so I bought the Freeds. I hope Miss Snow doesn't get too mad. Maybe she won't notice. They shouldn't take as long to break in either. I always take a magic marker and draw a heart inside my shoes to give me good luck.

Going back to school and ballet was good. (Except for lacrosse, I hate lacrosse.) Allegra met a cute guy in Atlanta, but her parents wouldn't let her out of their sight. She said, Zadi, that's why you never want to get caught cause they panic and think they can't let you go to the bathroom by yourself ever again. She said that because I asked her to write another note for me. I am like dying to slide with O again tomorrow. I was hoping we could do something on Good Friday because school was closed, but he didn't get my page or whatever.

Wednesday, April 7th
gray mini
leopard print top
Chinese slippers from Fla.

Dear Sistergirl:
I'm at school writing in my notebook. Allegra says she'll do another note for me, but she's worried that if I get caught, she'll get in trouble, too. I told her that if that happens, which it won't, then I won't tell who

*wrote it. I'll just act like I wrote it myself. I'll already be in trouble. She
was like, dang, you must really be pressed to sex O. I'm like yes, I am.
Like Janet says, I get lonely sometimes.*

*Forget it. Allegra just came over to my carrel. She is on my nerves—
panicking, so I'm just going to write the early dismissal note myself.
There's a new receptionist, so I'm taking that as a good sign because she's
never even seen my mother's handwriting before. O's meeting me at
Metro Center in two and a half hours. Thank goodness I write down
what I wear. I could look back and make sure I didn't wear the same
thing to meet him as last time. Cause I damn sure started to wear the
black Parasucos again today. Even though it is like seventy degrees.*

| *Twenty* | Returning to her office from washing out her cup and spoon in the ladies' room, Moxie notices Octavius in the elevator lobby, staring at Reebok's |

picture on the bulletin board. She stops midstride, still drying her cup with a brown paper towel. It's only eleven A.M., so he obviously didn't go to school. "Octavius. What are you doing here this time of day?" She starts walking back to her office, knowing he'll follow. He comes behind her through the metal door she holds open for him. They enter her office, and she sets the cup and spoon down on her desk, pointing Octavius to the wooden chair beside it.

"They said I missed too many days and I need a note from you. I know I missed some appointments, but they need something to say I have a counselor or something."

She leans her elbows on her desk. "Who are they? And what am I supposed to say in this note?"

He sinks low in the chair, seemingly staring at the bottom of her desk. "Them people at school. They want something that says . . . that I been coming here and having appointments with you. So they know I'm not just out on the street."

"Octavius, it's too late. It's over. The jig is up. I don't know how else to say it. Once again, you haven't returned my calls. Once again it's been weeks and you think you can show up with no appointment and a tired excuse. Well, I don't think so. Ron D was ready and waiting for you to come in. I don't know if they still even want you after all this time. You make promises and then you fall short. I called your school, the lockups, and the morgues, so I knew you were still out there somewhere." She's tired of always being angry with him, but he's beginning to resemble his pal Reebok a bit too much. Maybe, as Von says, she needs to figure out how to care less. She doesn't even like the way Octavius holds his head, arrogantly tilted to one side. As they accept the silence between them, Octavius's pager goes off. He glances at the number, hits a few buttons, and puts it back in his pocket.

"Do you need to make a call?" she asks wearily.

"Naw. It can wait." He shifts around in his chair. His cell phone rings. He pulls it from his pocket, looks at the caller ID and turns it off. "Sorry."

"Octavius. I'm going to stop lecturing you because it gets us nowhere. I'll write a letter to say that I am your probation officer, and that's it. I want you to be able to go to school, but I'm not going to say that you keep your appointments because you don't. And maybe it's better if you don't have this job with Ron D. What assurance is there that you'd remember to show up on time?"

"I would, Miss Dillar. It ain't the same thing like coming down here."

"Well, where you're getting ready to send yourself, you won't need a job, anyway."

"What you mean?"

"I mean I have to go back to court on you next month. Make sure you show up for that. And I hope you understand what I'm going to have to recommend."

"Oh, man! Come on, Miss Dillar. I ain't been in no trouble. Can't I still try the job?"

"Like I said, I know what recommendation I have to make—detention or boot camp. The court might listen if you have a job you actually show up for and if you're going to school. Maybe they'll overlook what I recommend. You need to call the radio station and see if the position is still available. I don't know why I'm even telling you this. It might be too late, anyway."

"Don't know what to say to him."

"Just ask whether the job is available, Octavius. You can call from here." She wonders how hard it was for him to admit not knowing what to say. His lack of social skills and vulnerability, sloppily coated with a hard veneer, tug at her, but not enough to change her mind about her next steps. According to the rules she is supposed to adhere to, and considering all the leeway she's already given him, she will make the recommendation she indicated to Octavius. She writes down the phone number to the radio station and steps out of her office so that he can have privacy.

He opens the door to let her know he's finished. "They said I can go in for two days next week. Eight dollars an hour." He doesn't exactly smile, just moves one side of his mouth higher than the other. "Man, see, Miss Dillar, I just need another chance to do right, do the stuff I'm supposed to. My curfew, school, urines, my appointments with you, and all that. I'm a do all that right this time. For real." He still doesn't look her in the eye.

"I'm glad the radio station's willing to let you come, but your time is up, Octavius." She shrugs. "You didn't have an appointment, and I've got work to do." Moxie rises from her seat. "I'll fax a note to your school this afternoon. Our next appointment is your court date."

Octavius remains seated, pressing his boots firmly into the floor in front of him. "Why can't you gimme another chance? I thought you was gonna be different. But you just like everybody else. My teachers, the principal, the guidance counselor, everybody think I'm just a bum. Good thing your daughter ain't like you." He points to Zadi's picture on Moxie's desk. "Knew I shouldn'ta come up in this joint." He hurls himself out of the chair and through her office door. She goes after him, but he's gone. He must have taken the stairs instead of waiting for the elevator. She's given him more than enough chances, more than she should have, but she thought she saw something in him and felt for his situation. Sometimes even gut feelings are wrong, but what did he mean about Zadi? She replays his words. *Good thing your daughter ain't like you.*

The rest of her day is marred by the echo of distraction. Her thoughts keep bumping into images of Zadi and Octavius and the possibility of a link between them. Maybe they exchanged numbers at Reebok's funeral and have been talking on the phone. Zadi is always on the phone, and she gets calls late at night when Moxie is too exhausted to keep track of who might be on the line. She knows how much Zadi hates to be questioned, but she certainly will ask her about it tonight. She tries to focus on her work and get a few reports written.

In the midst of an intake interview with a new client, Moxie's intercom buzzes. "Sorry to interrupt but it's your daughter's school on line two," Brenda says. "I figured you'd want it."

"Excuse me," Moxie says to the young man, who keeps picking at the dirt beneath his fingernails. She presses down the button for the blinking line., "This is Moxie Dillard."

"Hello, Ms. Dillard. Sorry to bother you. This is Ms. Somerset in the office. We've had a bit of a snafu. Zadi brought in a note this morning requesting early dismissal for a doctor's appointment today. We've got a new staff person in the front office who dismissed her. Apparently it also happened the Friday before spring break. In any case the handwriting in today's note didn't match the last note, so it raised a concern in Lisa's mind and she brought it to my attention. Ms. Dillard, this is awkward, and I'm sorry it's so late in the day, but I thought, better to err on the safe side. . . ."

"She left school early today? And on some other Friday, you said? I didn't write any note . . . she didn't have any doctor's appointment that I arranged. I don't know where she is, but I'm sure going to find out. Thank you for calling." She hangs up quickly and tells her client she has an emergency and will set up another appointment with him. It is almost two-thirty. Where the hell could she be? Could she be somewhere with Octavius? She knows he's not in school either. She's got to think straight. Von's in a meeting. She goes to the front and tells Brenda to let Von know that Zadi's school called and she had to leave.

"Everything okay?" Brenda glances up at Moxie from her computer screen.

"I don't know."

Would Zadi have the nerve to be trysting in her house? She takes her front stairs two at a time, but once inside, she finds no sign of Zadi. She paces, thinking about what to do, where she might be. She remembers that Zadi has a pager, which Moxie hasn't had to use before. She finds the number in her purse and pages her. She paces again, waiting for her

response. Five minutes, ten, she pages again. Another five minutes. In
Zadi's room, she lifts her mattress, goes through her shoe boxes, rummages her dresser drawers, until she finds, on the very top of her closet
stuffed in an old music box, the diary that Norma gave Zadi. The key
glistens beside it. Moxie lowers herself onto Zadi's unmade bed, and
reads, beginning with the last entries first.

Even though it's Zadi's private world, she feels justified entering it
because of the level of deception she is confronting. As she reads, she
trembles over the things her daughter has done, the things Moxie was
never supposed to know about. Some of it she cannot bear to read; she
rushes past the harrowing words written in Zadi's bold and upright
script. The story they tell is worse than she feared. When she has read
enough, she closes the diary and returns it to its place. Almost an hour
has passed since she left work. Zadi, her child, must be somewhere
screwing as if she's a grown woman. The thought scalds her. Moxie
washes her face with handfuls of water, avoiding looking at her swollen
and reddened eyes. She grabs her purse and her car keys from the top
of the television. How could Zadi be so stupid? With Octavius—of all
the people in the world—why would she pick such a loser?

While driving over to Octavius's, Moxie tries to remember where
Ms. Johnson would be this time of the day. Her college class? Job training? She's not certain. All she knows is that if they don't answer the
damn door, she will break it down.

As she drives north on Minnesota Avenue, she sees Zadi and
Octavius walking toward the metro. Walking as though they don't have
a care in the world. Laughing even. He throws her book bag in the air.
Her book bag! She remembers Zadi coming back into the house this
morning saying she had forgotten her book bag. Now she understands
what that was really all about. She forgot it because she was too busy
scheming. Someone honks at her because the light has changed to
green and Moxie hasn't moved. She makes the turn and pulls into the
gas station on her right, leaves her car running, and steps out. She
screams, "Zadi!" cupping her hands around her mouth. "Zadi!" she
yells again, as if her life depends upon it.

Zadi sees her and stands still as a manikin, or as though she has just
been turned to stone. Moxie sees Octavius mouth, "Oh, shit." He

looks as shocked as Zadi. Moxie cannot believe that they have a relationship, unbeknownst to her, and obviously have had one for a while.

She waits interminably for Zadi to cross the street to her. Zadi's face contorts, as she looks back and forth at the traffic before she comes over to where the car is parked and Moxie stands beside the driver's side. Zadi looks around everywhere but at her. Moxie reminds herself to be as calm as she can; otherwise, she knows she will get nothing from Zadi. Her face burns as she waits. Zadi has one arm looped through the book-bag strap, but it's not quite up on her shoulder. She walks toward Moxie, frowning hard now.

Moxie tries to keep her voice from sounding shrill. "You wanted a pager so bad; I got you a pager. I paged you. What happened?"

"Don't know, maybe the battery's dead."

"That's a lie, Zadi."

"He was just walking me to the metro. I was getting ready to go to the library."

"Still lying. The day my daughter became a stranger—what a terrible day," Moxie says, realizing as she does that she's repeating her own mother's sentiments from years ago.

"Ma . . ."

"Zadi, get in the car. Don't tell me one more lie. Just don't tell me another lie."

Zadi hesitates and then walks around to the other side, but the door is locked. Moxie opens her own door and reaches across to unlock Zadi's. Zadi sits down warily. "What are you talking about? What lie did I tell?"

A bold-faced liar, too, Moxie thinks. Ponsey probably would have slapped Moxie at this point. He did she recalls, when Moxie lied about going to the movies with Johnny Douglas. "Zadi, you left school early claiming a doctor's appointment, and apparently you did the same thing before you went on spring break."

"How do you know?" Zadi stares down into her lap. She reaches out and turns the radio on.

Moxie slaps at Zadi's hand and turns the radio off. "I'm talking to you. Are you crazy? What kind of fool do you think I am?" Zadi snatches her hand back, and stares at it. "What exactly are you trying to do, what are you trying to prove—that you're grown, is that it?"

Zadi is sobbing quietly now. She shakes her head no.

"Well then, what? What, Zadi? Answer me, damnit. Did you sleep with him? Huh? Is that what you skipped out of school early for—to screw some juvenile delinquent?"

Zadi stares out the window.

"Don't you have any respect for yourself at all? Octavius Johnson doesn't give a damn about himself—what makes you think he gives a damn about you?"

"He does! He does. He cares more about me than you do!"

"Oh, right, because he calls you his 'boo' and his 'bun-bun'—those sound like ghosts and food to me—and what, because he says he'll pay for you to get your damn nails done! Give me a damn break!"

"You read my diary? You read my diary! I don't believe you! How could you? That's it! I'm never going to speak to you again!" Zadi opens the door and runs up the street toward the metro station.

Moxie sits there, repeating the conversation silently. Wondering where she went wrong when she is the one who was wronged in the first place, not Zadi. She wishes, though, that she could rewind the words and start over. She opens her window. "Zadi! Come back here. Zadi, come back here, I said!" She gets out of the car again screaming after her, demanding that she return, the way she used to when Zadi was a toddler wandering off in the supermarket. "Zadi, get back here NOW!"

Wednesday, April 7th

In the Minnesota Avenue metro station, writing in my history notebook. Just got out of Ma's car. She looked me dead in my face and admitted that she read my diary. That's how she found me over here near O's house. How dare she read MY FUCKING DIARY!!!!! That means she went all up in my room. I wanted to slap the shit out of her or scratch her fucking eyes out or something. I hate her fucking ass!!! She has no right to go in my stuff just because she's my mother. She has no respect for

*my privacy whatsoever. Fuck her—she still doesn't know me! She might
know what I've done, but she doesn't know ME. She said it herself—her
daughter, the stranger, or whatever the fuck she said. I'm not going home,
that's for damn sure. Not with her, anyway. I'll call Dad. That's what I'll
do—call his cell phone. This is the worst fucking day of my life. First
Allegra wouldn't do the damn note for me, and now this shit with Ma.
This is a really fucked-up, mother-fucking day.*

*Thursday, April 8th
Old Navy flared jeans
Alvin Ailey T-shirt
Chinese slippers (no other damn shoes
     over here)*

Dear Sistergirl:

Temporary diary. I'm at Dad's for good. I'm never going back to live
with That Woman. She's out of her fucking mind.

Got in trouble at school because of this shit. Have to go before the Peer
Review Board next week. I can write up an explanation of my behavior
if I want them to read it before I go in there. I don't know what to say. I
wrote the note cause I wanted to leave school early so I could do it to my
boyfriend before his mother came home. Come on now, how would that
sound? I told Ms. Somerset I was sorry and Lisa, the receptionist, too. I
even cried a little. I mean I don't want to get kicked out of school. Ms.
Somerset said it was a very serious infraction, and that I would be
notified about the Peer Review date and it would help if a parent came
with me. You know who it won't be.

Dad picked me up from school, and I told him about the Peer Review
thing, and he said he would go. He asked me why I did it, and I told
him I wasn't ready to talk about it. I told him I want to live with him
because That Woman invaded my privacy and I told him what she did.
He started making a damn speech and was like, Zadi, of course my home
is open to you, but if this is something unresolved between you and your
mother and you are just using me trying to get back at her, I don't think
it's a good idea. I was like, that's not it. I just had to get up out of there. I

have a few clothes over here but not much. Dad is about to go get some more. I told him what to get and where it was. I told him to get my damn diary even though she read all the shit already. I just want it out of there. I should have kept it in my backpack. Fawna hasn't really said much. And Tiffany has the flu, so she's mostly been in her room. Dad's talking to That Woman on the phone now. She better not ask to speak to me.

I called Norma. I had to. Was just glad to hear her voice. Haven't talked to her in a real long time. She helped me calm down. I told her I decided to stay at Dad's. She thinks it's still about the hair stuff because I didn't tell her what happened with O. That Woman can tell her about that. She said she hasn't talked to her in a while, though. I know one thing, That Woman needs to stop playa-hating everybody. That's her number-one problem.

Twenty-one Zadi has been at James's house for almost three days. Moxie hasn't even talked to her, only to James. Each time she calls, he says Zadi is sleeping or in the bathroom, as if Moxie is harassing her. Moxie is still angry at him for letting Zadi get her hair relaxed against her wishes. "Don't you understand she played us against each other? She couldn't do it if you'd communicate with me about important things like that!" She had yelled and screamed, but all James said was he would talk to Zadi about it. Like Zadi is a damn adult. It's as if he can't bear to believe how deceitful and manipulative Zadi can be, and on top of that, he can't bear to actually discipline her. Moxie remembers that when Zadi was little, she was the one responsible for doling out the discipline. He almost always caved in to her wants and seemed incapable of telling her no. When she did something wrong, James would say things like, "Don't do that again, okay, honey bunny?" He'd never spank or punish her. Moxie felt like an ogre because often, after chastising Zadi, James would come along and undo it all. He'd pick her up and give her a treat, rescuing her as though she were a damsel in distress.

All Moxie wants to do now is understand how her daughter came to think so little of herself. It doesn't make sense. Of course Moxie knows she made mistakes, all parents do. But when she talks to James, she comes away feeling like a failure. "Zadi knows what she did was wrong, and I've gotten on her case about it, too, but your problem is—you always cross over the line. You shouldn't have gone into her things and read her diary, Mox." "Mox"—she used to love him calling her that. Now it grates against her nerves.

"Oh, really?" she had screeched. "Did she tell you why she forged the note and skipped school? Did she tell you she did it in order to go lay up with one of my juvenile delinquent clients?" James was silent after that, so apparently, Zadi hadn't told him. He informed Moxie he'd be over to get some of Zadi's clothes.

She notices her hands shaking when she fixes herself a cup of tea in the morning. This frightens her because it indicates she could be back hanging on the edge of sanity. But this time Zadi has left her, and maybe she has really lost her. If so, what would be the reason for living? She clenches that thought to her, doesn't let it go. Would she really want to die? Maybe, is the answer. Maybe is not good.

Moxie forces herself to go in to the office, makes some phone calls, and then throws herself on Von's mercy. She slips into Von's client chair and tells her she has a crisis with Zadi and needs some more time off. Von reminds her of the week she took not so long ago and the mental health days she seems to regularly need every month. "Right now, I don't think I need to be helping other people's troubled teens when I have one of my own," Moxie says. Von comes from behind her desk and puts her arms around Moxie until she calms down.

"Did you ever call the therapist?" Von asks, in a soft tone, not her usual brash one. "If your stomach or leg hurt as much as your heart and soul do, wouldn't you call a doctor?" She hands Moxie the box of tissues from her bookcase and brings her own chair around in front of the desk. "Moxie, there are three kinds of people in the world. And all of them are sick. Including you and me. The difference is this: some sick people want sympathy so they act like they're sicker than they really are; others are sick but try to pretend they're not and that they don't need any help; and then the third kind, the ones to be admired, realize they're sick and get the help they need to get better. That's it. Only those three kinds. Now which kind are you?"

Moxie sniffs. "I don't know. I guess I'm the kind who acts like I'm not sick and don't need help, but I've been thinking about it more and more," she says, collecting herself. "I think I might need some help."

"How much time are you talking about?" Von holds one of Moxie's hands inside hers.

Moxie looks at her with gratitude. "I was okay right after she went to her father's, but today I realized she might not come back, and that hurts so much, Von." She blows her nose into the tissue. "I think I'll be all right if I can just make it a long weekend." Von tells her to print out her client list before leaving and urges her, again, to call the therapist. The same suggestion Norma posed to her over the years. Moxie certainly advocates therapy to clients but has been petrified by the thought of going herself, fearful that if she goes, she will discover something horrific.

She knows Norma and Von mean well, but all she needs is time at home with some Frankie Beverly, hot baths, and tea. The worst times ever were when Zadi turned the same age as she was when her mother died, and six years ago when she turned thirty-one, the age her mother was when she killed herself. Zadi was only a couple of years younger than Moxie had been. It was a terrible time—months of inexplicable sadness, crying bouts, and angry lashing out at those close to her. Norma helped a lot. That was when Norma first suggested counseling. The point is, though, she made it through. Came out on the other side. Felt the sun again.

After leaving work, without thinking about where she's going, she drives to her father's. Ponsey is outside talking to one of his neighbors. Moxie walks up and greets the neighbor, who then returns to her own house. Her father folds over the top of a plastic bag of Miracle-Gro and places it on the steps. The pale daffodils are in full bloom, and his rosebush has tiny leaves on it. She loves the order of her father's garden. Separate sections for different types of plants. Forget-me-nots, like little blue clouds, are in a spoon-shaped cluster in front of the windows to the basement. A rainbow of pansies loop around in front of the forsythia bush, whose flowers have come and gone. The grape hyacinths have purple pyramid blossoms that give off a wonderful fragrance. Moxie bends to take in their full perfume. "There was an orange butterfly around here for a good while today," her father says as if in the middle of a conversation. "I went in the house for lunch, came back out, she was still flying around. I think she liked the pansies. And some robins were here and a couple of goldfinches.

Moxie is pleased that since it's spring, her father can spend most of his time in his garden instead of in front of the TV or reading the tabloids. She's especially happy to see the tulips, imported from Holland lining the steps because her mother loved them so. Of all the flowers he grows, though, Moxie's favorite is the creeping phlox that remind her of tiny pinwheels spinning in the breeze.

She stoops, putting an arm around her father's shoulder. He is down on one knee packing dirt around the rosebush. "You've been out here a long time, haven't you?" she says, noticing his dirty apron and finger-nails.

"No, just a little while. Mostly thanking the earth and telling it what else I want. Thanking it for the strong tulips—they don't disappoint; every year they come back stronger than the year before. And for the plentiful daffodils. Look how they've doubled from last year." He points to his gems. "I tell the azaleas I want them to be lush and luxu-rious so Zadi can help me prune them. Old O. C. Scott died today. Remember him, Moxie? We were in medical school together. He was smart as a whip. His were the only notes I'd rely on other than my own. His wife called me from Chicago a little while ago. Can you give an old man a hand?" He reaches his arm out to her, sweater sleeve pushed up. She sees the way his flesh droops down and notices the age spots splat-tered across his skin. She pulls him up slowly, and they walk up the stairs together. She keeps his hand inside hers.

"I remember Mr. Scott. He and his wife came to my wedding, and didn't they stop in D.C. once on their way to Hilton Head? I'm so sorry, Daddy." She rubs his back as he walks into the living room.

He lowers himself heavily into his armchair. "I'm going to miss him. We'd catch up with each other on the phone every couple of months. Most of my buddies are gone, you know. Lost four last year. O.C.'s the first one this year." He stares off past her, as if momentarily he is with those friends or wondering what that day will be like for him. "Treasure your friendships, Moxie."

She nods, not wanting to get into that discussion.

"How's Norma anyway? Haven't seen her or heard you mention her since the exhibit."

"To be honest, we're not speaking right now, and I don't really want to talk about it."

"All right, if you say so. Kind of early for you to be off work, isn't it?"

"I needed a break. Want something to drink?" she asks, and goes into the kitchen to see what there is. When she returns, her father asks her to move his ottoman over and she does. He puts his socked feet up on it and takes a deep sip of the orange juice Moxie hands him. Moxie looks around the house. "Haleem do anything else?"

"No. He's got plenty to do at his place. I told him he did enough over here. Sit down, would you?" He sounds irritated. "You always dashing here and there. No wonder you look stressed out. I don't like to see you like this."

She sits and picks up one of her father's plant-and-flower magazines from a pile on the floor and begins flipping through it. "Did you order anything new this year?"

"Just my bulbs. And a Christmas rose bush. Should be beautiful. Don't change the subject—what's the matter with you?"

His question is enough to start the tears. "Everything," she says.

"Oh, Moxiegirl. What is it?" He leans toward her.

She tells him about Zadi and Octavius, the diary and the resulting estrangement.

He breathes heavily. Maybe she shouldn't have told him. It might be enough to give him a heart attack. He lifts his eyebrows, compressing the skin on his forehead into tiny rolls. "She hasn't left you. Give her some time to figure things out. I'm thinking about what your mother used to say even though she couldn't seem to make it work for herself. She'd tell me, 'Ponsey, life isn't about pain. It's about how you get through the pain.' It's probably a good thing for Zadi to be with James right now, Moxie. A child needs two parents."

"But I only had you!"

He looks hurt. "For eleven years you had a damn good mother, too."

"Oh, I know that, but I shouldn't have gone to camp that summer. Just tell me, why did you make me? Remember how I pleaded? She might not have died if I stayed home."

He reaches across to her chair and shakes her by the arm. "No, Moxie. You couldn't save her. I couldn't save her. No one could, because the truth is, she didn't want to be saved."

Moxie gets out of her chair and sits at her father's feet, looking into his eyes. He places one hand on her locks and rubs her head. He picks up a lock at a time, caressing it, the way she used to do with Zadi's braids. She cries into her hands.

Before she leaves, she goes upstairs as always, into her mother's sewing room. The sewing machine. She still hasn't taken it to get repaired. She takes out the cloth to dust it and notices that someone has already dusted it. Impulsively she inserts a swatch of fabric, steps on the pedal and it works, stitching a neat line so quickly she has to move her fingers out of the way. She runs down the stairs, yelling to her father. "Ma's machine works! It's not broken anymore!"

He looks up from the newspaper. "I thought I told you. Haleem fixed it last week or so. Said it was something simple."

"Haleem fixed it?"

"Yes. I told you he was a good guy. Wish I could do something to repay him."

"He says you've done enough by being a kind neighbor."

Moxie leaves her father's house about four-thirty, thinking that Zadi should be at dance by now. She is armed with a bit more strength to handle what's before her. Ponsey walks her out to the porch. He smiles wearily, creases etched at his eye corners and circling his mouth. He waves when she's on the walkway and goes back into the house. Impulsively, Moxie decides to thank Haleem.

Jupiter is outside playing with a yo-yo. "Jupiter, where's your dad?"

"He's home."

"Is he busy?"

"No, he's just chanting."

"Oh, I shouldn't interrupt him, then. Tell him I stopped by."

"You can just knock. He won't mind. He finished doing gongyo—I mean, his prayers. That's the only time you can't interrupt him." Jupiter never once looks up from his yo-yo.

"Sure?" Moxie asks. Jupiter nods. When she gets to the front door, she hesitates at the low humming sound. Listening closer, she realizes the sound is unfamiliar words being repeated over and over. She rings, but there is no answer. She tries the door and goes inside, following the chanting sound to Haleem's large living room. She sits down in an armchair, diagonally behind Haleem. He is on his knees with his hands, palms together, clutching a pair of wooden prayer beads. Directly in front of him is a low table with lighted candles, a bowl of fruit, and two vases that hold evergreen branches presumably from her father's shrubbery. Haleem stares directly at a scroll with Chinese lettering encased in a mahogany cabinet, repeating the odd sounds she heard from outside. She watches, strangely soothed by the rhythm of the words. The lowering sun outside peeks through Haleem's window to the left of him, covering his dining room table with a soft, warm glow.

She looks around. The walls appear to be recently painted and the woodwork stained. Several African masks hang in the room as well as a large reproduction of the South African voting ballot the year Nelson Mandela was elected. The couch is covered with a large mudcloth throw, and a vase filled with dried flowers is in the center of the coffee table. On the wall to her right are the framed words: "Faith alone is what really matters." Moxie sits back in her seat and listens to the way Haleem's sounds reverberate throughout the room.

Haleem reaches out and, with a wooden stick, hits a small bell atop an embroidered cushion. Then, after chanting three more times, he rises from his knees, shaking out his legs. He seems slightly surprised to see her. "Hi. I was just finishing my evening prayers."

Moxie stands up. "Sorry to have interrupted you. Jupiter said it would be okay. He said you had finished."

"You didn't interrupt me. I had finished the prayer portion and was chanting before ending it." He points back to the armchair. "Have a seat. I'm surprised, shocked really, to see you. Pleasantly, though." Moxie sits again. "Can I get you something to drink? Take your coat?"

"No, thanks. Just stopped by for a minute. What were the words you were saying?"

Haleem sits on the end of the couch from her. "I was chanting, 'Nam Myoho Renge Kyo.'" When she looks puzzled, he adds, "It's a phrase that connects me with the universe."

Moxie nods, not sure what to make of Haleem's statement. Instead of pursuing it, she studies the small, tightly wound sprouts of hair on his head. "I see you started locking. Did you call the loctitian I recommended?" He nods, smiles briefly. "They look good."

"Thanks."

"Haleem, I came over to thank you for fixing my mother's sewing machine. I tried to fix it myself, and then I was going to take it somewhere. But I got sidetracked by my life and didn't follow through. I don't know how to say what that sewing machine means to me. It's all I have of her." She crosses her legs underneath the chair. They both turn toward the door as Jupiter comes in, picks up a basketball lodged in one corner of the room, and goes back out.

Haleem stretches his arms along the top of the couch. "Your dad told me the sewing machine wasn't working, and I took a look. I don't know what it is, but I never met a broken appliance I didn't try to fix. When the sewing needle broke, the bobbin case got broken, too. It was just a matter of replacing the bobbin case." He rubs the palms of his hands together. "No big deal."

"Well, it is a very big deal to me. She loved that sewing machine and made me such beautiful creations with it. I used to get so much comfort when I came home from school and heard her working on it. That meant she wasn't in a 'mood'—that's what my father and I called her depression. I got the same kind of comfort visiting his house and turning it on. So when it wasn't working, I was really upset." She hesitates. "Did my father tell you . . . about her?"

"Yes. I'm sorry."

She looks over to the window on the other side of the room. The sun casts an orange haze now as it sinks lower in the sky. "It's been really hard. No one could have told me it would be this hard for this long." Moxie stands. She looks at the framed words on his wall again. "Do you believe that—'faith alone really matters'?"

"With all my heart," Haleem says. Moxie walks toward the front door, and he opens it wide for her. They both walk onto the porch. Jupiter is shooting his basketball into the hoop erected in the driveway.

"See you later. Thanks again." Moxie smiles at Haleem and descends the steps. "See you, Jupiter."

"Bye," he says, dribbling. "Hey, Dad, one-on-one?"

"In a sec," she hears Haleem answer as she waits for a car to go by before crossing the street to her own car. "Moxie," he calls.

She stops at the curb. He comes down from the porch and out of his fence's gate. He slips his hands into the pockets of his jeans, takes out one of his business cards, scribbles something, and hands it to her. "Here—I wrote down the words I was chanting. Try repeating them to yourself sometime. They'll help with whatever, I promise."

"Thank you."

"You know—I hope you don't mind me saying this—but just because your mother took her own life doesn't mean she didn't love you."

"My father has been telling me that forever, and I do know it in my mind, but I'm just starting to know it in my heart." She thanks Haleem again and leaves.

Friday, April 9th
Tommy Jeans
red/black stretch top
Nine West Mary Janes

Dear Sistergirl:

Still at Dad's. Haven't talked to That Woman and don't plan to.

Went to ballet rehearsal after school. It was personally one of the best rehearsals I've had. I think because I could become someone else. I didn't want to deal with how I am still feeling kind of messed up right now. I was glad to become Odette/Odile. Next week we start rehearsing on Wednesdays, too, to get ready for the show.

Talked to O tonight. He was like what happened? He thought Ma beat my ass. I was like, she better not try to do that. He was like, she looked like she was going to. I told him what she did, but he didn't think that was as bad as if she had beaten on my ass. And I said it was worse. He said that she gave him a hard time earlier that day, too. He started working over at that radio station, so that's cool. He's going to the Black Hole with one of his friends. Playas, he calls them. I realized I never even met any of his friends. He never met mine either, except Allegra. He wants me to go to the Black Hole with him next weekend. He always says the gogos I've been to are fake. This is supposedly the real deal. He wants me to hear Northwest Youngins instead of what he calls the lollipop bands from somebody's basement that they have at private school gogos. According to him, the Youngins are crucial. When I told him that at private school gogos you have to dance like a foot apart, he laughed and said at the Black Hole you can lay on top of somebody if you want to. Dad might not want me to go because big mouth (That Woman) told him about Octavius and he got on my case. But I think I convinced him that me and O were just hanging out. I told him we weren't having sex, but I crossed my fingers behind my back, so I wasn't really lying. I definitely am going to stop lying. But Dad was trying to act really strict. He said, Zadi, this is serious. You cannot forge letters and play hooky. It is totally unacceptable. What am I going to have to do to impress this fact on you? What kind of punishment do you think you should have? I said, I guess I shouldn't be able to go to the movies or the mall or anyplace for a while. I should just be able to spend the night at Allegra's. He didn't say anything. But going over there shouldn't be a problem cause Dad doesn't do all that calling and checking with the other parents, like she does. He trusts me more than That Woman does for real. Even now. Anyway, next weekend I can go to the gogo first and go to Allegra's after. I got to call her and see what's up. Her situation is just the opposite. Her pops is the one always on her case. Her mother is more chill, but since they're together, they can influence each other. That's why she's always telling me I'm lucky my parents are divorced. I guess she's right.

Twenty-two | Norma hasn't wanted to face her feelings about Lawrence moving out. He did promise not to move until Bernard is gone, which is three weeks away. She overheard Bernard suggesting they look for a place together, which he said would speed up his departure, but she couldn't make out Lawrence's response.

When Norma and Miles enter the house for the evening, they are immediately blasted by the Four Tops singing "Sugar Pie Honey Bunch." Even Miles covers his ears. "Too loud, Mommy." She storms through the house, her mind raging. Bernard has turned up all the speakers, and the sound is deafening. She goes straight to the stereo in the family room and shuts off the CD player. Miles runs around behind her.

"Hey! What the . . . ?" Bernard comes out of the living room with a beer bottle in one hand and a cigarette hanging between his lips. "Oh, man." He looks at his watch and turns away from her, slightly wobbly on his feet. He is barefoot, wearing sweatpants and a V-neck T-shirt. "Damn. Watch must have stopped. I wasn't expecting you all for another hour."

"How many times do I have to tell you—no smoking in this house—at all!" She glares at the bottle in his hand. "And no food or drink in the living room! What were you doing in there, anyway?"

He drops his cigarette in the bottle and it makes a sizzling sound. "Nothing, Queen Bee. Just trying to give the room some action. Seems like nobody ever goes in there. Bunch of rooms in here you all don't use."

"Have you completely lost your mind?" she shrieks at him. "You need to stay in the basement. You don't belong up here!"

"Hey, little man." His voice and eyes soften as he looks down at Miles. He rubs his head, and Miles sidles next to him.

"I cut my finger at school, see?" Miles shows Bernard his colorful Band-Aid.

"Oh, but you're brave and tough like your Uncle Bernie, aren't you?"

"Yeah, I'm brave and tough."

"Miles, I need to talk to Bernard, okay? You can choose a video to watch until dinner's ready." Norma helps Miles with the VCR and then beckons for Bernard to follow her into the hallway. He walks up close enough for her to smell the smoke on his clothes and in his hair. "We made a grave mistake letting you stay here. I better not catch you upstairs roaming around again." She keeps her voice low because of Miles, but nonetheless, she is screaming.

Bernard acts as if he's making a layup shot and tosses his beer bottle into the wastebasket. He moves past her, but instead of going toward the basement, he returns and gets down on the rug with Miles. Unfortunately for Norma, Miles actually enjoys his company. She says nothing.

In the kitchen, she heats up some of Mrs. Coleman's spaghetti in the microwave. Lawrence told her he would be late tonight because he is meeting with partners from the other law firm he's considering joining. When she carries a plate in to Miles, he and Bernard are lying on pillows and laughing. Miles rolls away from Bernard, who is tickling him. "Can you play Lego with me?" Miles asks as he pulls his Lego bin out from under the television.

"Not right now." He grins at his nephew and slides his arm from around him. "I better go downstairs because the witch is back." He stands and glares at Norma.

"What witch?"

"Ask your mama." Bernard leaves.

"Where's the witch, Mommy? Uncle Bernie said the witch is back."

Norma shakes her head, exasperated. "There's no damn witch, Miles! Eat your dinner now! It's almost bedtime." It's not really, but once he's in bed, she'll have a better chance of sorting out her feelings.

His food remains untouched while he continues building a Lego statue. "Miles, I said EAT! Now!" She bends down, grabs his fork, and starts scooping the food into his mouth. He holds the spaghetti in his cheeks instead of swallowing it and starts to cry. "All right, then. No dessert. No ice cream for you! Let's go. You're going to bed now!" She pulls him up by his right arm, and the Lego in his fist falls to the floor.

In Miles's bathroom she only runs enough water to cover his thighs and doesn't add any bubble bath. "Can I have the little animals in my water?" Miles asks, still sniffling.

"No animals! Just get in the tub, Miles!" His bath is brisk, and she is relieved to finally get him in the bed. She doesn't feel like reading a bed-time story but knows that it's her duty. She selects one from Miles's bookcase and races through it, randomly skipping whole paragraphs. Miles whimpers when she kisses his forehead. She leaves on the light in his closet, hoping that will compensate.

Returning to the kitchen with Miles's barely touched plate of food, she hears laughter trickling from the partially open basement door. Mixed in with Bernard's guffaws is the giggling of a woman. She puts the plate on the counter, goes down the basement steps two at a time, and pushes open the door to the room Bernard occupies. Only a dim lamp illuminates the room. She has to get closer and narrow her eyes to see. The sofa bed is fully opened, sheets twisted around two bodies. Items of clothing dangle from the bed, and the room gives off a salty smell—a fusion of heat, sex, and sweat. A bare-chested Bernard sits upright when she enters. He removes his right arm from around the naked shoulders of a woman wearing blond crochet extensions. "Excuse me! Ho-tel's closed now—time for you to go, miss!" Norma stares incredulously at the woman and at Bernard. She hears the phone ringing upstairs.

"You shouldn't be so damn rude. Busting in here like that." He pulls the sheet across his lower body and tries to nuzzle back against the woman, but she grabs her discarded blouse from the floor and starts dressing.

"Sorry, ma'am," she says. "He said it would be okay. I don't want to be in the middle of nothin', though."

"Smart lady," Norma says. "Show her the door, Bernard, and you better damn well go through it right behind her!"

Bernard leaps up, wearing only his underpants, and follows her to the basement hallway, where they face each other in the muted light. "Maybe Lawrence lets you talk to him like that, but I don't play that shit! Understand?"

"Get the fuck out of my face, Bernard. Fun and games are over. You're out of here! Understand?"

"You don't rule me, bitch! I don't leave until Lawrence tells me to." His words spit out onto her face.

"Well, he'll be telling your ass to leave as soon as he gets here. You must be fucking crazy!" She stomps up the stairs and tries to reach Lawrence on his cell phone. When only the voice-mail message comes on, she slams the phone down and stands by the front window, pushing the drapes aside. Whoever called earlier left no message; she's sure it was Lawrence on his way home. She's so irate her whole body is trembling. Lawrence should be driving up any minute, though. He'll make Bernard leave when she tells him what happened. She should have told him about the other things even before this. All week long Lawrence has been home before seven o'clock. It's approaching ten. After a few minutes she sees the shadow of a figure running up the street. She looks harder. It's Bernard's woman friend. He didn't even have the decency to take her to the metro or put her in a damn cab.

Norma knows standing by the window is not going to make Lawrence arrive any quicker, so she leaves her post. She takes a forkful of Miles's cold food that she left on the kitchen counter. It tastes like paste in her mouth. Then she tries calling Lawrence again.

She pours herself a glass of wine and carries it upstairs to the bedroom, resting it on the night table. She sits on the edge of the bed, fuming. Even though instinctively she didn't want Bernard to stay, she never dreamed he'd go this far. She tastes the wine slowly and listens to the silence in the house. The only sounds are a soft rain outside and the pattering noise of cars traveling along Sixteenth Street. An ambulance wails, immediately followed by a howl from the neighbor's rottweiler. When that's happened before, Miles says the rottweiler "copies" the ambulance.

The bed yields to her form as she does her relaxation exercises. Still tense, she puts her hands to her neck and presses deeply with her fingers and rubs. She turns on the lamp near her bed, gets up, turns off the overhead light, and with one smooth motion, removes her slacks, tossing them onto the back of the chair in front of the vanity.

Norma lies across the bed, with her eyes closed, waiting for Lawrence. She dangles on the edge of sleep, until she hears a sound outside her door. Not knowing whether twenty seconds have passed or twenty minutes, she calls out, "Lawrence?" as she sits up and rubs at her eyes. She doesn't want him to assume she's asleep and head straight for the other bedroom. The door opens all the way, and Bernard stands there. She glances at her slacks on the chair, wishing she hadn't removed them.

"'Lawrence?'" He exaggerates her query into a high-pitched echo. "Trying to sound so sweet and innocent calling for your husband. After you just got finished cussing me out like I'm some shit you stepped in. I've had about as much of you as I'm going to tolerate. You and all your damn rules. Rule for this; rule for that. No smoking in here. No drinking over there. Bernard, don't do this. Bernard, don't do that. Bernard, don't breathe the fucking air! You *always* thought you were some better brand of nigger than me, didn't you? But lo and behold, you're nothing but a cheap whore!"

She looks around the room to see what she can throw if she has to. There's a ceramic vase on the night table that might suffice. It's on the other side of the bed, though. "Get out of my room, Bernard. I already told you to get out of my house!"

"Oh, still the tough-girl act, huh?" He steps into the room and stands at the foot of the bed with his legs splayed. "Let's see how big and bad you really are."

Reflexively, she grips the bedcovers tightly in each hand. "I said— get out of here," she repeats. "I mean it!"

"Oh, yeah? Who's going to make me?" He moves beside the bed, towering over her, shifting back and forth on his feet.

"You don't scare me," she lies. Norma feels trapped in this position but begins slowly inching over toward the vase. Bernard sinks one of his knees down onto the bed, brushing against her thigh. He grabs her shoulder, just as she reaches out for the vase. She cannot quite get her whole hand around it, touching only the outer edge. When Bernard exhales, she can feel the heat of it on the side of her face. He pushes his knee further down onto the bed. The phone rings again. She knows it's Lawrence and desperately wishes she could answer. Bernard grabs a handful of her hair, snatching her neck back so fast it makes a soft cracking sound. His scent alone is enough to suffocate her. He holds on to her hair while he folds his other hand around her neck and continues his harangue. "You must think your pussy's gold or somethin'." He yanks her neck again, jerking her head farther back still.

Norma's breath comes in quick, short pants. "Let . . . go . . . of . . . me," she says with difficulty, as the tight pulling on her hair forces her eyes to the ceiling. But she is able to move one more time and firmly grip the vase without him paying attention. She lifts and swings it, bringing it with as much force as she can muster to the left side of Bernard's face. The vase falls to the floor and Bernard loses his balance.

"Shit!" He touches the side of his head. When he discovers there is blood, he grabs her shoulders again and shakes her. "You crazy bitch, I'll whip your fucking ass!" He repeatedly smacks her across the face. She tries to scratch him when he grabs her hands. A shadowy feeling passes over her eyes, as if she might faint.

"Uncle Bernie, why are you hurting Mommy?"

Bernard lets go of Norma abruptly, and then he runs from the room, knocking over the vanity chair. Miles comes to Norma and looks up at her with deep concern. "Mommy, your nose is bleeding!" Norma, coughing and hyperventilating, pulls Miles onto the bed with her. She tries to catch her breath as she holds Miles tightly with her arms wrapped around him. "Don't cry, Mommy," he comforts.

She hugs Miles closer to her, rubbing her face into his tiny beads of hair. "Oh, Miles, you saved Mommy. Do you know that? I'm going in the bathroom to wash my face, okay?" He follows, grabbing on to her leg while she uses a washcloth to wipe away the blood collected around her nostrils. After, they make their way down the hall to Miles's bedroom, where she sits on the bed, cradles his head in her arms, and tries to get him to sleep again. Her neck is so sore that she has to move very slowly as she attempts to lie down with Miles. He clutches at her, not willing to release her, and they lie there, in his narrow bed shaped like a race car, holding on to each other. Miles drifts off to sleep, still clutching her hand. She disengages his fingers and pulls the covers over him.

She returns to her room and eases her now severely aching body onto her bed, stuffing pillows behind her, trying to relieve the burning in her back. She wonders if Bernard is still in the house. At the thought that he might be, she starts to tremble and cry uncontrollably. Then she hears the front door opening, closing, and being locked.

"What the hell happened in here?" Lawrence looks at the overturned chair and the vase broken on the rug near the wall. Norma tells him, feeling the terror again as she watches it appear on Lawrence's face. He says he tried to call. He sits on the bed and holds her, gently, so it won't hurt too much, while she cries onto his chest. "Jesus," he says more than once. "We'd better get you to the hospital."

"No. I'm okay. Just sore. If Miles hadn't come in when he did, I probably would have needed the hospital. Or worse. I'll call my doctor in the morning."

"Are you sure?"

Lawrence carefully massages her back and neck in the spots she points out. He listens to her describe how frightened she was. "I just didn't want to die. That's all I remember thinking—I'm not ready to die." She cries again. She convinces him she wants to rest and to know that Bernard is gone.

After pulling the comforter over her and making certain she is comfortable for the moment, Lawrence leaves to find Bernard. Norma drifts in and out of an agitated sleep, and has no idea how long Lawrence is gone. When he returns, though, she can tell he's been outside. He is also out of breath. "You won't have to worry about Bernard anymore," is all he will say. "I'm so sorry, Norma. Damn. I guess I didn't take his problems seriously enough. Thank God you're all right." He caresses her though the comforter. "What can I do for you?" he asks. "Is there anything I can do?"

She thinks back to the night Moxie came to her, under almost the same circumstances. All she did was give her wine and Frankie Beverly. At the time, she didn't know what more to offer, what more Moxie might need. "Just keep talking to me. Keep holding me. Don't leave me alone . . . I'm scared if I go to sleep, I'll see Bernard's face again." Lawrence nods as she speaks. He helps her get up and go to the bath-

room, where she almost collapses at the sink. He carries her back to the
bed and promises her each time she asks that he's not going anywhere.

Monday, April 13th
Express Classic Fit jeans
silver Bebe shirt (borrowed from
* Windy)*
blk Nikes

Dear Sistergirl:
  *We had the Peer Review hearing this afternoon. Dad came, and the
whole committee questioned me. The committee is made up of six
students and two teachers. Nobody black on it this year. Windy is on the
committee, but she had to recuse herself because we're friends. Some of
their questions seemed like they were just trying to be nosy. Like, why was
it so important for you to leave school early that day? Why couldn't you
wait until school got out? I was not about to tell them all my business,
but I didn't want to totally lie either. Dad was just sitting there rubbing
his hands together. He looked so sad, and that made me feel really bad. I
told the board that my reason was probably not going to sound like a
good reason to them and so I'd rather not say except that it felt to me like
something that couldn't wait. Zadi, do you have any regret or remorse
about your actions? Yes, I do because it upset a lot of people, and I would
not ever do it again. Really, I didn't know what else to say. The board has
to meet in private, and then they send out a recommendation to you in
the mail. They can recommend suspension, expulsion, or that you write
an essay about what you did wrong and have you read it to the whole
school. The head of school makes the final decision.*
  *I walked Dad to the parking lot, and he said he hopes I realize that
Octavius is bad news and that he thought I knew better than to be
dealing with any of my mother's clients. I tried to tell him how O is a
musician like him, but he didn't want to hear about it. He said he knows
I'm smart and will make better decisions from now on and that not
seeing O anymore should be one of them. I had my fingers crossed when I
said okay.*

Fawna and Tiffany picked me up after ballet. We went and got Chinese food. The rabbit in Tiffany's classroom died, so she was kind of quiet and didn't get on my nerves too much.

I just realized I am going to need a whole rack of clothes for New York. I don't hardly have any summer clothes. Definitely need some platform sandals. What did I wear last summer? I said something about New York when I was talking to O, and now he is tripping. He says I never told him I was going to New York for six weeks. I was like, I told you about the auditions at Duke Ellington way long time ago and how I got in and everything. He just doesn't remember. I am going to miss him for real, but nothing, not even a booty call, can stop me from going to New York.

Dad made me talk to That Woman just now on the phone because he said it's been almost a week and that's long enough. She said something about how she understands that I felt violated but that she felt deceived, too, and that is why she had to do something so drastic as reading my diary. I didn't say anything because basically she already said this to me and I don't think that's any excuse. She said she understands that I need some space and hopes I'll come home soon. I didn't really know what to say because I definitely need a break from all the tripping she does about everything. It's so much less stressful over here (even with the two chicken-heads, Fawna and Tiffany). That Woman said, Zadi, I love you and miss you very much. I didn't say anything, and so she acted all frantic, saying, did you hear what I said? I was like yes, I heard you. Basically.

Twenty-three | On Tuesday, the day after Bernard's assault, Lawrence takes Norma to see her doctor who X-rays her neck and back, the most tender areas of her body. There are no fractures, just bruises and a strain. He prescribes a removable medical collar and suggests she take it easy for the next couple of days. Lawrence calls in to his office and stays home with her, preparing meals, offering very gentle massages, and taking Miles back and forth to school. Lawrence has been sleeping in the master bedroom, and has returned his toiletries to their bathroom. They both seem to instinctively sense, however, that the road back to intimacy should be at an unhurried pace. She sleeps most of the time, but sometimes she awakens in midremembrance of Bernard's hands clutched at her neck.

On Thursday, while Lawrence is at the grocery store, Woody phones her. He apologizes for calling her at home, but he's been worried. They haven't spoken in weeks. She tells him she's been thinking about him, too, that she's been under the weather but is feeling much better and wants to talk to him in person. She can hear the shreds of anxiety in his voice. Woody and Norma agree to meet the next day at a small park near her studio.

She arrives at the park before him. She's glad they decided to meet outside because it's another perfect sixty-degree day. The sky looks like a lovingly painted canvas, the blue of it startlingly fresh, as if just washed. There are a few people jogging around the small park. One black and one Hispanic woman walk by pushing white babies in strollers. The tiny park is not in the best of shape. Patches of dirt, resembling ring-worm scars, spread between the sparse patches of grass. Lopsided bushes shoot up as if spit from the ground. Most of the trees seem frail except for one thick oak with bark like an elephant's trunk. A white couple, both in shorts, has brought a blanket out onto the grass. Norma watches them spread the blanket. The man carries a wicker bas-ket, which he places on the grass beside him when he sits. The woman leans across him to open the basket, but he takes her hand and puts it around his neck so he can kiss her.

Norma looks away, across the street, to the children playing in the school yard and smiles at their yelps of laughter. Several wait their turn on the steps of the large plastic slide, while others are being pushed back and forth on the swings. A group of small boys plays basketball without a net. The one dribbling reminds her of Miles, because of his slightly bowed legs. A man in dingy, heavy winter clothing, whom she noticed at the other end of the park when she first arrived, comes up to her and asks for money to buy a cup of coffee. He smells like stale chicken soup. She rustles through her wallet and gives him a crisp dol-lar bill. He grins. "Thanks, you got a cigarette?" he asks through his grimy lips.

"No," she says and looks away, hoping he'll disappear. He slinks away toward the couple on the grass. She sees Woody from afar. Everything she's tried to hold in her head, about what she wants to say to him, seeps out as he walks over. When she started seeing him, she never contemplated that she might hurt him. She never thought the relationship all the way through. He waves at her wildly, and he quick-ens his pace after spotting her. His tie flutters in the breeze, and he flicks his unruly hair back from his face with one hand. In the other hand he carries a white plastic bag.

"Hey there!" he says, slightly breathless. Blotches of pink appear on his cheeks. He brandishes the white plastic bag. "I brought those chicken salad sandwiches you like." He sits beside her on the bench.

"Thank you." She doesn't reach for the sandwiches.

He inquires about the neck brace. "Just a strain," she says.

"Do you want to stay here?" he asks, examining their surroundings.

"It's fine," she says. A slight breeze blows a piece of paper onto Norma's foot. She kicks it away.

He reaches out to touch her arm through her jacket. "So? We haven't seen each other in forever. On the phone, when I said I wanted to see you, you said we needed to talk. Sounded like different things to me, or am I being paranoid?"

"No . . . I said I wanted to talk because . . . some things have changed." She tries to smile at him, but he doesn't smile back.

He takes out his cigarettes. "Well, I knew something happened. That day at the studio you said you were going to call, but you never did. What if I hadn't called this week? Would I have ever heard from you again?" He looks down at the bag of sandwiches on his lap.

"Woody, I do care about you. . . ."

"Uh-oh," he says. "Should I expect the violins? This sounds like a line from a tragic romance." She glances at his profile while he stares straight ahead. In their short time together, she hasn't witnessed displays of anger or bitterness before. Strands of hair he has pushed behind his ear become loose, and he tucks them in again with the tips of his fingers. He inhales deeply.

Norma feels as though she has to keep talking. "I'm not saying that everything is going to work out with Lawrence. All I know is I want to try. I would have called you, soon."

"Let's get out of here," Woody says. She's not sure why but thinks maybe it's because of the couple on the blanket, nuzzling each other between bites of their picnic lunch. As Norma and Woody leave the park, Woody tosses the bag of sandwiches to the homeless man, now sitting beneath the large oak tree. Slowly, they walk up Third Street in the direction of Pennsylvania Avenue. Woody removes his sports coat and tosses it over one shoulder. He looks up at the sky. Norma looks, too. The sky has a gray tinge to it, and the clouds have merged. "Good. It's going to rain," he says. "That idyllic park setting was getting to me. So, I guess there's nothing to say?" He stops walking and leans one arm on a parking meter. "I went into this with my eyes open."

Norma feels teary. "I didn't intend to hurt you. I hope you know that."

"Once you told me that you loved me. Did you mean it?" He begins walking again. She does the same. The least she can do is let him decide when the conversation should end.

"I meant it when I said it, Woody. Please don't underestimate your importance—you gave me some of myself back. Here, we're at my car." They come together awkwardly and hold each other briefly. He kisses her on the side of her face. His lips feel out of place against her skin. Norma climbs into her car and watches as he continues walking up Third Street. The sound of thunder cracks overhead, and beads of rain begin to dot her windshield. Then the rain suddenly bears down, slapping against the glass. She can still see Woody. She didn't ask where his car was or whether he wanted a ride to it. He seems undaunted by the rain. She sits riveted, watching him hold his jacket up over his head, his form gradually becoming smaller. She widens her eyes until finally she can no longer see him. "Well," she says aloud. Norma is rather surprised that it has ended so quickly and cleanly. If someone were to ask her how she feels, she would not know how to describe it. Partially relieved and partially hollow, she would say if pressed for an answer.

Instead of going back home or to the studio, on an impulse, she drives down the street to Miles's preschool. She knows it is almost the end of nap time. The children lie on their cots and the lights are dimmed. One of the teachers puts snacks out on the table in the playroom; another is reading a paperback and eating an apple in the corner. The aide in Miles's classroom catches Norma's eye and smiles at her. She gestures toward Miles with her elbow, an expression of inquiry on her face. Norma shakes her head no, she's not in a rush. As if some silent alarm has gone off, several of the children begin to stir and whine. Miles raises his tiny rearend first and then his head. He sees Norma standing near the cubbies and comes to her, rubbing at his eyes, and says it's not time to go home yet. She tells him she wanted to surprise him and take him somewhere. He sits at the small table and eats his orange slices and juice. Afterwards, Norma proudly carries the shoe box that Miles finger-painted and reaches for his hand on the way out of the door.

They stop at the Fairy Godmother, a childrens' store on Capitol Hill, and she buys him the bathtub animal pills he likes and a kite that looks like a friendly dragon. Then they drive downtown and park close to the Washington Monument, where Norma remembers having come for a kite festival years ago. She removes her camera case from the trunk of her car. There is no festival today, but the rain has stopped; there are light wind gusts, and there is a hill. Norma reads the instructions and puts the kite together, pleased with herself for not reacting to Miles's impatient tugging. They stand on the hill and fly the kite. They run up and down the incline as the dragon kite streams out behind them. Norma stops for a few moments and shoots one shot after another of Miles running and laughing, using up an entire roll of film.

Another parent and child with the same idea are flying a kite that resembles a spaceship. The two children dash toward each other, and the kite strings tangle. After the child's father untangles them, the children know to move apart. She and Miles laugh until their stomachs hurt and fly the kite for hours. It falls to the ground a lot, but they begin again and again until they wear themselves out.

At home she lets Miles help her with dinner. He washes the lettuce and puts butter on the French bread. She broils swordfish and cooks red potatoes in the microwave. Norma cuts green pepper, mushrooms, and tomatoes for the salad, enjoying the rhythm of chopping. What do her mother and sister mean, she can't cook? Searching for the box of croutons she knows she bought, Norma ponders again about how her six months with Woody was dissolved in under an hour. Lawrence comes home when dinner is almost ready, and Miles excitedly recalls their afternoon of kite flying. After Miles is tucked in, Lawrence finally tells Norma the story of Bernard. How he threatened to turn him in to the police if he didn't leave, and bought him a one-way bus ticket. How they almost came to blows. Norma and Lawrence agree to tell Miles, who has been inquiring, only that Bernard went away for a long time because he did a very bad thing.

Later that night in bed, Lawrence puts his arm around her shoulder and asks if it hurts for him to do that. "No, it's okay." She whispers for no other reason than it's nighttime and it's dark and it seems appropriate. "It feels nice." She lays her head against his shoulder, listens to his breathing, and feels his chest moving in tandem with the breaths he takes. She can tell when the patterns change and he coasts into sleep. A picture of Woody comes to mind, how he looked earlier today when he walked up the street, away from her. How he walked, as always, leaning forward on the balls of his feet, looking like someone who, with a slight push, might topple over.

Friday, April 16th
blk lycra jeans
white T-shirt
blk Chinese slippers

Dear Sistergirl:

In study hall. So excited I can hardly do my work. I'm supposed to be studying because we're having a biology test Monday, but I will just have to study hard starting tomorrow.

This is the plan: I told myself that I was going to do my best not to have to lie to Dad anymore, but I couldn't take any chances that I wouldn't be able to go to the Black Hole tonight with O. So I told him I'm going to spend the night at Allegra's after dance, which I am, except not right after dance. Fortunately Dad has a gig downtown, so he won't be just sitting around at home wondering about me like Ma does. He said, how are you going to get to Allegra's? I was like, Dad, it will still be light out, I can take the metro and they'll meet me. (I didn't say who would meet me, so that part's not really a lie.) He said, have you done that before? I said yes (which is true). But really I am going to change my clothes in the bathroom after dance. The main problem is I won't be able to take a shower or anything. I brought a washcloth so I could wash up, though. I guess I'll be sweating in the Black Hole anyway, so it won't make that much difference. I was hoping me and O might get to slide a little bit and I wouldn't want to be all sweaty, but I don't know if we will. He thinks he's going to have the Blazer again. I don't know about doing it in a car, though. Anyway, the outfit: I have a black lace top I borrowed from Allegra and a black camisole (both she ordered from Victoria's Secret) in my dance bag and clean underpants and the black boots. Except I can't decide if I'd rather be comfortable in the Mary Janes or cute in the boots. My backpack is going to be heavy as a mug either way. O's going to meet me at the bus stop on Georgia Avenue with or without the car. If he doesn't have the car, we can take the bus up Georgia, so whatever. Now the problem is what to do when it's time to leave. I can't get to Allegra's too late. The gogo doesn't even start till ten, he said, so I'm thinking I have to be out of there by twelve, like Cinderella, and then take a cab to Allegra's. We just can't figure out where to tell her parents I'm coming from so late. I told Allegra to make up anything, but she's trying not to lie that much, especially when it doesn't have anything to do with her. We'll think of something between now and the end of school. Damn, I'm late for Geometry.

Twenty-four | Moxie has spent ten days without Zadi. She's ready for it to end, for Zadi to come home. They've talked, but only briefly, and it's been unsatisfying, like eating chips when you're hungry for a full meal. She has thrown herself into her work and tries to think about each client as some other mother's troubled child. Something she didn't always do before. She submitted a request to transfer Octavius to a different PO, without giving Von all the gory details. Let someone else, unbiased, decide what should happen with his life. She's sure he'll be locked up or sent to boot camp within the next few months.

Her master plan is to call James this weekend, set up a time to sit down with him and Zadi, and gently spread the issues out before them. Together they will decide when, not if, Zadi is going to return home.

With that settled in her mind, she doesn't allow herself to get melancholy, even though it's Friday. Facing the weekend with no Zadi seems especially difficult. No nine-to-five occupying her mind, no chauffeuring to ballet, no library runs. After leaving her office, Moxie snaps her seat belt into place and mulls over how to spend her evening. When she decides to pretend Zadi is simply on vacation again and that she has free time to splurge, her whole body feels lighter. She drives uptown and sees *Shakespeare in Love.* It is light and buoyant and captivates her mind for three hours. A love like that doesn't last anyway, she tells herself at the end of the movie.

She takes her time traveling out of the upper Northwest neighborhood. Even in the dark, the houses, and their invisible occupants, appear stressless and problem-free. She knows it's a superficial, non-

sensical assessment, but block after block of spacious, sturdy residences
with thriving grass and gardens, bikes and kiddie cars trustingly left on
lawns, lead her to draw such conclusions. Resentment nags at her,
threatening to drag her down from the evening's relative high. Passing
Sixteenth Street, she wonders if Norma is still cavorting with her
Woody.

Back in her Northeast neighborhood, Moxie stops at a Chinese
take-out restaurant near her house and orders moo-shu chicken with
two extra pancakes, the way she usually does when she's going to share
with Zadi. She remembers, as she carries the warm bag of food to her
car, that she didn't need the extra pancakes and thinks about facing the
remainder of the night alone.

It is close to eleven-thirty when she arrives home. She can hear the
phone ringing as she turns her key in the lock, but she is too late. After
she turns on all the lights and drops her coat on a chair, she checks the
messages. There are three new ones. She presses down the button to
hear them. It's her father's voice telling her to come right away to
Washington Hospital Center's MedStar unit. Zadi is all right, but
there's been an accident. Moxie grabs her purse and keys and is out the
front door.

Her father said she was in the MedStar unit, which Moxie knows
means something serious, but he also said she was *all right*. That
thought keeps her steady and able to proceed without giving herself
over to panic. What were those chanting words Haleem told her to try?
Her free hand searches through the chaos of her purse for the card he
gave her. She pulls out several other cards. Finally, she retrieves the one
she wants and glances, intermittently as she drives, at what Haleem
wrote out. *"Nam Myoho Renge Kyo."* She repeats the strange words over
and over, unsure of the pronunciation, but sensing an undercurrent of
calm trying to reach her.

She rushes into the hospital following the signs for the MedStar unit
and searches for her father. Haleem comes up to her from behind. She
turns and presses her fingers into his arm. "Where is she? Can I see
her?"

"Moxie, I know you're upset. We haven't seen her yet, but they
assured us she's okay. They want you over at the registration desk," he

says. She follows him past people watching television or sleeping and several children talking loudly while playing. She sits down in front of a booth, frantically looking for Zadi's insurance card. A woman comes from the other side of the booth, and Moxie hands her all of Zadi's information. "Can I see her?" The woman tells her the doctor will be out to speak with her shortly, and meanwhile, she can wait in the family waiting room. Haleem shows her where it is, separate from the other large waiting room. Smaller and with more comfortable chairs. A nicer room for those with more serious concerns, she worries. Jupiter is there, staring up at the elevated television. Her father sits on the couch, looking small and sunken, like air has been sucked from his cheeks. "Daddy!" She bends to him, and he puts his arms around her. "Do you know what happened?"

Her father touches her cheek with one finger as she stoops before him. He shakes his head and looks at her, his face a mass of sags below his tired eyes. "Cops said there was a shooting at a gogo on Georgia Avenue."

"A shooting!" Moxie straightens up.

"Said they got Zadi in the leg. I was getting ready to call you again. They need to operate, take the bullet out."

"What? Zadi—got shot?" Moxie places one hand on her chest, the other over her face. Haleem asks if she's all right, if she wants to sit down. She doesn't know.

"They're doing something preliminary, cleaning the wound, doctor says."

"Nobody's seen her? I have to see her!" Moxie paces in the small room.

Her father wipes at the corner of his eye. "They said the doctor will be back out, Moxie. Tried to reach James. No one was there. Do you have some other number for him?"

Moxie collapses onto the couch beside her father. "A shooting. Zadi shot. Where are they? Why aren't they telling us anything?" She gets up again and goes to the door, looking down either end of the hallway. A man in scrub clothes wheels an IV by the door. "Excuse me," she says. "My daughter was brought here—a shooting—I need to find out what—"

"Ma'am, as soon as possible, somebody will be with you. I know it's agonizing to have to wait." He smiles at her and continues down the hall.

Haleem stands beside Jupiter, one arm resting on his shoulder. Jupiter looks at Moxie with concern. She feels dizzy and leans against the wall. "Why don't you have a seat?" says Haleem again, pointing to a space on the couch beside her father. They are the only people in the room. "If you have a number for James, I don't mind calling."

"I'd better do it," Ponsey says.

Moxie clutches at her thoughts, desperate not to let them stray to the worst scenario. Finding a piece of scrap paper in her purse, she shakily writes down James's cell phone number and gives it to her father. A young white woman, holding a manila folder, comes into the waiting area, and Moxie and her father look up expectantly. She tells them she's a social worker whose job it is to sit with the family while they're waiting to learn about a loved one. She has a gentle voice and manner Moxie appreciates. She pulls a chair over to the couch and shakes everyone's hand. "We don't know anything yet. Just that she was shot in the leg. I'm her mother," Moxie says, barely recognizing her own voice. The woman tells them that, yes, Zadi was injured in the shooting, that she was conscious when she arrived at the hospital, though in some pain. She reiterates that the doctor will speak to them shortly.

Ponsey leaves to call James. His back is bent and his shoulders slump as if too heavy to lift.

Twenty minutes pass before a middle-aged black doctor enters the waiting room and introduces himself as Dr. Monroe, the chief surgeon on Zadi's case. The social worker gives him her seat, and she moves onto the couch with Moxie and her father. Dr. Monroe says the area of the wound has been preliminarily cleaned of debris and fragments. He needs Moxie's permission to operate and remove the bullet. It appears to have fractured her femur, but he'll know more once he operates.

"Will she be all right? Her leg—Will she be . . . able to walk?"

"We'll have better answers to all your questions when we can assess exactly what the bullet did."

"How long will the operation take?" Ponsey asks.

"I'd say about two hours, maybe less."

"Can I see her before you do that?"

"We've given her something for the pain, so she may be a little out of it, and she's still quite messy with blood. But you can go in briefly. Also the police are going to want to talk to you."

Moxie scribbles her signature onto the consent form and follows the doctor through two sets of large metal doors into one of the operating rooms. Several nurses and doctors are working around Zadi. Their gloved hands are bloody. Zadi's eyes are closed, and her hair is matted around her face with specks of blood decorating the strands. Her hands are crossed, resting on her chest, rivulets of dried blood staining them. A spearlike ache catches Moxie in her side, as if something is stuck between her ribs. A short screen has been erected across Zadi's middle to separate the area of the wound. From where she stands, Moxie can see only her toes, which appear pale and puffy. Moving closer, she sees that Zadi's pants have been cut away to her groin area. The pillows and sheet under her leg are crimson with her blood. Moxie wants to shake her, make sure she's not dead, even though she can see her chest moving. She begins to weep. A nurse, who is adjusting an IV, comes over and reassures her. She tells her she can speak to Zadi if she'd like.

Moxie tiptoes, as if instructed to be quiet, over to Zadi's side. She touches her face, which is also blood splattered. Zadi slowly lifts her eyelids and stares with a startled look at Moxie. Her lips part. Tears cloud her eyes, and her voice sounds scratchy as she moans, "Mommy." She tries to sit up, but the effort makes her shake almost convulsively.

"Everything's all right, Zadi. Don't be scared. I'm here and I love you."

Back in the family waiting room, Moxie buries her head in her father's shoulder. "James is on his way," he tells her. "The police came when you were with Zadi. They'll be back."

In a few minutes, two policemen return and ask questions about Zadi and Octavius, what time they went to the Black Hole, whether they frequent the club on a regular basis, who their enemies are, whether they had any involvement with drugs. She doesn't know; she can't answer. She holds her stomach as she listens to the police talk. "Black Hole is the right name for that hell hole," the black officer says, looking at Moxie skeptically, as if she granted Zadi permission to go there. "Kids go in there and come back out in boxes. They got metal detectors at the door, so the little hoodlums sneak in with the band or through the exit door or something."

"What kind of gun was it?" Haleem asks.

"Nine millimeter Glock," the white officer answers. "Good thing most of these punks never had any target practice. In your daughter's case, it could have been much worse. And as usual, nobody saw nothing." Moxie tells them Octavius Johnson is her client, and that he has a juvenile record. The policemen say they'll need to question him and Zadi later. She learns that Octavius was treated and released from the regular emergency room of the same hospital.

"I hope I never get shot," Moxie hears Jupiter say to his father.

James arrives after the police have gone. "Where is she? How's she doing?" He removes his jacket and holds it over his arm.

On the verge of tears again, Moxie screams at him. "She's been shot, James! She's covered with blood! You were supposed to be watching her! She was staying with you!"

James looks as if he is going to cry, as well. "She—said she was going to Allegra's . . ."

"You fell for another one of her lies? After the last time? What the hell is the matter with you?"

"Moxie, I didn't think . . ."

"That's right! You didn't think!"

Ponsey holds his hand up. "It's not going to help Zadi for you two to have an argument. The doctor said he'll be able to answer our questions after the operation. Why don't you get yourself a chair, James?" As if just realizing Ponsey's there, James takes his hand and shakes it hard. Ponsey introduces him to Haleem and Jupiter, who decide to go find the cafeteria.

James paces from the waiting room out into the hallway and back again. Moxie and her father remain on the couch. David Letterman signs off on the television, but no one is watching. Moxie can't concentrate on anything. Ponsey pats Moxie's hand, restless in her lap. "She'll be all right, sweetheart," he says. "I know she'll be all right. Have faith."

Moxie can't stop picturing Zadi with all that blood on her. Things that carried such a weighted significance have instantly cascaded to a level of minute importance. Zadi's hair—does it really matter if it's straight or natural, when it's now caked with blood? Zadi's lost virginity—how important when compared with a lost life or no ability to walk?

Shortly after two A.M., Dr. Monroe reappears. James and Moxie spring up almost simultaneously. Moxie scans his face trying to read answers in it, but all she can discern is that he's weary. "Let's sit down," he says. "She's very lucky. She has a single break in her mid-femur, or thigh bone. There was no vascular or neurological damage. We had to insert internal pins to make sure the fracture heals correctly, and we put her leg in traction." Dr. Monroe removes his head-covering and smiles apologetically. "I know that's a lot to swallow at once. I'm trying to tell you everything quickly because I'm sure you're anxious to see her."

"Can we?"

"She's still in recovery. When she comes out of there and we put her in a room, you may see her."

"How long will she have to . . . ?" Moxie's father begins.

"She's in a cast from her hip down and will stay in traction for, oh, probably four to six weeks. She can go home after that, and the cast will stay on for another month or so."

"She'll be able to walk?" James asks at the same time that Moxie says, "Will she be able to dance?"

"Walk, oh, yes, definitely. With physical therapy, of course. Dance, it's too early to say."

"But what does that mean?" Moxie asks, reaching out to grip her father's hand tightly.

Dr. Monroe closes Zadi's file and places it on his knees. "I mean, we'll just have to see how she does. A lot will depend on how determined she is and how hard she works at physical therapy. I don't want to make any predictions that far down the line."

"No recital," James says, searching Moxie's face.

Dr. Monroe tells them that when Zadi comes out of recovery, only two of them may go in at a time and they shouldn't stay long.

Moxie and James take the elevator up to Zadi's room. It's a double room, but right now she is the only patient in it. She lies flat in the slender bed with the metal bars pulled up around her. Her whole left side below her waist is in a cast, resting on what looks like a long aluminum tray elevated by traction pulleys. Her eyes are closed, and there are several IV pumps in her arm.

"What's in the IVs?" James asks the nurse in the room.

"We're replacing her fluids. She lost quite a bit of blood. Also an antibiotic and some pain medication that she'll be able to control herself." The nurse sticks a thermometer into Zadi's mouth. Zadi opens her eyes slowly. She appears drowsy and disoriented. Moxie leans over the metal rail and kisses her forehead. James stands behind Moxie and reaches across to touch Zadi's cheek. Zadi begins to cry silently. "Sorry," she says, and closes her eyes again. Tears seep from them. James puts one hand on Moxie's shoulder. She looks up at him and sees that his face is contorted as he tries, in vain, not to cry. They leave the room. James moves slowly, as if his bones hurt.

In the waiting room, Moxie tells her father that he can see her but warns him that she looks pretty bad. Haleem gives her father a hand rising out of the chair. "She's alive, though," Haleem says softly. "I can wait and take him home."

"That's all right. I'll take him," Moxie says.

"If you need anything at all or you just want to talk, please call me," Haleem tells her. Moxie thanks him and takes her father back up to Zadi's room. He doesn't let go of her arm the entire time they are with Zadi, who is now asleep. The nurse tells them she's stabilized for the evening and they might as well go on home.

Moxie returns early Saturday and spends her day at the hospital standing by the bed observing Zadi breathe. She is mesmerized by the way her nostrils flare slightly and her lips part, as if she is about to say something. Watching this way reminds her of when Zadi was a baby and she would stand over her crib and sometimes put her head down close to her chest to make sure she was breathing.

The nurses have cleaned her up so there is no more dried blood on her face or in her hair. Because they washed it, her hair encircles her head like a puffy halo. A hospital staff person brings in a tray of several liquids for Zadi's lunch. Moxie thanks her. When Zadi wakes, Moxie is in the rocker, turning the pages of some magazines she bought yesterday at the gift shop; reading material that requires no thought. Moxie stands and adjusts Zadi's pillows and partially raises the bed to a semi-upright position. Zadi grimaces when she moves even slightly. Moxie pulls the tray table with the food over to Zadi. Zadi looks disappointed when she sees it is only broth, tea, and juice, but she pries open the plastic containers.

"Don't worry. I don't think you'll have to eat like this for long."

Zadi takes a sip from one of the containers. Moxie stands nearby in case anything spills or she requires help drinking. "Ma. I'm never going to dance again, huh?"

Moxie studies Zadi's expression. She wishes she were the injured one. "Yes, of course you will. The doctor told us how lucky you were. Your recovery will take some time, but he expects it to be full and complete."

"Tell me the truth."

"I'm telling you the truth, honey. It would be really hard, but if you were never going to dance again, I wouldn't lie to you about it. And if you don't believe me, you can ask Dr. Monroe when he comes." The door opens and a different nurse enters. She is cheerful as she takes Zadi's blood pressure, pulse, and temperature, and gives her medication. She tells Zadi not to get too used to having a single. There's bound to be a roommate in the next day or so.

"Ma, I can't even feel my leg." Zadi resumes their conversation when the nurse leaves.

"Not right now. It's in a heavy cast, honey."

Zadi begins to cry again.

"Ma, is this my punishment?" Zadi's eyes seek an honest response.

Moxie intertwines her fingers with Zadi's, pressing herself against the hospital bed. "Sweetie, I don't know. It might be mine. Zadi, I swear I'm going to do better at loving you. You have to help me, though. Thank goodness you're all right. Thank goodness I have another chance." She cries onto her daughter's hand as she grips it tightly.

When James and Fawna arrive at the hospital, Moxie decides to go take care of a few things at home and come back later on. She drapes her jacket over her purse and stops downstairs at the cafeteria, thinking she won't have to cook anything at home if she eats there. The cafeteria has a wide selection of edible-looking food. She selects a salad plate and cream of broccoli soup and sits in a booth to eat.

Moxie is fixated on the idea that she has been somehow granted another chance. Another chance to correct the mistaken beliefs she has been living by. She thinks back on how she blamed Aunt BeJean for years after her mother's death. Even though her father showed her the suicide note and repeated over and over that it was impossible for BeJean to have been involved. Even when BeJean married and moved away, proving that she didn't have designs on her father. She winces at how much pain that must have caused BeJean, who loved her so. She was in college by the time she realized she had made a grave mistake and tried, through her letters, to make up for shutting her aunt out during what was also BeJean's time of sorrow and loss after her sister died. At least she got to apologize to BeJean before she died.

She drove to Philadelphia one weekend and stayed with BeJean and her husband. BeJean was riddled with cancer by then. Her head was bald, and she was extremely thin. A box that looked like a suitcase fit onto the back of her wheelchair and provided her with oxygen through a tube in her nose. She and Moxie sat in her kitchen. Sunlight splashed through the window onto Bejean's quilt-covered lap. They drank tea, and Moxie told her everything she needed to. The mistake she had made, the love she felt, the guilt that nagged. "Don't trouble yourself over what happened in the past," BeJean had said, taking long, pulling breaths between words. "The moment you're in is the only one that counts." Moxie tried not to focus on the years of that sort of wisdom she had forfeited. And while her aunt accepted Moxie's apologies and expressed forgiveness, Moxie could see that her pain was permanently etched in the shadows of her face. That was the last time she saw BeJean alive. She went into the intensive care unit the following week and never returned home.

Moxie finishes her salad and sips at the remainder of soup. She overhears two disgruntled hospital workers in the booth behind her discussing their delayed paychecks. Moxie reminds herself that along with her erroneous thoughts about BeJean's culpability, she continued to blame herself for not being more insistent about staying home from camp that summer. The lesson, firmly entrenched in her mind, was that if you compromise your beliefs in any way, terrible results will occur, even death. She wishes she had realized earlier that when those beliefs are false, the results can be just as devastating.

In the lobby on her way out of the hospital, Moxie sees Octavius and his mother at the information desk. Octavius has his back to her. His hooded jacket is draped across his shoulders and his right arm is in a sling. His mother, standing beside him, holds her purse close to her body. Moxie's first impulse is to keep walking, not even speak. She hasn't seen Octavius since the day she tracked Zadi down on Minnesota Avenue, near his house.

He sees her, though, before she can pass him. "Miss Dillar . . ." he says. Octavius carries a bouquet of red roses in one hand. Flashes of shame and sorrow crisscross his face in an instant. "We was trying to find Zadi's room. They say she ain't on the list."

"I just left her room," Moxie says, impatiently.

"The lady looked for her name," he says in earnest. "I spelled 'Dillar' for her and everything."

"Zadi's last name isn't Dillard."

"I didn't mean for Zadi to get hurt, Miss Dillar. You gotta believe me. We was just having a good time. For real, I didn't think nothing like that would happen. Not to Zadi."

His voice hurts her ears. She shifts her shoulder bag to her other arm. "Well, it did, Octavius."

Ms. Johnson abruptly reaches out and embraces Moxie. "So sorry about your baby. Told Tavius I wanted to come with him 'cause I've been praying for her." She continues holding one of Moxie's hands.

"Remember, this is a test of your faith. Hard times make us stronger—don't I know it!"

Moxie puts on the jacket she is carrying. "Her last name is Lawson, Octavius. Zadi Lawson. She's in room three-thirty-six."

Tuesday, April 20th
hospital gown

Dear Sistergirl:

Dad brought me my diary. This is the first day I felt like writing, though. Been here for five days. I can't move. Can't even go to the bathroom by myself. A nurse has to put a cold metal bowl under me. I get this deep kind of pain, worse than anything I ever felt. Especially at night. It twists around like a tornado inside my leg, like it's drilling a deep hole that keeps getting deeper until you could just pass out. That's when the medicine finally works, for a while. I'm trying not to think about missing the recital and Dance Theatre of Harlem. But sometimes I can't stop crying. Octavius has been here to see me twice so far. Watched TV and brought flowers. We didn't talk about what happened. I just remember lying in the ambulance thinking I was about to die. But I didn't. Ma and Dad come every day. Have a roommate now. An old lady with a broken hip. The nurse named Penny says I must be real popular. We're running out of room for all the flowers. Willow sent over a big basket of fruit today and a giant get-well card that everyone in my class signed. And Zora and Todd called last night from the studio. I must look really bad. Dad says Fawna doesn't want to bring Tiffany cause it might upset her too much. Almost everybody who walks in here tries not to but always ends up crying. Allegra and her mother just left. Allegra broke down and said I was the best best friend she ever had. Windy came after school yesterday and got all choked up, too. She told me she's never going to forget me. Then she kind of laughed and said she didn't mean it like that. She told me Peer Review had decided to suspend me for a week, but because of my accident they're just going to close my case. Octavius just called. He says he is my man and he's not going to be creeping while I'm in the hospital. He is going to wait for me no matter how long it takes me to be all right again. I said that could be a really long time.

Twenty-five | Moxie sits in her office, staring at the phone number for the therapist Von referred her to. She needs to adjust the ideas at the core of her life but doesn't have a plan in place for how to do it. She dials the number and is put on hold until an energetic voice answers, "This is Dr. Simms." She tries to discern Dr. Simms's race but can't be certain and doesn't allow herself to be thwarted by not knowing. When Moxie requests an appointment, Dr. Simms asks what kinds of issues she is interested in addressing.

"Well," says Moxie, "I miss my mother, who killed herself when I was eleven; I miss my best friend, who I haven't spoken to in two months; and I miss my daughter, who recently went to live with her father and is now in the hospital recovering from a gunshot wound. I'm worried that I might be depressed like my mother was."

"I see. Have you been in therapy before?"

"No."

"Sounds as if you've managed to hold yourself together through each of those very significant issues, but they're exacting a toll now. That doesn't necessarily mean you have a clinical depression. There's no way to know for sure over the phone, but I just want you to bear that in mind."

"Okay," says Moxie, beginning to relax.

"It's encouraging that you're showing yourself such compassion and courage by calling today. Let me tell you what I have open next week."

• • •

Moxie stops at her father's house after work and takes him to the hospital with her. "Zadi really is fortunate, Moxie. All of us are. You know that, don't you?"

"I'm starting to know that," she says. She removes an overnight bag she has packed for Zadi from the back of her car. Dr. Monroe suggested bringing in some of Zadi's special things to help her cope with the lengthy hospital stay. She has included several of her Janet Jackson pictures, her CDs, magazines, her pillow, and a stuffed animal from her bed.

Moxie and her father are both surprised to find Philandra Snow at Zadi's bedside, reading to her from a book she holds in her lap. Miss Snow puts a finger to her lips when they come through the door, so they won't interrupt her. Zadi appears to be mesmerized either by the words or Miss Snow's presence. The curtain between Zadi and her roommate is slightly parted. Moxie and her father wave to the older woman in the adjacent bed. Ponsey pulls up a second chair and indicates that Moxie should sit in it. She motions for him to, instead, and he does.

Miss Snow's head is bent over her book, a large worn-out paperback with yellowed, much-underlined pages. Her short, heavy legs are crossed at the ankles, one foot lightly tapping the floor to the cadence of her words. Moxie listens intently while she examines Zadi's face. Her eyelids are still thick from crying, but her expression is less strained than yesterday.

Miss Snow closes the book. "That is my absolute favorite novel of all times. It is the one I would take if I had to be trapped on a desert island with only one book. This is my third copy because I wear them out. Paule Marshall's *Brown Girl, Brownstones*. I am that girl, I am Selina. Zadi, did you know I am a Bajan?"

"No, Miss Snow."

"I will read you a chapter each time I come. There are so many lessons in it, and this will help your time fly by. Moxana and Mr. Dillard, how lovely to see you again!" She extends her hand to Moxie's father.

"Thank you for coming, Miss Snow," Moxie says. "I didn't expect to see you here."

"Of course I had to come. Zadi is my *prima,* my starlight, *ma chérie.* Of course I'd never tell her that in the studio. But I refuse to feel pity for her in here either, as she wants me to." She smiles wickedly at Zadi. Zadi looks down shyly. "Her body is of the strongest design, her mind even stronger. This situation can only be for her positive growth. That's what I've been speaking with her about."

"Thank you," says Moxie's father. "You're helping out this old man as well."

Miss Snow stands. She wears a lightweight black suit of vintage design. She goes to Zadi and lifts one arm. "Nothing happened to your arms, is that right?" She massages this arm tenderly and then the other. "You must promise to do *port de bras* every morning and evening. Let's see it now. One, two, and . . ." Zadi lifts her arms in tandem to the front and the sides, wincing just a bit. "That's right. Close your fingers. Yes. You must keep the arms working until the legs can join them."

"Miss Snow, the doctors don't know if I'll be able to dance again or not."

"They don't have to know. You know, and I know. Don't we?"

Moxie wants to answer for Zadi but doesn't. She presses her fingers onto her eyes to keep the tears in.

"I . . . don't . . . know . . ." Zadi looks pleadingly at Miss Snow.

"Zadi, my sparkling jewel, you are a dancer even if you can't move your left leg right now. You are a dancer because you are a dancer in your heart and in your soul and in your mind. Isn't it so? Being able to do *fouettés* and *pirouettes* alone don't make you a dancer. This accident is one of the crossroads of your life, one of the turning points to advance you as a person and a dancer. You will look back on this one day and say, ah, yes, that was the lesson, that was when I learned thus and so. And so, because you are a dancer, a dancer of prodigious talent I might add, you have to move whatever part of your body you can. If only your arms and your head. Once more with *port de bras,* please. Yes. Head up off your chest."

"Bless you!" Moxie's father claps his hands together as he watches Miss Snow with Zadi. "Moxie, why don't you write down what she said, so Zadi can read it when she needs to." Moxie obediently begins to scribble down what she can remember.

"Who is that woman?" Zadi's roommate asks, leaning forward to further open her curtain. Ponsey moves his chair closer and explains to her. She asks him to play cards, and he accepts, shuffling the cards on his thigh.

Miss Snow looks across Zadi's bed to Moxie. "Moxana, I have assured Zadi that when all is said and done, she will be a better dancer than ever before. And I will work with her, after she has healed, to make it happen. It is unacceptable, damaging even, for her to think that this is the end of anything. It is your responsibility to help keep her spirits lifted."

"I'll do my best." Moxie shows Zadi what she has brought from home and asks her where to place everything. Miss Snow helps Moxie move items around in the limited space. "Who pinned up your hair?" Moxie asks, when she switches Zadi's pillow with the one she brought from home.

"Nurse Penny. My hair's a mess, isn't it?"

"I could bring in the blow dryer," Moxie hears herself say. "Maybe I can rewash it and blow it out for you, if they let me."

"Would you?" Zadi looks astonished.

"Yes."

As Moxie bends to embrace her daughter, they hear someone say, "Knock, knock." Norma comes into the room. She carries a vase of irises and jonquils. A nurse comes behind her and takes them from her.

Zadi, wincing as she tries to sit up, squeals, "Norma!"

"This girl is close to winning the award for the most floral arrangements," says the nurse, adding them to an additional portable tray being used solely for Zadi's flowers.

Norma goes straight to Zadi first and takes her face in her hands. "Oh, sistergirl, what did you go and do?" She kisses Zadi on her head several times and rubs noses with her. Then Norma greets Miss Snow, hugs Moxie's father, and briefly clasps Moxie's hand.

"Talk about me; what happened to you?" Zadi points to the neck brace Norma wears.

"Oh, sistergirl, it's a long story, better left until later."

"Moxie," says her father. "Can you get an old man a cup of tea from the cafeteria? Maybe Miss Snow wants something, too."

"Oh, no. I'm fine," says Miss Snow.

"Norma, you go on to the cafeteria with her," Ponsey says. "We'll all be right here when you get back."

Outside the room, they take measured steps toward the elevators. They pass the nurse's station, where a woman behind the desk waves and smiles at Moxie.

"My father called you, didn't he?" Moxie asks.

"Yes, this morning. He said he didn't know what was going on with us and he didn't care. That you and Zadi needed me. And then he told me what happened. Are you angry that I'm here?" They leave the unit, and Norma stops next to two large artificial plants. She wants to see the truth in Moxie's face, no matter what her words.

"No. I'm glad he called you. I'm glad you came," Moxie says, releasing a grateful smile, relieved that despite everything, Norma's warm, brown face still welcomes her. "My father thinks he's slick, you know. Sending us both to get him tea."

"Yes, that Ponsey Dillard is something else."

"Damn, I missed you."

"I missed you, too." They embrace and then continue on to the elevators, arm in arm.